THE
BUG
DIARY

THE BUG DIARY

Amber Fraley

Anamcara Press LLC

Published in 2021 by Anamcara Press LLC
Author © 2021 by Amber Fraley
Cover image and illustrations by Lana Grove
Book design by Maureen Carroll
Chaparal Pro, PT Sans, Franklin Gothic
Printed in the United States of America.

Book description: While experimenting with substances in the university library, Kymer is confronted by a ghost from KU's past: Carrie Watson, the librarian who is the library's namesake. Carrie gives Kymer the insect field journal of Flora Ellen Richardson, the first woman to graduate from KU. When Kymer reviews the bug diary, she realizes there's a bee in Flora's journal that's never before been described by science. A wild ride ensues changing the world of entomology, and Kymer, forever.

ANAMCARA PRESS LLC
P.O. Box 442072, Lawrence, KS 66044
https://anamcara-press.com

Ordering Information:
Quantity sales. Special discounts are available on quantity purchases by corporations, associations, and others. For details, contact the publisher at the address above. Orders by U.S. trade bookstores and wholesalers. Please contact Ingram Distribution.

ISBN-13: The Bug Diary, 978-1-941237-79-3 (Paperback)
ISBN-13: The Bug Diary, 978-1-941237-81-6 (EBook)
ISBN-13: The Bug Diary, 978-1-941237-80-9 (Hardcover)

FIC012000   FICTION / Ghost
FIC061000   FICTION / Magical Realism
FIC027240   FICTION / Romance / New Adult

Library of Congress Control Number: 2021942074

This book is dedicated to my 4th and 5th grade teacher, Mrs. Richter, who always told me I could be a writer.

"There has been no movement for the benefit of her community or for women and children that did not receive her ardent support. Women's suffrage, the women's rest room, the various plans to provide high school privileges for rural pupils and the farm bureau for rural women, each in their turn were things she was untiring in her efforts to secure."

—*Nellie Colman Bigsby on her mother, Flora Ellen Richardson*

"Miss Watson tolerated me."

—*William Allen White on KU's Head Librarian, Carrie Watson*

Contents

1

MAGICICADA

As I passed through the doors of Oliver Hall to the outdoors, I was engulfed by two sensations: one, the blast of heat like opening an oven door, and the other, the deafening sound of a few million cicadas singing their little guts out, desperate for a hook-up. I could relate.

I walked to a small grove of trees just off the parking lot, appreciating the shade. A few hundred yards away was the men's baseball diamond, and though I could see the players, I couldn't hear the announcer over the piercing noise of the bugs. In the grove of trees, the cicada noise was ominous, starting as a low hum, building to a deafening buzz, then dropping to a low hum again, over and over and over: zzzzzzZZZZZZZzzzzzzZZZZZZZZ. You could hear them indoors. You could hear them while driving down the street with your car windows up, the air conditioning on and the radio blasting. Everyone was complaining about it. People were also pretty much over the brown papery skins the cicadas left everywhere after molting. I thought about shipping a box of them home to my little brother, Cade, since he'd think it was hilarious and our mother would be repulsed, but I hadn't gotten around to it.

The leaves of the trees were dotted with the cicadas, lazing around like fat, loud, alien berries. All I had to do was reach out and coax one into my hand. I sat down in the grass to get a good look at him. I'd be in my mid-thirties before I'd see these little beauties again, and I wasn't going to miss the opportunity to study one up close. I knew he was a he because he was buzzing, though it was a quiet purr, as opposed to his full-out song, probably because he was a little freaked out at being held. It's the male cicadas that sing to attract the females. My new friend crawled to the end of my finger and crept around on the tip, tickling every nerve. He had an exoskeleton so dark blue he was almost black, with stained-glass orange wings. He stared at me with his shiny-red, beady eyes, and I couldn't help but smile back at him.

He was beautiful.

This was a bug experience I knew I'd remember the rest of my life: a seventeen-year cicada emergence during my freshman year of college. The seventeen-year cicada spends seventeen whole years as an ugly, wingless nymph underground, sucking the juices from tree roots to survive. When seventeen years are up, they claw their way out from underground, molt, and that's when they get their wings and stylish new exoskeletons. These aptly-named Magicicada would live for a few, brief weeks, mate, and the females would lay eggs in the ground to ensure the next brood. The adults would all die after mating, and it would be another seventeen years before anyone would see them again. Not that most people wanted to see them, even though they didn't bite or sting or chew on anything.

They were just loud.

I pulled out my phone and took a million photos of him from all angles, until he gave a startling BUZZ! and flew back up into the tree. I was sad to see him go, but also kind of glad, because it meant I could go back into the air-conditioning. Still, it had been nice to get away from the bustle of the dorm for a bit.

So... I'm Kymer Charvat, but don't call me KC, because I hate it. And I suppose it's helpful to know my name isn't really Kymer. It's Kylie, which is perhaps the most vomit-inducing name ever. Thankfully, I learned about chimerism in a particularly enlightened biology portion of my sixth-grade science class, and I was so taken with the concept that I adopted it as my nickname, much to my mother's dismay. If you've never heard of chimerism (pronounced ky MER ism), it's incredibly rare and sounds like something out of a sci-fi story. You know how one twin can absorb another in utero? Well if they're fraternal twins, then their DNA doesn't match, which means there are a few individuals walking around on the planet who are made up of two distinct DNA profiles. Wild stuff.

Anyway. Once every seventeen years! Walking back to the dorm, I was super jazzed. I would've given anything to have kept the little guy in my live bug collection, but I didn't want to piss off my new roommate, and he'd simply be too loud to keep. So far, my new roommate, Siren, seemed pretty cool.

As I pulled the heavy glass outer door of the dorm toward me, the refrigerated air washed over me in cool relief, giving me goosebumps. There were already a handful of students waiting to take the elevator up, so I opted for the stairs instead, which were stuffy and warm. Walking up the nine flights made me even sweatier. Back in our room, I fell onto my bed. It was late in the afternoon, and I was tired after walking up the hill to classes that morning. I was lying there, listening to the cicadas singing away outside, when Siren burst through the door. She was wearing her server outfit, which consisted of a black miniskirt and a tight t-shirt that said BAZONGAS across the chest, the name of the breastaurant where she worked. She tossed her purse on her bed, dug into the pockets of her miniskirt, and pulled out a wad of money. She placed the money on her desk, plopped down in the chair and began smoothing out the bills, putting them in order from largest to smallest. Then she counted it. Twice.

"Dammit. Fifty-six and change. I still have to make another two hundred dollars payment toward my tuition this month. If I'd known the rediculous prices they charge for books in college I would've saved up more cash before I got here." She stood up, pulled her t-shirt over her head, sniffed it and wrinkled her nose. "Ugh! The fried shrimp appetizers are on sale right now and it's disgusting. I am so sick of smelling like greasy fish." She tossed the t-shirt toward her open closet, where it landed in her hamper.

"How was your shift?" I asked, trying to make small talk. "I mean, besides not making enough tips."

She sighed, putting on a clean t-shirt. "Oh, I mean, normal I guess," she said, taking off her sneakers. "Mostly the business-lunch crowd. A couple of families."

"Really?" I sat up on my bed.

"Really what?" She pulled the scrunchie out of her hair and tossed it on her desk.

"Both of those things. The business-lunch crowd and families? At Bazongas?"

She shimmied out of the miniskirt, throwing it in the direction of her closet. "Oh, hell yes. This is America, Mama! Tits and ass are the free appeteasers, don't ya know."

"Gross. Not gross you, I mean. Gross that people want boobs with their lunch." I wasn't sure what I thought about her calling me *Mama*.

She shrugged her shoulders. "Use 'em if you got 'em is my philosophy. You know what they say. Big tits, big tips." She shrugged off her bra and threw it at her bed, then grabbed her bathrobe off a hook and drew it around her, slipping off her underwear and tossing it in her hamper.

"Fair enough," I said, wiping some sweat off my forehead.

She looked at me. "What happened to you? You're all sweaty... You go for a jog?"

I laughed. "Definitely not. I don't jog. I went to have a look at the cicadas."

"Ohh, right. Of course you did," she said, smiling and nodding. Then she glanced at the shelves above my bed and the smile was gone. "Oh, God."

"What?"

"Is that another bug?"

"Uh... yeah," I said, glancing up at the two mini-terrariums. My second night at the dorm I'd collected about a dozen Big Dipper fireflies (*Photinus pyralis*) out on the lawn and brought them inside, and Siren had seemed to like the soft blinking. But that morning I'd been lucky enough to find a gorgeous, chartreuse praying mantis with red eyes (*Stagmomantis carolina*), in some hedges on the lawn in front of the architecture building on my way down the hill after English class. She was big, about sixty millimeters (two-and-a-half inches) long, and resting on some twigs I'd collected from the hedge. Siren walked over to get a closer look.

"I was hoping to have four terrariums of bugs in total," I said, and her eyebrows went up. "I wasn't going to keep anything noisy or messy or anything..." I said quickly "... but if they make you uncomfortable, I can get rid of them."

She furrowed her brow, looking skeptical. "I guess it's okay. As long as they're quiet... and they don't stink."

"Oh, no," I replied. "I'll be sure to keep their terrariums clean."

"Okay," she said, though she still didn't sound convinced. "And nothing too disgusting either."

"Disgusting?"

"You know. Nothing that's gonna make me want to yack. No slugs, nothing slimy or creepy or with too many legs," she shuddered. "No centipedes."

"Okay. Um... slugs aren't insects."

She gave me a look. "You know what I mean."

Centipedes and millipedes I could live without. "What about spiders?" I asked.

She looked at me pointedly. "Spiders aren't insects."

She had me there. "True... but I do like to study arachnids as well as insects."

She plopped down on her bed. "Ew. Maybe. It depends."

"Depends on what?"

"On whether or not it's a spider that freaks me out," she shuddered.

"That's fair," I said. "I'll try to stick to cute bugs." I was glad she was letting me keep any bugs at all, so I didn't push it. I wanted us to get along, seeing as how we were going to be living with each other all year.

She grabbed a handful of her thick, dark blonde hair and smelled it. "Ugh. Welp, I am going to shower now, because I smell greasy. I feel greasy." She grabbed a towel and her basket of toiletries and turned to look at me. "You wanna come with? You look pretty sweaty."

"Uh... sure," I said, trying to feel casual about showering in a bathroom we shared with fifty other girls.

I still wasn't quite used to the whole community bathroom thing. I'd already learned to avoid it in the morning, when all the other girls showered and did their hair. It was a steamy, loud, wet, giggly mess. Ugh. I never understood how some women could hang out naked together and talk. Siren was definitely one of those women who was comfortable in her skin. She never batted an eyelash changing in front of me. I, on the other hand, tried to always change my clothes as quickly as possible, or even better, when I was alone.

But I was learning dorm life meant I had to get over being undressed around the other girls. The worst was trying to find alone time in the bathroom to poop. I could not deal with anyone being in the bathroom with me for that.

We gathered up our towels, baskets of toiletries, and put on our flip-flops, click-clacking our way down the hall to the bathroom. The bathroom was the ultimate in utility, tiled in black and white. It was big and cold and echo-y when no one else was in it, like now. Most of the girls on our floor were hanging out in their rooms, studying or watching TV or on social media, since it was so hot outside. I actually kind of liked the bare function of the dorm bathroom, compared with my mother's fussy bathrooms at home, with towels and soaps we weren't allowed to touch. I just wished there was more privacy.

"I'm supposed to go see Gabriel in his room tonight. His roommate will be out," Siren said. "You want to come with?" She'd met Gabriel during the first week of school, and they'd hooked up almost immediately. I'd already had to spend two evenings out in the commons area so they could have some *alone time* in our room.

"I mean, if you want me there, I will," I replied. "But if it's okay, I'll stay in tonight and give you two some *alone time*."

"Oh, okay." She said it casually, but I was pretty sure she was relieved.

As soon as we passed through the bathroom door, before the door had even swung shut, Siren dropped her towel. She was long, tall and smooth with caramel skin. She had slim hips and really big boobs. Bigger than mine, which was saying something. I kinda felt like a pale dumpling next to her. We turned on our showers, waiting for them to heat up before stepping in.

"Oh my god, I need to tan again," Siren hollered over the shower noise.

"You do? You're so dark."

"Nah. This is light for me in the summer. Hey! I have time after my improv class tomorrow to lay out. You wanna lay out with me?" She stepped into her shower, and I stepped into mine.

"No way!" I said. "I never subject my skin to solar radiation when I don't have to. I don't tan, I burn. It's not fair your skin is so dark when your hair is blonde."

"Well, I do get my hair highlighted, so it's not actually this blonde. But my mother's side of the family is Lebanese, and I ended up with, y'know, what she calls 'olive skin.' But my brother is pale."

"Huh. Both my brother and I are light," I said, soaping up. "Like pasty light. And we both have brown hair. Our heritage is all Northern and Eastern Europe. You know, Czech, English, Scottish... I think there's some French in there, somewhere."

"Yeah, you are kinda pink," she laughed. "It's funny. There's a big population of Lebanese people that settled in Wichita years ago. My great-great-grandmother is the one who came over from Lebanon. To this day, there's actually a bunch of Lebanese-owned businesses in Wichita. My mom moved to Hutchinson later."

"That's interesting. So I bet your family has lots of great recipes."

"Oh my God, I'm almost tired of it." She laughed.

"Really?" I asked, soaping up my hair.

"Every holiday of my life has been nothing but kibbeh and stuffed grape leaves and kanafeh.

"What's kanafeh?"

"Um... it's sort of like Lebanese cheesecake deep fried inside a sweet, crunchy crust," she said. The farty noise of Siren squeezing a shampoo bottle echoed through the room.

"That sounds amazing!" I said, rinsing.

She laughed. "Yeah. I guess it kind of is."

"I think I would love that. Our holidays consist of all the regular, boring, holiday stuff. Turkey and dressing and mashed potatoes..."

"See, I would love that. I would give anything to have turkey and dressing at Thanksgiving or Christmas. And sweet potatoes and pecan pie... or a ham at Easter. But every holiday in our family we're stuck in the kitchen rolling up rice in grape leaves. It takes forever. So what's family life like in Bethesda?" she asked.

"Um, you know," I said. "Pretty basic, boring, suburban stuff."

"What does your dad do?" she asked.

"He's a computer programmer," I said, realizing I missed him.

"Tech guy, huh? What about your mom?"

"She's a realtor." Victoria loved selling oversized modern monstrosities to other suburbanites. She was damn good at it, too.

"And your parents are still together, right?"

"Yep. Thirty-one years," I said. I only knew that because last year my mother had thrown a huge thirtieth anniversary party at our house.

"Jeez. I can't even imagine what it'd be like to grow up in a nuclear family like that. My parents split when I was three. It's been me and my mom and my brother for as long as I can remember. And Travis is five years older than me, so mostly it's just been Mom and me."

"Wow. Do you know where he is?"

"My dad?"

"Yeah."

"Oh, yeah. He lives in New York City. He's an artist—a painter. I mean, I don't hate him or anything. I don't know him that well, but I like him. I've visited him twice in New York, and we talk on the phone two or three times a year."

"Wow," I said, not quite sure what to think. "Is he successful?"

She laughed. "I mean... not really. He manages to feed himself most of the time, but sometimes he ends up crashing on other people's couches. He seems happy living that way. It's not what I'd want, though."

"I know what you mean. I don't think I want what my parents have, either."

"How so?" she asked.

"They're just so... basic. I'm not even sure they're happy. They just seem to kind of exist together."

Siren laughed. "See, I think that sounds chill. My mom was gone a lot, between working and partying. She and my grandmother taught me to cook from the time I was like five years old. By the time I was nine, I could make dinner for the both of us. I learned to do my own laundry when I was ten."

I paused, squirting conditioner into my hand. "Aw. That sounds lonely."

"I mean, I didn't mind it. In fact, I think I liked it too much. I got used to kind of running the house myself and doing what I wanted when I wanted. Of course, it left me lots of time to get into trouble, too, you know? I had lots of friends over, played a lot of spin the bottle. That kind of thing. Almost burned the house down a couple of times. But I always cleaned everything up before she got home. It was more annoying when she'd bring her loser boyfriends back to the house and hang around. I've had to call the cops on three of her boyfriends over the years."

"Holy crap," I replied.

"I know, right? I love the woman, but she is one flaming-hot dumpster-fire."

The sound of the showers filled up the silence until my curiosity got the better of me. "So... why did you have to call the cops?"

"Let's see... One time when I was about ten or eleven, she and the guy she was dating at the time came home from a night at the bar and were screaming at each other at the top of their lungs in front of the house at midnight in the middle of the week. I didn't even go outside. I just called the cops. I figured if I didn't, one of the neighbors would anyway. And then a few years later—I remember I was seventeen because I'd just bought my car—she came home with a black eye. I drove her to the police station myself and made her file a report against the dick-bag. Luckily my brother Travis was home from boot camp."

"Yikes! Did the guy come back?"

"No, thank goodness."

I was done with my shower, so I shut off the water and toweled off behind the white shower curtain.

"Are you already done?" Siren asked.

"Yeah," I answered.

"You're fast! It always takes me a while to condition all this hair."

"I bet!" I said, drying my legs. "So what happened with the third guy?"

"Oh yeah. So one night Mom goes out to the bars at like nine o'clock, and at ten thirty, I hear this weird clicking noise at the front door."

I stepped out of my shower with a towel wrapped around me. "Clicking noise?"

"Yeah, like *tick, tick, tick* at the front door. I look out the peep hole and it's my mother. Which was weird, because it was way too early for her to be home. So I open the door, and her friend Tanya is with her, holding her up. She could barely stand. She was trying to get her key in the lock. Turns out someone slipped her a roofie at the bar. Thank God Tanya was with her."

"Jesus."

"Right? I called the cops, and they came out and took a report, but they never called us back."

I stood in front of one of the many sinks and mirrors, combing out my hair and applying product. Usually I let it air dry. "It's nice you and your mom get along, though," I said. "She's lucky you look after her."

"So you and your mom don't? Get along, I mean?"

"No, not really."

"How come?"

"I don't know. I don't get her and she for sure doesn't get me. She's into all these dumb clubs full of fake people." I parted my hair on the side and combed it out again.

"Clubs? What clubs?"

"Oh, you know. Like the Businesswomen's Association and Rotary."

"Rotary?"

"Yeah, it's like this charitable organization," I said, readjusting my towel, which had come loose, and made a mental note to buy a terrycloth robe.

"That sounds okay."

"Well, yeah, it is, but I mean, some people belong to Rotary because of the charity. Other people belong to Rotary because of the business connections and being seen." Having finished with my hair, I sat down on a bench against the wall and wondered how much longer it would take Siren to finish showering.

"Oh, I get it. Your mom's a social climber," she replied.

"Absolutely. Our whole house looks like something out of a magazine. She has a lawn service come out weekly to poison the lawn and mow and trim our perfect grass."

Siren laughed. "See, now I think you're the one who's crazy. Most people would kill to grow up like you. I know I would."

"I think you'd get bored. And it pisses me off that she has all those chemicals poured all over the place. She still has an exterminator come out twice a month."

"That bitch!"

"Seriously. She hates that I want to go into entomology. She hates bugs."

Siren stepped out of the shower, sans towel, and I tried not to blush. She bent over, twisted up her big mass of hair and wrung the water out of it. Then she put it up in a towel-turban on her head. "Still, I don't think I'd ever get bored not having to worry about money or whether or not some scumbag might kill my mom," she said. She took her time putting a towel around herself. I was having trouble concentrating on her face.

"You're right," I said. "I'm sorry. That was a dumb thing for me to say."

"Oh, no worries. It's all relative, right? I know a lot of people who'd feel sorry for themselves if they had my upbringing." She took herself in, in the full-length mirror, adjusting the turban. "Except, you know, the being poor part. That part sucks, but most of the time, we figure out how to make it work."

"Are you worried about her?" By now I was getting into my clothes and Siren was carefully drying her hair, massaging the big diffuser into her scalp. A couple of girls walked in to use the restroom.

"Worried about my mom?" she asked.

"Yeah. Now that you're off at college and not there to look after her."

"Not for now, anyway. She's actually with a decent guy right now. As long as she doesn't sabotage it, Rick is taking care of her."

"And what if she screws it up?"

Siren stood up, shook her hair out and checked herself out in the mirror. She shrugged. "Everybody has to grow up sometime, right?"

2

Life in Oz

*H*ow's life in Oz?" That's the text I woke up to a few days later, from my boyfriend Zach who was attending school at the University of Maryland, home of the Terrapins (or Terps), which is a turtle native to the Chesapeake Bay. He and all our friends back home had been giving me non-stop crap about going to school in Kansas. Still, it made me smile.

Haha. I texted back. *It's great. Lots of cool bugs here.*

Well at least I know you won't be meeting any new guys until you've finished studying all the local vermin.

Vermin. That's how Zach referred to insects. That or "pests." *Speaking of vermin, meet any hot lady turtles yet?* I typed, wondering if he'd tell me the truth if someone had caught his eye.

Long pause. *Oh, there are a few pretty shells around, but nothing compares to your gorgeous beak.*

I rolled my eyes. So dumb. *You're full of it.*

I miss you Lampinator.

Lampinator. A bastardization of Lampyridae, the Latin name for firefly. Goofy, but okay when Zach said it. No way I'd let anyone else call me that.

I miss you too, you bloodsucking lawyer, I typed.

You miss parts of me, he replied.

Yup. Especially the big throbbing one.

That's my girl. always go for the brain

Always

Got 2 go. Contracts class starting

OK have fun! I typed, and he texted back a kissy face. Aw. It made me miss him. And then I thought about how I wouldn't see him until Christmas, which was five months away, and I stuffed the feelings down. It didn't do any good to miss him, because it wasn't going to work out between us, anyway, and I had to get ready for my English class. I put on my favorite pair of shorts and a button-up sleeveless blouse. I made sure to put on a cute pair of earrings and necklace, too, and a little mascara on the eyelashes and lip gloss. I didn't bother with more than that because I'd sweat it off. I smoothed my hair into a careful ponytail, grabbed my backpack and took off for class.

Outside, it was already hot and humid. Luckily, the breeze was cool, because I didn't feel like waiting for the bus. I made my way up Naismith Drive and past Allen Fieldhouse, the place where basketball freaks worshiped on game days. This part of the walk was the easiest. Just past Allen Fieldhouse, though, the hill got steeper. As I trudged along, checking out dudes from behind my sunglasses, I tried to imagine the perfect college freshman-year friend-with-benefits. He'd be a chill guy. Kinda cute, but not a pretty-boy. Definitely smart. We'd have fascinating conversations and hot, hot sex in his apartment, because who wants to have dorm sex? It would be simple and uncomplicated, a relationship that was fun, without being too serious. I wanted to concentrate on my schoolwork. And maybe party once in a while. Nothing too crazy. I was excited about the possiblity of a new sex partner. I still loved Zach, but we were both young, after all, and it wasn't like we were going to be together forever.

The steepest part of the hill was the last bit before the summit. The more out-of-shape folks were huffing and puffing by this point, and everybody was happy to reach the top. Once on top of the hill, the main thoroughfare, Jayhawk Boulevard, was flat. As usual, the sidewalk was packed with students heading to and from classes, most of them wearing earbuds. Buses packed with students trundled past, along with the occasional university vehicle, but general traffic on campus was prohibited during the week. Vehicles that did move through campus did so slowly, as the students never gave traffic the right-of-way. Students pretty much wandered across the road wherever they wanted, like animals on a preserve.

Once you passed the Chi Omega fountain, which sat in the middle of a traffic roundabout, the buildings on campus were a hodgepodge of styles. Many were built of native Kansas limestone, while others were utilitarian and concrete. Some were modern, others traditional, some even gothic, complete with gargoyles and turrets. My English class, Nineteenth Century British Authors, was in Wescoe, which was considered to be the ugliest building on campus. Campus lore told it had originally been built as a parking garage, but then for some unknown reason the architect lost his mind and converted it into a building.

I liked my English class, for the most part. The grad student who taught it was British, but not like regular British. He was like a character out of a Monty Python skit British. His name was Basil Bunting (pronounced bazz-uhl). He had a dirty blonde afro, round, coke-bottle glasses and a round belly to go with.

We had just started reading Heart of Darkness by Joseph Conrad and were discussing it in class. It was dark and disturbing, and it contrasted the stiff antiseptic nature of British life against the wildness of jungle. It was creepy and mysterious.

"Let's talk about the significance of color in Heart of Darkness," Basil said, after everyone had shuffled in and found seats. "Notice that the word color is spelled correctly throughout the story, with a 'U,' which you Americans bafflingly opted to drop from your bizarre lexicon." Several of us laughed. I was sitting in the middle of the room and saw the guy whom I'd come to think of a DudeBro Number One roll his eyes at his friend, DudeBro Number Two. They were sitting a couple of rows in front of me.

"Specifically, let's talk about the significance of the colors white and black in this story, because it's already apparent that these two colors are recurring, persistent themes."

A few students put their hands up, myself included. "Yes, Susan," Basil said, pointing at a girl who liked to twist her hair around her index finger.

"Well, I mean, like... there's a lot of... contrast... between white and black? Like one is like as light as it can possibly be and the other is as dark as it can possibly be... and so there's a lot of contrast between those colors... " There was a pause as though no one was sure if Susan was done talking or not.

"Yes, yes, that's true," Basil said, finally. "There is perhaps no more contrast that can exist between two colors than the colors black and white. But what is the nature of that contrast in the story?"

"Well, like... so... black is everything dark and bad and evil, and white is like..." her hair-twisting hand flailed in the air, "...white is like everything light and good and pure."

"Yes, one might say that," Basil said, adjusting his thick, round glasses. "But does that metaphor also extend to the characters of the story?"

"I don't agree with that at all," DudeBro Number One interrupted. "Obviously in this story, the white people are bad and the Black people are good."

"Is it really that simple, though?" Basil asked.

"Um, yeah," DudeBro One said. "I mean, isn't that the way it always is? The whites are always portrayed as being bad and wrong."

"Well sort of," I put in, and suddenly everyone was looking at me. "Marlow isn't all bad. And there is this idea that the whites are almost god-like with their technology."

"Yes!" Basil said, flipping through his copy of the novella. "Kurtz says here in chapter two that the whites must 'necessarily appear... in the nature of supernatural beings.'"

"But let's be honest. Ultimately, the white people are bad, right?" DudeBro One said.

"Well, yes, one could definitely argue that," replied Basil.

"That's what I said," he huffed and folded his arms.

"Well, in this story, *aren't they* the bad ones?" I said, a little too loud.

DudeBro Number One and DudeBro Number Two turned in tandem to look at me. "How? By taking advantage of resources the natives are too dumb to even know what to do with and teaching them to not be so backwards?"

"By invading a country that isn't theirs and stealing resources that don't belong to them?" I shot back. "By forcing people into subservience and slavery? Is that what you'd call *good*?"

"If it's the only way to get some people to quit being so ignorant, maybe it's not so bad," DudeBro Number Two replied. I was stunned.

"Surely you can't be serious," Basil said, and someone snorted a laugh.

"Yes, I'm serious," DudeBro Two blustered. "If those people understood what kind of resources they had available to them, they wouldn't be walking around half-naked in the jungle."

"Those people? Wow." There was one Black girl in the class. She usually sat near the back of the room and didn't say much. Now she was the center of attention.

"No offense," DudeBro Number Two said, twisting further in his seat to look at her.

She looked him dead in the eye, arms crossed. "None taken," she said in a tone indicating to everyone offense was very much taken, then under her breath she muttered, "Fool," and most of us heard it.

I laughed out loud. If looks could kill, DudeBro Number One would've vaporized me on the spot, but he didn't say anything. He turned away.

"Alright, then, let's leave the question of black and white characters aside for now and discuss how black and white—or rather light and dark—are used in the landscape of this story," Basil said, trying to steer the discussion back on the rails. I refrained from participating, still mad at the DudeBros but also wondering if I'd been too loud and harsh.

The ominous tone of the campus steam whistle signaled the end of class. I packed up my stuff, trying to avoid looking in the direction of the DudeBros, taking my time so they'd leave first. When I walked out into the hallway, they were still there, hanging around. They started walking slowly, talking. I decided to follow at a distance.

"Bullshit fucking class with their bullshit crybaby liberal crap."

"And we have to put up with four years of this."

"Four years? It takes more than four years to get a master's in business, dude."

"Yeah, but at least we'll be out of these bullshit classes and in our real classes by then."

"Yeah. I don't know how much of this I can deal with. My Western Civ prof is such a bleeding heart she makes me want to fucking puke."

Outside Wescoe, they headed off down the sidewalk in the opposite direction I needed to go, thankfully, as I didn't really want to listen to their priveledged bullshit anymore. I heard enough talk like that at home in Bethesda, where I routinely found myself wanting to slap random clueless socialites for being heartless monsters with their heads firmly inserted up their bleached assholes. I had another class in three hours, so I walked back to the dorm to study and grab lunch. Thankfully, it was all downhill.

When I got back to the room, I found Siren cutting up a hot pink t-shirt while watching an algebra lecture on my computer. I had a nice one, and I let her use it when I didn't need it so she didn't have to always use the computer lab.

I checked on the Carolina mantis, who seemed to be healthy. Her color was good, and she was still fat and sassy.

"Hey, Caroline," I said.

"Who?" Siren asked.

"Oh... this is a Carolina mantis. I think I'll call her Caroline."

"You are so weird," Siren said. "Dammit. I'm going to have to watch this video again. I was hoping if I understood more about quadratic equations I could memorize the formula. No such luck." The t-shirt had been folded up like a snowflake, and Siren had cut strategic little holes all over it in an intricate design. She snapped open the t-shirt with one hand, a pair of scissors in the other.

"Damn," I commented. "That looks fantastic."

"You think so?"

"Yeah." I meant it, even though I'd never wear something like it myself.

"I can make you one," she said. "Or I can show you how to do it."

"Thanks, but I don't think I'd actually wear it."

"Why not?"

"It's not my style, that's all," I said, trying to put a look of sincerity on my face. "It'll look great on you, though."

She started the process of crafting her look for the day, which was a thing with her. She put on a cute bra and a black cami with lace trim and layered her new t-shirt creation over the top. Then she changed in and out of various shorts and skirts before settling on a flouncy skirt that was black with pink and purple flowers. She went to the mirror, running her hands through her hair, putting it up in various ways, securing it with a hair tie and stepping back to take in her reflection. It was funny though, when she just rolled out of bed in the morning, she was kind of a hot mess. But after a few minutes and a little makeup, she was absolutely gorgeous.

After messing with her hair and makeup for several minutes, she was satisfied with her reflection. "I'm starving," she said. "Let's get lunch." Just then, her phone rang. She looked at it and rolled her eyes.

"Hey, Bubba," she said, flatly, answering the call. "Whassup?" And I knew it was her brother, Travis, because I'd listened to a few of her conversations with him. He seemed to call every three or four days. Of course I could only hear one side: "Yeah, I'm fine. Yes, I like my roommate. She's ah-mazing," she turned and winked at me. "Yeah. She's tight," she rolled her eyes.... "Yes, I'm going to my classes. Yes, I'm doing my homework. No, I am not having unprotected sex.... You're not my dad, Travis.... Yes, I know. Yes. Yes, I will. I swear. I SWEAR. I WILL. Stop it! I love you too. Don't kill anyone.... YOU stink.... YOU do. Eat shit, Marine. Bye!" and she hung up. "Ugh. I have so had it with my brother. He thinks he's my dad!"

On the way out the door, we grabbed our KU IDs, so we could eat in the cafeteria. We were meeting our friend, Mattie, who lived down on the fourth floor. He and Siren had an improv class together, and the three of us had started having meals together.

Out in the common area, the RA for our floor, Cheyenne, had her arm around this girl named Staycee, who lived a couple of doors down from us. Staycee was from Chicago. She was straight-up bawling—tears and snot and everything—with her face in her hands. Cheyenne the RA patted her back and whispered: "It's her little sister's birthday, and she's missing her family." Siren gave Staycee a quick hug before we stepped into one of the elevators and rode it to the fourth floor.

When the elevator doors opened, Mattie was there, waiting. He was tall—at least six foot—and thin, with gangly arms and legs, a cool, fade-locs hairstyle, and oversized, square-rimmed, white glasses. He seemed to have an endless collection of brightly colored high top sneakers, tight t-shirts and super-slim jeans that were always white or black, but never blue. He was chatty and friendly and funny as hell, and weirdly, he was a townie born-and-raised, the first I'd met since I'd moved to Lawrence. Mattie was studying film at KU, and since Siren was studying theater, they crossed paths on campus a fair amount. Today, his purple t-shirt said OH HELL NO in silvery, glittery font, and I laughed out loud.

"Love your t-shirt," I commented.

"Why thank you, Kymer!" he replied. As soon as the doors of the elevator slid shut, he turned to us. "Okay, ladies. You need to keep Friday evening open, because I have managed to get my hands on some rare—let's call them *ingredients*—and the three of us are going to have a tea party, because you two are my new best friends in Oliver, and thank goodness. There is a little too much testosterone down on my floor, if you know what I mean."

"Tea party?" I asked, skeptical. And what did Mattie mean by *ingredients*?

"What tea party?" Siren asked.

"I have a special treat all worked out for us, but you can't have any other plans, for serious. For at least," he looked at his watch, "three to five hours. No studying, no dates, no virtual sex appointments with males on the internet... or females... Nothing."

"Okay," I said. "That should be easy for me, anyway. Well, I do have that biology quiz Monday."

"Oh please," Siren said. "You'll have the whole weekend to study, you big nerd."

"True," I said, though I knew I was going to need the whole weekend. I learned in my first week at KU that college biology was a hundred times tougher than high school biology. Never once in high school had I doubted I'd get an A in biology class. Now it was looking like I'd be lucky if I managed a B.

Siren shrugged her shoulders. "I'm free."

Mattie clapped his hands. "Excellent! We'll need to head out to the library around eightish, I think."

"The library?" Siren said, wrinkling her forehead with confusion.

"It's that big building between Fraser and Stauffer-Flint," I said.

She play-slapped my shoulder. " I know where the library is."

"Ow. Sorry," I said, rubbing my shoulder.

Siren tossed her hair. "I'm just saying, the library seems like a weird place to have a tea party," she said, crossing her arms. "There's got to be a better place to hang out than the library."

"Don't knock it till you've tried it, Sister," Mattie said, pointing at her. Then he clapped for our attention. "Ladies! I'm going to need you to have a good attitude for our tea party Friday! If we don't have a good attitude, we won't have a good time. All of your questions and concerns will be addressed. You just have to trust me."

3

WONDERFUL WATSON

Watson Library was like something out of my dreams. My good dreams. First of all, it looked like what I imagined a European cathedral looked like, at least on the outside. Inside, it was a cathedral of books. The smell was amazing. Everyone referred to the miles of bookcases as "the stacks," and the stacks went down underground like a labyrinth. It was cool, and creepy, and kind of disorienting, and easy to get lost.

As we traipsed up the hill and away from the dorm, the cicadas buzzed away at a deafening volume. It was almost eight-thirty and the sharp heat of the day had lessened, just slightly. The library would be open till 2 a.m. to accommodate studying students.

Mattie wore a purple sequined top hat that was almost blinding to look at in the setting sun, and a black satin backpack. Mattie and Siren were debating whether *Vagina Monologues* or *Mule Bone* did a better job at getting their respective messages across. Mattie was in favor of *Vagina Monologues*. I thought Siren was also for *Vagina Monologues* but was arguing in favor of Mule Bone because she liked to debate.

"The *Vagina Monologues* is kind of the point in history when it finally began to be OKAY to say vagina," Mattie said. "I mean, nowadays, vagina is almost passé. But when that play came out? It was downright subversive."

"Okay, yeah, I get that, but *Mule Bone* is operating on SO many levels: There's race, socioeconomics, religion, gender," she ticked them off on her fingers.

"Pssh. You think *Vagina Monologues* doesn't have all that? It has literally all of that."

I'd never seen either play, so I listened to them talk, I looked up the summaries of both plays on my phone and read them over. Interesting. The sun loomed big and low in the sky, and fluffy clouds blazed orange and pink. Kansas had gorgeous sunsets.

We made our way through campus, Siren and Mattie chatting away. I'd been so busy in those first weeks of school I wasn't even missing Zach that much. Sometimes we only texted once a day, right before bed. Some nights I'd just get: *Sleep tight Lampy!* And I'd text back: *You too!* And that was all. Which was okay. It was kind of how I thought things would go.

Victoria texted every two or three days, usually to ask how the weather was or to tell me she'd sold a house. Dad texted a couple of times a week wanting to know all about campus and my classes. It was cute. He was clearly reliving his college days and was happy I was at KU. Cade never texted me unless I texted him first. Usually I'd say something like, *Hey Fartbreath!* and he'd text back, *Sup, Mouthbreather?* And that would be about it.

"Kymer!" Mattie said, breaking into my thoughts.

"What?"

"Siren says you all have talked about drugs like weed and such, and... like... you're down with all that kind of stuff, right?"

"I mean... sure... I guess so."

"Well now, what does that mean?"

"I mean... I've smoked marijuana a few times. But, y'know, not all the time."

"Mmkay, then. I just wanted to make sure we're on the same page. And what's your opinion on hallucinogens?"

"Like LSD?"

"Yeah. Like LSD. Or peyote."

"Well, peyote, from what I understand, makes people vomit violently before they hallucinate."

"Oh, well, we don't want to do that, then," Mattie said, and he gave Siren a look. She laughed.

"But theoretically... sure, I'd try it."

"Oh my God, you've never tripped?" Siren asked. She grabbed my shoulder. "You have to try it. You have to. You'd love it. I can't believe you've never done it."

"No, I haven't. But like I said, I wouldn't be opposed to trying it. As long as I was in a safe environment, and I trusted the source of the drug."

"So what I'm hearing you say, Kymer, is you like your drugs to be organic and clean," Mattie said, and Siren snorted.

I shrugged. "Of course. I'm not taking random chemicals from some random person. I always look up the side effects and the likelihood of physical addiction, too."

"You're serious, aren't you?" Mattie said. He looked at Siren. "She's serious. She researches her drugs before she takes them."

"Oh she's serious," Siren said. "She researches everything. She probably researches her tampons before she buys them." And we all burst out laughing.

"I do," I wheezed, and none of us could breathe from laughing so hard. Mattie collapsed on the sidewalk.

Siren helped him up. "I told you so," she said.

"Just to be one-hundred-percent clear, Miss Kymer, you would be okay with taking an all-natural, organic drug that grows out of the ground, isn't addictive and is fun as hell?" Mattie asked.

"Sure," I said, assuming he meant marijuana.

We were still laughing as we struggled up the front steps of the library. We breezed through the heavy front doors, lowering our voices.

"Where are we going?" Siren said in a stage whisper.

"This way," Mattie gestured, and he took the lead. He walked briskly across the library, cutting through seating areas and past study stations, with the occasional student glancing up to see us scurry by. We followed, giggling, trying to keep up. He turned and admonished: "Settle down, ladies. People are trying to study." I snorted and we all laughed, louder than we should've, as Mattie snaked us through shelves of the reference section, and then the DVD collection, to a door on the east wall of the building marked **2 East Stacks**. Mattie flung open the door, and we followed. His nimble feet, though large, took the stairs at an amazing rate, and Siren and I struggled to keep up as he rounded the first turn in the stairs before we were even halfway down the flight. Down, down, down, we went, our laughter echoing in the stairwell.

"Dude! Wait up!" Siren exclaimed, though at this point she was ahead of me by a flight of stairs while I was at least two full flights behind Mattie—I could see his purple sequined hat bobbing up and down below me. Just when I wondered how many more stairs there could possibly be, and what a pain it was going to be to climb back up all of them, we were at the bottom, facing another door with a small window. Through the window were stacks and stacks of books.

"Ya'll ready?" Mattie asked.

"Ready for what?" Siren asked.

"For the fun," Mattie said, and he opened the door, motioning us through. "Ladies first." Siren and I walked through the door, then waited to follow Mattie, who made a right turn, walking past the aisles of books that seemed to go on forever in every direction. Siren and I followed, and I marveled at the stacks, packed top to bottom with books, all the way to the ceiling. The walls, and the floor, down here were concrete. The light was a sickly, flickering, yellow-green, the fluorescent tubes buzzing overhead. The air was still and stale and smelled of old books. There was nothing down here to make any noise except the three of us. We were alone. We passed through one room, then another, and finally another, the rows of books seemingly endless. Mattie finally stopped walking when he reached the corner of the third room. He took off his backpack and set it on the floor. He unzipped it and removed a small, flowered tablecloth. He snapped it open, and I laughed.

"SHHHHHHHH!" he said, smoothing it out on the floor. Then he sat down cross-legged and patted the floor next to him. He was still wearing the crazy hat. Siren and I sat down criss-cross applesauce, she next to him and me across. On the concrete wall behind him was a bee stenciled in stark black, likely done by some free-spirited art student. Then he produced an old thermos from the backpack

"Jesus," I said. "Where did you get that amazing artifact?" The thermos was one of those old-style metal and glass ones with vinyl plaid printed on the outside.

"My pops likes to fish," he said, as though that explained everything. He then pulled a box out of the backpack, set the box down on the tablecloth, and removed the top with a flourish. It was an honest-to-god kids' tea set. White china with delicate pink and green flowers. Even though Mattie's family lived in Lawrence, he'd moved into the dorm to get some separation from them. Especially since he also worked for the family business.

"Matthew," I said, "What is all this?"

"DON'T call me Matthew," he said, continuing to unpack the tea set. Then, more quietly: "Only my moms gets to calls me Matthew."

"Sorry. Okay, Mattie. What is all this? What are we doing?"

"Will you please keep your voice down? It is a tea service, obviously. It's my little sister's. I swiped it from the playhouse out back. Our dog Lola almost licked me to death before I got out of there. I *told* you we were having a tea party." Mattie set places for all of us, complete with tiny spoons, a little sugar bowl and a baggie with lemon slices. "I apologize for not bringing milk, but I don't think it'd taste good in this, anyway," he said. He poured a tea-like liquid from the thermos into the tea pot and began filling the tiny tea cups.

"What kind of tea is this?" Siren asked, wrinkling her pierced nose.

"It's my special infusion," he said. "You'll want to add sugar for sure, and I prefer it with lemon as well."

"Oh my god, Mattie, this isn't..." Siren said.

"Isn't what?" he asked, innocently.

"Oh my god, it is, isn't it? Say it is," Siren's eyes lit up.

"It is, love. Now, before we get started, I would recommend you take small sips of your tea. Remember, we have lots of time for this. Pinkies out!"

I added sugar and lemon, and stirred with the little spoon, but it smelled awful. I didn't want to be impolite and not drink Mattie's tea, but I didn't think I could deal with sipping it, so I downed the whole thing. I couldn't keep the disgust off my face.

Mattie looked at me with horror. "You were supposed to sip it!"

"Why?" He was making me nervous. Siren was looking at me funny, too.

"It's mushroom tea, you big doofus," she said.

"Mushroom tea?" I still didn't understand.

"You know. Mushroom tea," she looked at me expectantly. "Psychedelic mushrooms?"

I can't lie. I was furious. I'd never had psilocybin mushrooms before. "You dosed me?"

"Oh, Sweetheart. Please know that I would never do that to you. You drank it before I could say anything. I didn't know you'd go grabbing your cup like the Incredible Hulk with absolutely no manners whatsoever."

"The Hulk!" Siren collapsed on the floor, laughing.

"This is not funny," I said. "You do not give someone unauthorized drugs."

"Unauthorized drugs?" Mattie said. He put his hand on his heart, his eyes bugging out of his head.

"Unauthorized!" Siren wailed, still rolling on the floor.

"Drugs not authorized by the person taking them," I said, louder, frustrated.

"Oh, you're fine," Siren said. She grabbed my hands and began rubbing them. She looked into my eyes. "Just relax and enjoy this. Mattie and I will make sure you have a good trip. We'll keep you safe. We promise."

Her lips were perfect. Plump and the color of sparkly berries. My anger dissolved. I knew they didn't really mean to hurt me. Dickheads.

"Okay," I said. "I'm trusting you."

"These are pure, unadulterated mushrooms, Miss Kymer, from a source I trust implicitly. I promise," Mattie said. "I guess we'd better catch up." He and Sired picked up their tiny teacups and clinked them together. They sipped at the teeny cups while we continued to chat.

I felt myself begin to relax. Siren rubbed my shoulders while the three of us chatted, waiting for the effects to kick in. Twenty minutes later, I felt relaxed and happy. The feeling began to deepen, and when I turned to look at the books on the shelf next to me, one lit up like it had a light bulb inside it... That one went out and a light came on inside another book... The books were flashing on and off, and it was fascinating. I looked at Siren, and she was so beautiful I thought I might cry. Then her right eye, her beautiful, big brown right eye with the impossibly long lashes, grew three times its normal size, while her full mouth slid up the left side of her face. Suddenly, I was talking to a real-life Picasso. I laughed.

It felt so good to laugh. That's when any final traces of being angry melted away.

As it turned out, the room we were in was home to books about the history of the ancient world. While I flipped through books, staring at old maps and illustrations—sea serpents slipping from the depths and such—Mattie and Siren cleared the cups and thermos off the table cloth and were sitting on it, eyes closed, massaging each other's faces. I, on the other hand, couldn't sit still. I could feel the air—like water—so I swam around the room, enjoying the effect.

The floor boiled and rippled all around me. The leather bindings of the books became scaly dragon hides, even as I held the books in my hands. Illustrations buckled and roiled on the pages. My sense of perspective shifted from moment to moment so that bookshelves seemed twenty feet high one moment before shrinking back down to normal size the next. Aisles of books looked like canyons that didn't end.

"This is like *Alice in Wonderland*," I said.

"Those are called 'visuals,'" Siren said, laughing. "I told you you'd love it."

She and Mattie were still having their tactile love-in. "Wait, how does this feel?" Siren asked, massaging Mattie's temples.

"Amazeballs," he groaned with pleasure, and Siren laughed.

I wandered into the stacks again, just sort of swimming along, until a fuzzy bit of movement on the floor caught my eye. It was a house centipede (*Scutigera coleoptrata*). It had crawled out from under one of the book shelves and was skittering down the aisle in front of me. It was the biggest house centipede I'd ever seen. Its hundreds of hair-like legs worked up and down as it appeared to float across the floor, and I couldn't help but follow it. When I reached the end of the aisle, I was surprised to see that behind Mattie and Siren, instead of the wall with the graffiti bee, was a new room of books.

I stopped to orient myself in the room. "Hey… Did you two move?" I asked. They ignored me. "Um … friends?" No response. "PEEPS," I said louder, trying to break up their freaky love-in.

"WHAT?" Siren asked, eyes still closed, smiling like a lunatic.

"Open your eyes and turn around."

"Oh my gawd. Please don't tell me there's a monster behind us," Mattie opened his eyes and looked. "What?" he said.

"What do you mean, what? The wall you were sitting next to. It's gone."

"No," Siren said. "That's how it was. There was no wall."

"Yeah, girl," Mattie said. "There was no wall."

"Come on," I said. "You two are not that messed up. There was a wall there. It had a bee symbol stenciled on it."

"I don't know what you're talking about," Siren's eyes were closed again, her hands running up and down Mattie's back. "You're having a really good trip. You seem to be experiencing waaay better visuals than we are."

Just to make sure, I walked around the perimeter of the room. No bee stencil anywhere. Once I was back where I started, I considered the new room in front of me. It appeared to be similar to the room we were in, another concrete, bunker-like room full of books, but, somehow, even larger. Much larger. I approached slowly, stepping around Siren and Mattie, and started looking around. This room was so much bigger than the other book bunkers, it seemed odd to be located so far down underground. The light in here was even dimmer, the dingy bulbs giving off a strange shade of yellow haze. The air shimmered around me like a mirage in the heat, which I assumed was a visual effect of the psilocybin. I waved my hand through the air, watching it react as though I'd run my hand through water.

She materialized about twenty feet away from me. As soon as she appeared, the air became warm and suffocating. Thicker. I couldn't move. But my brain shifted into overdrive: Oh my god where did that woman come from no one else has come down the stairs unless there's another door somewhere in this room maybe that's not a woman at all maybe she's just part of the visuals it's just a weird shadow or something if I could look away from it and look back again

I bet she won't even be there except I can't look away because if I look away she might do something freaky and then I'll die and now she's moving oh holy God she's walking right toward me and why is she wearing that weird old fashioned dress I guess Halloween isn't that far away I bet that's what's going on, she's in costume or doing cosplay or something...

And then the woman spoke: "Here is the book you're looking for."

Her voice was clear and solid. So was she. She wasn't a visual. She was a person. And in her extended hand, a book. A book with a black cover, and on the cover, stamped in gold, something that looked extraordinarily like the bee symbol on the missing wall.

What. The. Fuck.

"I'm sorry?" I stammered. "The book I'm looking for?"

"Yes. Obviously you're looking for it, or you wouldn't be here, and we wouldn't be communicating," her brow furrowed with impatience. "Well, here it is. Take it," she leaned forward.

I reached out tentatively, wondering if I would feel—anything—and she shoved the book into my hand. It was solid. Real. But her hand hadn't touched me.

"Oh for goodness sake. It isn't as if it is a snake," she said, clearly annoyed. She pointed at me, critically. "You need to take that book and get going. Who knows how long this will last?"

"How long what will last?" I asked, having no idea what she was talking about.

She looked at me pointedly. "Our interaction, child."

"Okay," I said, turning the book over in my hands, still stunned that it was a physical object. "Um... Thank you? Is there anything else I should know? Anything else you want to tell me?"

She adjusted her steel-rimmed spectacles. "For one thing, you and your hooligan friends need to clean up your so-called 'tea party' and remove yourselves from my library. The library is NOT the place for such activities. The library is for reading and study. It is not a bar, nor a brothel. Secondly, always remember that when you pull a book off the shelves, if you aren't positive about where to reshelve it, place it on one of the carts located at the ends of the aisles." She motioned. "This lets the librarian know it needs to be returned to its home on the shelves."

The air was becoming thinner, and I felt the need to back away from her. "But what's this book for?"

"I don't know, exactly. Something that's unknown needs to be set right. That's what universities are for, after all. Education. Learning. Knowledge. You'll figure it out. You're not a *stupid* girl."

"But... I'm sorry, I don't understand... What needs to be set right?"

"I don't have that information. All I know is this book is important, and you're the mortal who can reveal what's been overlooked."

I pretended as though she hadn't just called me a 'mortal,' because that involved so many questions, and I just didn't know if I wanted to go there. "Asked? Asked by who?"

"Apparently, that is none of your concern, nor your business. Your job is to set things right. Why are you still here blathering at me? *The window is closing.*"

I turned to go.

"Young lady," she snapped.

I turned around. "Yeah?"

"Do not attempt to check that book out at the front desk."

"Won't the sensors go off if I don't check it out?"

"That book has not been tagged," she stood up straight and proud. "I have always been, and will always be, the head librarian here and I am entrusting that book to you and you alone. You'll be free to leave with it, under my authority."

"Yes ma'am."

She flicked her hands. "Now go." And I was dismissed. So I went.

I stepped back into the other room, staring at the book in my hand. I looked behind me, but she was gone. In her place? The concrete wall. Without the bee symbol.

"Aw man," Siren said, startling me. She stood up and stretched into mountain pose. Her voice cut through any remnants of mental haze that had been hanging in the air. "How long have we been here?"

Mattie looked at his phone. "A little over three hours."

"I think I'm starting to come down," she said.

"Me too," said Mattie. He stood up, stretching his long limbs.

"Yeah, I mean, I still feel it some, but it's definitely fading." Siren put her arms around me. Her hair smelled wonderful. "How you doin', Hot Mama?"

"Um, I'm okay." Because I wasn't really sure what to say.

"Did you have fun? You don't seem like you had that much fun," she let me go, her lower lip stuck out in a pout.

"Oh, I had a blast," I said, which was true, until the old lady had scared the bejesus out of me. "This has been... crazy."

"I'm so glad!" said Mattie. He clapped his hands. "I feel like we're at a point in our trip where we should move on, though. My body is craving movement."

"Me too!" Siren stood, legs set apart, and proceeded to do side lunges.

"Yeah," I said, looking at the leather-bound book in my hand. "We should probably get out of here."

"Where should we go next?" Siren asked, but I wasn't up to going anywhere else.

"It's getting late," I said, "I'm kinda tired." I faked a yawn for good measure.

"Stop it," Siren said, also yawning.

"I agree," said Mattie, looking at his phone. "It's after midnight and we still have to walk back to the dorm. The walk should be fun, though."

We cleaned up our tea party, placing everything back in the backpack. I considered stashing the book in Mattie's pack, but then decided that was crazy. When we reached the main level of the library, I headed straight for the front doors, ahead of Siren and Mattie. I couldn't wait to get out of there.

"Hey!" Siren said. "Don't you have to check out that book?"

"No," I said. I kept walking, not looking back. "It's not a library book. This lady gave it to me..." but I stopped short, because there on the wall, next to the checkout desks, was a black-and-white photo of a woman. A woman who coincidentally looked exactly like the creepy old lady who had given me the very book I held in my hand. MADAM LIBRARIAN, the caption on the photo read, and then, in smaller type, **Carrie Morehouse Watson**. It was her. The cranky librarian. Her and her spectacles and her lace collar and all. Holy shit. The whole damn library was named for her. I stopped briefly to read, and as it turned out, Carrie Watson had been KU's first, most longtime, and most beloved librarian, even though she was also known as kind of a grump. *She died in 1943.* I gaped at the photo.

"What?" Siren asked.

"Nothing," I said, turning away from the photo and heading toward the door. "I thought I saw something, but it's just the 'shrooms wearing off." When I reached the door, I shoved it open and walked outside, not bothering to hold it for either of them. I ran down the big front steps and kind of collapsed on the sidewalk. I mean, I didn't fall down or anything, I just had the overwhelming need to sit because I felt... drained, somehow. So I did, on the sidewalk in front of Watson Library, under a streetlamp swarming with moths of all sizes. The night was cooler than I'd expected. Mattie and Siren came scrambling out of the library and down the front steps a couple seconds later.

"Hey! Wait up! Kymer! Did you just steal that book?" Mattie asked.

"No," I said, not wanting to talk about it. I stood up and walked. They followed.

"Where did it come from?" Siren asked. "You didn't bring a book into the library, did you?"

I shook my head. "I told you. A lady gave it to me."

"What? Why?" Siren asked.

"I don't know," I said, and it wasn't a lie.

4

Flora and Carrie

You might be wondering what career path one can look forward to with an entomology degree. There are a few options, and I honestly wasn't sure what I wanted to do once I graduated. There were some things I knew I absolutely wouldn't do: pest management, for one. This can be government work, where you decide when and where to spray insect pests for the public good. Like spraying whole towns to kill mosquitoes in order to manage the spread of a mosquito-borne illness, or spraying a city block for large-scale cockroach infestations, that kind of thing. I would also never go to work for a private chemical firm to develop pesticides. Don't get me wrong, pesticides are sometimes necessary, but I had zero desire to kill insects or contribute to the killing of insects. Zero. Other people could do that. Not me.

Then there are entomologists who inspect goods coming into the country and establish quarantines in order to stop the spread of pests. Again, obviously necessary, but I didn't think I wanted to do that either.

Now forensic entomology—working with dead bodies, coroners, police and detectives, and the insects that colonize and breed on a dead body to determine when someone died—that was kind of intriguing. I thought I could learn to deal with dead bodies, but the number of insects you encounter in that kind of work tends to be limited... mostly flies and certain beetles.

Then there was the purely academic application of entomology...
going to school to become a researcher and teacher. That had a lot of
appeal to me—at least, the research part. I wasn't so sure about the
teaching part.

But there were private researchers, too, who worked in agriculture
to better understand how to breed and use insects to humanity's
advantage, in order to increase food yields. There was lots of new
research going into protecting bees and other pollinators. Ironically,
honey bee colony collapses were a sort of controversial concern in
the field of entomology, since modern honey bees (*Apis mellifera*)
aren't native to North America, anyway, but most entomologists
seemed to come down on the side of wanting to protect the honey
bees, because, well... honey, not to mention food crop pollination.
And a career in the agribusiness of insects seemed as though it might
be a good career fit for me. I hoped school would help me figure it out.

Because I was a freshman, I didn't have any actual entomology
classes yet, which kind of sucked. But I was taking the honors Cellular
Biology class, which was turning out to be a lot more difficult than
I'd anticipated. A lot more difficult. I thought I could pass the class,
but my professor wasn't making it easy. Well, that's not fair. She was
insisting we learn about biology properly, which meant going into far
more detail and specificity than my biology teachers in high school. I
realized, now, that we'd been taught a sort of dumbed-down version
of biology, when the real science was far more complicated. There
were just so many more chemicals to know, formulas to memorize,
and steps to remember. The photosynthesis I'd been taught in high
school, I was learning, barely touched on the highlights of the process,
which was incredibly problematic and frankly, inefficient.

College was definitely not like high school. In high school I hadn't
needed to study too hard for my science classes. So far, the college
experience had taught me to take thorough notes and review them
later. A lot of students recorded their professors' lectures on their
phones, but I retained the material better by taking old-fashioned
notes in a notebook. Something about writing the words down
helped them stick.

The first day I walked into my biology class, I was shocked. I
had no idea it would be so big. The auditorium in the student union

held at least five hundred people, and the professor's notes were a power-point presentation projected on a huge movie screen. The sea of heads all bent over the tiny desktops that unfolded like origami from the armrests was intimidating. I did like the anonymity of it, especially on mornings like this one, when I'd chosen to sleep in rather than shower, and fit a KU ballcap over my ponytail instead of washing my hair.

I fidgeted with my pen, nervous about the biology quiz. I'd studied some the night before, but somehow ended up in Mattie's room watching *2001: A Space Odyssey* until one in the morning, and then I couldn't fall asleep. I managed to snooze a bit until the sun came up, and it was time to get ready for the day. Now I had a slight headache and felt sluggish, physically and mentally. I put my head in my hands and closed my eyes, trying to visualize my notes. I had to make halfway decent grades if there was any chance of convincing Victoria she and Dad should continue paying for me to go to school in Kansas.

Professor Berg was up front on the stage as usual, a tall stack of papers on the stand next to her. She began doling out smaller stacks of tests to the TAs—teaching assistants—and they walked to different sections of the auditorium, handing even smaller stacks to each row. "Take one, place it on your desk face down, and pass them on," the TA with short turquoise hair said to the guy at the end of our row, but loud enough for several people to hear.

Professor Berg was an older lady with salt-and-pepper locs. Gladys Berg. She covered a shit-ton of information every class, and she expected you to keep up. She also did not like to take up class time re-reviewing material when people messed up the quizzes, which, it seemed, a lot of students did. Professor Berg always gave ten-point fill-in-the-blank quizzes, one point for each question, and she always set a timer for fifteen minutes. When all the quizzes were distributed, she set the timer, which was projected on the big screen. "And begin," she said, and the rustling of five-hundred people turning over their quizzes quickly became silence.

I answered all the questions but two, the answers for which I was blanking on, hardcore. I couldn't believe it. I knew the answers. I knew I knew the answers. I just couldn't pry them from my tired brain. I scribbled down the last two answers just as Professor Berg announced, "Pencils down."

We handed our quizzes to the end of the aisle so the TAs could collect and grade them during the lecture as Professor Berg put up the graphic for the start of our next section of study: DNA. She lectured for the remaining period, and as class was nearing its end, the TAs handed back our graded quizzes. Damn it. I'd missed three answers on a ten-point quiz, and our quizzes made up fifty percent of our grade. For one of the answers I'd put down adenosine diphosphate instead of adenosine triphosphate, like a complete moron.

"You may leave when you've received your quiz," Professor Berg announced, and people began to get up here and there and file out of the auditorium. A hand shot up down front. "Yes?" Professor Berg pointed, and what sounded like a dude's voice said, "Will you be grading us on a curve at all?"

Professor Berg chuckled. "Uh, no." Groans floated through the auditorium. Professor Berg was not having it. "I'm not sure what's going on with the students in this course, but about half of you are going to fail if you do not pick it up. And believe me, I do not have qualms about doing that. I have done it before, and I'll do it again. Would it be a shame to fail half of a class of four-hundred-eighty-some students? Yes it would. It would be a shame for you. And for your parents, who are probably the ones paying good money for you to have the privilege of being here. Is the system of photosynthesis complicated? Yes! Yes, it is complicated. But we're not going to skip steps just because it's difficult. Photosynthesis is the basis for most life on this planet. So we're going to give it the treatment and respect it deserves."

She was right, of course. I liked her, even though she made us work.

"What did you get?" The girl sitting next to me asked her friend as they got up to leave.

"Five out of ten. What did you get?"

"Four. Can you believe that shit? Four points out of ten. Why does that bitch have to make an entry level class so hard? I'm going to have to drop the class." As they left, I never wanted to pop someone in the mouth so bad.

By the time I got back to our dorm room, I was warm from the walk, still tired from the night before, and dying to look at the book from our library trip. I dropped my backpack at the foot of my bed and retrieved the book from the bottom of my underwear drawer. I'd tried flipping through it while we walked back to the dorm from the library the night before, but after tripping over a curb and falling on my ass—much to the delight of my so-called friends—I'd given up. I'd gotten chills, though, when I'd glimpsed pictures of bugs. Bugs!

I fell back on my bed and flipped through the book. Siren was in her English 101 class, followed by her improv class with Mattie, so I had the room to myself for a while. The book, as it turned out, was a hand-written field journal. An insect journal. A really good insect journal, complete with detailed notes and detailed sketches.

I flipped to the front of the journal, being careful with the aging pages. Flora Ellen Richardson was hand-written in cursive in the upper right hand corner of the inside cover, along with the year: 1871. The handwriting style was old, but since everything was written and drawn in pencil, nothing had faded. The pages were browning and smelled of vanilla, and I turned them carefully. The book was about an inch-and-a-half thick, with the black leather cover and the gold foil honey bee stamped on the front. The entries only took up the first half or so of the book; the rest of the pages were blank.

There were all kinds of bugs in the book, and I realized pretty quickly that it was a field-identification journal of insects Flora had seen around campus and around town. Most of the entries of common insects only took up a page, with a few notes ascribed to them. But the bugs that were a little more unusual had three or four pages devoted to them, with multiple sketches depicting the insect from various angles, and detailed notes. For those entries, Flora had noted the insect's genus and species, the location she'd found it, what it was sitting on, what time of day it was, the weather conditions, what it was eating if it happened to be munching at the time, and of course, the date. Sometimes she'd even describe how she was feeling at the moment of discovery. They were almost like diary entries:

September 20, 1872
Sunny, 10 a.m., 71 °F
Hummingbird Hawk-Moth
Macroglossum stellatarum

Sighted a beautiful hummingbird hawk-moth feeding in a patch of purple asters on my way to University Hall this morning. The handsome little insect was about two inches long, with black, gold and pink stripes on his fuzzy abdomen, and translucent wings, with a black proboscis as long as the body. It was in a feeding frenzy, flitting from blossom to blossom every few seconds. The weather was lovely this morning; the sky was cerulean blue with a smattering of downy clouds. The air was lovely with a slight breeze and low humidity. The thermometer outside the window of my Biology laboratory read 71 degrees Fahrenheit. As luck would have it, I was early to class, so I had time to stop and make some quick sketches in the field and was able to fill in the details later. I am fairly certain this is an example of the male of the species, as I believe I have located the single frenulum under his forewing, but I'm hoping Professor Snow will be able to confirm this.

It was a really nice journal. I couldn't believe the amount of work she'd put into it. I put the book down on my bed and looked up Flora Ellen Richardson on my computer, but the only information I could find was provided by the University of Kansas. As it turned out, Flora had been part of the first graduating class at KU, and the first graduation took place in front of a building called University Hall, which I wasn't familiar with. In a graduating class of only four people, she was the only woman, and the Valedictorian, at that. As part of the graduation ceremony, she'd given a speech titled *The Uses of Superstition*, about how she thought superstition could be a tool to lead people to be more curious about the natural world. A sort of religion-leads-to-science kind of thing. After a few minutes of research I figured out the University Hall she mentioned had been razed in the 1960s and replaced with the current Fraser Hall.

I thought back to the incident in the library, which was now very fuzzy—not fuzzy in my mind's eye—I could see it all fine. But it was a fuzzy feeling, as though the whole night had been a dream. I assumed that it was a side effect of the mushrooms, but it was still disconcerting. When you've had a dream, you know you've had a dream, and that's how last night felt. It felt... not real. Like a movie I'd watched. But I knew for a fact we'd gone to the library, and I had the book. So I must've met the old lady. But the old lady was dead, and had been dead for over a hundred and fifty years. It had been going around and around and around in my head all day, driving me nuts.

After reading through the bug diary for a couple of hours, I stashed it in my underwear drawer, left the dorm and walked back up the hill. I wanted to go back to Watson Library to see if there was any additional material there on Flora and Carrie Watson that wasn't available on the internet. When I arrived at Watson, I headed straight for the section of the library devoted to KU history. I did some preliminary searches and discovered a few newspaper articles and some research papers on both Flora and Carrie. Some of the documents were so old they had been photographed and collected on microfilm. A student working at the library retrieved the specific rolls of film for me and showed me how to work the viewer. I spent the next couple hours researching both women, and this is what I learned:

Flora was born in Monroe, Wisconsin in 1851. She moved to Lawrence in 1870 with her family. She and her brother George enrolled in spring classes at KU that year, but Flora returned to Lombard University in Galesburg, Illinois in the fall, where she had taken classes previously. She must have missed Lawrence, though, because in 1872, she returned and enrolled at KU full time. By then, Flora and George's younger brother Albert was also attending KU. Neither of the brothers graduated.

The next thing I read sent chills through me. *Flora collected and pinned KU's very first entomological collection of 140 insects, under the supervision of her natural history professor, Francis Huntington Snow.* Snow would later become chancellor of the university. Snow Hall was named for him. Though I didn't have any classes in that building, I always remembered the name because the building made me think of

Snow White's castle, complete with crenulated turrets.

Though Flora wasn't the first female student to attend KU, she was the first woman to complete an undergraduate degree in June of 1873. By 1875 she had completed a Master of Arts degree. After graduating from KU, she settled in Lawrence, got married and had seven kids—four girls and three boys. She was a fan of women's suffrage and worked to make sure that the local schools, including some of KU's buildings, provided restrooms for women.

In other words, she was amazing.

Carrie Watson, on the other hand, seemed like kind of a character. First off, as a kid, she had survived Quantrill's Raid on Lawrence in 1863. This was during the Civil War, when a man named William Quantrill, a Southern sympathizer from Missouri, came through Lawrence with a band of attackers. At the time, slavery was legal in Missouri, and Kansas had just entered the Union as a free state. Quantrill and his men burned down all the wooden structures in Lawrence—houses, hotels, stores—and killed over 160 men and boys. They let the women live. I had heard my dad mention Quantrill's Raid a couple of times, I guess, but I'd never really thought much about it. Carrie survived the raid, attended KU and graduated in 1877. In 1878 she was hired by KU as an assistant librarian, but the library at the time was located in Spooner Hall, which was now an anthropology building. Nine years later, she became the head librarian. She was known to be kind of a curmudgeon, and a good procurer of books, but she was also unorganized. When the library outgrew Spooner Hall, KU built a new, bigger library. It was added on to and remodeled several times to accommodate all the books Carrie acquired for the university, which was how Watson Library ended up a maze of stacks. She retired in 1921, but the library wasn't named for her until 1924. She died in 1943.

The whole incident with Carrie had me pretty freaked out, and I was a little afraid of seeing her again. On the other hand, I did want to see her again. I had so many questions. What had her life been like? What was it like curating an entire major university library from the ground up? And she would've been doing it at the time the West was expanding across the United States, when most women didn't have careers. Crazy.

Before I left, I gathered up the courage to go back down to the room where we'd had our tea party. I had to. I made my way down, down all the steps again, and weaved through the stacks until I found it. Then I stood there, trying to figure out... anything. Did I feel odd? No, not really. It all seemed... pretty normal. I hung out for about ten minutes, waiting for... something—though I didn't know what—to happen.

Eventually, I left.

As I walked back across campus and down the hill to the dorm, all I could think about was The Carrie Watson Incident, as I was now referring to it in my head. Had it happened? And if it had, was she real? Was she a ghost? Was I developing schizophrenia? After all, people did, at my age.

Finally, I decided to accept the known facts: Some lady, who may or may not be Carrie Watson, but who looked exactly fucking like Carrie Watson, had given me a book. That book appeared to be the diary of a former KU student named Flora Richardson who had been dead nearly a hundred years. The lady who had given me the diary could be:

A) A local whacko who liked to dress in period clothing and hand out random diaries to tripping college girls. (Kind of likely in Lawrence.)

B) A complete figment of my mushroom-addled mind, and I'd somehow picked up the book myself. (Also likely.)

or

C) An actual ghost. (Far less likely, since I was pretty sure ghosts were bullshit.)

Those were the facts, as I knew them to be, with my limited human senses and faculties.

And, for the moment anyway, I left things at that.

5

Diaries and Dildos

Once in a while our RA Cheyenne scheduled a floor meeting to discuss some matter or another—noise after hours, leaving huge messes in the bathrooms—etcetera. Of course I attended the first floor meeting, which happened that very first evening after we'd all moved in, because it seemed the natural thing to do, but the whole thing felt a little—nanny-ish to me—so I'd avoided the other floor meetings. I'd come to college to get away from my mother, not gain a different one. But Siren had seen the posters in the hall: *Let's Talk About Sex! This Sunday in the Common Area with Cheyenne, 4 p.m.*, with its cutesy graphics and thought it'd be fun to go. The one thing I did not want to talk with my RA about was sex. I liked Cheyenne, but it wasn't like she was my mother, either. Still, Siren was insisting we attend.

"Do we have to?" I groaned. What I really wanted to do was take a break from studying and stare at my bugs for a while. We were right in the middle of the semester, and I was crazy-busy with tests and papers and projects. Now I had a little bit of free time, and I wanted to lie around the room and do nothing. Besides that, I needed to find a cricket or something for Caroline to eat. She was starting to look a little thin.

"C'mon you antisocial weirdo," Siren said. "We live here. Let's act like it."

Caroline wasn't going to starve right away, I knew, and Siren made me feel like kind of an asshole about not wanting to go to the meeting, so I went.

Cheyenne was standing in the back corner of the common area. It was a drizzly Sunday afternoon, and the light coming in through the windows was muted, the air a little chilly with all that cold tile.

"Welcome! Welcome!" she said, waving us in. Cheyenne was almost always cheerful and confident and willing to help or listen to any of the girls. She was a good RA.

"Come in, ladies! Come and sit and be comfortable. Go grab a blanket from your room if you like. Grab a pillow. I want everyone to be nice and comfortable." I sat down cross-legged on the cool tile floor, near Staycee and Lila. They lived a couple doors down from us. Like Staycee, Lila was also from Chicago. They were friends from high school. They were pretty cool. Then there was Emily and Kayla, who were both from some suburb outside of Kansas City. There was Sonya and Brittany and Alexis and Destiny and Emma Kate and Emma... oh, and Grace, who was... odd. Grace brought her dead stuffed gray Persian cat Mr. Princie with her to school, which kind of freaked out her assigned roommate, Emma Kate. Emma Kate said she could deal with Grace, but she did not appreciate sharing the room with Mr. Princie. Grace was from Oklahoma, and her uncle was a taxidermist. He'd stuffed Mr. Princie after he'd died, so Grace could forever have her cat. Creepy.

There was also a gaggle of girls from Phoenix at the far end of our hall who seemed kind of snooty. They ignored Siren and me, and we ignored them back. Most of the girls in our wing of the floor seemed pretty chill, though. I didn't know anyone from the other wing.

After sitting on the cold floor for a couple minutes, Siren said, "Screw this," and she strode over to the far side of the commons area and dragged a big stuffed chair across the floor. Then she sort of draped herself over it, with her long legs bent casually over the armrest.

"Yes!" said Cheyenne, with her trademark enthusiasm. "Siren has the right idea! Make yourselves comfortable. I want this to be a safe, inviting space for everyone for the next hour or so while we chat."

Girls from both wings of the floor filed in slowly, taking various spots around the floor, many of them in their jammies and slippers, until the commons area was packed.

As usual, Cheyenne's cup runneth over with zeal, her voice booming throughout the commons area. "Are we all here? Yes? No?

A few more? Excellent! Please, cop a squat."

When it looked as though everyone who was going to show up to the floor meeting was there, Cheyenne whipped her hand from behind her back. "Hooray for the vibrator! Hooray for the vibrator!" Because she was indeed holding a vibrator. A purple jelly one. It quivered in Cheyenne's hand. The room exploded in noise. Siren burst out laughing. Several girls said, "You have a vibrator?" all at the same time. Staycee covered her mouth with her hand and said, "Oh. My. God." In her best Chicago accent. Someone else said, "Ew!" Grace looked grim and uncomfortable. I sat quietly, taking in the range of reactions over a sex toy. Hilarious.

I'd learned my junior year of high school that a vibrator was an absolute necessity in my life, especially when I didn't have a boyfriend. It was my friend Chloe who clued me in, and it was her older sister who'd encouraged her to buy one. In fact, Chloe made me skip sixth hour math with her and drug me to this crazy sex store in a strip mall—Cupid's Arrow. "Trust me, Kymer," she'd said. "Once you have a vibrator, you will *not* be able to live without one."

She wasn't wrong. It almost made me feel sorry for the sheltered girls who hadn't yet discovered the climatic joys of assisted stimulation. Cheyenne continued:

"The answer to that question is, yes, I do have a vibrator, but this is not the one I use. This vibrator is for demonstration purposes only," and she switched it on. It rotated and buzzed, while a cool blue LED light pulsed at its base. Again, the girls fell to pieces. So silly.

"Now, this is not going to be a sex talk, per se. I am going to assume that all of you understand how all those things work, and you've had those conversations with your parents, and so on and so forth."

"Lila hasn't," Staycee piped up.

"Shut up!" Lila said, smacking her on her leg. There was lots of laughter and Staycee snorted, which caused more laughter.

"Well Lila, sweetheart, if you want to have that conversation with me sometime, make an appointment, and we'll talk," Cheyenne said, clasping her hands with earnest.

"I don't need to," Lila said, nudging Staycee. She turned bright red.

"There is no shame here," Cheyenne said, raising her voice over all the giggling. "No shame! This is a shame-free zone." She waited for everyone to settle down. "What I am here to talk to you all about today is staying safe and honoring yourselves. And sometimes that means using a vibrator instead of jumping into a sexual relationship with a partner in an unsafe situation."

"That's easy for you to say," Kayla said. "You're in a room by yourself."

"Well yes, that's true, but where there's a will, there's a way. You know your roommate's schedule. You know when she'll be gone. Or maybe the two of you could work that out with each other, somehow."

"A masturbation schedule?" Siren asked dryly.

"Yes, if need be," Cheyenne said over the laughter. "Whatever works. But we also need to remember, when we're out or when we're bringing boys—or men—back to the dorm, we need to remember to always use condoms, which is why this condom bowl will be available in my room with lovely condoms provided by Watkins Health Services." Watkins was the school health center. She handed the bowl to Kayla. "Everyone take two or three and pass it on. Don't be shy. I don't need anyone waking me up at two in the morning because she doesn't have one. That's right. And feel free to come by and pick up more, anytime... well, anytime I'm awake, that is." She nodded approvingly as the bowl was passed around the room. I noticed that Grace declined to even touch the bowl, as she white-knuckled Mr. Princie. I grabbed three, considered how full the bowl was and picked out three more before passing it on to Siren, who grabbed a handful and stuffed them into the pocket of the hoodie she was wearing.

"We need to also remember to always have a buddy with us when we go drinking," Cheyenne said, as the bowl continued to travel. "Even though many of us here aren't of legal drinking age, we know that sometimes alcohol happens, and we need to watch out for each other. Remember to never leave your drink unattended."

"Why?" Grace asked, quietly. She was stroking Mr. Princie so hard it looked like she might give him a bald spot.

"Well, because sometimes certain..." Cheyenne hesitated.

"Fucking shitbag rapists?" Siren offered.

"Yes, thank you Siren. Certain... people who would like to engage in rape find it easier to commit their crimes by drugging people's drinks."

"That happens?" Grace asked. She looked terrified.

"Yes, ma'am, it does," Cheyenne said. "Look, the majority of boys and men out there are perfectly nice people. But it is a real danger that exists. So, just to be safe, keep your drink with you, you know? Or ask a girlfriend to hold it while you use the restroom.

"Of course there is no alcohol happening here in the dorm, correct?" Cheyenne said, pointing the vibrator at us for emphasis.

"Oh, never," I said, knowing that Siren and I were not the only ones who snuck in booze on the regular.

"Where can you even get those?" Emily asked, referring to the vibrator.

"There's a sex shop on 23rd Street," Siren said, and everyone turned to look at her. "What?" she said. "I'm just saying. There is."

"Yes, thank you, Siren," Cheyenne said. "It's across the street from the Dillon's grocery store on the corner of Twenty-Third and Naismith Drive."

After the meeting, I tended to my bugs while Siren highlighted her hair. After I'd pulled a few strands of her hair through a bleaching cap, I cleaned out my bug terrariums. The fireflies had all died, so I dumped the twigs and dead bugs in the trash and considered what species the next occupant might be. It did make me a little sad that so many insects had such short lifespans, but I guess I learned to not get so attached to the ones that lived only a few days or weeks, and it was always interesting to be able to observe new bugs on a regular rotation. Like I didn't name the fireflies individually. They were just "the fireflies," because I knew they'd be gone soon. Caroline, on the other hand, might be around for several months, and losing her would be more difficult.

I removed the dying leafy twigs from Caroline's container and picked out all the frass (poop). Then I rode the elevator down to collect a few more fresh leaves and twigs from outside. While outside, I was lucky enough to find a grasshopper for Caroline to munch on, and a gorgeous little metallic blue-green dogbane beetle (*Chrysochus auratus*) to go into the terrarium formerly occupied by the fireflies. I collected some of the dogbane leaves for him before taking him upstairs. I thought I'd call him "Chrysler," since he was shiny like a car. Once I had him settled, I realized I had no idea how long he'd live, so I looked it up: six to eight weeks.

After messing with the bugs, I retrieved the bug diary from my underwear drawer, laid back on my bed and propped myself up on a couple of pillows to leaf through it. Siren came back from the showers, having rinsed the bleach from her hair. She removed the towel turban from her head and began the long process of drying her hair in front of the mirror above her dresser. Her new highlights looked fantastic. She glanced at me in the mirror. "What is that book, anyway?" she yelled over the dryer. "Is that the one you stole from the library?"

"I told you, I didn't steal it." I hoped she'd drop the subject.

"Then where did it come from?"

I sighed, not really knowing what to say. "This old lady gave it to me," I said, still hoping she'd drop it.

"What?" she laughed.

"Yeah, I know, it's weird, but... The night we tripped at the library? There was this old lady there and she gave it to me."

"Wait, I'm confused. Is it a library book?"

"No," I said. "It's a diary. A bug diary. See?" I turned the book around so Siren could see the inside. She turned off the dryer and came toward me, squinting. She had terrible eyesight without her contacts.

"Bugs," she said, wrinkling up her nose. "How did she know you're an entomology major?"

"I have no idea," I said, which was true.

"Wait, whose diary is it?"

"It seems to be the diary of a woman who attended KU years ago."

"Well, that's cool she gave it to you. But still. Weird." She turned the hair dryer back on and didn't ask any more questions, thank God. I opened the diary somewhere near the center:

June 18, 1873
3 p.m. Sunny, dry, hot 98 °F
Spiny Elm Caterpillar
Nymphalis antiopa

This afternoon I observed large spiny elm caterpillar resting on the bark of a large elm tree in the grove behind the Pi Beta Phi house. The caterpillar develops into the dour-named Mourning Cloak butterfly, which is actually quite beautiful in appearance. This particular caterpillar was a handsome fellow of black with brilliant orange spots, and a number of ferocious looking spines. He was approximately three-quarters of an inch long. I didn't attempt to collect him, as I dislike the method for preservation of soft-bodied insects, and I don't know if I'd have the heart to drown the little fellow in alcohol. Additionally, I would far rather have the option to collect the imago version of the species, and now I will know to keep on the lookout for Mourning Cloak butterflies.

"Out of curiosity, I went to my desk and looked up the spiny elm caterpillar online, and though I'd never seen the caterpillar, I realized I had seen the adult form, the Mourning Cloak butterfly, in Maryland, and Flora was right—it's beautiful. It's a deep brown butterfly, edged with a cream-colored stripe and decorated with bright blue polka dots. It was named for its resemblance to the dark mourning cloaks people wore back in the day when a family member died. Instead of migrating or going into a pupa state in the winter, when temperatures begin to fall, the Mourning Cloak produces antifreeze in its body and shelters in place, hiding in the bark of a tree or some other nook. As soon as temperatures begin to rise, the adults emerge, and the males sun themselves, trying to attract the females to mate, so that by late spring, the babies can emerge from their eggs.

As I paged through the diary, I realized it was easier to stay at my desk because Flora had cataloged a lot of insects I'd never heard of, and it was fascinating to be able to look them up on the internet to see them in full color, after reading her descriptions and poring over her pencil drawings. It made sense, though, that she had seen firsthand so many more species than I had. The more humans developed the land, the more insects were pushed to undeveloped locations or even became extinct. In her time, Lawrence was just getting started. The landscape would have been crawling with insects.

She'd cataloged insects like the flower fly (*Scaeva pyrastri*), cottonwood borer (*Plectrodera scalator*), banded net-winged beetle

(*Calopteron discrepans*), and tons more, which was one of the reasons I was attracted to studying insects. Their sheer variety and numbers. It was pretty much a given no one was ever going to discover a new species of elephant, but humans have barely begun to document the millions of insects out there, which means the possibilities for new discoveries is almost limitless.

The more I read, the more I liked Flora. She was smart. And clever. And observant. And funny. I thought she was brave, too, being one of the only women on campus. Sometimes she talked about what that was like: *I would have stayed longer to sketch this morning, but I needed to use the toilet, so I had to pack up my things and hurry back to Pi Beta Phi as there are no rest rooms for women on campus.*

I'd been flipping through the diary for a good hour, chatting a little with Siren as she put on her makeup and got dressed, when I came across an entry that was different:

> *July 6, 1873*
> *Sweat Bee?*
> *Halictidae???*
> *Approx .75 inches*
>
> *Sighted this beautiful bee on a Lady's Slipper on my walk up the hill today, in a patch of wildflowers. She's a beautiful metallic gold, and her wings made the sweetest, high-pitched buzz as she went from blossom to blossom, drinking nectar and collecting pollen. I cannot recall having seen another bee like her before. I'm including several sketches that I hope may aid in her identification. I'm sure Professor Snow will have some insight into her classification.*

For this entry, Flora had included detailed drawings of top and side views of the bee, as well as three close-up sketches of the bee's wings, because wing shape is crucial in identifying bees. I wondered how she'd gotten so lucky to have the bee sit still for her for so long. She had to have been right on top of it for some time to see all of that amazing wing detail.

"Whaddaya think?" Siren startled me out of my diary-induced daze. I looked up. She had fixed her hair, which was spilling everywhere in cascades of golden-streaked perfection. She was wearing typical Sunday-afternoon lounging attire: cutoff sweats and an off-the-shoulder old t-shirt. Still, she was hot.

"You look amazing!"

"Thank you, dahling," she said. "I'm so glad this worked this time. Last time I streaked my hair myself I ended up having to pay seventy-five bucks to get it fixed. I looked like the Bride of Frankenstein."

Siren's phone made its text-alert noise for Mattie, which was Prince singing Kiss. I usually kept my phone on silent, so I'd never be the idiot whose phone made noise during a lecture. I checked my phone, too, and Mattie had texted us both: *Fantastic conversation and virgin cocktails will be served in the room of Matthew V. Walker @ 7:30. Dress is casual. Being boring is forbidden.* Siren read it and smiled at me. "Well, I guess we've got plans in twenty."

6

Mattie & Shirley

Mattie's dorm room was decorated with all his favorite movie posters, most of which were old, like, *What Ever Happened to Baby Jane?* and *Blackboard Jungle*.

I was kind of surprised Siren was there with us. She had a new guy... Well, she still kind of had the old one, too... and she'd been gone a lot in the evenings, as of late. I got the impression she was getting bored with Gabriel, and he'd soon be relegated to her past. All she could talk about lately was some Drew guy she'd met in her math class. He was studying music therapy and played the trumpet. It hardly seemed fair. I still hadn't hooked up with anyone, and she had two guys at her beck-and-call. At that moment, I realized Zach hadn't texted me in three days and a pang of longing went through my heart and loins. While Siren was busy with Gabriel or Drew, and neither of us had to study, Mattie and I hung out in his room. When she wasn't busy with one of the her guys, the three of us hung out in Mattie's room. We liked to pop microwave popcorn and drink diet Shirley Temples (he kept a supply of diet ginger ale, grenadine and maraschino cherries in his mini-fridge), while enjoying his favorite old classic movies. He had a soft, purple shag rug on the floor, with bright throw pillows and beanbags scattered around. He called it his "pleasure palace." Siren was nested in a tye-dye beanbag. I was hugging a big, fuzzy, lime-green pillow.

"I love it when we can be lowkey together, ladies," he said, getting out the Shirley Temple ingredients. He began mixing the drinks.

"Sometimes, I wish you two were queer, though. That way you could come to my LGBTQIA-plus meetings. I mean, you could come if you wanted, but it's nice for us to have our group of queer folks, you know?" He handed us the Shirley Temples. They were pink, cheerful and bubbly, each with three red cherries sitting on top of the ice. "It's supportive, but nobody makes me laugh like you two crazy bitches."

I sipped at my Shirley Temple and a thought occured to me. "Do you run into more discrimination for being Black or being gay?" I asked, genuinely curious and hoping Mattie wouldn't' be offended by the question. From the time I'd spent with him, though, he seemed to be unshakable.

"Ummm…" he said, stirring his drink with a red straw as he considered. "I mean, it's kind of not really straightforward like that, you know? Because a lot of the time if a stranger has a problem with me, I'm not sure what their problem is. I don't know if it's because I'm too fem for them or if it's because I'm Black. Sometimes I'm pretty sure it's both. And I haven't been harassed by the cops for being Black… but then, this is a pretty small town, and my uncle is on the force, so that probably has a lot to do with it, now that I think about it… I know other Black folks around town get harassed." He paused to sip his drink and continued. "I do know the hardest thing I ever had to do was come out to my parents."

"Really?" I asked, surprised. For some reason I'd assumed his parents were always accepting of him.

"Yes, really. I mean… it was weird because everyone knew I was gay. Everyone knew I was gay. From the time I was three years old, I was dressing up in my older sister's clothes and singing old Janet Jackson songs. Moms loves Janet. But, I think that being so religious, my parents didn't want to think it might be true. They wanted to believe that I'd marry a woman and have grandkids for them someday, and my mother had to kind of grieve through that. So, there was definitely some tension in the house for a week or so."

"How old were you?" Siren asked.

"Fifteen," he said, taking a sip of his drink. "I was fifteen, and I just couldn't take it anymore. I couldn't take not saying it to my family, you know? I mean, everybody at school knew it, and my brothers and sisters knew it, but Moms and Pops weren't acknowledging. So, one day I kind of exploded out of frustration and made a big old scene.

It was a scene worthy of an Oscar. I wish someone had gotten it on video. Anyway, I remember it had been a really rough week—like a couple of Neanderthals had messed with me at school, and this other boy at the other high school who I liked, who acted like he liked me, ended up breaking my heart, and I was just a teenage mess, and I broke down in front of my parents and told them I needed to hear them say that they knew I was gay and that they accepted me for me."

"And what did they do?" Siren asked. We were transfixed.

"Moms started sobbing right then and there. I mean sobbing. It almost killed me. I have never seen her cry like that. For real. My parents are emotional rocks. And then my Pops hugged her and yelled at me, 'Why are you trying to make your mother cry?' and I was like, 'I am not trying to make her cry! I need you both to tell me that you know I'm gay, and I hope you still love me.' And Pops said, 'Of course we love you, you damn fool. Your mother needs time to process this. Now get out of here.'"

"So, I left the house for a few hours, went to my friend Hailey's house—I need to text her—and I stayed there for a while. When I got home late that night, Moms and Pops were in the living room, and Pops called me in, even though I wanted to go straight to my room and cry. For some reason, I remember they were watching an old rerun of Family Feud... Anyway, Pops said, 'We love you very much, Matthew. We will always love you and support you.' And then my Moms gave me a big hug, and that was pretty much it.

I thought about what my parents' response would be if Cade or I were to come out. Dad would get over it, I was pretty sure. Victoria, though? That probably wouldn't go well.

"Like I said," Mattie continued, "things were tense with us for about a week after that. Moms asked me one day if I was *sure* I was gay, and I was like, 'Momma, I'm wearing a t-shirt right now with Brittany Spears on it.'"

Siren and I laughed.

"Anyway," he continued, "after about a week or so, it was all okay. They still don't really talk about it much, or actually say the word 'gay,' but they don't freak out when I talk about boys who I think are cute, or when I talk about maybe moving to San Francisco and such," he looked thoughtful, "except of course Moms doesn't want me to move so far away."

"I didn't know you wanted to move to San Francisco," I said, munching a cherry, and Mattie's demeanor seemed to brighten with talk of the future.

"I'm not sure," he said, thoughtful. "I'd like to try San Francisco—because, you know—it's like homo heaven or whatever. But, I've read that Baltimore is actually pretty LGBTQ-plus friendly, and I'd kind of like to try living someplace where there are lots of Black folk, because I've never had that before. No offense, girls, I love you, but Lawrence is very white. San Francisco is probably a better place to be to make movies, if you're not going to be in L.A. And then, of course, there's New York City, but the whole idea of New York kind of scares me, for some reason."

I hadn't really thought about it, but Mattie was right. Lawrence was predominately white. But then, so was Bethesda. Even more so. "New York is pretty cool," I said. "So much there is so amazing. The museums, the Broadway shows, the food... But, there's too many humans there to suit my taste. Now, downtown Baltimore is nice," I said.

"Yeah?" Mattie said, looking interested.

"Yeah, it really is. They've cleaned it up a lot. There's a world-class aquarium there, right on the bay," I said. "There's great shopping and food."

"You mean it's better since they moved all the poor Black folks out?" he said, smirking. His comment took me completely off guard.

"No!" I replied. "That's not what I meant at all."

He laughed. "Oh, sweetie, I'm just messing with you."

"I want to move to New York," Siren said. I was grateful for the change of subject.

"You do?" I said. For some reason, I was surprised.

"Oh, hell yes," she said. "I want to get the fuck out of this backwater part of the country. People are so goddammed closed-minded in this state. I can't stand it. Besides, I want to act, and if you're not going to be an actor in Los Angeles, New York is really the only other place to be. I mean, unless you want to get into sketch comedy, which might take you to Chicago. But that's not what I want to do," she grabbed her hair and twisted it into a bun. "I want to get out of the Midwest and work in the theater... or maybe television. Either or both would be fine. I don't care so much about movies."

"Where do you want to end up, Miss Kymer?" Mattie asked.

I thought about it for a few seconds before answering. "I honestly have no idea."

Siren laughed. "I find that very hard to believe."

"Why?" I asked.

"Yeah, why?" said Mattie.

"Because we're talking about Kymer Charvat. The woman who researches everything to death. How can you possibly have no idea where you want to live after you graduate?"

"I don't know. All I know is, I don't like where I'm from, and I do like it here. Maybe I'll want to end up somewhere else entirely." I shrugged my shoulders. "I haven't seen any of the U.S. west of Kansas—except that one vacation we took to Hawaii. I've never even been out of the country."

"Oh my God I want to see Paris before I die," Mattie said all of a sudden. "And Egypt. I must see Cairo before I depart this earth, as Moms would say. And I will make it to Cannes someday. Even if I never have a movie at Cannes, I just want to experience it, you know?"

I did know. "I feel that way about the monarch migration. I want to visit the forests of Mexico to see where the monarchs overwinter."

"They do that?" Mattie asked.

"Yeah," I said. "They migrate from all over North America— Canada and the U.S.—and spend the winter in a small area of these old growth forests outside of Mexico City. People go down there to camp and see them. The monarchs fill the trees and cover the ground. It's a sea of orange and black wings. Like something out of a fairy tale." I shivered with the thought of seeing most of the world's monarchs in one place. Like magic.

Mattie saw me shiver and giggled. "Kymer, I think you wanna see those bugs more than I want to go to Cannes."

"So what are you gonna do with your degree, Kyma-jyma?" Siren asked.

"I don't know that either," I admitted.

"What?" She said, in response to me. Then, abruptly, "Mattie, do you have any chips? I want to munch on something."

"Up in that cabinet," he pointed, "there's popcorn." She got up, retrieved a bag from the box of popcorn and the room began to fill with the smell, as it turned in the microwave, puffing up like a balloon.

"So, you're telling me you're getting a degree in bugs," Siren said, grabbing the steaming bag from the microwave and slamming the door shut, "and you don't know what you're going to do with it? You're so logical about everything. I just figured you knew exactly what you were doing after college."

I shrugged my shoulders. "I'm not that worried about it, yet. I'm hoping I'll figure it out while I'm in school. That's what school is for, right? Figuring out who you're going to be?"

"That's not what I think school is for," Siren said, downing the rest of her drink.

"What is it for, then?" Mattie said, handing her the big red-and-white striped popcorn bowl.

"School is for getting out of the shitty place you're in and making your life better," she said, pouring the popcorn in the bowl and munching a piece. "I may not be able to afford Juilliard, but I'm going to get every dime's worth of acting experience out of this little Midwest degree."

"She will wring the last drop of value from it," Mattie said, making a wringing motion in the air, and it gave us all the giggles.

"So, what do you think school is for?" Siren asked Mattie.

"Honestly, I think you're both right. I mean, I hope to use my degree to direct movies, but I'm also realistic enough to know I want to have a degree, in case I *don't* end up directing movies. Like, hopefully, I'll still work in the field somehow. Maybe costuming or makeup or casting or something. Does that make sense?"

"Sure," I said. "You have a degree to act as a fallback."

"There's that, but also maybe while I'm here I'll take an underwater basket weaving course and fall in love with it and forget about movie-making altogether. Or maybe I'll take a history class and decide I want to make historical documentaries. I mean, you really never know how any experience is going to guide your choices, right? But also I think school is for finding romance. I'd like to get a boyfriend while I'm here, for goodness sake. Because I've never really had one."

"Really?" I asked. "Why not?"

"I don't know. There were only so many gay guys in my high school, you know? Kind of a small dating pool. It just didn't work out," he said.

"I just want to get through college without getting pregnant," Siren said.

"Me too," I said.

"Well that would probably be best," Mattie said, and he took a big sip of his drink.

We talked until eleven o'clock that night, until Siren and I agreed it was time to get to bed. "Good night, beautiful ladies," Mattie said, blowing us kisses as we left.

As I lay in bed that night, I was having trouble falling asleep, because I was fixating on Mattie's comment about Baltimore. I couldn't stop thinking about it. He was right... I had said something kind of racist and shitty, and I'd had absolutely no idea I was doing it. And it sucked, because I thought of myself as such a progressive and open-minded person. But... the truth of the matter was, before Mattie, I'd never had a good friend who was Black. Certainly not a close friend. Now, gay friends, sure. Or genderqueer or bicurious or genderfluid or whatever. I had plenty of friends like that. Then I thought again about how Mattie had said Lawrence was "white," and here I'd thought of it as being so cool and diverse, especially compared to where I came from. But Mattie had also said even in Lawrence sometimes the police hassled Black people, which blew my mind. I knew it happened in D.C. all the time, but Lawrence? It was crazy how different the world was for different people and it made me feel ... bad. I knew I wouldn't be able to sleep if I didn't address the issue with him. I grabbed my phone and typed out a message to him, deleting it several times until I settled on something short and simple, but wondering if it was enough. *Hey! I want to apologize again, for what I said earlier about Baltimore.*

I set the phone down on the nightstand, and tried to fall asleep, hoping he'd reply, because if he didn't, it was going to be a long night. But after fifteen minutes or so, the phone buzzed on the table. I couldn't wait till morning, so I picked it up: *Oh, Sweetheart. U R A peach to still be worrying about that. I've had 2 educate so many of my whyte friends over the years. It's important UR listening & learning. Srry 2 B breif but I need my beauty sleep. Kisses! Sleep tight!*

I felt a wave of relief wash over me. I loved Mattie. I was glad he was in my life. Siren, too. There was no way I'd be able to navigate my freshman year without them.

My mind drifted to the diary. I was grateful for it, as well. Grateful that Carrie had entrusted it to me. I thought about the cool bugs in there. The butterflies and the bees and the stick bugs and roaches... and that weird caterpillar that was called a slug but was really a caterpillar. That's when I thought of the entry itself. I could see it in my mind: *I haven't yet worked out a method for preservation of soft-bodied insects, and I don't know if I'd have the heart to drown the little fellow in alcohol.*

That was when I realized how stupid I'd been. Flora hadn't been sketching live insects. That would've been ridiculous. She'd probably had a "kill jar," which was just a jar with a cotton ball soaked with something like ether or chloroform to kill bugs quickly and humanely. Then she would've pinned the bugs later to draw them. I guess it hadn't occurred to me because that wasn't how I did things, in this day and age. I had a camera phone on me at all times, and I could catalog the bugs with digital photos. In fact, that was how most entomologists were doing things anymore. I had pinned a few bugs because my high school biology teacher, Ms. Hernandez, had insisted I learn how. But I always hated killing bugs, so I'd never started my own pinned collection. I simply uploaded my bajillion bug photos to the cloud. Flora didn't have any choice but to kill and pin her bugs. The diary was her version of my smartphone photos... small, compact and portable.

That's when I thought back to the article I'd read about her and how she'd curated KU's first entomological collection... If the collection still existed, I realized, the mystery bee might be in it.

I fell asleep, with that single thought in my mind.

7

Golden Job, Golden Ticket

Sometime around the first of October, when the last of the magical cicadas had expired and the trees were once again quiet, I realized I should probably get a job. Mattie already had a job, working in his parents' barbeque restaurant. That was the deal in his family: There was an understanding that if they worked in the family restaurant, Mattie's parents would pay for all their kids to go to college, but only if that college was KU. Siren was still working at Bazongas several days a week, sometimes in the afternoon, and when she was lucky, the dinner shift, since she always brought home more tips. But on those nights, she had to help close the restaurant and she didn't get home until after midnight.

I was pretty sure I didn't want to do restaurant work, and jobs were tight in Lawrence, what with all the college kids. I decided my best bet might be to apply for campus jobs. I was sitting at my desk one afternoon on the campus jobs website when my dad called and asked what I was up to. I told him I was applying for jobs at the Natural History Museum, the library and the visitor center.

"Job website?" he said. "Ha! Back in my day, you had to actually walk to the building you wanted to work in and fill out an application. Bunch of spoiled pansies is what you kids are."

I managed to land a job at the Natural History Museum on campus, which was amazing. After all, I could be running a cash register in a grocery store or a maybe a boutique downtown, but I was going to get to work inside an actual natural history museum, and one of my favorites, at that. Though my parents paid for all my school expenses, any spending money I had to earn on my own. I'd saved up some money before high school graduation by doing some odd jobs, and I'd received a decent amount of Christmas, birthday and graduation money. But I'd managed to blow through all my savings in only two-and-a-half months, what with my fancy coffee addiction and a few frivolous clothing purchases.

The Natural History Museum gig was my first real job. I'd worked a few of the snack bars at our high school football and basketball games, only because my mother had arranged it through a friend of hers who was head of the snack bar committee. It had annoyed me at the time, but as it turned out, having snack bar experience was actually a plus, since I had previously run a cash register and handled money. I was now working in the museum's gift shop.

The Natural History Museum was in Dyche Hall. (Pronounced "dyke." Yes, ha ha ha, hilarious.) Dyche had been named for the explorer Lewis Lyndsey Dyche, who had personally shot and stuffed most of the animals in the diorama that took up the entire ground floor of the museum. He'd been an explorer, and naturalist, and professor at KU way back in the day. I knew this, because my new boss, Ms. Rockson, had given me a brief history of the building after she'd hired me. The museum itself I was familiar with because our Kansas grandparents—Grandma and Grandpa Charvat—had taken Cade and me there a few times when we were little kids.

The first time I'd seen the panorama of animals of North America, at about the age of seven, I'd been overwhelmed. Mostly it was the polar bears and walruses that did it. They were so big, towering over me, I was awestruck. They looked a little smaller now that I was grown, but not much. The panorama had been a huge draw at the 1893 Chicago World's Fair. I had to forgive Lewis Lindsey Dyche for shooting all of those gorgeous animals because, well, that was just a thing back then, and I was super glad that mostly wasn't the case anymore. Since modern people were becoming more icked out by taxidermy, natural history museums were relying on it less and less, which was why so many taxidermy specimens in museums across the country were getting to be old and even in some cases, kind of ratty. I hadn't noticed it as a little kid, but several of Dyche's specimens were showing their age, with small tears and moth holes here and there.

Once, when Cade and I were about five and seven years old, Grampa looked at Cade and I, bent down and put his finger to his lips. "Shhh. If you're really quiet, you can hear the ghosts of the polar bears growling because they want to go home to the North Pole," and he cupped a hand behind his ear. Cade and I listened intently for a few seconds, and I was afraid I might actually hear a ghost bear, until Grandma's authoritative voice broke the silence: "Don't listen to Grampa, kids. He's full of beans." Her statement echoed throughout the big space. But the thought of ghost polar bears growling forlornly for the North Pole haunted me for weeks afterward, and now it occurred to me maybe Grandpa hadn't been so full of beans after all. If KU could have a ghost librarian, why not ghost polar bears?

The exterior of Dyche Hall was like a castle, complete with turret and gargoyles, and fanciful carvings of beasts and flowers, real and mythical. I knew Dyche was built of Kansas limestone, because Grandpa Charvat told me so. Even though I was excited beyond belief to be able to be inside one of my favorite buildings on campus, the absolute best part about landing a job at the Natural History Museum was that I could find out if Flora's bug collection still existed—and not only Flora's collection—KU had a massive entomological collection, and I couldn't wait to get a look at it.

My school day ended early on Tuesdays and Thursdays, which left me with a few hours in the afternoon to work at the Natural History Museum. I was also working Sundays and every other Saturday.

The first couple of weeks I worked I didn't even have time to worry about the bug collection—or any of the collections—at the museum because there was a fair amount to learn about working in the gift shop. I had to learn how to use their cash register and count down and balance the drawer at the end of the night. Then there was learning how to place inventory on the shelves and post prices, updating prices and inventory in the computer, and learning the answers to visitors' most asked questions. There was also sweeping, dusting and general tidying of the shop. But I enjoyed it, and I was super jazzed when I got my first paycheck two weeks later. I went out and opened a bank account, all by myself. They even gave me a debit card with a Jayhawk on it.

My job got pretty comfortable pretty quickly, and once I got the basics down, and the museum was slow and there was nothing left to clean or straighten, I'd end up wandering into the panorama room, staring at all the animals frozen in time. The animals were definitely showing their wear. Most of them had been collected in the mid-1800s and were starting to look a little faded and worn. Still, the collection was impressive.

"The largest collection of its kind in North America," my boss, Ms. Rockson, told me. There were animals as small as prairie dogs and pheasants, and as large as elk. The panorama started at one end in a jungle setting, with monkeys and snakes and birds, moved into a desert landscape with coyotes and rattlesnakes, then a forest setting with mountain lions and wild turkeys, into a plains setting with the prairie dogs and deer, a mountain setting with mountain goats and elk, and ended in the Arctic setting with the polar bears and walruses.

One night, a couple of weeks after I'd started the job, I stopped in at Ms. Rockson's office to ask about the entomological collection.

"Most of the entomological collection isn't located in this building," she said.

"It's not?" I was shocked.

"No. There are a few soft-bodied insects kept in liquid in the collections downstairs, but mostly what's in this building are bird and mammal specimens, and some fossils. The entomological collection outgrew this building years ago. It's located on west campus. Just out of curiosity, what exactly are you looking for?"

Her question caught me off guard. "Oh, um… y'know. I love bugs."

She raised an eyebrow. "Well, thank goodness you're an entomology major. Speak to one of your biology professors, and you should be able to get a pass."

"Okay," I said. I backed out of the office and gave a little wave. "Thanks for the information."

"You're welcome, Kymer. We'll see you Sunday. You're doing a good job here."

The following Monday, I waited outside Professor Berg's office during her office hours to talk to her about getting access to the entomological collections. She was a stickler about office hours. She absolutely wouldn't talk to students after class. It was always funny when someone would try. She'd wave the person away with her hand, while packing up her stuff. "You may come by during my open office hours or schedule an appointment via email." She'd say the same thing every single time, but there were always students who thought she owed them special attention, and they always got shot down for their efforts.

Dr. Berg's office, like much of the Biology department, was located in Haworth Hall, a sort of nondescript modernish building partway down the hill from the main drag. As I sat in the hallway outside her office, waiting for my appointment, my mind churned away with the reason I was going to give for wanting to get into the entomological collections. Obviously, I couldn't tell the truth. And if it turned out the bug diary had really been Flora's, the university was probably going to want it. And it wasn't that I thought the university didn't deserve to have possession of it. They definitively did. But Carrie Watson had given it to me. She had entrusted it to me. And I wasn't done with it yet. When I was, I figured, I'd turn it over to... someone. Until then, I intended to keep hold of it.

Professor Berg's door opened, and a student, a guy, walked out of her office. He didn't look happy. "As I said, Mr. Tidwell, you may turn in extra credit worth up to five percent of your grade. But no more than that." She said this to his back as he stomped away. She looked at me. "Ms. Charvat?"

"Yes, ma'am."

"Please, come in. Have a seat." When I stepped inside her office, I was shocked to see bugs all over her office walls. All preserved and framed under glass. My mouth dropped open as I took them all in. There were hundreds. They were everywhere.

She didn't seem to notice. She sat down at her desk and asked, "What can I assist you with today?" She tapped away at the keyboard in front of her computer. I sat down in the chair across from her, but I couldn't stop looking at the bugs. "So... I'm a biology major..."

"Yes," she said, looking at her computer screen. "I see that here. And which area of study do you intend to go into?"

"Entomology."

"Oh!" she said, surprised. She looked up from the computer screen and over her glasses. "That was my area of study as well. Obviously." And she smiled.

"Your collection is incredible," I said.

"Why, thank you," she said, brightening. She looked around the room. "I am quite fond of my collection."

"Did you collect them all yourself?" I asked.

She looked around. "Yes, most of them." She pointed to a section of particularly colorful insects on one wall, which included several butterflies, moths and beetles. "These are from a trip I took to Brazil." She pointed to another set of frames on another wall. "And these are from Africa. Egypt and the Sudan, mostly." There were beetles of all shapes and sizes, some of them gargantuan. There were walking sticks, spiders of all kinds, a couple of scorpions and several species of ginormous ants. "I'm hoping to travel to India next winter on sabbatical," she said.

"Oh wow. That would be so dope!" I winced inside after I said it. "I understand there are some crazy leaf bugs in India." Dammit. Why couldn't I stop using slang in front of my professor? I barely used it in real life.

"Yes. Crazy indeed. Now, how can I help you today, Ms. Charvat?" Suddenly she sounded all business.

"So, like I said, my interest is also in entomology, and I've been doing my own digital collecting for several years now," I pulled out my phone and began swiping through my bug photos for her. She pulled down her glasses to peer at them. "I also recently started working at the Natural History Museum."

"Well, I'm sure that's a lively place to work... Oh! What a gorgeous Swallowtail!" she said, zooming in on the brightly colored butterfly.

"Yeah, so, I mean, I love bugs. Love them. I even have a few in my dorm room—live ones—that I take care of. So, what I was wondering is, I really want to be able to keep building my digital bug collection, and, I mean, I know what most of these bugs are, but there are still a few that I need to identify for sure, and it can be a little difficult to identify some of my photos from photos of specimens on the internet, so what I was hoping..."

"You'd like me to give you permission to access the entomological collections." She took her glasses off. "Normally, we don't let freshmen access the collections, but seeing your obvious enthusiasm, and also that you're wanting to advance your knowledge of insects on your own, I think it's safe to allow you into the collections on the collections. I trust you'll treat them with the care they deserve."

"Oh, absolutely," I said.

She opened a top drawer of her desk, thumbed through a few papers then selected one and filled it out. "Be sure to take this permission slip with you in case someone asks you for it, though they probably won't. You know where the collections are located?"

"I'm told they're on west campus?"

"Yes. The busses go there," she moved her mouse around, looking at her computer screen. "Ms. Charvat?"

"Yes, ma'am?"

"I see that you're earning a low C in my class right now. Congratulations. Most of your peers are failing. But if you're going to continue in the entomology program, there's no reason you shouldn't be making an A in this class. This is all basic material. Things are only going to get more difficult from here on out."

Ugh. Her words felt like a punch in the gut. "Yes, ma'am. You're right. I'll... I'll study harder."

"Well, it can be a little distracting when one is young and suddenly has all this freedom thrust upon her." She looked at me with a spark in her eye, and we laughed. "Taking this class from me now will serve you well later. I teach some of the upper level entomology classes as well, so you'll already know what I expect from my students."

"I look forward to it," I said, and I meant it.

"If you can manage to make an A on my final, you have a very good chance of receiving a B for the class."

"Yes, ma'am. I will definitely dig in and study more. For real. Thank you. For everything." She handed me the permission slip for the entomological collections, and I felt like Charlie with the Golden Ticket.

8

Bugs, Glorious Bugs

The next afternoon, after my Intro to Finite Math class, I took a bus to the west side of campus. I was buzzing with excitement. If Watson Library felt like church, the entomology collections felt like home. It was a large, warehouse-like space, and the air was tangy with the smell of preservation chemicals. It was also cold, since cool, dry air was best for keeping the specimens in as good of shape as possible for the long term.

There were rows and rows of mammoth-sized, steel cabinets on rails, and each cabinet had a sign on the side indicating what specimens it contained. In order to save space, they were stacked one right up against another, but because they were on rails, they were moveable. Each cabinet had a hand crank on the side in order to make space between one cabinet and the next to be able to open the drawers. I knew that if I were to slide out any one of the drawers of any one of those cabinets, it'd be full of pinned insect specimens.

I scanned the rows of cabinets, which were arranged in taxonomic order. I chose one at random, marked Coleoptera (beetles), cranked it apart from its neighbor, and opened the door to reveal rows and rows of drawers. Every drawer in this particular cabinet held beetles in the superfamily Scarabaeidae—scarab beetles. I reached for a drawer, slid it out, and beheld the glory within. They were beautiful. Like gems in a jeweler's case. Some were striped, some spotted. Some were tiny as the head of a pin and others as big as walnuts. The colors were dazzling. Some were shiny, some iridescent, some matte. Some had huge mandibles—the pincer-like mouthparts—and others had extra-long antennae. I slid the drawer back in, carefully, and slid another one out. I did this over and over, taking in all the shapes, all the colors and sizes.

They were gorgeous. Each one represented hours and hours of discovery, hunting, seeking, collecting, preserving, identifying and pinning. Though some of these beetles were flightless, most of them sported specialized wings that were folded up carefully under their elytra, the hard, colorful wing covers. The elytra popped up to allow the wings to unfurl, sort of like a soft-top convertible.

Taking them all in, knowing that there were hundreds of drawers to open and thousands more species and varieties of insects to gaze at and study, I was overwhelmed. It was kinda stupid, but a couple of tears slid down my cheek.

I pulled myself together and headed toward the cabinets marked Hymenoptera (bees, wasps and ants). Like the beetles, there were several cabinets for Hymenoptera. I took off my backpack and set it on the floor. I retrieved Flora's diary from the backpack and flipped to the page with the mystery bee. I wanted to be able to compare her drawings with the specimens. Then I started opening drawers, starting with the bee family Halictidae.

As I scanned the bees, I gravitated toward the Augochlorini tribe of sweat bees, since Flora described the bee as being "metallic gold," and Augochlorinis tend to be metallic. It was at this point I wished Flora's sketches were in color. Without color to help in identification, I was going to have to rely on wing shape, head shape, and antennae length.

I spent two-and-a-half hours that afternoon poring over the sweat bees. I squinted at their wings and antennae, picked them up in their little specimen boxes and peered at them from every angle. While I was there, a couple of grad students came in—a guy and a girl—who glanced at me curiously. Then they spent a few minutes looking at the cockroaches and chatting about some project they were working on before they left. Other than that, I was by myself. But none of the Augochlorini bees seemed quite right. There were a handful of individuals that looked like they might be candidates, but there was always something that was a little off. Still, I took photos of the ones that looked like the best matches, so I could reference them later.

Honestly, I was disappointed to not find the smoking bee, as it were, but I also hadn't lost hope. That's the thing about science. You never know where you might find the answer you're looking for. There were still plenty of species of bees in the collection to go through. There was also the slight possibility that Flora's unknown insect wasn't a bee at all, but some other insect masquerading as a bee, like a fly or an ant, although that didn't seem likely, since the drawing was so detailed, and it had all the earmarks of a bee. Beyond that, I trusted Flora's intuition it was a bee.

I was startled when my phone buzzed in my pocket. *Where RU woman??? We R hungry. Fuck it. We R eating.* It was Siren. She and Mattie and I had a standing dinner date in the cafeteria at the dorm, at 5:30 p.m., though those were getting fewer and further between what with all of us having jobs. My phone said it was 6 p.m. I knew I'd been looking at bugs for a long time, but I hadn't realized it was that long.

Sorry, guys. I typed as I walked to the bus stop. *Looking at bugs on west campus. Lost track of time. Go ahead & eat. Be back soon!*

When I got on the bus and sat down, I realized that a guy across the aisle and a few seats down was looking at me. There were only a few people on the bus. I kept glancing away, but when I'd glance back at him, he was still looking. He smiled. I smiled back. He had dirty blonde hair, thick eyebrows and he was wearing a black t-shirt with a Storm Trooper on it. It said *I had friends on that Death Star.* He was cute. I had a thing for nerds.

Christ. I hadn't had sex in weeks and my boyfriend was nineteen hours away by car. As long as I didn't think about it too much, and kept busy with my school work, it wasn't too bad. But now... the guy was looking cuter and cuter. I realized I had looked at him too long and blushed. Dammit. I looked away. When I glanced at him again, he was smiling even bigger. I looked away again. I zipped open my backpack, fished out Flora's diary and pretended to read it, even though I couldn't concentrate. I let like a whole two or three minutes go by before I looked at him again. This time, he was looking at his phone. I was both relieved and disappointed.

When the bus pulled up at Oliver Hall, I had to walk by him to get off the bus.

"Oliver," he said, smiling at me. "I'll have to remember that."

I gave him a pointed look, determined not to blush again. Then I flipped my hair and de-bussed. My heart did a little flip-flop, and my stomach growled as I headed to the cafeteria. I hoped to run into him again.

9

Smokey Jo's

Now that Mattie was spending more time working at his parents' barbecue restaurant, the three of us hung out there at least two or three times a week. It didn't hurt that his parents, Coretta and Lee, insisted Siren and I eat there for free. "I want you to call me Moms," Mrs. Walker told us. "And everyone calls Lee 'Pops,' so you might as well not be any different. In fact, I think I'm the only one who calls him Lee." Moms was short, shorter than me, and kinda round, with a sweet, quiet-but-firm voice. She was friendly and kind, but you got the idea that she wasn't the kind of mom you could disobey, either. She wore athletic outfits in bright colors with sneakers to match— she had several pair—and her purple cat-eye glasses glittered with rhinestones. She always wore a hair net and plastic gloves at the restaurant, and she made sure everyone else working there did as well. Pops was a large man with a booming voice who talked a lot. The customers loved him. He knew most of them by name, and when he wasn't tending to the smoker, he chatted them up like crazy.

The restaurant was called Smokey Jo's, named after Mattie's grandmother, Josephine. Mattie said she was the one who had developed most of the recipes. It was located kind of at the south end of downtown, across the street from South Park, the big city park where summer band concerts and art festivals were held. When Mattie wasn't working, we'd take our food and hang out in the park. I'd already put on five pounds eating the Walkers' barbecue a couple times a week, not to mention the potato salad, mac-n-cheese and the pies. Lordy, the pies, as Mattie would say. Moms always had three varieties of pie available in the pie case. "I like to keep one fruit, one custard, and one cream pie in the case at all times," she told me. Lately, they'd had blackberry, lemon meringue and Mississippi mud. It was mad tasty.

When the Walkers had food to throw out at the end of the day, Moms would box up meals and walk around downtown delivering them to homeless people. Mattie's parents were so different than mine, and really any of my friends' parents from home. They laughed and teased each other all the time. Pops would sometimes pat Moms on the butt as he passed. "Lee! Stop that nonsense!" she'd say, playfully slapping at his back.

"Finest backside in the Midwest," he'd say, and I'd notice that Moms looked pleased that he still flirted with her. I couldn't remember if I'd ever seen my parents touch each other. Then there were Mattie's brothers and sisters: his littlest sister Olivia was thirteen and very into boy bands. We'd see her around the restaurant when she wasn't in school. His two older brothers were named Ethan and Isaac. Ethan was still at KU, majoring in Education. He worked at the restaurant when Mattie wasn't there. I liked Ethan. He was funny and super cute. Shorter than Mattie, but with a toned physique and very hetero. He always flirted with Siren and me, and I was hoping that over time, he and I might get to be better friends, until the day his girlfriend came in to visit. She was a chemistry major and gorgeous. I was definitely bummed.

Isaac had recently graduated KU. He worked in a suburb of Kansas City at a drug research company, so he didn't work at the restaurant anymore, but every weekend, he hauled meat and wood to the restaurant in his pickup. Apparently the Walkers had arrangements with farmers in the area for both. Siren and I hadn't yet met Mattie's oldest sister, Eva, who was a lawyer in Topeka.

The warmth and closeness of Mattie's family was fun. That Saturday afternoon, Siren and I came to the restaurant to eat and take Mattie back to the dorm with us when he finished his shift. Siren and I grabbed a booth in the back corner, while Moms piled up some plates with smoked turkey, ribs, coleslaw, fries and pie and set it all down on the table in front of us. "Here you go, ladies. You don't want to get too skinny. Those college boys want something to get hold of."

"Thank you, Moms!" Siren said.

"Yeah, thanks. This is soooo good!"

"Well, you are welcome. You girls let me know what you think of that blackberry pie. I seasoned it with some fresh lime zest this time."

After Siren and I had gorged ourselves and he'd finished his late afternoon shift, Mattie took off his hair net and gloves, sat down with us and picked at the food. He ate one rib, a few fries and a few bites of blackberry pie. He was usually a light eater. We helped him take out the trash and restock the fire wood for the smoker before we thanked Moms and Pops again and left.

Before going back to the dorm, we wandered over to South Park and settled on the swings. The cicadas had all died off. Now, the air was filled with the sound of crickets, which I loved. Such a peaceful sound. In the butterfly garden planted there, I found the new tenant for my empty terrarium: a gorgeous black and orange Woollybear caterpillar (Pyrrharctia Isabella), munching on a sunflower. She was fuzzy, black on both ends and orange in the middle.

"Aw," Siren said, "She's adorable!"

Mattie held her for me while I drove us back to the dorm, where I put her into her new home with a few of the sunflower leaves and some other twigs and leaves I picked in the park's garden. I hoped I could get her to pupate into a tiger moth. When I read up on the process, I learned my best chance of getting her to pupate in captivity was to let her winter as she would in the wild. That meant once the temperature outdoors dropped, I'd need to move her to the ledge outside our dorm window, because she had to freeze in order to pupate.

Later that night, the three of us were hanging out in our room with the door open, trying to decide what we were going to do for entertainment that night, when Staycee popped her head in. "Have you heard? There's a Halloween party up on ten, tonight."

"At what time will these festivities occur?" Mattie asked.

"Um… I think it starts about nine-ish?" Stacycee said.

"Costumes?" Mattie asked.

"Of course," she answered.

"Room number?"

"Ten thirty-nine."

"Thank you, darling," Mattie said, as Staycee left to spread the news down the hall. "Well that settles, it," he said. "I'll have to run home to find my Uma Thurman from Pulp Fiction wig and costume."

"Aw, man. I want a costume," Siren pouted.

I checked the time. "We could run out to Walmart or Target real quick. The stores downtown will be closed by now."

"You girls can come with me to my house," Mattie said. "I have plenty of clothes, wigs and makeup to choose from. It's all from my days in the theater. And... you know... I just like to dress up."

Mattie's house (or, more specifically, Mattie's parents' house) was a large, creaking old Victorian on the east side of town. Mattie's bedroom was on the second floor. "My parents have said I can keep my room for a couple more years, but Moms wants to make this her sewing room, because my room always had the biggest closet," he said. Then he gave us a look, "Yes, I do hear how that sounded."

Mattie's bedroom was a lot like his dorm room, with movie posters all over the walls. Except this room had old wood floors, Victorian crown molding and doors with glass doorknobs and old keyholes. Mattie's room was painted mauve. "Your room is cool," I said, thinking of the modern monstrosities my mother liked to push on up-and-coming young couples and hip retirees.

"Well, thank you, Miss Kymer. I like to think of this room as my sanctuary."

"It's beautiful," Siren said, gravitating toward a hat rack covered in boas, scarves, strands of beads—and also hats—and began stroking the boas and scarves. "Where did you get all this stuff?" she asked.

"I've been collecting play clothes and stage outfits since I was twelve or so. I used to sort of try to hide things at the back of my closet, but at some point it all just came spilling out, you might say," and he chuckled. "Siren, you need to try this one!" he exclaimed. He pulled a lime green marabou boa from the hat rack and draped it over Siren's shoulders. Naturally it looked great on her statuesque frame, because of course Siren could pull off a boa. "I know what you need now," Mattie said, walking over to an antique dressing table covered in wigs. He open a drawer full of sunglasses and dug around. "Here they are," he said, putting an oversized pair of white sunglasses on Siren's face. "You don't even need a wig," and he fluffed her big blonde curls. "But you could use a hat," and he grabbed a wide-brimmed black-and-white striped sun hat from the top of the coat rack and placed it on her head. He stood back and considered her.

"Fierce," he declared.

"But who is this?" Siren asked, flinging the boa around her neck dramatically.

"Lady Gaga?" Mattie suggested. Then his face lit up. "Oh!" he exclaimed. "I have the perfect dress for you! He opened a door in the wall to reveal a walk-in closet, pulled the lightbulb chain and began flipping through clothing. "Here it is! This is my Cher dress!" He held out a long, low cut, slinky dress sparkling with blue and silver beads. I couldn't help but feel a pang of jealousy that I'd never be able to pull it off. Just when I was about to feel sorry for myself, Mattie said, "Miss Kymer, I have just the outfit for you, too," and he presented a poodle skirt with a baby-blue satin jacket. "We could put your hair up in a pony tail with a scarf around it," he said. "Though I doubt you could fit into my big ol' saddle shoes."

I spied a fedora on the closet shelf, pointed and squealed. Mattie laughed and reached for it. "You like this?" he said, putting it on my head. "I bought that when I was Mr. Green in the play Clue my junior year of high school."

Siren and I riffled through the clothes and accessories, changing outfits several times. At one point Mattie dressed up as Uma Thurman from Pulp Fiction, but then settled on 1970s Pam Grier, complete with afro and giant hoop earrings. Siren picked up his Uma Thurman discards—white dress shirt, black Capri pants and ballet flats—and Mattie helped her tuck her blonde hair under a black bob wig. Since Mattie was going in drag, I decided to go in drag as well. In keeping with the movie theme, I decided to go as Indiana Jones. I even used one of the stipple-sponges in Mattie's stage makeup kit to create a five o'clock shadow on my chin. He even had the bomber jacket and a whip. I thought it was a pretty sweet costume. I put my hair up in a bun under the hat. And just so everybody still understood that I was a girl, I wore a mini skirt and a bra under the leather bomber jacket... but no shirt.

Siren reached out and cupped one of my boobs. "How ironic. Tonight I'm the one who's fully clothed and you're the one dressed like you work at Bazongas."

By the time we got back to the dorm it was ten-thirty. The tenth floor RA was a guy who was notorious for being gone on Saturday nights. We didn't have any problem finding which room the party was in, because it had spilled out into the hallway. In fact, the guys living there had decorated the entire hall in that wing of the dorm; Oliver Hall was technically co-ed, but single-gendered by floor. The boys of floor ten had strung up orange lights from the ceiling, which glowed under a stringy mass of fake spider webs. Plastic spiders and bats and a couple of bloody body parts hung down from the ceiling. It was kind of impressive.

The tenth floor boys had managed to sneak a pony keg of beer upstairs in a mini-refrigerator box. Clever. It cost three bucks to buy a plastic red cup. Several people were already totally drunk. I recognized several girls from the ninth floor, including Sonya, who was dressed as Dorothy from the *Wizard of Oz*, sitting on a bed draped over some guy who was dressed as a soccer player. Weirdly, Grace was there, though she wasn't wearing a costume. Thankfully, Grace had left Mr. Princie in her room. She didn't have a drink and she looked very uncomfortable. She had her arms wrapped around herself, with a death grip on her elbows. She bit her lip and glanced around, clearly not knowing who to talk to or what to do. Her roommate, Emma Kate, was around, somewhere—I'd seen her, dressed as a hippie— but she seemed to be keeping her distance from Grace.

Siren, Mattie, and I stood in a circle in a corner of the room for a while, sipping our beers and talking to each other. But the more we drank, the more we drifted apart from each other and mingled. At one point I looked around and saw Mattie talking with a guy who was shorter than him, muscular, with a great tan and tight green t-shirt. He had dark, curly brown hair, and a stubble-beard. I was pretty sure this guy was flirting with Mattie, because Mattie was crazy flirting with him, talking even louder and waving his hands more vigorously than usual. Siren was talking to a guy, of course, because there were always about twelve guys who wanted to be in her company, no matter where she went. She'd quit seeing Gabriel and had only been seeing Drew, but this dude was definitely not either of them. At one point, she threw her head back and laughed, loudly, so that all eyes were on her. Somehow, I ended up talking to Emily and Kayla, two girls from our floor. Emily was dressed as a cute black cat with headband ears, a black feather boa tail and fuzzy black slippers that looked like paws. Kayla was dressed as the Little Mermaid, with a long red wig and a green dress. They were telling me about all the famous people who had attended KU. There weren't many.

"Oh my God, there's that one old guy... He used to be on that cop show... *Miami Vice*," Kayla said.

"Tom Cruise?" said Emily.

"No."

"Don Johnson?" I said.

"Yes!" Kayla said, pointing at me. Kayla was beginning to slur her words. We were all yelling at each other over the noise of the party. The boys had some great R&B thumping in the background. The sexual tension at the party was palpable, but here I was, stuck talking to two straight girls, with nothing but dudes and dick on my mind. I kept glancing over their shoulders, trying to keep an eye on Mattie and Siren, but also checking out the guys in the room. There were definitely a few candidates who caught my eye.

"And then there's Paul Rudd, of course. Oh em gee, I love him so much! Oh, and that guy from the Princess Bride!"

"Cary Elwes?" I asked, surprised.

"No, no, no," Kayla shook her head. "You know, that guy... 'My name is Inigo Montoya, you killed my father, prepare to die.'"

"Mandy Patinkin?" I said.

"Is that his name? I don't know. That guy."

"And all the basketball players," Emily said.

"Well of course the basketball players," Kayla said.

I guess the three of us appeared to be the most non-threatening group at the party, because Grace wandered over and joined us. "I like your costumes," she said. She was so quiet I almost didn't hear her. We all thanked her, and then I blurted out, "So... not that this is any of my business, but—"

"Why am I not wearing a costume?" she said.

"Yeah." My face started to turn red, as I realized I might've overstepped.

"We don't celebrate Halloween in our church," she said. The way she said it made me think she'd been asked that particular question a lot. She twisted a lock of hair around her finger. "I never minded missing out on the candy, really, or, you know, going door to door, or whatever, but I've always loved the costumes. You make a really cute cat," she said, looking at Emily.

"Thank you!" Emily said, sloshing her beer.

"You could try on a costume on a regular day," I suggested. "I mean, if you put on a costume when it's not Halloween, then you're not technically breaking any rules, right?"

She looked uncomfortable. "I don't think it would be right for me to be purposely disrespectful to my church like that."

Oh shit. "I'm sorry, Grace, really. I was teasing. I didn't mean to poke fun at your beliefs. I just meant that I thought maybe you could..." I searched for the right words "...explore your curiosity about costumes...without being disrespectful to your church... I mean, you could try one on, right? And sort of...observe what it's like to wear one... You wouldn't have to enjoy it or anything." My hand flailed uselessly in the air as I dug myself deeper and deeper into my verbal hole.

She looked at me curiously. "Maybe... Do you know that movie *Friday the 13th*?"

"I mean, I haven't seen it, but I'm familiar with it."

"You know the man with the hockey mask?"

"The demented slasher-guy? Sure."

"I want to dress up as him," she said, her eyes widening with excitement.

"What?" I giggled. I couldn't even believe what I was hearing. Emily and Kayla perked up.

Grace barked out a laugh that sounded slightly unhinged. "Oh, I love him! He's so scary! He makes me so... scared." She grabbed her arms and shivered, but her eyes lit up, as though the thought of being scared was the most wonderful feeling in the world.

"Your parents let you watch *Friday the 13th*?" I asked.

"No. But I used to watch it when I'd spend the night at my cousin's house. My aunt and uncle don't care what they watch. I never told Momma and Daddy."

"Why, Grace," I said. "You little minx, you."

"Do you think so?" she said. She looked alarmed.

"Of course not," I said. I patted her on the arm, which was weird, but I did it. "I'm teasing you. I think it's awesome." She breathed a sigh of relief.

"Oh, good. I was afraid you might think I was strange," she said, and somehow I managed to smile, but not laugh.

From behind me, a male voice interrupted, "Somebody's in my Western Civ lecture."

Startled, I turned. There was this big guy, right behind me, with sandy hair, and I had to look up because he was about six inches taller than all of us. He was dressed as a pirate, with the weird triangle hat, an eye patch and a Van Dyke beard that looked like it was scribbled on his chin with a Sharpie.

"What?" I said.

"Sheesh," he said. "Self-absorbed much? You usually sit a row or two in front of me."

"I do?" I was surprised. Somehow I had missed noticing this guy in class, and I did a fair amount of people-watching in Western Civ.

"Every day. I always make sure I'm behind you. You know, for the view."

Ick. He'd been watching me, and I didn't know it?

"You're lucky," he said. "Normally I'd be weirded-out by a girl with a beard, but since I know how cute you are most days, I'll let it slide."

"Oh, well, thanks for your approval."

"You're welcome, m'lady," he took off his pirate hat and bowed, apparently unfamiliar with sarcasm. Ugh. He stuck out his hand. "I'm Troy. And you are?"

"Kymer," I said, reaching out reluctantly. His hand was giant and sweaty. Thankfully, he let mine go after just a second.

He laughed. "Kymer? What kind of name is that? Are your parents hippies?"

"Um, it's my name, and not in the slightest." I was smiling at him, hoping he'd say something that didn't make me want to punch him in the face.

"I'm kidding. It's a cool name. For a cool girl." He nudged me, which I didn't love. I decided to bring up something boring to get him talking, and then I'd have to figure out a way to excuse myself.

"So, what do you think of Mr. Wheaton?" I asked, not sure where I should even start with a conversation. Mr. Wheaton was our Western Civ teacher, a grad student.

"Oh, I love the Wheat! He's my man!"

"Really? He seems like kind of a doofus, to me," I said, taking a sip of my beer.

Pirate-man looked surprised. "In what way?"

"Oh, y'know, the way he goes on and on and on about how the government is responsible for Nine-Eleven... It's kinda... maybe... not appropriate for a classroom setting?" I said, giving Troy a look like, "Are you even serious with that bullshit?"

"Well, I happen to agree with him. There's no way the fire in those buildings could've gotten hot enough to melt steel. Clearly those were controlled demolitions." And right then and there, I knew I didn't want to waste any more time talking to Troy.

"Hey," I said, finding Siren in the crowd. "I see my friend over there. It looks like she needs me." She was nose-to-nose with the guy she'd been talking to, unaware of anything going on around her. "It was nice to meet you, though."

"Oh, no," he said, putting his arm around me and pulling me into his sweaty armpit. "We are not done here. I've been wanting to talk to you for a long time. Why don't we get out of here and go to my room and talk? It's too loud in here." And he started to walk us toward the door. I'd dealt with pushy guys before, but this dude had to be kidding. I twisted out of his grip.

"That's okay. I'm going to stay here. I'm with my friends." I looked around again. Kayla and Emily and Grace had moved away a few feet but it was so loud they couldn't hear me. I couldn't see Mattie. Siren wasn't looking my direction.

This time he grabbed my wrist. Hard. Like, it hurt.

"Come on, don't walk away. You're so pretty. I've been wanting to talk to you for weeks."

"Please let go of my arm," I said. "You're hurting me."

He let go. "C'mon. That didn't hurt."

"Um, actually it did." I said, rubbing my arm and trying to back away.

"I'm sorry. I really didn't mean to hurt you. I swear. It was totally an accident. I didn't realize you were so delicate," he ended the statement with a weird smirk that made me want to punch him in his moronic face.

Delicate? "Oh what the fuck ever," I said, and I turned to walk away.

"Hey, you stupid bitch. I can't believe I ever thought you were hot."

He fucking yelled it. Everyone looked.

"No, asshole. She's not the bitch. I am." Out of nowhere, Siren was in his face. She was only a couple inches shorter than him, and frankly, she looked like she could beat the shit out of him. Her face was pure fire.

"Jesus Christ. I didn't know this was rug-muncher night," he said, backing away.

"That's right, fuck-face. And my dyke self is gonna kick your scrawny ass if you don't get the fuck away from my girl." She grabbed me and pulled me to her. If I wasn't so freaked out, I'd have laughed.

"Whatever, you crazy bitches," he said, heading toward the door.

"You'll find out how big a bitch I am if you don't leave, now," Siren said, and took off her wig. Oh shit. I did not want this to get physical. Did I have the nerve to back her up in a fight if it did? Thankfully, he kept walking.

He poked his head back into the room, "Whatever, you ugly cunts!"

"Oh, go fuck yourself, you piece of shit," Siren called after him. Her face was flushed with anger. He was already gone, but she yelled: "It's the only way you're ever gonna get any!" I wished she'd be quiet. Everyone was still looking at us, and I wanted to cease to exist.

"What in the great holy hell did I miss?" Mattie said, joining us. He had his wig in one hand, the other over his heart. The cute bearded guy was still next to him. At least the music was still bumping loud, so people went back to talking, but they glanced at us uneasily.

A random guy came up to us. "Hey, are you okay?" he asked.

"Yes," Siren snapped. "We're fine."

"Okay," he said, holding up his hands in surrender. "Listen, I'll leave you alone. I just wanted to make sure you're both all right. Look, I'm Jordan and this is my room, and I'm really sorry if that guy was out of control at my party. I don't put up with that shit. If I'd known he was gonna be a dick like that I never would have let him in here."

"Thank you," I said. And then, for whatever reason, I burst into tears. I wanted to die. Whoever heard of a bawling Indiana Jones? Fuck me.

Siren hugged me. "It's okay," she said.

I did not want to cry in front of everyone. "I have to get out of here. This is fucked up."

"I'll walk you back to the room," Siren said.

"I'm fine," I said, but she and Jordan were looking at me with so much pity I could hardly stand it. "Really," I said, trying to wipe the tears off out of my eyes without smearing my makeup. "I'm fine. I don't know why I'm crying. I need to get out of here."

"We'll walk you back to your room, sweetie," Mattie said.

"Yeah, totally," Jordan said. Oh, great. Apparently he intended to be part of my rescue party as well. Jesus. I felt like such a baby.

"No," I said. "Really. I'm okay. I just need to leave."

"I'll walk her back to the room," Siren said, waving everyone else off.

"Okay," said Mattie. "Text me when you girls get to your room safely."

"You don't have to leave the party," I said, glancing back at the guy she'd been canoodling with. He looked concerned, seeing his potential hookup getting away.

She led me toward the door. "Him? He's no big deal." She turned and wiggled her fingers at him, dismissively. He rolled his eyes. "He was getting on my nerves, anyway."

I guess I was glad she walked me back to our room, even though we only had to go down one floor in the elevator. I sure as hell didn't want to run into that Troy asshole again, at least not by myself, and not tonight. I wondered if he lived in our dorm or somewhere else. Also, it occurred to me that going to my Western Civ lecture was going to be awkward from here on out.

I didn't realize how drunk Siren was until we got back to the room. She shut the door and locked it, but she was stumbling. I was a little tipsy, but mostly tired. The lava lamps were pulsing around my computer and the moon was almost full outside our window, so we didn't bother to turn on any lights. We sat down on her bed, and I took my jacket and hat off.

"I feel so stupid," I said.

"Why would you feel stupid? He was the one being a dick. I saw him grab you like a piece of meat, and I wanted to kick him in the nuts."

"I don't know," I said. I felt so tired. "You can go back to the party. Seriously. I'm fine."

"I'm not going back to that stupid party," she said, and started pulling the bobby pins from her mass of hair. "Oh, I have to text Mattie and tell him we're okay." She grabbed her phone, typed out a quick text and hit send.

"I wonder how Mattie's doing," I said. "That guy he was with is really cute. I wish I'd had a chance to meet him."

"I know," Siren said, giggling. "I hope he's nice. Mattie deserves someone nice. But I'll kick that guy's ass, too, if he mistreats Mattie."

"Hey, thanks for coming to my rescue tonight," I said.

"You're welcome, mama," she said, smiling at me. "Turn around. I'll take the pins out of your hair." I did as she asked, this time grateful for her fussing over me. As we chatted, she pulled the bobby pins out of my bun one by one. Once she had removed them all, she ran her hands through my hair, combing through the sticky hairspray and fluffing it out. "You have such pretty hair," she said.

"Are you kidding? You're the one with gorgeous hair. Mine is straight and brown and boring."

"It's really soft," she said, continuing to comb her fingers through it. "It's so... silky. Mine's always a crazy, tangled mess. Turn around and look at me. Let's get your beard wiped off." She grabbed her makeup remover wipes from the top of her dresser and began wiping my beard off my face. I felt kind of like a kid, except this was... pleasant. I don't even know how it happened, but the next thing I knew we were making out. I'm pretty sure I didn't lean in first, but I don't think she did, either. I don't know. It just happened. And I am not going to lie: It was hot as fuck. Siren was a great kisser. Her lips were so big and soft and she knew exactly what to do with her tongue. It didn't hurt that she was still wearing the bright red lipstick from her Mia Wallace costume, which made her mouth even more gorgeous than it always was. I reached out for one of her beautiful, big boobs and she pulled away.

"Oh, mama. We can't do this. It would be too weird. I do love you, though. You know that, right?"

I was crushed. And I was so horny I thought I might die. But I also knew she was right. It was weird. Fuck. "I'm sorry," I said, feeling stupid again.

"Don't be sorry. No worries at all," she said. She gave me a mischievous look. "You're a damn good kisser."

"So are you," I said. I was exhausted from the stupidity of the night. "I'm going to bed."

"Me too. But I'm going to take a shower first." She grabbed her shower gear and kissed me on the forehead. "Good night, sweetie. You'll get a hookup soon, hot mama."

I knew she meant it to be nice, but it made me feel like shit. When she left, I was glad to be alone. I was even more grateful that I fell asleep before Siren came back to the room, and didn't wake up when she got ready for bed. The next morning was way less awkward than I thought it would be. Siren behaved as though nothing had happened, and Mattie texted to make sure I was okay.

The following Tuesday, when I walked into my Western Civ lecture, I arrived at class early and took a seat at the back corner of the room, where I could see everyone. Eventually, I saw Troy come in and take a seat in the middle of the room, near where I used to sit. He kept to himself, and I was relieved when he left at the end of class without looking for me.

10

Bees & Thanksgiving

O ver the next few weeks, I visited the entomology collections several times, whenever I wasn't studying or working and Siren and Mattie weren't bugging me to hang out. (Haha.) After looking through the entire Augochlorini tribe of sweat bees (*Halictinae*), I moved on to the other tribes of Halictinae, glancing past the ones that were obviously wrong and taking photos of the specimens that looked closer to Flora's drawings. Still, I couldn't find a bee that was a good match to Flora's detailed drawings and notes.

As Thanksgiving approached, I eventually made it through the university's entire bee collection, which was no small feat, considering KU claimed it was one of the world's largest. When none of the bees panned out, I moved on to the wasps, and finally the winged ants. By the time I made it through all those bugs, I was pretty darn sure Flora's unidentified insect was indeed a bee, and probably somewhere in the Augochlorini tribe of Halictinae, which was exactly where I'd started. That was okay, though, because it was, in my opinion, just as useful to be able to exclude candidates as to include them. But I was frustrated. What was I missing? Had I overlooked something, somehow?

The other thing was, I wasn't really looking forward to going home for Thanksgiving, mainly because I was so happy at school. I mentioned it one afternoon when the three of us were hanging out in Mattie's room, watching *Who's Afraid of Virginia Woolf*, because I'd mentioned we were reading *To the Lighthouse* by Virginia Woolf in English class and then Siren and Mattie insisted I needed to watch the movie, which had nothing to do with Virginia Woolf. It was good. Kind of batshit, but good.

"Ugh," I said, taking a handful of popcorn from the bowl in Siren's lap. "This movie reminds me I have to go home for Thanksgiving."

Siren laughed. "I hear you."

"Kymer, just come to my family's Thanksgiving," Mattie replied. "It'll be at the restaurant. There's plenty of food. Plus you can meet my older sister and my cousins and all my aunties and uncles. It's a blast!"

"Are you serious?"

"Hell yes, I am serious. We have so much food every year we could feed half the town. In fact, half the town will be there. Our whole family will be there, and my mother is always inviting most of the church and all the homeless people downtown. She would love it if you came."

I really wanted to. The thought of my family's stuffy, uptight Thanksgiving seemed suffocating.

"I don't know," I said.

"I'm telling you, just come to ours!"

"It's not that I don't want to come to your Thanksgiving," I explained. "I do want to come to yours. I don't want to go home to mine. But, I don't want to hurt my mom and dad's feelings, you know? My parents are probably looking forward to seeing me." Not to mention Zach...

"You're worried about seeing your old boy-toy, aren't you?"

"No," I said, a little too impatiently.

"Ooo. That sounds touchy," Mattie said, clutching his metaphorical pearls. "Okay then. Well, listen, you call your mother and ask her permission to stay in Lawrence, and then you come to our Thanksgiving at the restaurant. Sound good?"

"Yeah," I sighed. "Okay, I'll try."

"Good. Just tell her you have studying to do."

"I could tell her that. It does sound like something I'd say, and this time, it happens to be true."

Mattie looked over his glasses. "You doing okay in your classes, Miss Kymer?"

"No. Not really," I said, laughing, because it was true.

"How is that possible? You study more than anybody I know."

"I don't know. I never had to study this much in high school. There's just so much more material to memorize, and even when I think I have it all down, I sit down to take a quiz or a test and all of a sudden I'm having a panic attack, and I can't remember the answers, or the questions are weirdly phrased or presented, and I can't figure out what they want for an answer." Just talking about it was making me feel panicky.

"Oh, I see," he said, nodding knowingly. "You don't really know how to effectively study because you've never had to do it before."

It was such a truth bomb I didn't know what to say. He was right. Before I could answer, he said, "I used to have problems studying, myself, so this is what I started doing." He got up, went to his desk and retrieved a stack of cards from the top drawer. Then he showed me his method of converting his notes to flash cards, color-coordinating each class. His English flash cards were written in pink, math in green, sociology in orange, theater class in blue, etcetera. "That way it's easier to visualize and remember your flash cards in a test," he explained.

"That's genius."

"Why thank you, love. My big sister taught me that. It's what got her through law school. I hope it helps."

"You guys! Shh!" Siren said impatiently. "You're missing the best part of the movie!"

But after the movie was over and Siren and I had returned to our dorm room, did I recopy my notes to flash cards? Nope. I lay down on my bed and read Flora's diary before I had to go into work.

That evening, I called Victoria to talk about Thanksgiving. I explained I was having trouble in my classes and was invited to my friend Mattie's Thanksgiving dinner. Instead of freaking out, she said, "You know what, sweetheart, that will work out fine."

"Really?" I was prepared to beg, or even claim my boss asked me to work at the Natural History Museum over break.

"Well, you know... your Kansas grandparents are going to be in Colorado for Thanksgiving this year with your Uncle Bob's side of the family, and my sister has plans with her in-laws instead of our family this year, so it's just going to be Daddy and Cade and I, and honestly, I've been so busy lately that I don't really want to cook. I'll just book us a table at the club. They always offer a Thanksgiving meal, and then your father and Cade can watch football at home afterwards. They'll be thrilled."

I wasn't sure what to make of this development. On the one hand, I was super glad I had a guilt-free green light to spend Thanksgiving with Mattie's family. On the other hand, I was kind of insulted.

Well, it's on, I texted Mattie as soon as I got off the phone with my mother.

What's on?

I can spend Thanksgiving in Lawrence

Yass girl! U will not regret!

He was right. I did not regret it. I slept in late that morning, awakening to Mattie's text: *Food prolly won't be ready til 4, but U should come hang when U get up*

I took my time taking a shower and getting ready, and pulled up outside Smoky Jo's around 1 p.m. There were so many cars parked outside it looked like a Saturday afternoon after a KU basketball game. Inside, the restaurant was packed with people. They had put out extra tables and chairs, and every table was covered with a black tablecloth, with leaf-shaped red, gold and orange glitter scattered for decoration. A plastic banner tied to the wall proclaimed: *Happy Thanksgiving from the Walker Family!* with a cartoon turkey holding a knife and fork. Toward one edge of the room were two extra-long tables covered in black cloths. One had industrial-sized food warmers where the main dishes were obviously going to go, while the other table held a smorgasbord of snacky-type appetizers, deviled eggs and cookies and chips, and I felt rude for not thinking to bring something to share.

Mattie wasn't kidding. It looked as though half of Lawrence was there. People milled around, talking, laughing, sitting, standing. There was hip-hop thumping in the background, and all three television sets in the restaurant were muted and tuned to different football games. The noise was deafening in a happy way: it was a party. The soundtrack to Thanksgiving at our house was usually Frank Sinatra, at Victoria's insistence, which was kinda nice in its own way I guess, but nothing like this.

Mattie came sashaying out from the kitchen wearing a hair net, gloves and an apron. He looked around, spotted me, and made a beeline straight in my direction. "How are you doing, Miss Kymer? Did you just get here? Have you met anyone, yet?" He continued before I could answer. "You don't have anything to drink. Let's get you something to drink, and then I'll introduce you around. What would you like to drink, darling?" He gestured to a serving table. "You can get your regular soft drinks from the soda dispenser on the wall, of course. On the table in these drink coolers we have lemonade, sweet tea and water," he gestured to several coolers under the food tables, "or we have beer in the coolers under here. If you'd like some cognac or whiskey to go in your cola, you'll have to talk with my uncles out back. Come on," he gestured. " I'll introduce you around."

I followed as he wove a path through the happy, noisy crowd of people—"excuse me, excuse me, excuse me"—and stopped in front of a group of women of differing ages and sizes. "Kymer this is my Aunt Bernice, my Aunt Liz, my cousin Shanice, my Auntie Bethany, my cousin LaTisha and my Auntie Francine," he said, gesturing. As we all smiled and shook hands, he continued, "This is my friend Kymer from the dorm. She's from Maryland, but she can't help that. She's good people, though," and we all shared a polite laugh.

"Well, welcome to Kansas," Auntie Bethany said.

"I think we've converted her into a certified Kansas City barbeque lover now," Mattie said, looking me up and down.

"It wasn't difficult," I said, patting my stomach. "Mr. and Mrs. Walker are amazing cooks," and we all agreed this was true.

"Aunties, do any of you need your drinks refreshed? No? Well, I'm going to keep showing Kymer around," he said, and led us back into the crowd. I loved the way he said "ont" and "ontie" instead of "ant" and "antie." Some kids cut through the crowd, giggling and shouting and chasing after each other. Mattie pointed after them. "Those are some of my little cousins, Benjamin, Katrina, Sasha and Darius and you know my littlest sister Olivia." Olivia stopped, turned and stuck her tongue out at Mattie. "Aren't you supposed to be in the kitchen helping your mother?" he called after her as she ran away. He waved his hand in defeat. "Fine, go play. Let's see, you haven't met my older sister Eva and her husband Xavier yet," he said, and led us to a young couple. "This is my beautiful older sister Eva, whom our mother is pressuring the fuck out of to get pregnant."

Eva laughed. "She sure is. I keep telling her, 'Momma, I need to put in a few years at the practice before I go having a baby,' but she does not want to hear it. She wants grandkids."

"All her friends have grandkids, Eva," Mattie said. "Why are you so selfish?"

"Shut up, Matthew," she said, play-smacking his shoulder. "You are not even funny. You know I can still beat your skinny ass at arm wrestling."

Mattie ignored this. "This is one of my new best girlfriends, Kymer, I've told you about. Well, not girlfriend, but friend who is a girl, obviously. Our friend Siren had to go home to Hutchinson for Thanksgiving, and Kymer is from Maryland."

"Nice to meet you," Eva said. She was a mix of Pops and Moms in the face, tall like Lee, but a soft voice like her mother. I shook hands with her husband, too; he seemed nice.

"And this fine lady is my grandmother, Josephine, the founder of our family barbeque legacy," Mattie said, leading us toward a chair in the middle of the room. He placed his hand on the old lady's shoulder. She was cute as fuck in that old people way, obviously seated in a place of honor. She was dressed in a lavender pantsuit, with a lavender scarf bundled up high around her neck. On her head was a beautiful white hat with a wide brim and black lace. She was shriveled and bony, but you could tell she was tough. I shook her hand and could feel the strength in her work-worn knuckles.

"I love your barbeque," I said, patting my stomach. "I'm getting seriously fat being friends with your grandson."

She laughed. "Why thank you! I did always pride myself on trying to keep the community well-padded." We chatted for a bit. She asked me what my major was, that kind of thing. Just when I was starting to wonder if I could possibly remember the name of everyone Mattie was introducing me to, he said, "Don't worry, Miss Kymer. You don't have to remember everyone's names. There will be no test, and everyone here is friendly," he glanced around the restaurant. "Oh, except for my cousin Richard over there," and he pointed to a tall man in his forties or so. "He's kind of an asshole, so I would steer clear of him if at all possible. Now, I'm really sorry I have to do this to you, but if I don't get my tiny butt back in that kitchen, my mother is going to come out here and murder me. Will you be alright out here mingling by yourself?"

"Absolutely!" I said, patting him on the shoulder. "Go, get back in the kitchen before your mother kills you! I'm fine."

"Okay, Miss Kymer! I'll see you soon!" He went off through the crowd toward the kitchen, and I navigated to the drink dispenser for a diet cola. Then I meandered through the throng of humanity. I thought about walking back over to talk with Eva and her husband to find out what Mattie was like when he was little, but they were busy talking with another couple. So, I wandered over to the other side of the room where there were a few tables of people playing games. There appeared to be a game of spades at one table, a game of hearts at another, and two tables of people playing dominoes. I guess I'd heard that people play dominoes, but I had no idea exactly how one did that. Curious, I hovered near one of the tables and watched the game, trying to figure it out. The two men playing were both older gentlemen, one whom I guessed to be in his seventies, and the other guy looked like he might be a couple of decades younger.

"Henry, my good sir, you have just made your fatal mistake," the older man said, placing his domino on the board.

Henry's face fell, and his shoulders sagged as he considered where to play next. "Don't 'my good sir' me, you old fool," he grumbled. "You just got a lucky draw from the bone-pile."

"I may be old, but I don't think I'm the fool this time." The older man played his last domino, and from the younger man's reaction, he had obviously won.

"Aw, man! Admit it, now, Patrick. You a cheat. Somehow you are cheat-ting. You never have a run of luck like this. Tell the truth."

"When one has skill, there's no need to cheat, my brother," Patrick said, and Henry shook his head. Henry tallied up the score from his remaining dominoes he hadn't been able to play, and those points were added to Patrick's score. It looked like an interesting game.

Patrick turned his attention to me. "Hello, there. Would you like to join us?"

"Oh, I don't know how to play," I said. "I hope I'm not bothering you by watching."

"No bother at all. We can teach you. It's simple," Patrick said, helping Henry turn all the dominoes face down, so dots were hidden. "Well, let me clarify that, like any good game, the rules are simple, but once you get the rules down, the strategy of dominoes can be quite complex." He pulled up an extra chair to the table, so I sat. They pushed the dominoes to the center of the table, mixed them up, and we took turns drawing five dominoes each.

It turned out Patrick was right—dominoes was easy to learn, but the strategy was challenging. Apparently the two of them had been friends with each other more decades than I could comprehend, and they had both been friends with the Walker family since they were kids. Listening to Henry and Patrick trade verbal jabs was hilarious.

"Hey, Kymer, you know what?" Henry said to me at one point.

"What?" I replied.

"You know how old my man Patrick is?" he asked.

"How old?"

"Patrick is so old, his Social Security number is five," Henry said, holding up five fingers, which cracked me up.

"Kymer, don't listen to Henry," Patrick replied, gesturing to his friend. "This is what happens when children are left behind."

We played for the next hour, until Henry looked past Patrick's shoulder and said, "Praise Jesus. Here come the food," and the three of us stopped playing to watch a parade of people hauling out catering-sized pans heaped with sweet potatoes, mac 'n' cheese, mashed potatoes, greens, cornbread dressing, regular dressing and gravy. Mattie's dad brought out two turkeys: one plain-smoked and the other spicy-smoked, and then some men I assumed were Mattie's uncles brought in two smoked hams and a pile of beef brisket. While all that was going on, Mattie's mom and some other older ladies brought out the pies: sweet potato, pecan, apple, cherry, blackberry, banana cream, chocolate cream and coconut cream. It was total, complete food-porn, and I was in heaven. It was nothing like Victoria's dry turkey and creamed peas with pearl onions on the good white china. This was like food-church, and I had found the altar, hallelujah. I had been hungry earlier, but by now I was dying. I hadn't had anything to eat, and my stomach made a crazy noise like a kitten being stepped on. Thankfully, it was so loud in the room, no one but me could hear it.

Mattie's dad hollered over the crowd for quiet: "Can I get everyone's attention, please? Hello, everyone! Thank you for coming. If you all don't mind, Pastor Lucas is here from our local AME church. I've asked her to lead us in prayer before the meal." We all bowed our heads. Some people folded their hands under their chins and closed their eyes. As the pastor spoke, my stomach churned with the anticipation of shoving food into my face, and I prayed my stomach would be quiet.

I don't remember everything she said... I remember it was nice, though. Like, it was genuinely uplifting and not at all fake or hokey. Her voice was like sitting by a fire when you're really cold. It made you feel good. And it made me feel good to be there with Mattie's family. There was a general feeling of warmth, and everyone was smiling and happy, like an electric goodness in the room. At the end, she said, "Keep the spirit of Thanksgiving in your hearts every day of the year. When we invite our fellow man into our homes and offer them nourishment, we offer God himself. And when we talk about nourishment, we're talking about all types of nourishment: food... shelter... love. When we nourish our neighbors' stomachs, shelter their bodies and show them love, we show them God's mercy."

It was kind of awesome.

Once the prayer was over, the crowd migrated toward the buffet tables and lined up, and the line proceeded to move way too slowly, but eventually I piled up my plate, and when I went to sit down, I was surprised when Mattie tapped my arm and pointed to two empty seats at a crowded table. "I saved you a seat with my family. I'll be right there," and he joined the line, which was thinning out now, to fill his plate.

The whole Walker family was packed around one long table, along with their spouses. All the kids, though, were at their own table, and it was a total madhouse of adorableness, with kids laughing and wiggling and shoving food into their faces. Everyone was there, including Pops. Everyone with the exception of Moms.

"Where is Mama?" Mattie's sister Eva asked.

"You know how she is," chuckled Pops. "She won't sit down and eat until the very last person is sitting down to eat thirds. She'll wait until everybody else has theirs and then she'll let herself eat."

Mattie squeezed in next to me with his plate and sat down. "Who?"

"Moms," said Eva. "Did you see her when you were up?"

"Moms is in the kitchen right now making up a special gluten-free plate for old Mrs. Jones, and you know how she is. So particular. But Pops is right. Moms won't sit down to eat until everyone else is good and settled. And I should be a good son and go help her, but I am sorry, I am starving," and he took a big bite of mac 'n' cheese. His plate was piled dangerously high, and he worked his way through the whole mess of it, until he was scraping the plate clean. Then he grabbed for his piece of sweet potato pie and shoveled it in, bite after bite. It was the most food I'd ever seen him eat. When he was finished, he pushed back from the table and rubbed his belly. I swear to God it looked like he'd swallowed a basketball. "Oh my lord, I am full," he said, rubbing his belly.

Just then, seemingly out of nowhere, Moms appeared with her plate, taking a seat next to her son. "Please, let's not take the lord's name in vain on Thanksgiving," she said calmly, tucking into her food.

"Ooooo. Mattie's in trouble!" Eva laughed.

"I'm sorry, Moms," Mattie said, leaning on his mother.

"Don't apologize to me," she joked.

Mattie looked skyward. "I'm sorry, Lord."

"That's better," Moms said, as everyone at the table laughed.

I could never say this to Mother Victoria, but it was the best Thanksgiving I'd ever had.

11

Christmas & Zach

From Thanksgiving to Christmas, school became... intense. There were so many papers to write and so much studying to do for finals before winter break and fitting all that in around work and a little social time to keep from going nuts meant there wasn't much time to just sit and relax.

It was the Friday of finals week, and I was in my last English class of the semester. It was snowing outside, and there was already a good six inches on the ground, but classes hadn't been cancelled because apparently KU was notorious for not ever cancelling classes. I hoped the weather would cooperate when I was supposed to fly home tomorrow. The thought of spending the night at KCI Airport seemed less than desirable.

We were taking our final on the novel *Mary Barton* by Elizabeth Gaskell. Rather than assigning an essay, Basil had given us three essay questions to answer and we were all furiously scribbling our extended answers in the paper "blue books" we had to purchase from the student union, trying to get all our thoughts down before the class period ended.

I had to give it to Basil; I really liked the novels and short stories he picked for the curriculum. Once you got used to the archaic language, the stories were basically about how hard life can be and how much it can suck. Especially when you love someone who doesn't love you back. "Unrequited love" was what it was called. I liked that. I think people tend to have this romanticized view of the past, and act like people back in the day were somehow more innocent and good, but the truth is, people pretty much live the same dramas over and over and over again. There are always jerks trying to make life more difficult for other people. There are always people who get married for the wrong reasons. And there always will be.

My phone was silenced and in my backpack, like we were supposed to do during a test, but it must have been wedged in there in exactly the right way, because when it vibrated, it made this embarrassing, loud, buzzing noise right in the middle of the test.

"Oh, bruh!" DudeBro Number One said, waving his hand in front of his nose as though someone had farted. "Bruh. That is nasty." DudeBro Number Two laughed.

I felt my face redden. Motherfuckers. I couldn't stand those guys.

"Sorry," I mouthed to Basil, grabbing my phone and glancing at it. It was a text from Dad: *What do you get if Santa comes down your chimney when the fire is ablaze?* I smiled. My dad loved corny puns and jokes. I shoved the phone back into the backpack and picked up my pencil again. I needed at least a B on this final if I wanted a B in the class.

As soon as class had ended and I'd handed my blue book to Basil, I fished my phone out of my backpack and texted: *I don't know. What?* as I made my way out of Wescoe. There was a pause. I smirked at my phone, walking, glancing at the sidewalk, trying to make sure I didn't trip and fall.

Crisp Kringle

I snorted in the quiet snowfall, and a couple of people walking through the concrete expanse in front of Wescoe, known ironically as Wescoe Beach, looked at me funny. The joke was so my dad.

The phone buzzed again. But this time it wasn't Dad. It was Zach.

Hey, Lampinator!

I stared at my phone as I walked in the snow. *Still with the Lampinator talk?*

I know you're probably in English right now, but I had to let you know how happy I am you're coming home and I can't wait to see you.

Ugh. I felt my shoulders getting tight. Zach had been texting a lot lately. Like, every day, sometimes several times a day. He seemed to be really looking forward to winter break and us getting together with our old friends from high school. Like, really excited. Like, way more excited than I was.

I mean, I wanted to see him, and all our friends—Chloe, Erin, Aubrey, Brent, Will and Austin. Zach and I were part of a friend group that had started our sophomore year with a few people coming in and out, but had gelled our senior year. I liked our group because none of us was particularly popular or stuck-up or entitled, which was rampant at our school. Of course, Zach and I were dating, Erin and Brent were dating, Will and Austin were dating, Aubrey had a girlfriend named Aimee who went to a different high school, and we all knew Chloe wanted to be dating Zach, but none of us ever really talked about it. She dated a few guys here and there and it was usually a little awkward when our friend group would have to incorporate Chloe's new guy. Usually we didn't have to suffer through the awkwardness for long—she usually only dated a guy for a few weeks and then he'd be gone. The only guy Chloe seemed to be consistently interested in talking to was Zach. At first, I didn't even notice it. It was Aubrey who pointed out how Chloe would use every excuse in the world to sidle up to Zach whenever she had the chance. As soon as I'd move away from him, she'd get closer. I guess I didn't notice because everyone in our friend group liked to talk to each other to some degree or another. Once I saw it, I couldn't believe I hadn't noticed before. "Oh, Kymer," Aubrey said to me, shaking her head, "you can be sooooo naive." It had made me laugh.

Weirdly, I liked Chloe. We were decent friends. She had a great, goofy sense of humor and more than once we laughed ourselves silly, until our stomachs were sore. In fact, sometimes I wondered why Zach dated me and not Chloe. In the high school social pecking order, we were almost the same person. She was just as funny as me, same-ish intelligence. Objectively, though, I thought she was prettier than me: a bit taller, a bit skinnier, definitely prettier hair, wavy, with an auburn tint. Her family was about the same, income-wise, as mine, not that Zach really gave a crap about that kind of stuff.

Occasionally, I worried Chloe might make a move on Zach—when she was drunk and our group was all together—but even when she'd get flirty, Zach never showed any interest in her that I was aware of, so I just let it go. There didn't seem to be any point in fucking up a perfectly great group friendship over a little flirtation.

Zach and I meshed pretty well—in bed and in conversation. He liked to talk about the same kinds of nerdy things I did, and we shared a special language of dark sarcasm I not only thought was funny, but kind of hot, too. In addition to knowing a lot about law, Zach knew a lot about weather and a little about astronomy. Once, after we'd had sex at his house during a thunderstorm, he explained the whole storm scientifically—how it had come about because of high pressure in the Gulf and low pressure in Canada, and updraft and electrons and protons and lightning and the speed of light versus the speed of sound and it was so insanely sexy. I shivered at the memory and the cold. That was back when Zach made me feel full of butterflies. Lately it felt more like moths endlessly bumping a streetlight in the dark.

I was on the steepest part of the trek back to the dorm now—downhill—and the powder was a little slippery. You could see people's elongated tracks where they'd started to slide. I inched down the hill, trying to stay on my feet. Up ahead, a couple of guys who had been kicking snow at each other accidentally locked shoes and fell down, laughing, calling each other "asshole," in the cold, dead air of muffled sound trapped in fluffy snow. It looked as though at least another inch of powder had collected on the ground since I'd started down the hill, and it occurred to me I should get Victoria to take me shopping for some cute snow boots while I was home.

Home. That was a weird word. Maryland didn't seem like home. This seemed like home to me now. I loved my new friends, and my classes, and unlike a lot of the other girls on our dorm floor, I didn't mind being away from where I grew up. I didn't mind being on my own much, at all. In fact, I was kind of loving it. And then there was the bug diary… I hadn't talked with Professor Berg about it yet, because we'd been reviewing for the big test before winter break, and I wanted to get through that before I tried bugging her about Flora's mystery bee. The phone buzzed again. It was Zach: *U don't have to answer. I know UR sitting through a lecture. Only one more sleep till I get to see you!*

My stomach fell. The phone buzzed again, and it was Dad: *See you soon, kiddo! Don't forget to take a photo of your parking space at the airport.*

Oh! That's a great idea! I typed back. *Thanks, Dad! Love you!*

Love you, too, kiddo!

I decided not to respond to Zach and let him think I was still in English class. Thankfully, the phone stayed quiet. I did miss that little punk, Cade, and my Dad. Zach, however, was annoying to me for some reason, and I also wasn't looking forward to seeing Victoria. She would want to hear all about my classes, including who was in them and what the professors were like. She would want to know if I was exercising and eating right, since she always thought I was fat. She would also grill me about any friends I'd made. She'd want to know their names and if they came from "good" (i.e. upper middle class) families. She wouldn't approve of Mattie or Siren, not that I cared, but I'd have to sit through the disapproval. She'd shame me for wearing too much eyeliner, and she'd want to know whether or not I was I behaving myself, which was Victoria-speak for not having too much sexual intercourse, which, hooray for her, I wasn't having any. She was also going to want to know about my grades, and I wasn't looking forward to that conversation. She was already not happy about me going to school in Kansas, and it was going to be difficult to convince her to continue paying my tuition when my grades were less than stellar. It wasn't even like I could get around her and go through Dad on this one. She held the purse-strings at home and paid all the bills.

And what the hell was going on with Zach? I honestly thought he'd have a new girlfriend by now. To be fair, though, I guess I'd assumed I'd have a friend with benefits, myself, by this point, and that hadn't happened. I was looking forward to seeing him because I desperately wanted to have sex, but I also didn't want to rekindle any sort of serious romance between us. As far as I was concerned, I was ready to move on. I thought Zach was moving on too, because we'd been texting less and less as the semester had gone on. Now, though, he was acting like everything was supposed to be the same between us, exactly like our senior year of high school. But maybe he was just jazzed about break and Christmas and all that sentimental stuff. Maybe once I saw him it would be all casual and good. The two of us could hook up, and party, and hang with the gang for a bit before going our separate ways again, and maybe for good.

That afternoon, I worked on doing a load of laundry and packing to go home for the break. The dorm had a festive, but kind of frenetic, buzz about it. Several of the girls had decorated their rooms or hung wreaths on their doors. It was the last day of finals, and everyone was bustling around, trying to finish up their studying while packing to go home over winter break, since the university closed the dorms over the long holiday.

Siren was putting in an early shift at Bazongas, trying to make a little more money before Christmas. She apparently had several little cousins to buy presents for. I didn't know what Mattie was up to, but I assumed he was probably Christmas shopping or working or taking a test.

I was waiting for my load of laundry to dry. Somehow, I'd managed to find a free washing machine and dryer, even though the laundry room was bonkers with people trying to get their laundry done before they went home. I decided to only wash the essentials, pack my suitcase with dirty laundry and wash it when I got home. Or, even better, maybe I could convince Victoria to do it for me, since that was kind of her thing.

Siren tried to do a load of laundry in the laundry room in the basement of the dorm every few days. I, on the other hand, let my dirty clothes pile up in the closet for three weeks or so, until they were a good two or three feet deep, and then Siren would hang out with me at a local laundromat for a couple of hours to get all of it done at once, even helping me fold everything. "Why can't you just do a load every few days?" she'd ask, but I never had a good answer for her.

I opened my underwear drawer and grabbed all the clean underwear, socks and bras in the drawer, which wasn't much, since most of those things were in the laundry. The bug diary was there, too, so I grabbed it as well. I packed all the underwear and socks (and my vibrator), then sat down on my bed to page through the diary. Something about Flora's handwriting and sketches was always soothing to me. The fineness and detail of her drawings was kind of mesmerizing. And sometimes the text cracked me up. Like this entry: *It was both fortunate and unfortunate that professor Bailey tripped and fell in front of Blake Hall this afternoon. Two young men helped him up, and upon standing and seeing the hole in the knee of his trousers, he swore, not realizing there was a young lady present. When he saw me he turned every shade of red imaginable, apologizing profusely. The fortunate part of this incident is that the fracas caused me to pause next to a large pine tree where I discovered this pine sawyer beetle resting on one of the boughs.* A couple of times, when I was looking at the diary late at night while lying in bed and feeling really relaxed, I thought I'd felt something—close-ish to the feeling I'd had when Carrie Watson appeared in the library, but not quite. It was like chasing an orgasm: I'd kind of get there, but as soon as I thought about it too much, the feeling would go away, and I'd wonder if it had been real, or if I was just imagining things. I looked through the diary until the alarm I'd set on my phone went off, so that I'd know when to go down to the basement and get my laundry from the dryer.

As I left the room, I almost bumped into Staycee, who was walking down the hallway. "Hey, Kymer! You ready for break?" She generally spoke at a high volume, in the up-and-down timbre of her Chicago accent.

"Almost," I replied. "I have to go get my laundry from downstairs, so I can finish packing."

"You haven't packed yet? I was packed yesterday." I bet you were, I thought. Staycee was notoriously fastidious, to the point of being anal-retentive. Sometimes she kinda drove her roommate Lila crazy.

"Oh, I'll be done before I go to bed," I said.

"What time is your flight tomorrow?" she asked, twisting her hair absentmindedly around her finger.

"Not till nine."

"Oh my gawd! How did you luck out like that?"

"I don't know," I shrugged. "It's nonstop, too. Crazy."

"You total whore! I hate you right now. I have to get up at three-fucking-thirty in the morning because my flight leaves at five-thirty," she said, though I was pretty sure that was about the time she got up most mornings anyway, judging by the number of times I'd had to get up to pee at 6 a.m. and she was in the bathroom blow-drying her wavy, brunette hair in front of one of the foggy mirrors.

"That sucks," I said, hoping I looked sympathetic.

"Right?"

We moved out of the middle of the hall so the snooty girls from Arizona could get to their room. "So, are you finished with your all

Christmas shopping, then?" I asked, and that's when things became uncomfortable. Staycee looked at me, her eyebrows raised, not saying anything. The change in the mood of the conversation was palpable. I looked back at her. Had she not heard me, maybe? "Have you finished your Christmas shopping?" I asked again. She continued to stare. That's when it dawned on me I must've said said something wrong. But what was it? My mind whirled for a couple seconds and then stopped: Oh. My. God. Jewish. She's Jewish. I'm a fucking idiot.

"Oh God, I am so sorry." I was mortified.

"That's okay. I knew you'd remember."

"No. It was... dumb."

She smiled at me, and it was kind of unnerving because it was a real smile. She was forgiving me, but I knew it was a question she'd probably had to field a million times over. "We're totally good, Kymer." She turned to walk back to her room. "Go get your laundry. And have a nice holiday with your family!"

"You too."

When I got back to the room with my laundry, I set the basket on the bed and started folding the warm clothes. My phone buzzed. I grabbed it and looked: Ugh. Zach.

Hey, Lampinator! I can't wait to get my hands on you! ;)

I had a range of emotions: first, mild annoyance. Then, mild amusement. And then it occurred to me that it was kinda hot, especially considering I was about to explode from lack of sex. Maybe Zach missed me more than I missed him, but I was still looking forward to hooking up.

That sounds good, I typed back.

I miss you so much

Ugh, why? Why did he have to miss me so much? *I'm looking forward to fucking, I mean, seeing you, too*, I typed.

That's my girl. Always the poet

Immediately I typed back, *Don't you know it!*

When do I get to see you?

Um... not sure. I typed. *My parents will want me around the first night. Maybe after that?*

Okay. Let me know as soon as you get to your house, though.

Sigh. Will do!

The next morning, I woke up, got dressed, gathered my suitcase, phone, coat and hat, cracked open one of our windows and felt the icy air blast me in the face as I carefully set the wooly bear caterpillar's terrarium on the ledge outside the window. Then I placed a brick on top of it (which I'd found on the ground outside the art building), so that the terrarium wouldn't blow away, because Kansas could get windy. I closed the window and put on my coat and gloves as quietly as I could. Siren didn't have to leave as early as I did, since her drive home wasn't that far, so she was still snoozing in bed, and I didn't want to wake her. She'd ended up putting in a double shift at Bazongas the day before, because the money was good. I was kinda nervous about driving to the airport and getting myself through check-in and security and on a plane, and I ended up accidentally knocking a container of pens off my desk. Siren stretched and yawned.

"Oh, hell no. You were not going to leave without saying goodbye."

"I didn't want to wake you up."

"Come here, you," she said, reaching out from her bed. Her hair was a hot mess like it was every morning, and her mascara was all smudged.

"Merry Christmas, mama!" She grabbed me in a hug.

"You too," I said, squeezing her. I was going to miss her. I kept thinking that it would be easier to handle my mother if I could take Siren or Mattie home with me, but that wasn't to be. I was just gonna have to suck it up and deal with Victoria all on my own.

I turned to check on the other bugs one last time. I'd cleaned all their terrariums and made sure they all had plenty of dry food and moisture cubes to drink from.

I shut the door carefully behind me. There were several girls with their suitcases out in the common area outside the elevators. The elevators could only handle three or four girls and their suitcases at a time, and there were already several girls waiting their turn to go down, so I hefted my suitcase and walked down nine flights with it and out to my car. I didn't want to take any chances being late to the airport.

Driving to the airport made me think about the drive from Maryland to Kansas with Dad. It was one of the best times I'd ever had with him. Actually, it was one of the best times I'd ever had with anyone. I laughed so hard my stomach hurt. We did the trip in two very long days of driving, and somewhere around Indiana, we got so punchy it was stupid. We started punning hardcore, about trees, for some reason:

"Willow you just relax?"

"Oh, that was tortured."

"You mean... orchard?"

"Is that really a pun, or just a rhyme?"

"I think it's up to your pine of view."

"Oh my God. Leaf me alone."

"Life's a birch."

"I might have to kick your ash for that one."

"Now you've junipered the shark."

"That was palm-thetic."

"Oak, I don't know. I think I could do worse."

"Could I get your persimmon to use that last pun?"

At one point Dad looked around and said, "They've really spruced this place up." And I almost died laughing.

I mean, I know it all sounds really dumb, but that was the point. It was really dumb. Super dumb. I always felt like I could relax and be myself around my dad. He got me. And I got him. Sometimes we got on Victoria's nerves. "Mark," she'd say. "Stop encouraging her," which I never could figure out. She had married the guy, so she must have, at least at one time, enjoyed his goofball humor.

I managed to get my car successfully parked at KCI, which my parents said I could use their emergency credit card to pay for. It was going to cost my parents at least a few hundred bucks, but they'd insisted they wanted the car covered since it was going to be sitting for a month. I managed to find my airline counter and get my bag checked. I was so freaked out going through security you'd have thought I had a bomb in my pants. I almost fell down taking my shoes off and I didn't realize I'd have to take off my coat and empty my pockets, and there were all these security people barking orders at me, but then they waved me through. Forty-five minutes later, we were able to file onto the plane.

I ended up sitting between a guy who immediately balled up his coat against his window and fell asleep on it, and a woman who, thank God, was too into her phone to make conversation. I put my earbuds in and listened to music while flipping through Flora's diary, which was stashed in my coat pocket.

12

Room of Doom & Sex

Dad and Cade picked me up from Dulles airport, and I couldn't believe how much taller Cade had gotten in less than six months. He was only fourteen, but he'd shot up all of a sudden and was now almost as tall as Dad. His voice had also dropped at least a couple of octaves. When I'd left for school, he'd been a squeaky-voiced little freak, but now he looked and sounded like an actual dude. It was truly weird.

When we walked into the house, it looked and smelled familiar, except, of course, Victoria had decorated for Christmas. My mother liked to make the house look as though a photographer from Beautiful Homes magazine might drop by at any moment to snap pictures. It was always too stiff and stuffy for my taste, with lots of stripes and ruffles and expensive knickknacks placed just-so. I never felt like I could hang out and be comfortable at my house, so I spent most of my time in my room or at friends' houses.

Our house was pretty much exactly like I remembered it. Over-decorated and impossibly clean. Everything was in its place. Nothing was dirty or dusty. There was no clutter lying around. But the most overwhelming sensation was the smell. The house always smelled like vanilla or cinnamon or sandalwood from all the decorative candles and scented pinecones, but since it was Christmas time, the smell was multiplied by, like, a thousand. And there was our artificial Christmas tree, all eight feet of it, decorated in gold and burgundy, since Victoria always picked a "color scheme" for the Christmas season—a color scheme she usually announced while we were eating Thanksgiving dinner—like anybody gave a shit. "This year's color scheme will be blue and silver," she'd say, like she was announcing the city where the next Olympics would be held. So annoying. As it all enveloped me, I realized how weird it felt to be home. Like, very weird. Way more uncomfortable than I'd even thought it would. It was an alien feeling, the way the dorm felt that first week. And I was going to be here for an entire month. Under the same roof with Victoria.

"Are you back, finally? What took so long?" That oh-so-familiar accusing tone rang out from the kitchen. Speak of the devil. "Kylie?" She hustled out of the kitchen, looking trimmer than ever. She'd clearly been to the hairdresser recently and she was wearing an apron. An actual apron.

"Hey, Mom." She grabbed my shoulders and sort of side-kissed my cheek. I patted her back and felt her pointy shoulder blade poking into my hand.

"You've lost weight," I said, knowing it would make her happy.

She smoothed the apron over her thighs and rested her hands on her hips. "Yes! Laura and I have been taking Carmine's Funky-cise! class. It's a hoot!" She looked me up and down. "You look like you may be falling prey to the freshman fifteen."

Ouch.

"Oh for Christ's sake, Vicky, she does not," Dad said, setting down my suitcase and hanging his keys on the hooks Victoria had cleverly hidden in the coat closet. "I think she looks good!"

"Well, I'm not saying she doesn't look good. She does look good! I'm just saying they're clearly not starving her at the dorm, which means we're getting our money's worth!" She touched my hair. "Your hair does look beautiful, though. So thick and silky!"

I smiled. "Thanks." I grabbed my suitcase.

"I can get that for you, pumpkin." Sometimes Dad called me Pumpkin.

"It's okay, Dad, really. I've got it."

"Alright, sweetheart, if you're tired, I suppose you can go up to your room and rest for a bit," Victoria said. I could tell she was annoyed with me, but I didn't care. The whole thing was giving me the heebie-jeebies so bad, I had to get out of there. I headed through the living room, to the kitchen, through the kitchen and up to my room.

Walking into my room was a worse shock than being back in our foyer. It was like I'd stepped into a hotel room. All of my posters were gone... the Vitruvian Man, Butterflies of North America, Walking Sticks of the World... the curtains and bedspread were completely different. My room had been decorated with geometric patterns in bright colors, and the walls had been light gray. This room was painted an obnoxious baby blue and decorated in nauseating blue-and-white flowers and white frills. The bed frame was the same, but they'd replaced my modern nightstand and the dresser with a fussy bedroom set painted white, of all things. On top of the nightstand was a Kleenex box covered with the most God-awful blue-flowered porcelain cozy that ever existed. I guess it was fair that they'd changed my room, since I didn't live there anymore and Cade hadn't wanted it, but jeez. It was like I'd been exorcized from the house.

I dropped my purse, coat and bag on the floor. Then I flopped down on the flowery nightmare of a bed. Victoria walked in a couple of minutes later.

"I see you didn't waste any time getting rid of my posters," I said.

She laughed. "Well, we could hardly host guests with that naked man on the wall."

"It's the Vitruvian man. You know. Leonardo DiVinci."

"I wanted a more... classic look," she said, splaying her fingers.

"More classic than DiVinci?"

She gave me a look. "You know what I mean. Tasteful. Dinner should be ready by six-thirty," and she left. I decided to let her go and not debate the tastefulness of the sketches of an Italian Renaissance master, because... whatever. As I laid on the bed, I remembered I was supposed to text Zach when I got home. Home. Whatever that meant.

Hey, I typed

Hey! What's up? Are you home?

Yes

When can I see you?

Um, not sure... I know Victoria wants me here for dinner tonight. I think I'm required to stay in

Yeah, my folks are being the same, even though school is only an hour away.

Maybe tomorrow?

Definitely. We need to make that happen. Love you!

Oh shit. *Love you too!* I typed it, wondering how much I really meant it.

Text me later

Okay

With naughty photos? Pretty please?

That made me smile. *Sure*, I texted. I trusted him… mostly. But I did insist on using one of those photo sharing apps that doesn't save photos. Since I wasn't completely stupid.

Excellent. Zachy like! And he texted a bunch of hearts and tongues and bananas and peaches. Dork.

Dinner that night was de-fucking-licious. I can't lie. Spinach lasagna and salad with Victoria's homemade Italian vinaigrette. One of my favorite meals. I ate until I was stuffed, and Cade ate twice what I did. Sexting with Zach that night was fun, and we got into it. Like really into it. Thank goodness I'd packed my vibrator.

Victoria wouldn't let me leave the house to visit friends the next day, either, but she did say I could go to a party that night. She made Cade stay home too, so we played video games most of the day, the way we did when we were younger. Zach picked me up at nine in his new Infinity he'd gotten as a high school graduation present. Of course he had to come in and chat up Victoria, because she loved him.

"Wow, you've really outdone yourself with the Christmas decorations this year, Mrs. Charvat." Zach loved to flatter Victoria, and she ate up every bit of it. He really knew how to handle her.

"Why thank you, Zachary. But I keep telling you to call me Vicky," and she actually batted her eyelashes at him.

"Are these genuine Charlie Radkey decorations?" He examined an ornament on the gigantic tree in the living room. He was really laying it on thick.

"You have such a good eye," she said. "They are. Those are from this year's collection."

"I thought so," he said, turning to smile at her. "I hear they make a good financial investment, as well."

"Well, I would never think of selling them," she said.

"Oh, no. Of course not. But still. It's a mark of quality that they keep their value."

"You are so right," she said, beaming. I was pretty sure she wished she could trade me for him as her firstborn.

He turned to look at me. "Ready, Lampinator? You look gorgeous, as always." He gave me a look like he was a man stranded in the desert, and I was a glass of water.

"You kids have fun," Victoria said. "But not too much fun."

"No worries, Vicky," Zach said, sliding his arm around my shoulders. "I'm the designated driver. I'll take good care of her."

I had been looking forward to the party. It was at Brent's house, and Brent's parties were legendary. His parents traveled a lot, and they trusted him to have parties when they were gone. He always sequestered the parties to the finished basement of the house, which consisted of a movie room and a game room, with walk-out access to their massive back yard. The upper floors of the house, though, were off-limits, and everyone knew that. As usual, there were kids all over the ground floor, inside and all over the back yard. Hip-hop blared from the stereo inside. And, as usual, there was a keg of cheap beer on the back patio and several bags of plastic cups.

Usually when we went to parties, Zach and I would kinda mingle around and chat with different groups of people. But all night long, Zach wouldn't leave my side, and he couldn't seem to keep his hands off me, either. He was either holding my hand, or had an arm around my waist with his face in my neck.

"Oh my God!" Chloe screamed when she saw me, and she came at me, fast, beer cup in hand. She collided with me and we fell down, but somehow she kept the beer upright. She laughed like a maniac. She was clearly drunk as shit, and it wasn't even ten o'clock.

"Daaamn, thirsty girl," I said, teasing. "I'm glad to see you, too!"

"It feels like forever since I've seen you, and you never text me, you bitch!" She was hollering in her high-pitched party-scream over the music.

"I know, I'm sorry, but you know what college is like," I yelled back, leaning in.

"I know, right? It's so much harder than high school! Nightmare!" Chloe's voice was at peak party screech.

I stood up and put out my hand to help her up, but Zach grabbed her arms and lifted her from the floor. "Ooo! That was fun," she said, in a flirty way. Zachary either didn't notice or didn't care.

"Yes," Zach said in his dry way. "Just like Disneyland." And Chloe laughed like a maniac again, flipping her good hair.

We all said our hellos and went through our hugs. Erin, whose hair had always been long and dark with a sort of raspberry wash over it, had cut her hair. It was now a short, sleek pixie cut, and her clothes looked a little different... more masculine. I wondered if she was going through a fashion phase or if she was exploring her gender identity.

They were all attending colleges in Maryland or the five-state area, and they all wanted to know what Kansas was like.

"Have you had any locust plagues?" Will asked. He was joking, but we had just come through the 17-year locust hatching there, which wasn't technically a plague, but I knew I wouldn't be able to explain the difference to a bunch of drunk non-science majors at a loud party.

"Um, well, kind of," I said, and I told them about the 17-year locusts, knowing that for the rest of their lives, they'd probably all imagine Kansas to be a hot dust bowl of locust plagues. Yay.

"Oh my God that is freaky!" Austin said. "I still cannot believe you're going to college in the Midwest. Do they all have really thick Southern accents?

I laughed. "No. They have Midwest accents."

"Oh. What's that like?"

"They sound pretty much like we do... I mean... there are differences, but it's not like they sound like they're from Mississippi, or anything. Some of them do say worsh instead of wash. That's kind of annoying."

"Have you seen a tornado yet?" Aubrey asked. Aimee wasn't with her.

"No," I laughed. "But there are tornado siren tests the first Monday of every month, if the weather is nice." They all looked like their eyes might fall on the floor from bugging so far out of their faces.

"Tornado siren tests? What the hell is that? What does that even mean?" Brent asked.

"They're sirens that go off when a tornado is sighted in the area and they test them once a month on a sunny day to make sure they're working."

Austin looked horrified. "Wait. Sirens inside? Or outside?"

"Outdoors, thank God," I said. We were all screaming at each other to be heard.

"So what are you supposed to do if there's a tornado?" Erin asked.

"Take shelter underground," I said.

"Oh my God!" Austin said. "Like in a bomb shelter?"

"No, goofball. Any basement will do. I might never see one. It's not like there's a tornado every other week."

I thought I had been looking forward to catching up with everybody, but as Austin droned on and on and on about how badly he wanted to be a psychologist, I realized how uncomfortable I was and how much I didn't want to be there. It was painful. It felt as though somehow, I had nothing in common with any of these people anymore. I got weirdly depressed, and all I could think about was Siren and Mattie and the Walkers and our dorm room, and it finally dawned on me I was homesick. Homesick for Kansas. Fuck me.

Zach was on my right side; I was talking to Austin on my left. All of a sudden, Chloe sagged into Zach's other shoulder.

"I might be a little big... I mean bit... I might be a little big drunk," she slurred.

"Yes... I agree you might be a little big drunk," Zach said, and everybody cracked up. He didn't push her off his shoulder, though.

I disentangled myself from Zach and pulled away. "I need to get a beer," I said, and I didn't even wait to hear his reaction. I turned and moved through the crowd, pushing and weaving and yelling, "Excuse me!" even though I didn't think anybody could hear me. I went out the sliding glass door to the patio, and thankfully, there wasn't a line at the keg. I filled a cup and downed it, as fast as I could, hoping it would cheer me up. As I filled my cup again, I heard Erin's voice behind me: "Hey, are you okay?"

I hadn't realized she'd followed me.

"Yeah, I'm good. I just needed to kind of... take a break, you know?"

"Yeah, I get it," she said, and she filled her cup until foam spilled from it. "Isn't it fucking annoying to try to have a long-distance relationship?" Brent was studying business at Loyola. Erin was at Georgetown studying graphic design.

"It is," I said, nodding, not wanting to explain that I really would prefer for mine to end. "How are you and Brent doing?" I asked.

"Oh... I don't know. We haven't seen each other much since school started, and now he's all over me tonight but I'm feeling like I might want to... explore... some... other... people..." She looked at me as though to say: You know what I mean.

Interesting. "I think I know exactly what you mean," I said, sipping my beer.

She gave me a look. "Oh, really? Do tell. Have you hooked up with... them?" I couldn't help but notice her use of a gender-neutral pronoun.

"Oh, I mean, there isn't anybody specific, yet. I'm on the lookout."

"I hear you," she said.

"Hey, is Aubrey still dating Aimee?"

"No, they broke up," Erin said, trying to fill her cup with beer, but getting mostly foam.

"Nobody tells me anything," I said.

"It's not like you've been texting us either," she said. "By the way, did you know Austin and Will broke up?"

"They did? It doesn't look like it."

"I know. It's weird. But I'm wondering if maybe neither of them has met anybody, so they're just looking to hook up tonight."

"I get that," I said.

She laughed. "Well, you might as well, right?"

"Yeah... I don't know," I said. "I feel like it might be wrong."

She looked thoughtful. "Zach does miss you a lot. Like... a lot." It was not what I wanted to hear.

"I know," I said. The thing was, I was going to have sex with Zachary. I just was. And then, at some point while I was still in Maryland, I was going to have to break up with him. I knew that, but he didn't. And I felt guilty. But not guilty enough to not have sex with him.

"Oh, well," Erin said, as though she could read my thoughts, "a few more beers, and you won't care."

We made our way through the party and back to our group. Chloe was hanging off Zach's shoulders, trying to stay upright.

"Pleeeeeeeease Zachy," I heard her say to him, but when she saw Erin and I, she straightened up.

"There you are!" she slurred brightly. "Dorothy has returned from the Land of Oz! Lemmie see your shoes!" I didn't move. I couldn't figure out why Chloe was making Dorothy jokes. All our friends knew it annoyed me. She bent over, wobbly, still holding onto Zach's shirt, to glance at my black Mary Janes. "Aw," she said, putting her lower lip out. "No ruby slippers."

"Left those in Kansas," I said, not bothering to hide my irritation.

"Oh no! How will you get back? There's no place like home!" She let go of Zach, laughing like a maniac as she tottered my direction. She threw herself at me and held on to my dress for dear life as I struggled to keep us both upright. "I love you, Kymer. I really do. We're like sisters, right?" Then she laughed again, gasping for breath. "Sisters who like the same mister!" She put her finger to her lips. "SHHHHHHHHHH!"

That's when Zach stepped in, taking her by the shoulders and pulling her off me. "Okay. It's quite apparent we've reached maximum capacity for alcohol, here. Let's get you outside before it's all over the carpet."

I watched them go, as Zach guided Chloe out the front door. It was typical of him, watching out for the rest of us when we were drinking, like that.

"What the fuck was that all about?" I asked, looking around at all my friends' uncomfortable faces.

"You know how Chloe is," Austin said, touching my shoulder. "She gets crazy drunk like that and doesn't know what she's saying."

"Chloe knows exactly what she's saying," said Erin, rolling her eyes. "And doing."

"What's that supposed to mean?" I asked. If she meant Chloe was trying to get in Zach's pants, well what the hell else was new? But where was her hostility toward me coming from? "Why was she fucking with me like that?" I asked.

"That's not all she's fucking," I thought I heard Will say, but Austin shushed him.

My head was starting to spin. My hands were sweaty and my face was hot. My beer buzz was starting to feel more bad than good. I felt my phone buzz inside the little clutch purse I was carrying and took it out to read the text: *You ready to go Lampinator? Chloe needs a ride home.*

Ugh. I was ready to leave, but why did we have to take Chloe with us? I knew the answer, though. It was typical Zach courtesy. True to form, he'd nursed the same beer all night, just in case somebody else needed to be driven home.

"It looks like my ride is leaving," I announced. "I guess I'd better go. But it was great to see all of you."

They all smiled and waved, and said goodbye, but it felt weak. Erin surprised me by sliding over and putting her arm around my waist. She wasn't one for mushiness. "It was good to see you, Kymer. Stay in touch dammit," she emphasized, squeezing me.

"I will," I said, surprised at her show of emotion. As I walked away, I turned back and could see Austin and Erin talking about something intensely, Austin waving his arms.

I wasn't falling-down drunk, but I was stumbling a little as I made my way through the crowd and to the front door, saying goodbye whenever someone from high school recognized me. I spotted Zach's car, which was running and doubled-parked out front. As I approached, I could see Chloe passed out in the back seat. I slid in next to Zach.

"Let's just get her home safe," he said. "Then we can go back to my house."

"She was pretty trashed tonight, huh?" I said, trying to make small talk.

He shifted in his seat and shrug his shoulders. "You know how Chloe is. She enjoys playing the part of the loud, drunk party girl."

"I don't think I've ever seen her that drunk. Is she doing okay? Like, is school going okay for her?" I asked.

He shifted around in his seat again, and glanced at her in the rearview mirror. "I mean, I think so. I haven't heard anything to the contrary."

I turned around to make sure she was still out. I could see the shine of drool at the corner of her mouth when we passed under a streetlamp. "She's always been a fun drunk, but tonight she was kind of being... an asshole."

"Was she?" he said, casually.

"I mean, yeah. To me, at least."

"I'm sure she didn't mean anything by it. She's just drunker than usual," he said, making a left turn.

"I guess," I said, letting it go. After that, I couldn't think of anything to talk with Zach about, which was uncomfortable. We'd always talked easily.

When we pulled into Chloe's driveway a couple minutes later, Zach put the car in park. "Chloe," he said, loud enough to wake her up. "We're here."

"Hmm?" she said, lifting her head a little.

"This is your house." Zach said, and opened her door. "C'mon, sweetie," he said, helping her out of the car. He walked her to the front door, up the steps and eased her down to a sitting position on the porch. In the car headlights, I could see her dig through her purse for a couple of minutes, before Zach took the bag from her, fished around for a second and found her keys. Once they determined which was the front door key and he'd managed to get the door open, he took her inside. He was gone for several minutes. I was about to text him to see if everything was okay when he finally emerged from the house.

"Safe and sound in bed," he said, in a satisfied way, sliding into the driver's seat. It made him happy to do the right thing like that.

When we pulled up to his house, it seemed even bigger than I remembered. His family was better off than mine, and their house was a lot larger, something that both vexed and impressed my mother. He guided his brand-new, two-door Infinity into the four-car garage and turned it off. "Stay there," he said, and he came around to my side of the car to help me out and into the house.

He took my hand, and we made our way through the dim house, up the big front staircase to his room. We always had sex at his house because we knew his parents wouldn't bother us, unlike Victoria, who'd be at my bedroom door faster than you can say "teenage pregnancy."

I still had a decent buzz, and when we passed by his parents' room, I giggled.

"Shhh!" he said, squeezing my hand. I put my free hand over my mouth. Finally. I was going to get laid.

Except things didn't get any easier between us. Things just got weirder.

When we got to his bedroom, he leaned in, solemn, and kissed me slowly, like I'd told him I had a fatal disease and it was our last night together. It was creepy and uncomfortable, and after a minute or two, I grabbed his face and kissed him hard, the way I liked it. I slipped one hand in his jeans and found his familiar erection. Thankfully, that seemed to snap him out of whatever fucked-up women's television channel Sunday romance movie moment he was having.

"Lay down," he said, and gently pushed me down on the bed. I complied. He pushed my dress up, pulled my underwear down and proceeded to work his oral magic. After a few minutes I came so hard my eyes rolled back in my head. It was such an amazing relief. Then we had sex. Real sex. He came quickly the first time, and thankfully, we didn't talk after. We made out until he was hard again and the second time we went at it for like a solid half hour. We collapsed onto our backs, next to each other, sweating and breathing heavily. He grabbed my hand and massaged it like he was kneading a hunk of pizza dough. I kinda wished he'd stop because his palms were sweaty and hot, and I was sweaty and hot and really didn't want to be touched at the moment, but I didn't say anything. Then I started thinking about how many days were left of winter break and wondered how many times I could have sex with Zach before I had to go back to school, because it might have to last me a while. Then I wondered how many times I could stand to have sex with him, especially if he was going to be a sappy dork about it.

"I really missed you, Lampinator."

Ugh. "I missed you, too."

"You sound so incredibly convincing." He said it in his dry, deadpan way, and it made me laugh.

"I'm just tired," I said.

"It's going to absolutely suck waiting for summer."

"What do you mean?" If I'd thought about it for a couple of seconds, I wouldn't have said it, but my brain wasn't at its sharpest right at that moment.

"Y'know. Waiting until you come home for the summer. Jesus. It's been torture." He let my hand go, rolled over and rested his hand on my stomach.

"Umm… I guess I haven't told you yet. I'm not coming home this summer."

"What?"

"Yeah… Siren and I are going to move out of the dorm and get an apartment together."

"Wait… you're moving in with Siren? I'm confused. Is she transferring to UMUC?"

"No. Why would she do that?"

"Wait… how are you going to live together?"

"Like I said, we're going to rent an apartment together," I shrugged.

"In Kansas?" He said "Kansas" like it was the stupidest place on the planet, which irritated me.

"Yes, in Kansas. In Lawrence. That's where I live now, remember?"

He stood up. "Jesus, Kymer. I miss you. I thought this Kansas insanity was some dumbass thing you were doing to please your dad for your first year and then you'd come back to Maryland." The tone of voice wasn't like him. Not at all.

"Why in the world would I go to college to please my dad? When have you ever known me to worry about what my parents think?"

"Oh, that's right. Nobody tells Kymer Charvat what to do. Kymer Charvat feels zero commitment to anyone but herself." He got up and put his underwear on.

"Oh my God, Zach. Did you actually think we were gonna get married or something? We're nineteen. *Nineteen*. You are going to have at least two or three more fairly serious relationships before you settle down with your Stepford Wife," I said. The look on his face was one I'd never seen before. I had hurt him.

"Do you always have to say things in that way? Do you have to be so fucking pragmatic all of the time? Once in a while can't you just be nice, for someone else's benefit? Can't you even pretend you still care about me for a little while before we fade out of each other's lives? I missed you so much and you just didn't care." He threw his hands up, and the next thing he said landed like a bomb: "I didn't even want to do anything with Chloe, but at least she treats me better than a convenient fuck."

"Oh my God," I said, as it dawned on me. Suddenly, everything that had happened that night made sense. "You've already slept with Chloe, haven't you? You've been having sex with Chloe, and all our friends know it. Everybody knew but me."

"Oh give me a break," he said, rudely, and I was surprised by his meanness.

"No, seriously, Zach. You have been having sex with Chloe and you didn't have the courtesy—none of our friends had the courtesy—to tell me that before I went out with you tonight? So you all knew and I was just standing there like a gullible idiot all night long?"

"Keep your voice down," he hissed. "My parents are asleep."

I lowered my voice. "You could have at least told me."

"Listen, I would've been perfectly happy to keep having sex with you if you'd chosen to go to school here. We could be hanging out on campus between classes, getting lunch together, studying together—we could be having sex on a regular basis. But you just took off to Kansas and would barely even answer my texts like I didn't mean anything to you. He stared at me for a moment. "You don't even care, do you?"

"Care about what?"

"You don't even care I had sex with Chloe. You're more concerned about looking foolish in front of our friends."

Ouch. I was speechless. We looked at each other, but I didn't know what to say, so I didn't say anything. I realized we had never talked about what was going to become of us. I had assumed we were going to drift apart. He had assumed something else entirely.

"Fuck this," he said, and sunk down on the bed. He wouldn't look at me. My alcohol buzz was wearing off, and I was super tired. I still didn't know what to say. After a couple of minutes, he got up and put the rest of his clothes on. "C'mon. I'll take you home."

It was an uncomfortable, silent ride. When we got to my house, I kissed his cheek as I got out of the car. He wouldn't look at me. He stared straight ahead.

"I'm sorry," I said. "I really am." I wasn't entirely sure why I was the one doing the apologizing, but it felt like the right thing to do.

"You know, having sex with her didn't mean anything to me, not that it matters to you. I was just horny, and she was here, and you weren't," he said, flatly. "She wants us to start going out, but I've been putting her off because like a fool, I didn't want to hurt your feelings. Turns out you never had feelings to hurt."

I felt a sob creep up my throat. "That's not true," I said, and it came out a whisper. "We all knew Chloe liked you. I just thought you liked me more."

"I did like you more. I *do* like you more. But you're not here. Chole is."

His words hit me in the chest, making the lump in my throat so big I gasped a sob. It hadn't occurred to me that Zach getting together with someone else would make me feel anything other than relieved. In that moment, I felt so many things. I wanted to take him in my arms and tell him I loved him and I'd transfer to Maryland and be his girlfriend again. I wanted to slap him for making me look stupid at a party in front of all our friends. I wanted to wish him and Chloe well, even though she was a backstabbing little whore who deserved to have a lock of that gorgeous hair ripped out of her head in a catfight with her former friend. I kept it inside, knowing there was no way in hell I was going to put my relationship back together with Zach and leave Kansas. I loved my new life too much. Breaking up was the right thing to do. It just hurt more than I thought it would.

"I'm sorry," I whispered, tears rolling down my cheeks.

"Are you?" His words stabbed at me.

"You're the one who cheated on me," I said, defensive.

Finally, he looked me in the eye, hurt anger all over his face. "Did I, Kymer? Really? Or have you been dying to cheat on us since you left?"

I was done arguing. I got out of the car, and the second I slammed the door he reversed out of the driveway, squealing the tires a little and speeding off down the street. Usually he waited to make sure I made it inside okay.

By the time I dragged myself up the stairs of my parents' house and into the room that wasn't my room anymore and climbed into the frilly bed that looked like a department store display, it was after four o'clock in the morning. I put Zach out of my mind and crashed. I slept until noon, then took my sweet time showering and getting dressed, in jeans and a sweater. I put my hair up in a pony tail and grabbed a couple of ibuprofen from my parents' bathroom on my way down to the kitchen. I went straight to a kitchen cabinet and filled my glass with the filtered water pitcher my mother always kept in the fridge. I threw the ibuprofen to the back of my throat and downed the entire glass of water. Then I filled the glass again, with a few cubes of ice, and sipped. Victoria was at the counter, chopping vegetables. "Oh good. You're up," she said. "Lunch will be ready in just a few minutes. Would you please carry this crudités platter and the hummus out to the dining room table when I get it finished? I need to make the sandwiches."

"Sure," I said. My voice came out thick and hoarse, and even with the shower, I knew I still had bags under my eyes. Victoria looked up from the vegetables. "You look like you had an eventful evening."

"Yeah," I said, shuffling across the kitchen slowly.

"Are you feeling alright?"

"I'll be fine once I get some food and caffeine into my system," I said, retrieving a cup from a cabinet and pouring myself a cup of coffee. I shuffled to the fridge for milk.

"So how is Zachary?" she said, brightly. " I haven't really spoken with him since before you left for school."

"I mean... I guess... he was okay... until we broke up," I said, taking a sip of coffee and feeling grateful it went down okay, with no resulting nausea. But I wasn't expecting her reaction.

"You broke up with Zachary? Why on earth would you do that?" Her eyes shot invisible needles at me as she held the knife in the air, hovering over the cutting board in mid-chop.

"Because he lives in Maryland and I live in Kansas?" I couldn't help it. I rolled my eyes. And then I felt like I was in the Twilight Zone, because it was apparent I was about to revisit the same Kansas conversation I'd just had with Zach a few hours ago with my mother.

"What do you mean you live in Kansas?"

"I live in Kansas," I said, feeling my head begin to throb.

"You're moving to Kansas?"

"I *have* moved to Kansas. That's where I live."

"Kylie that's ridiculous," she said, bringing the knife down firmly into the vegetables with a crunch. "You live in Maryland. I don't mind you doing a year, possibly two, of undergraduate work at KU, but you're going to finish your education at the University of Maryland."

"Um... no, I'm not. They have an excellent entomology program at KU. Besides, I hate it here. I always have. You know that."

"Mark... Mark!" Oh gawd. It was her screechy "someone's in trouble now" voice. Shit was getting super real, super quick. I couldn't even believe it.

"Yo!" Dad sauntered into the kitchen wearing his favorite bucket hat with the fishing lures all over. It was classic Dad. I couldn't help it. I burst out laughing.

"There is no part of this that is funny in any way, Kylie," Victoria said, and that did it. I set my coffee cup down on the counter and doubled over, dying. Dead. I looked up to see Dad struggling to not laugh as well, but he would be in so much trouble if he did. Somehow, he managed to hold it in.

"Kylie says she's moving to Kansas." She gestured at me with the knife.

"She has moved to Kansas," he replied, calmly.

"Told you," I muttered. She gave me the "don't take that tone with me, young lady" look.

"Why didn't you tell me about this?" It felt as though Victoria's voice was drilling holes into my throbbing head.

"Tell you about what?" Dad said. He was always a rock.

"Kylie is planning to do all of her schooling in Kansas."

"Oh. Well," he glanced at me, "I didn't think any final decisions had been made in that regard."

"I'm nineteen," I said. "You can't force me to move back to Maryland. I'm an adult."

"We're paying for your education," Victoria huffed.

"I have a job," I said, knowing it was a dumb thing to say as soon as the words left my mouth.

"It's not enough to pay for your education, and you know it. It's probably not even enough to pay rent on some hobo apartment there."

"Now, Vicky," Dad said. He was the only person in the world who could get away with calling my mother Vicky. "She is a legal adult. We can't very well tell her where to live."

"Oh, yes we can, and we will, as long as we're paying for her education." She picked up the knife and started chopping again, faster than before.

"But KU is a great school. I loved my time in Lawrence. And I can understand why Kymer loves it as well," he winked at me. "Even if she never does go to a basketball game."

I relaxed a little. If I had Dad on my side, I still had a chance. Usually Victoria steamrolled him, and he let her, but when Dad took a stand on something, he generally got his way.

"She has dumped Zachary. Dumped! He's a good boy. From a good family. And she'll end up with a degree from Kansas." She set the knife down on the counter with a firm whack.

"I have a degree from Kansas. Believe it or not, it's a respected school, and I for one don't have a problem with either—or both—of the kids going there. Secondly, we can't control who she dates, for Christ's sake. Or who she marries. You wouldn't have any problem with Cade going to school out of state, and I don't see any reason to limit Kymer, either."

"Her name is Kylie."

"What if I don't EVER want to get married?" I said. "How is that even your business?"

"How isn't it my business, young lady? I am your mother."

"Kymer, don't speak that way to your mother," Dad said.

"This is bananas," I said, knowing I was pushing it, but how long did Victoria think she could try to control me? Forever? Did I really have to conform to her wishes about my schooling, so they'd pay for my education?

"Vicky, you and I will talk about this later," Dad said.

"Oh, will we?" Victoria said, arms crossed, lips pursed in that way that made me nuts.

"Yes. We will."

"What the hell is going on in here?" Cade had wandered into the kitchen.

"Don't say hell," Victoria said, and she began scooping up the cut vegetables with two hands and depositing them in bunches on the platter, instead of carefully arranging them like she normally would.

"There's no reason to fight in front of the kids," Dad said. "We will discuss it later." Meanwhile, Victoria turned toward the kitchen sink, turned on the water full blast and banged some pots and pans around until we all drifted out of the kitchen.

Lunch was tense, to say the least.

"These sandwiches are great, Mom," I said, trying to break the silence.

She dabbed a napkin at the corners of her mouth. "Thank you," she said, quietly. She wouldn't look at me though, and she went right on eating, taking small bites and chewing thoroughly, the way she always did.

"Kymer, how is your biology class?" Dad asked. He munched a celery stick.

"Um... it's good," I said. "It's a lot of work, but it's worth it."

"You like the professor?"

"Yeah, I do. She's tough, but she's good."

"Is it a small class or is it one of those big lecture classes?" he asked, chewing a bite of sandwich.

"It's a big lecture class."

"If you transferred to one of our smaller colleges here, you could have smaller classes," Victoria commented, still refusing to look in my direction.

I took a big gulp of ice water. "I'm good. It was a little intimidating at first, but I don't mind the larger classes. In fact, they're kind of a nice change of pace from the smaller ones." I kept my temper, even though it was clear what Victoria was doing, making her subtle dig at my choice of school.

"Yeah, sometimes it's nice to be kind of anonymous in those big classes. When I went there, they used to have classes with twenty-five hundred kids at a time in Budig Hall... what they call Hoch Auditorium now, before it caught fire in the early Nineties. You have any classes there?"

"No," I said, taking a bite of sandwich. "Not yet, anyway."

"The next time we visit you, I'd like to wander in there and see what it's like now," he said.

"Sure," I said, shrugging. "We can definitely do that." Dad smiled at me.

"You're a dumbass," Cade piped up. "I don't know why anyone would want to go to school in Kansas."

"I agree," Victoria said. She didn't even bother to get on Cade for calling me a dumbass.

"Oh yeah? Where do you want to go to school?" I asked Cade, nudging him with my foot under the table, like we did when we were younger.

"University of Maryland, baby," he said. He ignored the nudge and took a big bite of his sandwich.

"And what are you gonna study?" I asked, scooping up some hummus with a cucumber slice.

"Sports medicine," he said, his mouth full of sandwich. "Obviously."

"The University of Maryland is a fine school to get a sports medicine degree," Dad said.

"You'll be a dork-ass turtle," I pointed out.

"Better than that red-white-and-blue chicken," Cade said.

"The Jayhawk is crimson and blue," I said. "It's the most badass mascot in the country."

"Psh. Whatever, dude. Looks like a crazy chicken to me." I didn't take it personally, though. Cade and I liked to pick on each other.

"What is with this 'dude' business?" Victoria asked. "Your sister is not a dude."

"Sorry, dude," Cade said to her, and I had to giggle. Victoria was not amused, and she frowned at him.

She stood up, picking up her plate. "Please put your dishes in the dishwasher," she said tersely. She disappeared into the kitchen. We heard the kitchen sink water turn on and then some general banging-around-in-the-kitchen noises.

Dad sighed. "And with that, I'd better help your mother with clean-up." He picked up the rest of the dishes and headed into the kitchen.

"See you haters later," Cade said, getting up.

"Where are you going?" I asked.

"Basketball."

I managed to avoid Victoria by reading in my bedroom that was no longer my bedroom until suppertime, which was thankfully uneventful. We kept the conversation light, talking about the one thing we all seemed to like: movies. Surprisingly, Victoria wasn't as uptight about movies as one might assume. She liked decent sci-fi movies like *2001: A Space Odyssey and Contact*. *Aliens* was a bit much for her, though. We made it through dinner that way, and later, we all settled in to watch one of the *Star Trek* films.

Much later that night, the most horrifying thing that ever happened in my life so far, happened. It was about midnight, and I was in bed, in my jammies, reading *Interview With a Vampire* per Mattie and Siren's recommendation, when I realized I was hungry. Victoria had made this amazing Thai noodle dish for dinner, and it was tasty. She was a good cook, which always made her digs at my weight sting a little extra. It seemed like a deliberately cruel trap she'd set up for me: Cook delicious food I couldn't resist, then nag me about my weight. Ugh. My stomach moaned *feeeeeed me*. Victoria would notice the missing leftovers in the morning, of course, then ridicule me for not being able to control myself, but it was so damn good it was worth enduring Victoria's saltiness.

I put on my slippers and crept out the bedroom door, shutting it softly behind me. I walked lightly down the hallway, and as I passed by my parents' door I heard it: "Mmmm spank me again, Daddy."

Oh my fucking God. My parents were having make-up sex after their argument. The argument that had been my fault. I held my breath and scurried, and I do mean scurried, as quickly as I could without making any noise through the hall and down the back stairs to the kitchen. I briefly considered pouring boiling water in my ears. Now that I'd heard what I'd heard, I knew I'd never forget it. Not ever. It would be seared into my brain for the rest of my life. Mmmm spank me again, Daddy.

Agh!

I made myself an extra-large bowl of noodles and warmed it up in the microwave. I had intended to take the food back to my room, but I wasn't going back down that hallway for anything. At least not right away. I sat down at the kitchen island and shoveled the noodles into my face. I couldn't help it. Stress always made me eat.

I sat there, staring at the empty bowl, wishing I'd brought my phone or my book down to the kitchen so I could entertain myself. Instead, I picked up and inspected the boxes of herbal teas Victoria kept on the kitchen island. She was convinced there was an herbal tea for every mood and ailment: weight-loss teas, calming teas, teas for a gassy stomach or menstrual cramps or a cold. Between the noodles and the tea-box reading, forty-five minutes had passed. Eventually I was going to have to go back up those stairs and down that hallway, past my parents' closed door. I shuddered.

I rinsed the bowl and placed it in the dishwasher, closing it with a click. Then I made my way up the stairs like a cat. My heart pounded. The worst, the worst would be if a floorboard were to creak outside their door. But as I passed, my feet padded noiselessly on the thick carpet. Victoria had insisted it be "lush."

Once I was back in my bedroom, I closed the door soundlessly behind me and breathed. *Made it.*

The next morning, all through a delicious breakfast of artisanal whole-grain French toast topped with orange marmalade and whipped cream, I waited for Victoria to mention the missing Thai noodles. I knew she knew. The container was right there, staring you in the face at eye level when you opened the fridge.

But she said nothing. In fact, she was in a good mood, chatty about some dumb garden tour she wanted our house to be part of.

"That's why I need you to dig up those ratty old evergreen bushes on the south side of the house, Mark, so I can put in some japonica bushes as soon as spring comes. We missed being part of the Blossoms and Butterflies tour last year, and I don't want to miss out this year." That's when I flashed back to the night before—*Mmmm spank me again, Daddy*—and I realized that the reason she was in a good mood was because she'd gotten laid, and I wanted to barf up my fancy orange French toast all over the kitchen island.

"Yes, Vicky. As soon as it is humanly possible, I promise to remove those bushes. I'll put a reminder in my phone for March." And sure enough, he pulled out his phone and entered the reminder. Instead of picking at him some more, this seemed to placate her, which was bizarre. She kind of smiled again while she pushed her French toast bites around on her plate with her fork. My mother did a lot of food pushing and not so much food eating.

"I know you will," she said, and the Ice Queen patted him on the arm. Shudder. Gag.

After breakfast, I bummed around the house, bored. I didn't want to read. All I could think about was Zach. Zach and Chloe. It had been a whole day, and I hadn't heard from either of them. Beyond the breakup, they were both my friends, and I couldn't stand the thought of everything being so tortured and awkward between all of us. I turned on a science-y channel on the television in the den and got comfy on the couch among the designer throw pillows, hoping to stop thinking about the two of them by watching a documentary about sea life in a coral reef, which I'd normally love. The colors were pretty, but after about twenty minutes I realized I had no idea what was going on in the documentary, so I picked up my phone and texted Zach.

Hey. I hate how we left things. Do you want to talk?

We agreed to meet at the Saphire Café that evening, a kind of dive-sports-bar Zach liked because you could play retro Nintendo games in your booth. Actually, our whole friend group liked the Saphire because of its chill vibe and the quirky little bands that often played there. I was surprised, though, when he didn't offer to pick me up, so I borrowed Dad's Subaru Outback and drove myself there. Ironically, I was a few minutes late—I'd spent the whole afternoon fretting about our meeting and then somehow didn't get out the front door on time. I'd been obsessed with getting my makeup perfect and finding the exact right outfit that somehow conveyed I was confident and not really all that upset about us breaking up, but still upbeat and totally willing to stay friends.

When I got there, I was surprised to see Chloe in the booth next to Zach. I hesitated, staring at them. They hadn't seen me yet, and for a split second, I thought about just leaving and blocking both their numbers on my phone. Then I took a breath. *No.* I wasn't going to freak out and run away. I was going to face them like a big girl.

A bluegrassy sounding band made up of hip youngish people with lots of piercings and tatoos wearing oversized Big Mac overalls was playing in the next room. They even had a standup bass and a banjo. As I approached Zach and Chloe's booth, I could see they were playing Super Mario Bros. Together. Usually I just watched Zach play, because I sucked at video games. But Chloe was good. In fact, she had a higher score than Zach.

"Hey," I said brightly, as though nothing at all was amiss. "Sorry I'm a little late."

"That's okay," Zach said, but he didn't look at me. Neither did Chloe. They both just stared at the screen.

"Agh!" Chloe exclaimed, just barely saving Luigi from walking off a scaffold and plunging to his death. Then she got a power up.

"Nice one!" Zach said.

"Thanks, babe," she replied, as if she'd been calling him "babe" forever. It was odd watching them play together, as if they'd spent many hours doing so, and I could feel a lump welling up in my throat, tears on the verge of ruining my perfect makeup. Thankfully, that's when our server walked up. She was maybe a little older than us, wearing shimmery purple eyeshadow, big hoop earrings and the most amazing afro pulled up into a topknot, held with a brightly colored scarf. She smiled at me. "Hey there! How are we doing tonight? Can I get you something to drink?"

"Could I get a diet cola, please?" Somehow I managed to get the words out. My voice caught a little, and I cleared my throat, but I didn't cry. What was wrong with me? Chloe and Zach getting together solved everything for me. It just hurt so much. I had been starving and looking forward to a juicy burger and fries. Now I was sick to my stomach. I sat and waited for them to finish the game, but they didn't. They just kept playing. The server brought my drink and sat it down. "I'll give you all a few more minutes to look over the menu, okay?"

"Thank you," I said. Zach and Chloe said nothing. I took a couple of sips of my drink, waiting for something to happen. After a few minutes of watching them play and being ignored I said, "Hey..." but Zach interruped me.

"Just one sec," he said, still focused on the screen. "I think we're just about to die."

Chloe gave a fake scream and the game played the little song that signaled Mario and Luigi had no more lives left. "Ha!" she said, "I beat you!"

"Yes you did," he replied.

"I still love you though," she said. She leaned over and pecked him on the lips, and the shock of seeing her do that with my boyfriend, right in front of me, like I wasn't even there, was a knife to the heart. *I can't cry. I can't cry. I can't cry.*

I swallowed the lump in my throat. "Look, I know this is awkward, but I just wanted to let you guys know that you're my friends, and even though this is kind of hard, I really am happy for you two if you're happy."

"Thanks," Zach mumbled. His eyes flicked up to catch my gaze for just a second. He took a drink of his iced tea, which I knew would be unsweetened, because the thought sweet tea was gross.

Chole looked defiant. "I'm not so sure you should really talk to Zachary anymore," she said. "Which should be easy, since you've basically ignored him since you moved away." She was looking at me as if she were a preschool teacher, and I was a toddler who had spilled my juice. I wanted to smack her.

"Zachary?" I said. "Seriously?" He hated his full name. Only his dad could get away with calling him Zachary. I had raised my voice so loud I could feel people looking at me. "I'm pretty sure Zach gets to make his own decisions about who he does and doesn't talk to, Chloe."

"Well, he should be able to make his own decisions, yes."

"What's that supposed to mean?" I asked, baffled.

"As if you don't know. As if you don't enjoy leading Zachary around on a leash."

"Chloe what are you talking about?" I leaned forward in the booth. Now I was not only sick to my stomach, but I could feel my face starting to get hot with anger.

"Just stop playing dumb, Kymer," she held up a hand. "Some of us are tired of your shit."

The juxtaposition of her rant against the happy bluegrass in the other room was kind of bananas, and I let out an angry laugh. I thought I was going to have a quiet, if awkward, meal and conversation with my ex-boyfriend. Now I felt as though I'd been thrust onto the stage of a bad talk show. "What shit, Chloe? What are you even talking about? Why are you being like this? We've been friends forever. Why can't we just calm down and work this out, and the three of us can go on being friends?"

She leaned forward, her voice hostile. "Because I know the sort of hold you have over Zachary, and I just don't think it's good for him. I think he needs a fresh start. You coming home for the holidays has been super stressful for everyone." I couldn't help but notice Zach wasn't saying a word. It was like he didn't know which one of us to defend, so he just opted to stay quiet.

"Oh, well, excuse me for coming home," I said. "Maybe things would have been less stressful for everyone if someone had bothered to tell me what was going on with you two."

She flipped her hair. "Well, that's the problem. That's exactly what I'm talking about. I couldn't get him to just tell you the truth. It was like he was afraid of you or something. But it's always been that way with you two. It's sick the way you're always controlling him." She sat back in her seat, folded her arms and glared at me. Zach was looking at his hands, silent.

I was stunned at her anger. I mean, I'd always known she liked Zach. I just never realized how much she disliked me. As far as her "controlling" accusation, I didn't even know what to do with that, because it was just ridiculous. I had never demanded Zach's loyalty; he was just like that. I almost said something snarky about how Zach couldn't wait to fuck me the second I got home, but decided it wasn't worth the additional drama it would cause. Just then, our server was at the table again. "What are we hungry for tonight?" she asked brightly.

I grabbed my purse. "I'm not eating," I said, my voice breaking. I scooted out of the booth. "I have to go."

I turned and rushed out of the Saphire, without looking back. I managed to drive a few blocks away from the Saphire when I had to pull off on a side street because I was sobbing so hard I couldn't see. I sat and cried in the Subaru for a good twenty minutes, glad it was dark, and no one passing by could see me. Eventually, I realized I was starving, so I called one of my favorite burger place and ordered a bacon cheeseburger with fries and a double chocolate shake. I checked my reflection in the rearview mirror. My makeup was totally annihilated. It almost looked as though I hadn't put any on, except for the remnants of my eyeliner, which had collected in dark circles under my puffy, bloodshot eyes, but at that point, I didn't care.

I had no choice but to go inside the burger place to pay for and pick up my order. I could tell the guy behind the counter wanted to ask me what was wrong and was glad when he didn't. "Thanks," I mumbled, when he handed me the greasy sack of food. Then I drove to a nearby park and ate alone in the car with the doors locked until I couldn't eat any more. I made sure to throw away all the evidence before I got home.

13

Queen Victoria

It was a loooong, slow winter break. Christmas Day was kinda fun. We ended up going to my Aunt Judy's house, Victoria's sister. Somehow Aunt Judy had escaped being born with a stick up her butt. I loved my aunt Judy. She was wacky. Judy and Uncle Jack lived in the historic part of town, and it always irritated Victoria that Judy's house was bigger and way more expensive than ours. Their house was so big, and so Victorian, and so romantic, it had even been in a couple of movies. Victoria was insanely jealous of the attention Judy's house got. But here's the weird thing: Victoria hated old houses, so it wasn't like she'd ever want that house, anyway.

Uncle Jack and Aunt Judy were both art and antiquities dealers and collectors. Their house was full of the craziest stuff. They even had an honest-to-God collection of shrunken heads. Three of them. Supposedly the largest collection in the country outside a museum. I always made a point of looking at the heads when we visited. Aunt Judy called them Tom, Dick and Harry. Judy and Jack were also friends with lots of what Victoria called the old money in town, which also made her crazy with jealousy.

My cousins were tolerable. They were a little older than me, in their early twenties, and had attended exclusive private schools. They were weirdly more like Victoria than their own parents. "Todd and Sandy are such good kids," my mother said, often. Todd was some sort of junior executive for a tech company, and Sandy sold luxury cars. I always had trouble talking to both of them. Cade did better. At least they could talk sports.

As we did every year, Cade and I got new pajamas for Christmas. I also got lots of cash, which was sweet, because I wanted to start getting together enough money to be able to pay the first month's rent and deposit for an apartment in Lawrence.

Victoria wasn't really working, since the real estate market had almost stopped for the winter. She had a few appointments showing houses, and her usual club meetings and whatever other social nonsense she participated in, but mostly, she was home, cooking and cleaning and flipping through her issues of Vogue and trying to get me to go to her Funky-cise! classes with her. Dad had taken the week off around Christmas, but he'd gone back to work, so I only got to see him in the evenings and on weekends.

I hadn't talked to any of my other friends since the shitshow at the Saphire with Chloe and Zach. Since I was the one moving to Kansas, I figured I should let Zach have custody of our Maryland friends. I didn't feel like making anyone choose between the two—I guess the three—of us, and I didn't want to find out how much everyone in our friend group had known about Chloe and Zach before I did. Occasionally I wondered how many times Zach and Chole had hooked up. It seemed like they had been seeing each other for a while. Had she waited until the second I'd left town to throw herself at him? Maybe she'd made her move one of those rare nights when Zach would allow himself to drink—usually when we were hanging in Erin's basement, because her house was just half a block from Zach's and he could walk home. That was probably what had happened. They'd been hanging out, both drunk, she started in flirting with him like she always did when she drank and maybe he was just buzzed enough that they leaned in and kissed... ugh. I couldn't think about it.

One day, finally, I did text Erin, when it became apparent none of my other friends were going to text me. I got right to the point: *Why didn't you tell me?* Thirty minutes passed before she answered.

I don't kno... I didn't kno what 2 say...didn't kno what u knew & also din't know if you'd care anyways...seemed like U were hooking up with some 1 in Kansas

I told you I wasn't

The last time we txtd was weeks ago...last time we txtd it sounded like U were done with Zach anyways...and even last nite it seemed like U were done!

I didn't respond. I didn't respond because she was right, and it made me mad. Erin was like that. Brutal with the truth. I loved and hated her for it. After a few minutes, my phone buzzed.

Look I'm sorry...I would have told U if I'd known you'd be upset...it's just awkward...I don't want 2 hv 2 pick sides...ur all 3 my friends & I just don't want 2 pick sides...it seems 2 me everyone is at fault in this situation...

You're right I texted back.

I mean no offense lol

But I took a little offense, and I sure didn't see anything to "lol" about. Still, she was probably right. Every single one of us had been too chicken to say what we really wanted. *Hey Kymer*, she continued, *U wanna meet up at sweetbean?* Sweet Bean was a coffee and pastry shop we all loved to hang out in.

Sure. When? I typed.

Now?

Erin picked me up and drove us to Sweet Bean in her boxy, silver Kia Soul she referred to as "the toaster," which she'd received as a Sweet Sixteen gift from her parents—just like my parents had given me a newish Toyota Corolla—and it made me think about Siren's beat-up old Nissan Sentra, with its sun-faded paint and tattered upholstery, that she probably had to buy herself.

Sweet Bean was kind of a dive that made great coffee and pastries, where people my mother didn't like hung out: poets, artists, musicians, activists... "hoodlums," Victoria called them. Sweet Bean was below street level, under the shops above, with just a little sunlight peeking through the narrow windows that faced the street. Inside, the shop was painted completely black: concrete floors, walls, ceiling tiles and all, and dimly lit with a crazy collection of vintage glass hanging lamps scattered here and there. The room where you ordered was small, but there were two other rooms off that one, with various booths and mismatched chairs and tables for seating. The bell on the door tinkled just like I remembered, and I breathed in the familiar Sweet Bean smell of coffee and freshly baked scones, muffins and sweet rolls. Punk music from the 1980s was playing—the Dead Kennedys, I thought, though I wasn't positive.

"Hey there," the barista called out. She was short and curvy with a nose ring, jet black hair and an oversized pink sweater. "What can I get started for you?"

Erin ordered a cappuccino with two shots of espresso and a butterscotch scone. I ordered a latte and chocolate croissant. The shop was mostly empty. A feminine-looking person with shock-pink spiky hair was typing away on a laptop, making faces at the screen. We collected our order and went straight to our usual booth in the back of the room farthest away from the front counter. On the way, we saw a big guy with a big, bushy beard and his tongue sticking out, working on a drawing of a poster-sized dragon. He ignored us.

"Thanks for asking me to coffee," I said, sliding in to the booth. "I'm going a little stir-crazy at home with Victoria."

Erin laughed. "What's Victoria up to these days?"

I took a sip of my latte. "Oh, you know. The usual. Selling houses and bossing Dad around. I think with me not there, she's got more time on her hands. She's taking more classes and getting more involved in community events."

"Your mom's always been a mover and a shaker," she took a bite of scone and chewed. "You watch. When your little brother graduates, I bet she runs for City Commission or something," her eyes narrowed, "and then, mayor."

I almost spit my coffee in Erin's face. "Ugh! I've never thought about it, but I bet you're right!"

Erin nodded. "Oh, heck yeah. It's in the eyes. She's a killer. Victoria wants to rule Bethesda."

"Oh God," I said. "She could have signs and postcards printed up— she loves that kind of shit—I bet her campaign colors would be royal purple and gold."

Erin knew my mother's proclivity for announcing her Christmas colors and snorted. "Really, Kymer. Purple and gold? How gauche. Now, forest green and silver? All the rage." We laughed about Victoria, but I was burning to know what was going on with Erin's new look. Today she was wearing khakis with a crisp, white button-down shirt and pin-striped suspenders with a pair of platform Oxfords. Her sleeked-down pixie was perfect, with no hair out of place, and the only really "feminine" things about her appearance were the diamond studs in her ears and the bright red lipstick she wore. For the first time ever, I found myself somewhat physically attracted to my friend Erin.

"I love your hair," I said. "I've never seen it that short on you. It looks great!"

She touched her hair and smiled. "Thanks. Brent hates it. He won't say it out loud, but I can tell."

"What is it with guys and long hair?" I asked, taking a sip of my latte.

"They say men like long hair because it makes us easier to catch when we're running away," she said dryly. She picked up a spoon and stirred her cappuccino, wiping out the decorative foam leaf the barista had made.

"Yuck," I said, touching my ponytail.

"Hey," she said, shrugging her shoulders sarcastically. "What else are they supposed to do? Shoot us?"

"So what's going on with you and Brent, anyway?" I'd been dying to ask her since the party.

She sighed and touched her hair again, smoothing it down. "I don't know... I mean, I do know. I just don't feel like the same person since I started going to college, you know?"

"I do know," I said, nodding.

"Right?" She leaned forward. "I just—Brent wants things to stay the same with us, but we're at different schools, and I'm meeting new people and—I don't think I'm that high school girl anymore." She slumped back in her seat. "Sometimes I don't even know if I still like guys."

Boom. Suspicions confirmed. "So... are you seeing somebody else?" I asked, peeling a bit off my croissant.

"No," she said, shaking her head miserably and sighing.

"But you want to?"

She looked up, shame washing across her face. "There is this girl. She's in my industrial design class, and she hangs out with the same design crowd I do, and we've gotten to be pretty good friends... except it feels like more than that, you know? We click and... I don't know how to describe it, but it's in a different way than I click with you or Chloe." She drifted off for a second, staring at the table, then kept going. "Also, I like the design students. I like hanging out with them. I like how they're big on individualism and don't give a shit what anybody thinks. They wear what they want and dress how they want, whether it's wacky or normal and everybody just seems to accept each other. It's not like high school, where I was trying to fit in all the time and have the right shoes and the right clothes and the long hair like all the it girls and the same backpack everybody else had... I'm tired of fitting in, you know? I just want to be... me."

"And you should," I said. "This is the age when we're supposed to reinvent ourselves, right? In college?"

"Yeah..." she said, sounding unsure.

"But it's confusing to Brent," I said, sympathetically.

She looked down. "It is. It's confusing for me, too, though. It's not like I hate him or anything. I just don't feel like I used to. About him or myself. And I'm not saying I've totally stopped liking boys. If James Dean came back from the dead tomorrow I'd be all over that for sure." We laughed. "But I don't know if I want to keep being the girlfriend Brent expects me to be. I'm tired of it. I'm tired of all of it."

"It sounds like maybe you need to be honest with him," I said, taking a sip of coffee. "No offense."

She laughed. "I know. I do." She traced a circle on the table with her fingertip. "But if I do that, it's probably going to be the end of all of us."

"Is there a stray asteroid I don't know about?"

"No, I mean the end of our little gang from high school. Between you and Zach breaking up and you moving to Kansas and Chloe losing her mind, if I break up with Brent that will probably be the nail in the coffin for our group, right?"

"Wow. That makes me feel bad," I said, putting the last bite of my croissant into my face.

"That's not what I meant." She placed her hands on the table. "It's not like things can stay the same forever. We're all moving on with our lives. This isn't high school anymore. Things are going to change, whether we want them to or not." She looked me in the eye, having made a decision. "You know what? I'm going to talk to Brent today. I can't keep stringing him along. It's not fair for either of us. It's stupid."

"Damn," I said, slumping back in the booth. "I feel like I came home and blew everything up."

She leaned forward. "Believe me, this is not on you. Not even. When you left, Chloe decided she couldn't hold in her feelings about Zach anymore and I guess she started being, like, aggressively suggestive with him. You know. Sexually. Zach told Brent he was weirded out by it, and he talked about you a lot. But eventually, I guess she kind of wore him down, especially when you weren't texting him back."

I held up a hand. "I don't want to hear any details about how they got together. I mean, I'm happy for both of them if that's what they want, but I cannot handle hearing any details. Not right now."

"Heard," she said nodding. Then she perked up. "Oh! I've been meaning to tell you. I talked with Austin, and he and Will are officially back together. So that's something good, right?"

"That's great!" I said, sipping my latte. "They're good for each other. Will helps to balance out Austin's..."

"Fabulousness?" Erin offered.

I laughed. "Exactly. So... I have another question for you."

"What's that?" she took a big drink of her now-warm espresso, which was how she always drank it.

"What's her name?" I asked, as she set the cup down.

"Whose name?"

"You know," I said, leaning forward. "The girl."

"Oh," she said, blushing a little. "Her name is LaShae," she paused. "She's from Oakland."

"California?" I asked, chewing a bite of croissant.

"Is there another Oakland?" she asked, raising her eyebrow.

"Just saying. That's a long way to go for school."

"She has a full scholarship," Erin said, smiling coyly and looking down at the table. "She's super smart and crazy-talented. She already sells her work. She has like, fans."

"Damn. That's impressive."

"Right?" She looked up and changed the topic. "Hey, thanks for getting coffee with me. It really helps to talk through this stuff." She threw her hands up. "What the hell am I going to do without you to talk to? You're not coming back to Bethesda, are you? To live, I mean?"

"I don't think so," I admitted. "I'm happy in Kansas. I like my roommate—her name is Siren—and we hang out with this other guy named Mattie a lot, and his parents own a barbeque restaurant, and they feed us all the time. Mattie and Siren are both from Kansas and they're both... really cool."

Erin laughed. "That's why I like you, Kymer. You've always been a little different, and you're not afraid to be yourself. Who the hell loves bugs and runs off to Kansas?" She held up a hand, "No offense about Kansas—but who does that? Only you. Only you would be brave enough to do something so freaking wild."

"Brave? I don't feel brave. If anything, I feel like I'm running away. Running away from Maryland and my mom and Zach."

Erin shrugged. "What's wrong with going for what you want? That's what everybody else is doing, right? Why shouldn't you?"

"And why shouldn't you?" I agreed. "You're braver than I am! Look at you! You're becoming an entirely new person. That's what I love about you, my friend. You always cut through the bullshit."

I spent a lot of time at home, reading, waiting for break to be over. After coffee with Erin, I didn't bother trying to get together with any of my friends because I didn't want to have to navigate the whole Chloe-Zach thing. Erin did text me to tell me how relieved she was to have finally broken up with Brent, even though he apparently took it pretty badly. My first instinct was to call Zach to see what Brent had said to him, and then I remembered we weren't together anymore. I tried talking with Cade, but he seemed to be gone most of the time with his best friend Josh and their other friends, which was kind of a bummer because I kind of missed him. Cade, that is, not Josh. Josh had always had a crush on me, from the first time he ever came over to our house, when he and Cade were second graders. I'd look up sometimes to see him gaping at me, open-mouthed, like a little weirdo, but these days he was apparently all cool and grown, because now I was barely worth a glance and a casual, "Hey, Kymer," in his creepy new man-voice.

I thought a lot about texting Mattie and Siren, but I refrained because I didn't want to disturb their holidays. They were probably having a great time at home, and I was the only loser with no friends. Thankfully, Mattie sent a group text one afternoon, about a week-and-a-half before the end of break: *Ahoy salty bitches! Hows yalls holiday?*

I replied immediately: *OMG I'm so glad to hear from you. I AM LOSING MY MIND.*

I'm sorry luv, Mattie said, then Siren jumped in: *TELL ME ABOUT IT. If I hv 2 put my mother to bed 1 more time I'm getting emancipated lololololol!!!*

Why doesn't her boyfriend put her to bed? I typed.

Bcuz Rick is passed out 2 but no way I'm putting his drunk ass to bed, she replied.

Siren! You are too funny! Mattie said.

I'm not kidding. Siren replied. *Ready 2b back at ku*

Are you having a good time with your family Mattie? I typed.

I mean it's fine it's like normal but I miss seeing Alejandro & you gals & Lawrence is kind of gray & boring & cold

Same in Hutch, Siren said.

Same here, I typed.

Kymer did you finally get your sexytime? Mattie asked, which cracked me up.

I did! I typed. *But then we broke up :(*

I thought that's what you wanted? Mattie said.

It is, I typed, but before I could say more, Siren said, *But U were hoping to keep having sex & brake up at the end of winter break lololololol*

GUILTY, I replied.

Do U miss Drew? Mattie asked Siren.

Naw, when I'm in hutch Hunter keeps me company lolol

SIREN. Mattie said. *WHO IS HUNTER???*

He's a friend of my brother Travis lol if Travis knew he'd kill us both lolololollll

That makes it more fun, I said.

You 2 R 2 wild! Mattie replied.

Before I knew it, a half hour had gone by when Siren texted, *Gotta go! Hunter's here & mom & rick are out lol.*

Me too, Mattie said. *The whole family getting together 4 holiday game night*

The WHOLE family? I asked, feeling jealous.

Haha! Yep! All my aunts & uncles & cousins & rum & eggnog. It will be LOUD

That's so nice! I typed, but really, I was bummed they both had to go.

On the morning I finished *Interview with a Vampire,* I mentioned to Victoria I wouldn't mind visiting a bookstore to pick up a couple more paperbacks.

"Oh, good," she said. "There's a darling little bookstore in that area they've been updating downtown. We can get lunch!"

"You mean that area of downtown they've been gentrifying for the past five years?" I shouldn't have said it, but I did. She gave me a look.

"It's a lovely area now. Real estate prices have tripled."

Well hot damn for real estate prices. I didn't say it out loud, though. The drive over was pleasant enough. It was kind of interesting to see my hometown. Not too much had changed, except that when I looked at it all, even though I'd lived there my whole life, it felt like I'd been gone a long time. I felt weirdly... removed from everything, and I didn't really care.

When we got to the bookstore, Victoria headed straight for the self-help section.

"I'm going to look at the fiction," I said, pointing to the opposite end of the store.

"I'll meet you over there in a few minutes," she said. "I'd like to get something for some light reading as well."

I quickly found the books I was looking for: *The Vampire Lestat* and *Queen of the Damned*. Then I took my time, browsing through the fiction section. There were several books that looked interesting, and I marked them in the book app on my phone. After a while, I noticed Victoria was also in the fiction section, looking at the romance novels. Eventually, she wandered my way. She had three books in her hands: STAMINA! Get it! Have it! Live it!, a bodice-ripper called Stalked at Midnight (ew) and, of course, The Nature of Food: A diet for life.

"Oh," she said, craning to see the books I was holding. "What are those?"

"Nothing," I said dismissively. "You wouldn't like them."

"Why not?"

"I'm pretty sure they're not your thing."

Before I could object, she took one of the books from me and turned it over, reading the back. "Oh. Are these those weirdo pervert vampire books they made movies of several years ago?"

I laughed. "Um, I wasn't aware weirdo pervert vampire was now a genre, but sure. They're my weirdo pervert vampire books, and I don't think you'd enjoy them." I took the books and gestured to the romance novel in her other hand. "You'd better stick with your regular perversions."

"Very funny," she hissed. "Not so loud." She glanced around, horrified that someone might be listening to us.

"Oh, for Christ's sake," I said, and I rolled my eyes. I took the books from her and headed toward the cashier. I knew I was pushing it, but the whole thing galled me. She was so concerned about what other people thought of her and we—Cade and Dad and I—were never supposed to "embarrass" her. Ever. Even though what she thought of as "embarrassing" I thought was stupid.

She came up behind me and grabbed my books. "I can buy them for you. Your father and I have always bought books for you kids. No matter how... out there they were."

I decided to let it go, since she was willing to pay for my books. "Okay. Thank you. I appreciate it."

"You're welcome," she said, tersely.

We checked out of the bookstore okay, and the ride home started alright... and then everything went to hell.

"I know you think I'm a prude," Victoria said, "but I really don't appreciate the way you had to try to embarrass me over my books. I don't have that many guilty pleasures, and romance novels happen to be one of them."

"Well, I suppose they are calorie free," I said, and that's when she lost her shit. For real.

"I will never understand your contempt for me and everything I do," she screeched.

"Oh my God. What?"

"Don't 'Oh my God' me. You have been rude to me since the moment you got home, and I have had it. I work hard to make a nice home for all of us. I work hard at my job, I work hard at home, I work hard to stay trim and maintain a certain look, and if you don't approve of how I do things, well you can keep it to yourself because I don't need any more of your criticism!"

"Wait, what?" I said, unable to contain a smirk. "You work hard to maintain a certain look? What does that mean?"

"You know, I... I like to maintain my weight and wear professional clothes because I am going for a certain... polished look." She sat up straighter in her seat.

"So what does that make me? Unpolished?"

"I never said that!"

"You don't have to. You let me know every day I'm a disappointment."

"I have never been disappointed in you."

"Okay, fine, maybe not disappointed, but definitely not proud."

"That's ridiculous. I've always been proud of you. I've always been proud of both of you."

"Oh really? You weren't disappointed when you found out I wasn't a virgin?"

"Well, you certainly didn't try very hard to keep it to yourself."

One of the few times my friend Alex and I had skipped school and had sex at my house when no one was home, we'd accidentally left a condom wrapper on my nightstand. (I was super paranoid about getting pregnant in my early days of having sex, so Alex and I always used condoms.) Instead of ignoring it, like a normal person, Victoria shoved it in my face that night, demanding an explanation. I wanted to know why she'd been snooping around in my room, but that was an argument I always lost.

"It may be your room, but it's my house," she said, like she always did.

By now we were home. She pulled into the garage, and we slammed our car doors, arguing as we walked into the kitchen. "Kylie, just because I didn't approve of the fact that you became sexually active so young doesn't mean I don't care about you. It certainly doesn't mean that I'm not proud of you, either. I do wish that you would have waited until you were twenty..."

"Twenty?" I said. That was like an old maid.

"Or at least nineteen, but I still love you, and I want you to be safe. There are STDs out there..." she whispered STDs as though it were a dirty word, and I wanted to scream.

"STIs," I said.

"What?"

"STIs. That's the new abbreviation. It stands for Sexually Transmitted Infections. It's a more precise term than disease."

"Well, thank you so much for the biology lesson, young lady. You knew darn good and well what I meant. We are talking not only about your reputation, but your health here."

"And why are we talking about my reputation at all? What does that even mean anymore? Is this 1955? Did we hop in the DeLorean and drive eighty-eight miles per hour?"

"What on earth are you talking about, Kylie? I have no idea what you're saying." She was waving her arms, her face pinched with angry confusion.

"I am saying that my reputation is none of your business! I am saying that my body is mine, and I don't care what you, or anyone else, thinks about what I do with it. I am saying there is no such thing as a reputation anymore."

"Oh, believe me, young lady, there most certainly is! Things like that can affect who you marry and follow you into the professional world and ruin your career."

And there it was. The reason I couldn't stand my mother. Because she couldn't stand me. I was fundamentally offensive to her. Damaged goods.

"Only if you buy into that whole uptight, privileged culture, Victoria," I yelled. "Stop perpetuating this insanely damaging myth that women who like sex are dirty! It's people like you who make being a woman so difficult. Let it go, already!"

"People like me?"

"Yes," I said. "People like you."

"You mean women like me, of course. Women who enjoy designer clothes and the golf course and Rotary Club and serving on the school board and not walking around looking as though I wandered out of a trailer park?"

"Oh my GOD."

"You know, it hurt my feelings when you first decided to go by Kymer," her arms were folded in that way that drove me crazy, her lips pressed together. "But I guess I understand it." My mother always wanted me to go by the name Kylie. I detested the formality of it. "You think I'm uptight? Do you have any idea what it was like growing up with my mother? She practically measured the hems of our skirts with a ruler before we were allowed to leave the house. That's why I chose the name Kylie for you. I thought it sounded... light... and cheery." She started to choke up, tears in the corners of her eyes, and I didn't know what to do. "I know you've always thought that your name is frivolous—and it is, I suppose—but do you know it has a meaning?"

I could hardly keep from rolling my eyes. I was sure she'd tell me that according to some baby book she'd bought in 1985, Kylie meant "peace" or "angel" or some other inane nonsense, and she'd held on to that name her whole pitiful life waiting until she could bestow it on a girl child.

"Kylie is 'boomerang' in Aboriginal Australian," she said. "I liked it, because I thought of it as meaning you'd always come home to us, no matter what." Her face softened, and all of a sudden, instead of looking like a giant bitch, she looked kind of sad.

My mind was totally blown. I had no idea my mother even knew Aborigines existed. Suddenly, I was the biggest asshole on the planet.

"That's... really... cool. It never occurred to me that my name meant something. I always thought it was just... noise. Kylie and Cade. I never even bothered to look it up."

She looked surprised—and a little pleased— that I'd said she'd done something "cool."

"Well, it's true," she said, wiping the corners of her eyes. "You can look it up yourself. I guess I should've told you a long time ago. Seeing as how words and definitions and facts impress you so much. It never occurred to me that it might make you happy to know." She threw up her hands as if to say, "Who would ever have guessed?"

I threw my head back and laughed, and her face fell again. "No, Mom, I'm not laughing at you," I said, and grabbed her in a hug. She put her arms around me and squeezed back. "I can't believe we misunderstand each other so much. It's so fucking dumb!"

"Yes," she said, laughing as her voice broke. "It is effing dumb."

And I laughed again, because she couldn't bring herself to say "fucking."

The next day, it felt like something had actually shifted with my mother. Instead of feeling defensive around her all the time, I relaxed. So did she. She let me get away with saying "shit" when I dropped a can of Diet Coke on my foot, and somehow, I kept myself from saying "fuck" for the rest of the day. I mean, I said it when I was alone, but I didn't say it around her.

The afternoon before I was supposed to go back to school, I was so ready to get on the plane. I had everything packed up by 10 a.m. I wandered the house, bored and aimless, each minute ticking by painfully slowly. It was times like those—and there were a lot—that I thought most about texting Zach. But I didn't do it. If he'd wanted to see me again before I left, I figured he would've texted me. I was staring at my phone, weighing the pros and cons of texting my ex-boyfriend when Cade came downstairs with a basketball in his hands, headed toward the front door.

"Where are you going?" Victoria said.

"I'm playing ball with my boys," he said. He and Josh and some of their other friends often shot hoops in the neighborhood park.

"Don't you want to stay home and see your sister? She leaves tomorrow."

"Aw, man," he said, bouncing the ball on the tile.

"You know better than to bounce that in here."

"It's okay, Mom," I said. "I get it. He doesn't have to hang out here. It's nice out today. Have fun, dude. Say "hey" to Josh for me."

"No way. I'll tell him you said "hi" after the game is over. If I tell him before, it might throw him off his game," and it made me feel kinda good to know that Josh was still crushing on me.

"Make sure you're home by six tonight," Victoria said as he left. "I'm cooking."

"Okay, Mom," he said, and he was gone.

"Speaking of which... I guess I'd probably better get to the store to pick up the ingredients I need," Victoria said, heading to the coat closet. "Do you want to go with me?"

"If it's okay, I think I'd like to stay here. I was thinking of finding Dad and having a chat with him."

"About what?" she asked, buttoning her coat.

"Nothing specific," I lied. "I just haven't gotten to talk to Dad much since I've been home, and I want to visit with him a little bit before I leave."

"I think that sounds like a lovely idea. I won't be long," she said, putting her purse over her shoulder.

"Where is Dad, anyway?"

"I think he's out in his shed."

Dad's shed was definitely his place to escape. He'd had it built when we'd moved into the house, and over the years, he'd added to it and improved it. He'd installed solar panels and a couple of small windmills on the roof to power the lights and outlets. One half of the shed was where all the lawn care and gardening equipment was stored, along with the riding lawnmower, but the other end was his "work room." His tools lined the walls, and there was a work table in the center of the room. That was where he tinkered with old video game systems and computer equipment. I had noticed when I was pretty young that whenever Victoria was getting on his nerves, he'd disappear to his shed.

I wandered out to the back yard, and I could see him through the window at his work table. When I entered, he had his glasses pushed up on top of his head, squinting intently at an old typewriter. Fluorescent lights buzzed loudly above his head. He seemed not to notice.

"What's that?" I asked.

He looked up, startled. When he saw it was me, he smiled. "This is a genuine 1917 Smith Corona folding typewriter with case. (He pronounced it gen-you-wine.)

"That's cool!" I said, peering at the funny round keys.

"Yes, I think so. I'm hoping if I clean it up enough, your mother will let me put it on display in the den," he picked up a rag and wiped some dust off it.

"You need her permission?"

He glanced up from the typewriter. "No, I don't need her permission. But certain things are... upsetting to your mother, and there's no reason to press those buttons if I don't have to."

As soon as he said it, my plan to subtlety get to the subject I wanted to ask him about went totally out the window. I blurted out: "What did you two ever see in each other? How did you even meet? What was that like?"

He looked super uncomfortable, and I wished I hadn't been so direct. He sat up, shifted around on his stool and put his glasses back on. "Your mother and I met not long after I moved to Maryland for my first job. On a blind date."

"You're kidding."

"I'm not. I was a young programmer for a big tech company, and your mother worked in the HR department there. We worked on different floors, but someone who knew us both—I don't remember who, anymore, but I'm sure your mother knows—anyway someone set us up."

"So, what was your first date like? Where did you go?"

"Let's see. We ate these fantastic crab cakes at this little joint in the Chesapeake Bay, and then we took a boat tour of the area."

"Mom got on a boat?" (I knew better than to call her "Victoria" in front of my dad.)

He chuckled. "She sure did. She managed to make it through the whole boat ride, too, without vomiting." We laughed. Victoria was known for her seasickness.

"Why didn't she just tell you it would make her sick?"

"You know your mother. I'm sure she didn't want to be rude or make a scene, since it was our first date."

"So, did you have a good time?"

"We did. Once the boat ride was over, I could tell something was wrong, and she finally admitted she was barely holding down her crab cakes."

"What did you do then?"

"We walked along the beach, talking. The sea air seemed to help her feel better."

"What did you talk about?"

"It's funny you should ask that, because I can tell you exactly what we talked about, even though that date was twenty-five years ago. We talked about *Terminator 2* and *Jurassic Park*... she even liked *Pulp Fiction* to an extent, though she'd never watch it again." He chuckled. "That one is a little much for her."

"I can imagine."

"And then... I seem to remember we talked about how beautiful the Chesapeake Bay is." He paused. "We haven't been back there in years. Thanks for reminding me. I should make reservations for us to stay there for our anniversary."

"So, that's what makes for a successful marriage? Having movies and the Chesapeake Bay in common?"

"It's a hard thing to explain. It's not something that makes sense.... It just kind of is. Something about her... about the two of us... clicked. I know she can be a little high-strung, but..." he looked me in the eye "... it's important to know that the person you want to spend your life with is on your side. That's the only way a marriage can really last." He kind of laughed. "It's the only way you can really stay sane for all those years with the same partner. There has to be a very basic level of trust. If you don't have that... then you don't have anything."

When he said that... it made me want to cry. It was so... sweet. I had always kind of assumed my dad just put up with my mom.

Turned out he liked being with her.

"By the way, you can be just as high-strung as your mother. That's why you butt heads." And my mouth fell open. He laughed. "Think about it, Kymer. You know it's true."

"So, what are you doing to this old typewriter, then?" I said. I decided to change the subject, because what Dad said was too real for me to deal with at the moment.

He brightened. "Oh, mostly general cleaning and ungumming the works. I've had to unbend some of these type bars," he said, referring to the spidery little arms that came up to bang a letter onto the page, and he grabbed one between his thumb and forefinger. "But this one I may have to replace. I know a guy who can get me parts."

"That's awesome, Dad," I said, and I hugged him.

14

Lewis Lindsay Dyche

It was so nice to get back to my dorm room after winter break. Siren was glad to be back, too.

"I love my mother," she said, dropping her bags, "but that woman wears me out. I spent the entire first day home cleaning the kitchen." And from that moment, things went right back to the way they were before winter break, and we settled back into the first few weeks of the new semester.

A few days later the university posted our grades from the previous semester.

"Yesss!" Siren said, throwing her fists in the air when she saw she'd received a D in math. "At least I didn't waste all that money. I didn't think I was going to pass. And thank God I only have to take one more semester of math to get my degree." She got an A in her theater class and Bs and Cs in the rest of her classes.

It was the first time in my life there was only one A on my report card, and it was in English, of all things. My stomach dropped when I saw the C for Cellular Biology, and dropped again when I saw another C for Western Civ. I'd studied so hard for that final. (Well, sort of. There was that afternoon the kids on the sixth floor of the dorm had made an impromptu slip-n-slide in their tiled hallway by pouring soapy water on the floor, and I took a break from studying to repeatedly launch myself head-first down their hall, jamming my finger when I smashed into a door jamb.) I decided I wouldn't mention my grades to my parents, and hope they didn't ask. Victoria still wasn't happy about me going to school in Kansas, and I didn't want to give her any more ammunition to use against me than she already had. Somehow, I needed to get more serious about studying, and quick.

Now we had new classes to adjust to, and it looked as though winter was finally coming to an end. The woolly bear caterpillar was still on the ledge outside our window, still buried under leaf litter, but I checked on her at least once a day. One particularly warm and sunny afternoon, there she was. She had come out of quiescence (insect hibernation), and was crawling around on top of the leaf litter. I went outside and found several different samples of spring leaves. I wanted her to start eating so she could get to work on her cocoon because she'd need the energy… the end result would hopefully be a tiger moth.

I was sitting at my desk, trying to study for my first Organismal Biology exam (no, not orgasmal), when Siren came up behind me and began massaging my scalp and running her fingers through my hair. She gathered it up into various pony tails and buns, which she did on occasion. Sometimes I liked it; sometimes it was annoying. She was always trying to get me to let her make me over and dress me up. A couple of times I let her do my makeup and hair, but generally, I declined.

"Whatcha doin'?" she asked, after a couple minutes of playing with my hair.

"What I'm usually doing if I'm not at work. Studying," I said, a little irritated. I knew I needed to take school more seriously, but somehow, I kept getting distracted.

"C'mon, Kymer. It's Friday afternoon. No one is studying. Let's go have some fun." I glanced sideways at the mirror across from us. Her nails were perfect; squared off and painted a bright shiny pink as she ran them through my brown hair.

She was right. Our dorm room door was slightly ajar and you could hear competing music coming from rooms up and down the hall. The snotty girls from Phoenix preferred pop. Lila and Staycee liked hip-hop. Emily and Kayla were fond of country and classical, respectively. Siren and I had our usual Eighties-Nineties mix going.

"I can't," I said, still not looking up from my homework. "I have to work all weekend because we're short-staffed at the museum, I need to write my stupid speech for stupid Speech class, and this Biology quiz is on Tuesday."

"So you have Monday to study!" She was still playing with my hair.

"Monday I'll need to practice my stupid speech, if I can ever get it written."

She pulled my hair up into a genie-style pony tail on top of my head, considered it for a few seconds, then let it go. "You'll get it written. Why are you getting so worked up over it?"

"I'm not 'worked up,' I'm freaked out. I hate speaking in front of groups of people." At this point, I wasn't really getting any studying done, but I wasn't going to give Siren the satisfaction of looking up at her. I just wanted her to leave me alone.

"Look, I'll help you out with it this weekend. I can give you a few breathing and speaking pointers."

"I'm working this weekend," I reminded her.

"You're not working the whole weekend. There'll be plenty of time to go over your speech. We can do it Sunday."

"I haven't written it yet," I reminded her.

"How long is it supposed to be?"

"Three minutes," I said, knowing what she'd say next.

"That's easy," Siren said, rolling her eyes. "That's nothing. You can get that written in an hour."

I sighed. I wasn't concentrating very well. And it was Friday afternoon. "Okay," I said, giving up and closing my textbook. "What do you want to do?"

She was still behind me, but suddenly a baggie of weed was dangling in front of my face.

"This!"

I turned to look at her. She had her mass of hair pulled up in a high ponytail, and she was wearing a long-sleeved KU t-shirt over leggings. She also had a huge smile on her face.

"Where did you get that?"

"It's a college town. Where can't you get it?"

"Well, we're not smoking it in here. You know we'd get kicked out of the dorm if we got caught," I said.

"Of course we're not smoking it in here, fool. We're gonna get Mattie and we're gonna go out to the parking lot and we're gonna smoke up in your car."

"Why not your car?" I asked.

She shrugged. "Because I like yours better."

Luckily, I had parked in a far corner of the lot, where things were quiet. It was a bright, sunny winter day. The air was crisp, but the sun was warm. The trees were still bare, and the vestiges of the last snowstorm were melting rapidly.

The sun streamed through the windows, so the car was almost toasty. I sat in the driver's seat, while Siren sat in the passenger seat, and Mattie was in back. Siren rolled up a joint on a spiral notebook, then lit it and took the first drag. She held the smoke in for several seconds, then blew it out in a big cloud. The inside of the car became hazy with smoke. I started to roll down a window. "No, don't," she said. "Let the car fill up with smoke. We'll get a better buzz." She handed me the joint, which felt solid and compact. The end was twisted beautifully.

"You're good at rolling these," I remarked.

"Yeah, one of my mom's boyfriends taught me when I was fourteen."

"Fourteen?"

She shrugged. "I actually really liked that guy. He was one of my favorites. I wish they'd stayed together." Then she changed the subject. "Hey, you know what they call this, right?"

I took a drag of the joint, coughed out the smoke and passed it back to Mattie.

"Call what?" Mattie asked.

"What we're doing right now," Siren said.

Mattie took a drag, then croaked out, "Toking on a doobie?"

For some reason this cracked me up to no end. I wheezed and laughed, which trailed off into coughing at the end.

"No, silly," Siren said. "It's called hot boxing." She accepted the joint back from Mattie as he exhaled.

"Um, the phrase hot box makes me uncomfortable," Mattie said, and we all dissolved into weed-induced giggles. "Speaking of hot box," he said, "Did you know there's this Seventies women's prison movie called The Hot Box? It's this weird, pseudo-pornographic, Blaxploitation-slash-softcore-porn flick. The prison is in a tropical jungle, but the women plan a jailbreak. There's sex and violence and explosions..."

"That sounds wild," I said, passing the joint back to him.

"It is wild. Like so messed up you wouldn't even believe it, wild. We should totally make cocktails and watch it sometime."

"Mattie! Shit or get off the pot," Siren said.

"What?" Mattie said, his eyes glazed over. The joint smoked lazily in his hand.

"Smoke or pass me the weed," she said.

"Oh!" he said, and passed the joint. "What was I talking about?"

"I can't remember," I said, and we cracked up.

Mattie and I only needed two hits and we were completely baked, but Siren kept hitting the joint. She looked so hot when she exhaled, the smoke blowing past her pouty lips. And maybe it was the weed, but her big eyes seemed exceptionally large and gorgeously defined by her makeup, and it was really difficult for me to stop myself from staring at her face. I giggled. "How can you keep smoking that? I am so high right now."

"She was so high she was literally out of her mind," Mattie said in this deep narrator voice he did sometimes, and we both fell apart laughing.

She shrugged. "Oh, hell. I've been getting high before my shifts at work just to get through them. I guess I'm building up a tolerance."

A wave of weed-enhanced sadness washed over me. "That's awful!"

She locked eyes with me for a couple of seconds, then snorted out a laugh. She touched my face. "Aw. That's so sweet! You look like a sweet, sad puppy," and both she and Mattie fell into a giggling fit.

"It's not funny," I said. "You shouldn't have to go through all that to go to college."

She shrugged. "What the hell else am I supposed to do? That's life. I do wish I could afford to take a job on campus like you did, but I'd never make as much as I do in tips. I'd love to work at the library."

The library... thinking of the library made me think of Carrie Watson. Then I had a weird thought: What if Siren did get a job at the library, and Carrie and Siren met and became friends? The whole notion was so bizarre, it made me snort and giggle uncontrollably.

"What's so funny?" Mattie asked.

I was laughing so hard, I couldn't catch my breath. "I don't know," I finally squeaked out, and we all died. We spent a while talking and laughing, until Siren said, "I don't want to sit in this car anymore. It's cramped." She was running her hands through her hair, grabbing it in big handfuls, putting it up in a ponytail then taking it out and making it into a bun, every few seconds, over and over. "Let's go somewhere."

"I'm not driving," I said. "I'm impaired." Mattie giggled and fell over in the back seat.

"So, let's catch the bus somewhere," Siren said, impatiently.

"We could go explore the library again," Mattie suggested.

"No," I said. "I know exactly where we should go."

The bus arrived on campus a little after 4 p.m. We tumbled off it, laughing, and walked down to Dyche Hall, giggling the whole way. Siren headed for the main entrance.

"No, not the front!" I hissed. "We're going in the side door. I don't want anyone I work with to see me stoned." Especially not my boss. I led them to the north door, where most of the staff entered and exited Dyche hall, since that's where the offices were located.

"Ohmygod!" Siren said, as if it were one word. "Let's go into the black-light room! Do they still have the black-light room? I saw it once when we came here for a grade school field trip."

I knew exactly what she meant. We headed down the stairs into the basement of Dyche, where the dinosaur and prehistoric exhibits were located. But to the left of the staircase, in a little room painted black, was a minerals exhibit. We crammed into the small space, giggling, and I flipped the light switch, which turned off the regular light and turned on a black light. The minerals in the display case lit up in fluorescent colors: purple and orange and green. We laughed at each other's glowing teeth. Mattie's shoelaces were electric-lime green.

Suddenly, all of the lights went out, and we were in total darkness. Mattie screamed and Siren yelled, "What the hell?" For a couple of seconds I didn't know what was happening. Then I clicked my phone on and checked the time. It was five minutes after five o'clock.

"Calm down," I said. "It's five o'clock. The museum is closed. They turned the lights off." As my eyes adjusted to the lack of light, I realized it wasn't totally dark. There was some light filtering in to the museum half of the building, from the half of the building where the staff offices were located. The two halves of the building were connected by open hallways, and even though it was a Friday night, I knew from my time working in the museum gift shop that some professors and graduate students would continue working in their offices until late.

"Do we have to leave?" Mattie said, disappointed.

"No," I said, lowering my voice. "As long as we don't act like total idiots, I don't think anyone will bother us. But let's get out of the basement."

"How do we get out of the building?" Mattie asked. "Are we locked in?" He was clearly experiencing some weed-induced paranoia.

"The doors will be locked from the outside, but we'll be able to leave," I said.

We hadn't been to the top floor of the museum, and it was my favorite. We used the lights on our phones to make our way up the stairwell, which was somewhat lit by windows. But the top floor of the museum was pretty dim, especially the farther into the exhibits we went. We explored the floor, giggling and whispering in the near darkness. This floor contained a bunch of taxidermy birds, and I had to admit the big ones—eagles, hawks and vultures—seemed to leer at us in the near-dark. The smaller birds were spooky, too, but in a different way, with their dead little glass eyes. Then there were the live snakes, in cubbyhole exhibits in the walls, behind glass, but they were so good at hiding we could only spot a few.

There was a taxidermy grizzly bear up here, as well, the only animal not behind glass. He'd been posed standing up, in a threatening position, snarling, with paws the size of baseball mitts. I stood in front of him for a moment, marveling at his mouthful of dangerous teeth. My head would easily fit in his mouth, and were he alive, he could smash it like a cantaloupe. Cool.

My favorite exhibit on the top floor was the honeybee hive. There was an honest-to-God, living, working hive housed in the hollowed-out trunk of an old tree. They'd installed a Plexiglas window in the tree in order to view the hive. The bees had recently come out of their winter clustering behavior and begun to venture out of the tree, through a clear plastic tube that fed out a window, so they could access the outdoors to gather spring pollen. The tube was drilled with small air holes, and lining the tube were hundreds of forager bees, either filing outside or coming back in. The forager bees made their way out the window empty-legged, while the ones coming in carried fat globules of bright yellow-orange pollen on their back legs, in structures called corbiculae, more commonly known as "pollen baskets." They hustled past each other, coming and going. A few sat stationary in the tube, buzzing their wings, acting as living fans to keep the air from becoming stagnant in the tube. The forager bees would bring the pollen back into the colony, where worker bees would mix the pollen with digestive juices and honey to create something called "bee bread," which they would feed to the larvae.

I watched the bees, transfixed. I imagined their short, frenetic little lives, which existed pretty much only to make honey, reproduce, and serve their queen, who would live three or four years. Siren and Mattie seemed relatively unimpressed with the bees and wandered off. At some point, they lost their minds and started racing up and down the halls, giggling. At one point, I stepped away from the bees, found a dark corner to hide in and jumped out as they rushed past: "BOO!" They screamed and fell into each other, a tangle of arms and legs on the floor.

"Oh my LORT," Mattie said, fanning himself. "I think you gave me a heart attack!" We laughed and then shushed each other, listening, but it didn't seem as though anyone had noticed us.

"C'mon! Let's go look at the snakes again!" Siren said.

"Ooo, I dunno. The snakes kinda freak me out," Mattie said.

"Don't be a baby!" she said, pulling on his hand. "They're behind glass."

"You guys go on," I said. "I want to look at the bees some more."

"Of course you do," Siren said. "C'mon Mattie!" And she dragged him away.

Watching the bees was so soothing. Like watching blood cells under an electron microscope. They buzzed and moved and vibrated and jostled past each other, all trying to do their jobs. I spent several minutes focused on the bees, until something shifted out of the corner of my eye, near the grizzly. I looked past the tree and was startled, but not surprised, to see a man standing there. I gasped out loud. He looked to be in his late twenties or early thirties. Weirdly, he was wearing an entire outfit made of fur—not fur trim, but full animal skins—which looked incredibly uncomfortable given the current temperature in the room, which had risen noticeably. The man wore a fur parka with the hood pushed back, fur pants and fur-lined boots that looked like they were skins turned inside out. In one hand, he held what looked like... a spear... no wait, the spear had a hooked point and a rope at the other end... it was a harpoon. His hair, which was several inches long, was disheveled and wild, sandy-colored, and he sported a dark walrus mustache. Though he was obviously still fairly young, his face was tanned and weather worn. This time, I knew exactly what was happening and who he was. It was Lewis Lindsey Dyche himself.

I couldn't speak. I stared at him, heart pounding. That familiar feeling of oppressively heavy air washed over me and I froze. Then he spoke.

"I see you like bees. I like them as well. I have to say, of all the modern additions to the museum, this one might be my favorite. It's absolutely delightful." He leaned over to peer into the hive and shook his head. "Amazing."

"It's one of my favorites too," I said, shifting my weight. "I mean— besides the—your—panorama."

He turned to smile at me. "Why thank you!" he said brightly, straightening up. "Although, I'm fairly certain you're far more enamored with this hive than I am. You don't merely like bees, do you? You love them." He rocked back on his heels, regarding the hive. "And how can one not love bees? They're such fascinating, highly organized creatures." I couldn't help but notice how he kind of... flickered... like an image on an old television screen. I was also surprised at how rapidly he spoke. I guess I expected him to speak with some sort of slow, Midwestern drawl, but his words were crisp and quick.

"Yes," I said, because I didn't know what else to say. I was fangirling so hard it was insane. I wanted to invite him to coffee and ask him questions—no, I wanted to tour the Natural History Museum with him and ask him questions. So many questions. I wanted to ask about his time in the Arctic, and at the World's Fair in Chicago, and where he'd been in Colorado, and have him describe the vast herds of bison thundering over the plains and the monstrous grizzlies he'd encountered in the Rockies, and the indigenous people he'd seen and ask what their villages had been like, and have him tell me stories about what it was like to grow up in a homestead in the vast plains of Kansas, and what it had been like to see the university buildings go up stone by stone on the top of Oread Mound. But I couldn't say anything, and somehow I knew that just like with Carrie Watson, our time together would be short. Before I could figure out what to say, he looked thoughtful and spoke again.

"In my early days at KU, my mentor, Dr. Snow, encouraged me to collect insects, and I did so, enthusiastically. Mostly moths. Eventually, of course, I became interested in collecting the larger varieties of wildlife, and all the challenges and dangers that come along with that. Still, I identify with your enthusiasm, and your love of the natural world and learning."

I still didn't know what to say, so I said nothing. He turned to look at me. "I was under the impression you would be a bit more loquacious. However, I can sympathize with your shock. In the interest of time, I'll get straight to the reason I'm here: The answers you seek are not located in the University's entomology collections."

"Answers?"

"The somewhat unclear task the crotchety librarian gave you. You've been searching for the identity of Flora's insect—and you have made a good effort—but you are... stumped, as it were." The edge of his mouth turned up, and I realized that, because we were standing next to the tree trunk, he'd made a pun.

"Oh, yeah," I said, nodding. "I am totally stuck."

"Correct. In order to complete your task, you must seek the assistance of your biology professor."

"Dr. Livingly?" I asked. Dr. Livingly taught the lecture portion of my Organismal Biology class.

"No, no, no," he shook his head. "You know. The entomologist. The negro woman."

"Oh," I said. "Professor Berg." I was startled by his use of the word "negro," but too dumbfounded to say anything about it. We stood there in silence for a couple seconds and then he said thoughtfully, while staring at the bees: "I never thought I'd see the day when negros would be university professors.... or women, for that matter. But I do like the progress. I've known a few women in my time who would've made fine professors, had that been the convention of the time." He paused again. "I must say I do like her—Dr. Berg, you said?"

"Yes," I said, nodding, though he wasn't looking at me. "Dr. Gladys Berg."

"She understands the discipline of biology, and she still goes out to the field to explore and gather specimens, traveling the world as every decent naturalist should. And she does not coddle her students. She is an exemplary teacher." He looked at me. "Universities need more professors like her."

He stared at me, and I realized he was expecting a response. "Yes," I said. "I like her too. She's my favorite professor at KU so far."

"Good," he said, nodding. "Too many students prefer the professors who hand out high marks without requiring the work needed to earn them." Then he smiled and cocked his head, thoughtfully. "I shouldn't have referred to Carrie Watson as 'crotchety.' She is a persnickety woman, but she does love her library, and she runs a tight ship. I must give her that." Pause. "What I would give to be back working on Mount Oread again. But such is life.... and death." That one-sided smile again. He began to back away, turning to leave, and I realized that the air was feeling different... thinner... and I panicked because I didn't want to stand there like an idiot and not ask him something.

"Hey!" I said. He turned back to look at me.

"Yes?"

For some reason I knew he only had a few seconds left. The bear caught my eye. "Was that bear... did he go... quietly?"

He smiled. "This handsome fellow? He did. I always tried to shoot from a distance... not so far away as to not make the kill, but still far enough away that the animal never even saw me. Though I did enjoy some aspects of the sport of hunting, in many respects I hated doing it... the killing. So much killing. But we could see the wildlife of the American west disappearing right before our eyes. The settlers came like ant swarms, thousands of them, and we built our cities and roads, and the habitats disappeared, along with the animals. It was a terrible, horrible irony. We had to kill to preserve. And we had to do it quickly because we knew the majority of the majestic beasts would be gone any day. Fortunately or unfortunately, we seem to have made the correct decision..." his voice was fading, and the air was so thin I was having trouble catching my breath. The air shimmered in front of me as he turned and left down the dark hallway. "Good luck," his voice came from the darkness. "Remember, you must speak with your professor. Tell her everything. Well... perhaps not quite... everything." And at the end, as though his voice was coming from far, far away... "Discretion is the better part of valor." As the air cooled and the sultriness went away, I caught my breath and knew he was gone. I could hear Mattie and Siren again, somewhere in the darkness, and I realized I hadn't heard them at all while Professor Dyche had been there. I stood, staring into the black hallway, for a good minute after he'd left.

Now I knew for sure: I was seeing ghosts. Honest-to-God spirits who were speaking to me. Whether or not those ghosts were real, or made up by my brain, remained to be seen. I didn't feel insane... whatever feeling insane felt like. I didn't think I was insane... but of course, how would I know?

I decided I wasn't insane. I still didn't understand what the hell was going on, but I'd just have to go with it.

15

Dead Car, Dead Bugs

The next day I scheduled an appointment to see Professor Berg, but our appointment wasn't until the following Monday. On the one hand, I couldn't wait to talk with her and tell her about the diary. If she believed me, and if she could confirm the diary was real, it was going to be a fun conversation. On the other hand, I was probably going to have to admit I'd lied to her by omission about why I'd wanted a pass to the entomology collection on West campus. That part I was not looking forward to.

The following day, my car began acting up. Sometimes it would start immediately, and other times the engine would do this weak chug-cough thing before starting. It was worrying, so I asked Mattie if he knew of an honest mechanic in town. He recommended a little mom-and-pop car shop in a part of town I'd never been in, over the river in what the locals called North Lawrence. "Marvin's," he said, without hesitation. "That's where my family takes all our cars. They won't cheat you there. I promise. That's where all the real townies take their cars."

When I called Marvin's, a cheery sounding woman answered the phone. I described the problem with my car and mentioned I was a student, living on campus. "Sure, bring it by anytime," she said. "We'll take a look. There's a bus stop down the street from us. You can take the bus back up the hill."

I took my car in later that day, after my last class was over. It died at two different stop lights on the way to the shop, and the second time it died, I wasn't sure it was going to restart. By the time I rolled into Marvin's Auto Shop, I was feeling pretty lucky I hadn't had to call a tow truck.

It was a small shop, tucked into an old neighborhood. There were several cars on the lot surrounding it. A bell rang as I pushed through the door to the office. The cheery woman I'd spoken to was at the front desk, talking on the phone. She looked like she was probably in her early 50s. There was a small waiting area, with a few old magazines. The whole place smelled like dirty motor oil.

"Uh huh. Uh huh," she said into the phone and winked at me. "Joe, I gotta go. Gotta customer. Okay, hon. Love you too!" She smiled at me. "I bet you're the college girl who called! If you leave your key with me, hon, we'll look after your car for you. It's a little late in the day today, but we should get back with you tomorrow to let you know what's wrong."

The following day I was walking to my math class when I received a call from a strange number, and I almost didn't answer it; then I remembered my car. Sure enough, it was the nice lady from the auto shop. She told me the alternator was going bad. She told me how much it would cost to replace it with a rebuilt alternator, and the price wasn't too expensive. In fact, it was reasonable enough that I was pretty sure I could pay the bill myself, which made me feel weirdly proud, like I was kind of, almost a grownup. I told her they could go ahead with the work. Then I texted Dad with the news and the cost, because I thought I'd better double-check with him. *Sounds okay to me*, he texted back. *But you don't have to pay for it, Pumpkin.*

I want to.

The following afternoon, the cheery lady called to tell me my car was finished. I rode the bus over the hill and across the river to the shop, where my car was parked out front. She smiled at me when I came in. I was always fascinated by people who seemed to be in such a good mood all the time. I couldn't even imagine going through life that way.

"Hey, there, College Girl!" she said. After I'd paid my bill, she said,

"Why don't you head out into the shop there ..." She pointed to a glass door across the room that provided a window into the shop. "Jakey wants to talk with you a minute before you leave with your car."

Jakey? "Okay," I said, kind of surprised, but then, this was my first time dealing with a car repair. The petroleum smell really smacked me in the face when I pushed through the door and stepped into the garage. An older, skinny, gray-haired guy in blue coveralls looked at me like I was an alien.

"Can we help you?"

A disembodied voice came out from under an SUV parked in the garage. "I got it, Earl," and a guy pushed himself out from underneath. He stood up, wiping his hands on a rag he'd pulled from his back pocket. "I'm Jake. Are you... Kymer? Or is it pronounced Kimmer?"

"Kymer," I confirmed, taking his grubby hand. He was young, probably not much older than I was. He was also wearing dirty blue coveralls, and a blue KU ball cap with greasy black fingerprints on the bill. He was a little taller than I was, and under the dirty smudges on his face, he was kinda cute, despite smelling like sweat and motor oil.

"That's a nice name," he said. "Different. Why don't we walk out front?" and he led us out of the garage to where my car was parked on the lot. "I wanted to let you know what we did here." He opened the hood and pointed, but the tangle of wires and pipes was meaningless to me. "We went ahead and installed a rebuilt alternator. It's in good shape—rebuilt it myself—and you shouldn't have any problems, but if you do, you be sure to bring your car back and if it's a problem with the alternator, we'll fix or replace it no extra charge. In fact..." he unzipped a pocket on the breast of his coveralls and pulled out a phone. "Why don't we get each other's cell numbers, so you can text me if anything goes wrong?"

"On one condition," I said, pulling out my phone.

"What?"

"Promise you won't send me any dick pics." And I gave him a cheeky smile, to let him know I was kidding. Sort of.

He shifted uncomfortably, adjusting his ball cap. "No, no, nothing like that. I swear. I'd hate for something to go wrong with your car, and I like to guarantee my work." His voice was older than his years.

I was pretty sure he was more interested in flirting with me than he was worried about my car. He seemed okay, though. Wasn't giving off a serial killer vibe, and I figured it couldn't hurt to know a mechanic.

"Okay, Rusty. What's your number? I'll forward you my contact info."

He told me his number and then asked, "Rusty? Who's Rusty?"

"You are," I said, tapping away at my phone screen. "That's how I'm going to designate you in my contacts."

"I've never been designated before," he smiled at me, and his warm brown eyes twinkled from under the bill of his greasy ball cap. At that very moment, electricity shot through my lady parts.

Oh, shit. This could get interesting.

When I stopped by Professor Berg's office the next day, her office door was cracked a couple of inches. I peeked in through the crack, but I couldn't see her. Just a wall full of... bugs. But I could hear the clickety-clack of her typing away at her computer. I took a breath. Here we go. I knocked lightly and said, "Professor Berg?" I pushed on the door a little. She looked over her glasses, from behind her computer.

"Yes, Ms. Charvat. Please come in and sit down. I'll be right with you."

I did as she asked, taking the seat across the desk from her.

"I apologize that I'm not quite ready for you. I have a few more thoughts I need to take down."

"That's fine," I said, and I waited. It was nerve-wracking the way her keyboard clicked away in the quiet, so I studied the bugs in the room. Her collection was impressive. Really impressive. Every time I thought I was done being surprised by some of her specimens, there was something else that caught my attention. She had a giant darner (Anax walsinghami), the largest dragonfly in North America; she had several giant walking sticks (*Megaphasma denticrus*) in colors ranging from green, to brown, to bright yellow and even red; and a stunning collection of royal moths (*Saturniidae*).

I kinda jumped when she said, "There we are," and clicked around with her mouse. "And save. I do apologize again, but if I don't get certain thoughts down when I have them, I lose them," and she chuckled. "I guess that's what happens when we get older. Now, how can I help you?" But before I could answer she said, "By the way, how are the entomology collections? Are you enjoying them?"

"Oh yes! Very much so. It's been amazeballs!" I died a little inside when I said it, but she laughed.

"Amazeballs, huh?" she chuckled. "Good! I'm very glad to hear it. Now, how can I help you?" She pushed her glasses to the top of her head and leaned forward, her gaze intense. I felt my insides freeze. I was about to launch into a story that was, frankly, too strange to be true, and I really didn't want Professor Berg to think I was some sort of drama queen at best, or a liar and a thief at worst.

"Well, I need to talk to you about something... and... I think it's important, but it's also kind of—awkward."

Her brow furrowed. "Well, that's intriguing. Do go on."

I launched into my story. Sort of. Discretion is the better part of valor... I couldn't tell the whole truth... but I also didn't have to totally lie. "I was in the library one afternoon—studying—and I found this book," I handed it to her and she took it, brow still furrowed. She put her glasses on to better see it, and I just kept talking. "Except it's not a book, really. It's a diary. Well, it's more than a diary. It's a field journal of local insects and arachnids from the mid-1800s." Of course, I didn't say I'd been there tripping on mushrooms with my friends, and I also didn't mention Carrie Watson being the one who handed the diary to me. As I talked, she looked at the outside of the diary, feeling the embossed bee on the front and turning it over. Then she opened it and began paging through it, slowly.

"It says in the inside cover that it belonged to Flora Richardson," I went on. She glanced at me, then checked the inside cover to confirm. I continued, "Flora was a student here at KU, part of the first graduating class. I looked her up."

"Yes, I'm familiar with Flora Richardson," she said, which for some reason, surprised me.

"Oh. Well... I really think this might be her field journal. And if you look here... may I?" I asked, holding my hand out. She raised her eyebrow and handed me the diary. I flipped to the page of the mystery bee. "There's this one bee Flora couldn't identify. So I thought maybe I could identify it, but I can't find anything that looks like it in the collections." I handed the diary back to her and was quiet. She took the diary again, and spent a couple of minutes reading the bee entry and considering it. She brought the diary close to peer at the bee drawings. After studying the bee entry, she flipped through the rest of the pages a little faster this time, not saying anything, looking the pages up and down. I couldn't tell from her face if she was pissed at me, or if she thought the diary was fake, or anything. It seemed like it took forever before she spoke again.

"So that means the first time you came to me, when you asked for access to the entomology collections, you weren't entirely truthful. In fact, you lied to me—by omission." It was a statement, not a question.

"Yes, ma'am," I looked her in the eye.

"Because, I assume, you didn't want me to know about the diary?"

"Yes, ma'am." I looked at my hands.

"Because you wanted to see if you could identify this bee on your own."

"Yes, ma'am. But I was going to hand the diary over to the university. I swear. No matter what I found. I was mad-curious about the diary and I wanted to see if I could find Flora's bee myself."

She stared at me for a few seconds without saying anything, and I crumbled inside, wondering if I'd just lost any and all credibility with my favorite professor who happened to be an expert in the very discipline I hoped to be in some day. It could make the next several years uncomfortable, to say the least. What if she hated me so much I had to change schools? I didn't want to think about it, but I couldn't help it, especially since she had gone back to being silent, looking over the diary.

Finally, she spoke. "Well please don't do that in the future. I don't care for liars. You say you found this? In the library?"

I nodded. "Yes, ma'am."

"And you removed the electronic tag from it? You stole university property?"

"No ma'am! It wasn't tagged. I swear," I looked her in the eye when I said it, hoping she'd believe me.

"Exactly where in the library did you find it?" her voice was crisp.

"In the history section," I said. Which was true.

"And you chose to remove it from the library." She had me there. I looked at my hands.

"Yes, ma'am."

She looked through the journal again, this time paging through it more slowly. She was quiet for a long time, and just when I thought I might die from the suspense, she finally said, "Well... it is possible this field journal could have been removed from the Spencer Research Library and left in Watson... though it doesn't seem to have the research library's stamp anywhere, and it's generally not permitted to remove items from the research library."

"Spencer Research Library?" I asked. I'd never heard of it.

"Yes, that's where the university's rare books and personal papers are kept... the personal papers of various university staff and influential people around Lawrence," she looked up from the diary. "I'll check with them tomorrow to make sure they're not missing this field journal, though to be honest, if it's been in our collection all these years, and I didn't know about it, I'm going to be a little irritated I wasn't aware of its existence before now."

Yeah, I doubt the Spencer Research Library knows anything about it, I wanted to say, but of course I couldn't say it out loud.

She went quiet again, studying some beautiful illustrations of a cuckoo wasp. After a while I couldn't take the silence any longer. "I'm really sorry I didn't turn over the field journal right away. That was wrong."

She didn't bother to look up. "I would be far more bothered by that if you hadn't shown any genuine interest in this field journal. Since you seem so sincere in your enthusiasm to investigate Flora Richardson's work..." she paused, flipping through the diary quickly, and I was on the edge of my seat. "Ms. Charvat, you do understand that if this diary is authentic, it's a valuable piece of history that is important to this university, particularly the biology department. Of course, it will have to be authenticated." Finally, she looked up at me. "We have staff here who can do that, but I will need to confiscate it."

Damn.

She must've seen the disappointment in my face. "However," she said, putting her glasses back on, "since you are so clearly invested in this diary, I'll tell you what. You and I are going to go through this field journal and cross-reference every insect in here against Flora's collection."

"Flora's collection?"

"Yes, the university is still in possession of Flora's pinned collection."

I almost fell out of my chair. "Where?"

She got up. "Well, as it so happens, as the senior most entomologist at the university, her collection is under my care." She walked to a closet door, opened it and went inside. She came out with an old wooden display case with a glass lid and several bugs pinned on what looked like yellowing white silk. She set the case down on the desk and I stood up to get a better look at the bugs. They were obviously old… faded… a few were losing legs and wings. But I recognized the handwriting on each of the tags. It was Flora's. I was sure of it. "There are several more of these cases. I keep the collection in the closet in the hopes the specimens won't degrade as quickly in the dark."

I couldn't help it. I gawked. Most of the specimens didn't look all that exotic, and they were definitely showing their age, but they were *hers*. She'd had her hands all over these insects. I was geeking out hardcore.

"Can I open the case?" I asked. I had to ask.

"Yes," Professor Berg said. "Just be careful."

I unlatched the case and opened it to get a closer look. The care with which she'd pinned each insect was evident. She'd positioned each one just so, in order to make every part of the insect visible to the viewer: legs, antennae, wings… she'd also done a great job of hiding the pins wherever she could.

"That is insanely cool," I said.

"It sure is," Professor Berg said. "As I said, we should be able to cross-reference the species here to the diary. If they're a match, that will go a long way toward proving that Flora actually compiled it." She bent down to look at the tags on the bugs. "The handwriting looks the same. But we'll have to build our case, and I'll need to get my colleagues to weigh in. We're also going to look into the bee in question—which I have to admit I don't believe I recognize, off hand—to see if we can identify it." She looked up at me. "Would you have time this coming Sunday to help me go through Flora's collection? I believe we can cross-check all of these in a few hours, if we don't mess around."

I was supposed to work that Sunday, but I was pretty sure they'd let me trade shifts, and I didn't want to say no. "Yes, ma'am! That would be amazing."

"Ms. Charvat, I understand your desire to keep hold of this diary. It's extraordinary if authentic. Certainly of interest to a entomophile, especially one attending KU. And you say you weren't able to locate an example of this bee in our collections?"

I kinda loved the way she called me Ms. Charvat. "No, ma'am." I shook my head.

"Explain your method," she said, with no nonsense in her voice whatsoever.

So I explained... I explained where and how I'd started, and the photos I'd taken, and my thought process and what I'd done to eliminate or include possible specimens. She asked to see my phone, and I handed it over to her. She put her glasses up on her head and peered at the photos on my phone as I spoke, studying each photo before swiping to the next. She listened the whole time I talked, without interrupting me.

"Very good," she said when I was finished, and she handed back my phone. "It sounds as though your procedure was fairly thorough. I'm going to need you to document exactly what you did." She put her glasses on and peered over them at me, with that piercing gaze of hers. "Can you do that? I need it documented on paper. Step by step."

"Uh..." Could I do that? Of course I could. "Yes, ma'am," I answered. "Yes, I can do that."

"Go back to the collections if you have to. Retrace your steps. Write everything down. The more complete your notes are, the better," she put her glasses on and looked through them at me. "Ms. Charvat?"

"Yes?"

"You may have accidentally, in your freshman year, stumbled upon your thesis. How about that?" Her eyebrows were raised, and to my relief, the corners of her mouth were turned up into what was almost a smile.

"Uh..." I said, but she cut me off.

"Well, let's not get ahead of ourselves. First we have to see what we're dealing with here. I will see you Sunday. We'll go from there."

16

Rusty Jake

I was comfy in the dorm room, lounging in my jammies and doing my chemistry homework, when my phone buzzed around nine thirty that night. Siren was at work. I didn't look at the text right away because I kind of assumed it was Mattie, but then it occurred to me it might be Siren needing a ride home from work because her car broke down or something, so I picked up the phone.

It was craziest text I'd ever received:

Hey collage girl remember me its Rusty from the shop who worked on your car,, Everythign ok?

I was kind of shocked he texted, because it had been a full week since I'd picked up my car from the shop. I'd almost forgotten about him. It was one thing lusting over him when I was standing there looking at him, but now that I'd had time to think about it, getting involved a blue-collar, non-college guy seemed too complicated ... and not prudent. We probably had totally different goals and values.

I typed back, *Yeah! It's running great! Thank you!*

A few seconds later, *Your welcome. How are you?*

And there it was. The real reason for his text.

I'm okay. Working on some chemistry homework.

There was a long pause.

I cuold make a chemitstry joke but I wont ,,,,

Ugh. Better not to encourage him. I needed to be firm, but nice. *Haha! Thanks for checking in. I appreciate it! I'll be sure to let you know if I have any problems.* I set the phone down and went back to my homework. We were learning to balance chemical equations, and I kinda liked it. Especially the tricky ones. There was something so satisfying about messing with both sides of the equation until they balanced.

Twenty minutes later my phone buzzed. It was Rusty again. Ugh.

Hope I am not interupting your studying,, but was wondering if I could take you out sometime

Oh God. Why, Rusty? Just why?

I waited a couple of minutes before I typed back: *So, do you do this a lot?*

do what

Sexually harass your customers

A couple more minutes went by... no response. Oh well. Scared him off. Maybe I'd been a little too forward, but I figured it was better for him to know who he was dealing with up front. Thirty minutes later the phone buzzed: *Sorry was cooking pork chops for super,, ...* long pause, then, *I usualy don't bother with college girls,,most are boring,, but once inawhile,,one of you is intresting*

I had to admit I was kind of digging the alternative spelling and grammar. Creative.

I'm so flattered I finally made the cut, I typed back.

I would of txtd sooner but I didn't think you would go out with a uneducatid grease monkey,, haha

So what made you finally text?

my mom likes you and she said I should getin touch

That made me laugh. Before I could answer, he said, *Yes ,, I'm a momas boy ,, and proud of it*

I typed back, *So if your mom hadn't told you to, you wouldn't have texted?*

Like I said,, I didn't think I had a shot but,,, she likes you and I thought maybe she has better taste in woman then I do

So would your mom go on the date with us? I texted.

If you want her to I gess so if that would make you feel safer

Aw! How sweet!

I'm a gentlemen like that

I'm sure you are!

So,,,,are you free this Saturday night

I stared at my phone. Was I free Saturday night? He was cute, kind of funny and not a serial killer, I didn't think. A couple of minutes went by and he typed: *I can pick u up at your dorm around 7?*

I typed back, *Yeah, that's not gonna happen, Rusty.*

Mom was right about you

What does that mean?

That your to smart for me and I will be damm lucky if you go out with me

I couldn't help it. I kind of liked his smartass flattery, despite his horrible spelling and grammar. Then he texted, *That's OK if you do not trust me yet we can meet someplace*

I took a couple of minutes before I responded.

Where?

You know where rickys is?

Who the hell is Ricky? I'm not meeting you at some random dude's place.

No,,,it's a sports bar over in nolaw

What's nolaw?

North Lawrence

North Lawrence. Over the river. Oh. I can find it. I'll meet you there at 7 on Saturday. But I'm gonna tell my roommate where I'm at so I don't end up roofied and tied up in your trunk.

I drive a pickup

Fine. I don't want to end up duct taped and under a tarp in the back of your truck

I wuold put u in a sleeping bag with a pillow

Like shoved down inside so no one could see me of course

Of course

Such a gentleman

You sure can type fast collage girl

Hey Rusty: Go fuck yourself

I have been practsing my yoga

Good thing, too

See you Saturday at rickys then?

I'll be there with bells on

That will make u easy to find

Weirdly, the texting went on like that for an hour or so, and I didn't hate it. In fact, I kind of enjoyed it.

Ok college girl im gonna say goodnite because im not so good at txting
Goodnight, Rusty
Looking forward 2 saturday

His name, of course, was not Rusty. It was Jake, but I had kind of forgotten that. Rusty-Jake had grown up on the other side of the river, which made him a River Rat or a Sand Rat or something... some nickname bestowed on residents of North Lawrence. Ricky's was in a kind of cool-old industrial looking building with a dark pine interior. The crowd was odd. It was a mix of townies and students, families with kids, professional people, and blue collar workers. But everybody looked comfortable hanging together, even though there was a table of women in office attire seated next to a table of sweaty guys wearing road-construction orange.

I could tell right away Rusty spent a lot of time there. He led us to a table as soon as he saw me come in, like he owned the place. I was pleasantly surprised at how cute he really was, now that he was cleaned up. He was wearing clean jeans, a surprisingly stylish Hawaiian shirt, nice sneakers, and had traded out his greasy KU cap from the autoshop for a fresh one.

He looked me up and down, trying to be casual about it. I was pretty sure I passed the inspection. Siren had insisted I wear one of her dresses and a super cute pair of black, sleek, knee-high boots. The dress was super short on her and the perfect length for me. It emphasized my curves but didn't look too slutty. She also put my hair up, did my makeup and loaned me jewelry. Okay, so Siren basically totally dressed me, even though I'd resisted at first. Oh yeah, she'd also sprayed me with perfume. Like a really nice perfume. I had to admit, she had done a great job. I was pretty scrumptious.

"You look nice," he said, pulling out a chair for me. "Whatcha drinkin'?"

"Umm... a diet cola?"

"Bullshit. Whatcha drinkin'?"

"A glass of chardonnay would be nice, but I'm not twenty-one." I knew I shouldn't drink, but my palms were sweaty, and my stomach was doing flip-flops, and a glass of white wine sounded really good. I hadn't been on a date in over a year, and this guy was way out of my comfort zone. I really had no idea what to expect, and I wasn't entirely sure I trusted him yet.

"Not a problem," he said, waving down one of the waitresses. I noticed that all of the bartenders and wait-staff were female, and most of them were wearing tight jeans and low-cut blouses. A gorgeous waitress with long, wavy brown hair a tiny waist and big brown eyes sashayed over.

She batted her eyelashes at Rusty, ignoring me. "Hey, sweetie, what do you need over here?"

"Hey, darlin'. How are you doing tonight?" Rusty-Jake said. Darlin? Did I fall asleep and wake up in fucking Texas? "Can we get a vodka on the rocks and a glass of chardonnay, please?"

Now the waitress looked at me. "Should I start a tab for you?"

Before I could say anything, Rusty-Jake said, "No. It's on me. Just put everything on my tab tonight."

"Oh!" she said, smiling at me as though she had just realized it was a date. Then she turned back to Rusty. "Hey, Jakey, are you gonna be able to look at my car next week?"

"Oh, that's right," he said, nodding. "Sure, darlin'. Bring it by Monday morning, and I'll take a look."

"Thank you, sweetie. I'll be right back with those drinks." And she sashayed away.

"So, you come here a lot?" I asked, already knowing the answer.

"Well, seeing as how I call this place 'the office,' I guess you could say yes," he said.

"Yeah... and seeing as how you call our waitress 'darlin.'"

He chuckled. "Yeah, that's Jess."

"And are you still having sex with her?" I asked. I figured it was best to get these things out of the way up front.

He looked at me, raised an eyebrow and smiled. "Who?"

"Jess."

He squirmed a little in his seat. "Well, no, not now. That was a couple years ago. We're just friends, now."

Well, at least he didn't lie. "Sorry, I can be kind of direct like that," I said. Only I wasn't sorry.

"That's okay," he said, looking me square in the eye. "I like it."

Jess showed up with our drinks and set them on the table. She didn't ask for my ID.

"Thanks, darlin'. Keep 'em coming. Oh, and can we get some menus? We'll be ordering food, too."

"Ooo, special!" she said, grinning at me again. Well... she didn't seem to be jealous in the least. But what if she was happy he had a date, because that meant he'd leave her alone?

He took a big swig of his drink and set it down again. "So, go on with the interrogation. What else do you wanna know?"

"How long have you worked as a mechanic?"

"Shit. My whole life, basically."

"Seriously?" I took a sip of wine. It was good.

"Seriously. Y'know how the shop's called Marvin's?"

"Yeah."

"Marvin was my dad. He died about five years ago, now, so now I run the shop. Mom still does the books."

"Oh no! I'm so sorry!"

He shrugged his shoulders. "S,okay. I mean... it's not okay. It was pretty much horrible. He died of lung cancer. I helped Mom take care of him." He took another big drink.

"That's awful," I said. "I mean... that must've been tough to go through." Thankfully, the wine was kicking in. My stomach had settled down, and to my surprise, the conversation seemed easy.

"Yeah," he nodded. Then he shrugged. "But, I mean... what else can you do, you know?" Then he changed the subject. "So how did you end up bringing your car over the bridge? We don't get a lot of college girls on this side of the river."

"My friend Matt recommended your shop," I said. "He's a film major from Lawrence. He goes by Mattie, actually."

"Mattie Walker?" he asked, raising an eyebrow.

"Yeah," I said, surprised.

"Oh, I know Mattie," he crossed his arms and chuckled.

"You do?" The wine was going down smooth.

"Sure. I dated his older sister Eva for a few weeks in high school," he chuckled. "I don't think her parents were thrilled, since me and my brothers kinda had a reputation for getting into trouble. So Matt's in film school, huh?" he chuckled again. "That figures. He was always quite dramatic." He made a little flourish with his hand and took another drink.

Dramatic? I felt myself getting pissed off. "You know he's gay, right?"

"Oh hell, Matt's as queer as a three dollar bill," he shrugged his shoulders. "Always has been, ever since he was a little shit. I don't care. I have a lot of queer friends... transgender... hell, I even have a buddy who thinks he's a pony," he laughed. "I love 'em all."

I laughed. Loud. The wine was hitting me hard. This guy was an honest-to-God redneck.

"What? Did you think the grease monkey from NoLaw would hate gay people?" he asked, smirking a little.

"Maybe," I admitted, shrugging my shoulders. "I don't know... I guess I hadn't really thought about it."

"Well I don't. See, that's why I don't like you snooty out-of-town college girls. You're way too quick to judge people."

"You know I woulda walked right out of here if you had been a bigot, right?"

He took a drink. "Same here."

"Wait a minute... did you call me snooty?"

He smiled that smile at me, his brown eyes sparkling as he took another swig of his drink. "That's right. Snooty. Whatcha gonna do about it, college girl?"

I snatched his hat off his head and put it on, clumsily, over my up-do. He was even cuter without the stupid hat. Good haircut. He laughed and took it back. "I'd let you keep it, but you're too pretty to have your face covered."

It was corny, but I liked it. "So you must be..." I calculated his age, based on him graduating high school three years before Mattie, "Twenty-one? Twenty-two?"

"Twenty-three. They held me back in the fifth grade. Discipline case."

"Oh yeah?"

"Yeah. I was always getting into trouble."

I took a sip of wine. "How come?"

He shrugged his shoulders. "I don't know. I was a real pain in the ass for my teachers. I just wanted them to leave me alone. I wasn't dumb, but I didn't want to be there, either. My favorite was my fourth grade teacher. When I was too much trouble for her, she'd send me out to the teachers' parking lot to change the oil in her car."

"That's hilarious."

"So how old are you?" he asked.

"Nineteen," I said.

"Really?" he said. "When you said you weren't twenty-one yet, I figured your birthday was coming up soon." He seemed genuinely surprised. Not like a twenty-three-year-old trying to get into a younger girl's pants.

"Nope," I said. "I'm a freshman," taking another gulp of wine.

"So what's college like? I can't imagine going to school voluntarily, let alone paying that much money for it."

"Yeah, well, I don't have to pay for it. Thank God."

"Oh, so you're snooty and spoiled. Figures." He downed a shot and signaled for the waitress to bring another round.

"I am *so* not spoiled," I said, leaning forward.

"You have a job?"

"Yes," I said, feeling defensive.

"How many hours a week you work?" He still had that little smirk on his face, but it wasn't unkind. More teasing.

"Fifteen or so. It depends," I took a sip.

"So just enough for spending money," he grinned.

"Well, yeah, but..."

"So your parents are paying for your college?"

"Yes."

"You see these girls waiting tables?" he motioned around the room. "All these women go to school. They also work full time. Some weeks more than forty hours. And they gotta get loans to pay for their school and put up with all these jerkoffs who sexually harass them all night."

"Okay, I get that, but I work hard at my classes," I said, knowing I was lying.

"See that girl, there?" he pointed to a cute blonde waiting on the table next to us. "Jade is getting a psychology degree. Making all A's too. See that girl?" and he pointed to a girl with long black hair and perfect eyebrows behind the bar. "That's Ember. She wants to work with disabled kids and she's getting her teaching degree. She also volunteers at the local homeless shelter."

"Okay," I said, taking a gulp of wine. "You've got me. I'm an asshole."

"Oh, I wouldn't go that far," he smiled. "You've just got some blind spots."

Normally, if a guy had accused me on a date of being some sort of elitist jerk, I'd be so mad. But honestly, he was right. I was spoiled. I'd never really thought about it because all of my friends' parents paid for their kids to go to school, but I knew there were people out there who didn't have that luxury. Like Siren.

So we talked about what college was like for a while, and he actually listened to me. It was sort of weird to explain college to someone who didn't have much concept of what it was like. I told him I was into bugs, which didn't seem to faze him at all. Some guys couldn't deal with it. I was telling him about my English class and my silly English professor who was unironically from England, and that's when I learned Rusty liked to read, so we talked about novels and movies we both liked. I talked about my family, growing up an hour from DC in an uptight, boring town that never felt quite right, and moving to Lawrence to go to school to study bugs. Once I said it out loud to Rusty, it again occurred to me that I sounded kind of selfish and ungrateful for everything I was lucky enough to have.

He talked more about his upbringing, which mainly consisted of him doing stupid shit with his two older brothers, like making extra cash selling weed and quarter sticks of dynamite, being arrested a few times and working on cars. He talked about how he practically grew up in his dad's shop, learning about cars from such a young age that he couldn't really remember a time when he didn't know how to work on cars.

In fact, the whole date went great. Even though he had no plans to ever go to college, he was pretty well-read, and definitely not stupid. I mean, he wasn't reading Tolstoy, or anything, but we could talk about Stephen King and J.D. Salinger and Diablo Cody. We sat there talking for hours, laughing at how different we were, but then again, how much we were alike. We ordered a pizza to share and lived at our table all night. The only thing that freaked me out was how much he drank. After downing three double-vodkas, the beers kept coming, and he drank all night long. I stopped at three glasses of wine.

We ended up closing Ricky's. Then we made out in the cab of his pickup truck in the parking lot for a full hour, and it occurred to me that the only other time I'd ever been in a pickup truck was on my grandfather's farm. No one I knew in Maryland had a pickup. No one. The making out was hot. Rusty definitely knew what he was doing, and it didn't hurt that working as a mechanic his whole life had left his muscles very well-defined.

I wanted to have sex so bad. So did he. Clearly. But we didn't. Because, much to my dismay, I kind of liked him. And I was pretty sure he liked me. So we just didn't do it. Instead we made out until there wasn't any makeup left on my face and his stubble had rubbed my cheeks raw.

When I finally got back to the dorm room, it was five o'clock in the morning. Siren was dead asleep. I collapsed on my bed and watched the sun come up through a crack in the curtains while I tried to will myself to feel tired. But I wasn't tired. I was tingly. Horribly, uncomfortably, sexually tingly.

And what about Rusty? What was I gonna do? Was I really gonna date a mechanic? I was in college, for fuck's sake. I was supposed to be meeting college guys. And my mother would hate him. Like hate him. Then I decided fuck it. I'm not going to worry about it, and fell asleep.

17

Rock Chalk

That same day, at precisely at 10 a.m., I showed up outside Professor Berg's office and knocked at the doorframe with one hand, while holding on for dear life to an extra-huge to-go mocha with the other. The door was cracked open, but when I peeked in, I didn't see Professor Berg. I was exhausted from the night before. I'd only gotten about three hours of sleep, and I wasn't exactly hung over, but I felt... off. Also, I hadn't showered, nor changed my stupid push-up bra from the night before, and it was digging into my skin. Even so, I couldn't wait to see the bug diary again and get a close look at Flora's actual freaking bug collection. I was starting to wonder if Professor Berg had blown me off, when from out of nowhere, she threw open the door. "Welcome, Ms. Charvat! Come right in!" I was startled by her clothes... she always dressed so professionally during the week. Today she was wearing jeans and a KU sweater... and KU earrings, and red and blue sneakers.

"Of course there's the basketball game tonight, so we can't be at this forever," she said, businesslike. "My husband and I are having people over at our place later. Do you follow the team?" She motioned me inside.

"I think my friends and I are the only ones in this town who don't," I admitted. It was kind of true. In Lawrence, more people watched KU men's basketball games than went to church. During the games, you could ask anyone in Lawrence what the score was, no matter where you were, on campus or off, and twenty people could tell you.

Lots of students camped out for hours on the sidewalk outside Allen Fieldhouse to try to claim a spot in the student section, but for some reason, Mattie and Siren and I had no desire to do that. We always had so much fun with each other, it seemed like the games would pale in comparison.

"Well, let's get at this, so we can get through it all." I followed her to the big walk-in closet in her office and flipped the light on. The closet was as big as a small room, with deep shelves on one side, and on the shelves rested the cases comprising Flora's bug collection. "Let's see here," Professor Berg said, flipping to the first pages of the bug diary. "Why don't we begin at the beginning, and work our way forward from there. Interesting. The very first entry is of a Rocky Mountain locust—more commonly known as a grasshopper—and the Rocky Mountain Locust went extinct by the early 1900s." She grabbed one of the cases from the bottom shelf and pulled it out. "I don't see a grasshopper at all here, do you?"

"No," I said. That particular case was full of beetles and butterflies. She slid it back into place and grabbed the next case over. We scanned several until she finally pulled out an insect case that had a large grasshopper in the upper left hand corner of the case. She took her reading glasses off her head and put them on. "I think this is it. The Rocky Mountain Locust. I'll be damned." She slid the case from the shelf, and I grabbed one end to help her out of the closet with it. "Let's take it to my desk and set it down." We set the sturdy old case down carefully. It was heavier than it looked. The grasshopper in question was a big one, about three inches long, and its color had faded to a dusty beige. She undid the latch and opened the case, carefully. She used her manicured nails to grab the wrinkled, yellowed, tag pinned next to the grasshopper and straighten it out. She pulled her reading glasses off her head, put them on and leaned in close to read the tag, but I could read it from where I was standing: Rocky Mountain Locust (*Melanoplus spretus*).

"If this is what I think it is... it is! Have you read the Big Prairie books?" Professor Berg asked.

"I have," I said, nodding. "I read them tons when I was a kid. Love them."

"Remember when the locust invasion wipes out their crops?" she asked.

"Yeah, sure," I think that was in the *Blue Skies Forever* book.

She pointed to the grasshopper. "That was these guys. They cost American farmers millions of dollars in crop damages around the turn of the last century. And then one day—just like that—they were gone, and we don't really know why. This is a fairly rare specimen... there are only a few examples in various museums around the country." She held it out at arm's length, squinting at it. "At first glance, it doesn't look any different from your average American grasshopper. I can't believe this has been under my nose this whole time."

We figured out immediately that the next entry in the diary corresponded with the insect to the right of the Rocky Mountain locust, a large wasp called a Cicada Killer (*Sphecius speciosus*). That was when we both kinda freaked out and got really excited. As we went through the diary, bug by bug, they were literally pinned in the order of the diary, and our excitement kept building. After we worked our way through the first case of specimens, we figured out which was the next case by locating the next insect in the diary located in the upper left hand corner of the case.

It was kinda silly—a couple of insect nerds geeking out—but it was exciting. It was also weird to be hanging out with Professor Berg and see her acting like a real person instead of a professor. We were having so much fun that I didn't even notice when late afternoon came and my stomach made an embarrassing noise.

"I'm hungry, too!" Professor Berg said, as we laughed about my stomach. She ordered delivery sandwiches and drinks for us from a little shop downtown, and when the food arrived, we took a few minutes to eat. "You have to realize Kansas was a brand new state when the university first began, and relatively unsettled. Well—you know—unsettled by the white man. Dr. Snow, the first Chancellor of the university, required all of the students—no matter their major— to collect samples of the local flora and fauna and turn them in if they wanted to earn their degrees, because so much of it had simply never been identified. Sometimes it was about identifying species already known in Europe or South America, but more often than not, it was about discovering brand-new species previously unknown to European scholars."

I swallowed my bite of sandwich. "But if Flora found a new species of bee, why didn't she name it?"

Professor Berg shrugged her shoulders. "Hard to say. Maybe she assumed it was a known species, but she never was able to identify it for sure. Or maybe they were cataloging so many new species they simply overlooked this one and never got around to naming it."

"I can't imagine forgetting to name a new species," I said, chewing. "That would be the most exciting thing like... ever."

"Oh! Ms. Charvat—I spoke with our friends at the Spencer Research Library, and they'd never seen this diary before." She threw her head back and laughed before continuing. "You should have seen the look on the librarians' faces when they realized I wasn't going to let them have it. But they looked through their catalog, and they have no papers on file for Flora Ellen Richardson, and I wasn't about to donate it to their collection. As far as I'm concerned, the Entomology Department is going to take ownership of it," and we laughed about screwing over the librarians, which made me wonder what Carrie Watson would think.

As we worked our way through the diary, identifying the corresponding specimens in Flora's pinned collection, and we neared the mysterious bee entry, we were both getting excited. It was palpable. When we reached the bee entry in the diary, Professor Berg read the whole entry out loud. And then we studied Flora's physical specimen. We were quiet for a while, looking it over. It was small—which I expected, because the diary said it was only three-quarters of an inch long—but it looked to be in perfect condition. All of its legs and antennae were there, and the membranes in the wings were still intact and shiny. It didn't look as though its color had faded in the least. It was shellac black and a bright, iridescent gold. I'd never seen anything like it. So I held my tongue and my breath, and I waited to hear what Professor Berg would say.

"I have to say, Ms. Charvat... I don't think I know for sure what this is. It's certainly a bee, because it has a stinger." She had pushed her glasses up on her head and was leaning in close, squinting at it.

"I think it's a bee, too," I said. "It's just... well, I mean, I know I haven't seen as many insects as you have, but I've never seen a bee quite like that."

"You know... I don't know as if I have either." We looked it over for several minutes and Dr. Berg took several photos of it with her phone, from a million different angles. I wielded a nice set of Dr.

Berg's calipers, taking measurements of all its body parts while she took down the notes. We counted its stripes, noted the wing shapes and lengths (it had four wings, as all bees do), eye size, stinger length, shape of the antennae, as well as the shape of the abdomen, thorax and head.

After we'd measured everything, written down all the specifics and discussed the specimen for a good half-hour, we eventually moved on to the next insect in the case. So far, there had been no omissions as compared with the diary. We worked at the collection like that, from ten in the morning straight through until five o'clock, until every insect in the diary was accounted for. You had to admire Flora's organization and precision.

"You said you don't watch basketball, but you're welcome to come to our place to watch the game, if you'd like. Some family and friends are coming over." Professor Berg reached for her jacket. "There will be plenty of food."

I was pretty sure she was inviting me to be polite, and I was happy to let her off the hook. As much as I kind of wanted to hang out with her—in a worshiping sort of way—I was usually uncomfortable in sports situations because I never knew what was going on or how I should act. Besides, now that the bug excitement was wearing off, I was dead tired.

"Oh, thanks," I shuffled my feet, "that's really sweet, Professor Berg, but I really don't know anything about basketball, and I had a late night last night. I just want to get back to my room and crash."

She gave me a look like a mom would, and we both knew she knew I had partied the night before.

"I understand, Ms. Charvat. I will see you Monday."

"See you Monday," I said, and started to leave. Then I turned. "Thank you, Professor Berg. This was a really great day."

"I enjoyed it as well."

I put my fist out. "Rock Chalk!"

"Oh, hell yes," she said, putting her fist up and bumping mine. And I almost died.

18

The Bridge Date

Friday rolled around again, and I found myself getting ready for my second date with Rusty. Frankly, Rusty didn't meet most of my expectations for a boyfriend, which, I rationalized, made him ideal. We could share a friends-with-benefits situation, and as soon as he was bored with me—or I was bored with him—we could go our separate ways. Or maybe we could even agree to see other people, as long as we were both safe about it. What heterosexual guy wouldn't want sex with no strings?

But on that second date, I didn't want to think about all the logistics of what our sex "agreement" would be or what it would look like. All I could think about was getting back to his place, tearing his clothes off and hoping he was halfway decent at sex and also not a murderer. Inside, I felt like he was a nice guy, but intellectually I knew two dates wasn't a lot of time to get to know someone.

We left Rick's a lot earlier that night. Out in the gravel parking lot, Rusty took my hand. The air was dry and cold. Rusty was wearing a denim Carhartt jacket, while I had opted for my stylish leather jacket over my dress, which, thankfully, was warm.

"C'mere. I wanna show you something," Rusty said, and he started to lead us away from Rick's, toward a line of towering trees between Rick's and the river, because Rick's was tucked down just below the bridge. It was dark in the dense thicket of trees, though, out of the lights of Rick's parking lot, even though the moon was almost full and glowing bright white.

"Oh, hell no," I said, pulling back, taking my hand out of his, feeling vulnerable in my short dress and heels in a dimly lit gravel parking lot at night. This was how horror movies started.

He knew exactly what I was getting at, and put his hands up in surrender. "I'm not going to attack you in the bushes. I swear. I just thought we could go look at the moon over the river. See?" he pointed. "There's a path through the trees that leads up to the levee. Seems like a nice night." He gestured toward my feet. "Figured you'd need a hand, since you're not really wearing the appropriate footwear for hiking."

It made me laugh, and I let him take my hand again. "Careful," he said, more than once, leading us on the dirt path through the towering trees that lined both sides of the river, and up the levee. "Lotsa big rocks on this path," he commented, helping me steer around the big stones and tree roots.

When we reached the top of the levee, it was a beautiful view. The crest of the levee was flat and smooth, with what looked like a nicely maintained crushed gravel path that disappeared in both directions as far up and down as the levee as was visible. I'd seen people jogging and riding bikes on it the few times I'd driven over the bridge. The river was flat and smooth, and in the moonlight, you couldn't see the mud-brown water, just a pretty, mirror-like sheen reflecting the moon and the black sky. The sound of water rushing over the dam roared faintly a few hundred yards away.

We held hands, looking out over the water, the slight breeze off the water chilly on my cheeks.

"It's pretty up here," I said, my breath ghosting out into the night.

"This view right here is why I live on this side of the river," Rusty said, looking into my eyes, the corners of his mouth turned up ever-so-slightly, his lips inviting, his eyes sparkling with that little smile they always seemed to have, and we did the whole corny, slow lean-in and kiss in the moonlight thing. It was pretty hot. Rusty was a great kisser, and his body was rock hard everywhere my hands wandered: His abs, his chest, his biceps, his shoulders... after several minutes of serious tongue play and hands venturing in to ever-more private places, I checked the most important part, and sure enough, it was rock hard as well.

He pulled away from me, gestured down the levee and said,

breathless, "I live just right over there," pointing downstream. Peering into the dark, I understood he meant we could walk down the levee path to his place, which backed up to the river. "If you wanted to come over," he said, shrugging. "No pressure, though."

My heart was pounding. I was so turned on, the thought of walking away from his hard, warm body and skillful lips seemed impossible. Two dates. Sex. Was that slutty? At this point, did I care? Turns out I didn't. "Sure," I said, brushing a lock of hair out of my face.

He smiled, coyly, pointing over his shoulder with his thumb. "You sure? Because a few minutes ago back there you thought I might be the Boston Strangler."

I laughed. Why did he have to be so weirdly funny in his Kansas hayseed way? I put my hand out, and he took it. "I mean... you get there has to be condom use, right, Rusty? I'm not doing anything without condoms. I mean it."

He looked taken aback. He took off his ever-present ball cap, rubbed the top of his head a couple of times, and put his cap back on. "Um... okay. Sure. That's fair. I'll have to run to the gas station real quick..."

I let his hand go, opened my purse and dug around for a few seconds. "Here," I said, producing a condom. "I have some."

"Holy shit," he said, laughing. He shoved his hands into his pockets and rocked back on his heels. "You're a regular girl scout aincha? Always prepared."

I shrugged. "Yeah, well, you know what they say. You can't be too careful. So yeah, as long as you're not the Zodiac killer, and we agree condoms will be used, and stealthing will not happen, then yes," I said, taking a breath and watching the words billow out of my mouth in clouds of steam in the cold, "We can go back to your place."

He leaned in and said, "I promise, Snooty College Girl," before kissing me again, which led to making out for a few more minutes. Finally, he pulled away, turned and took my hand. "C'mon. Let's get you inside before you freeze to death," and we started down the levee in the moonlight.

"So, what's at your place besides a dog?" I asked, teeth chattering. The cold was starting to sink into my skin. "Is it all fishing rods and shot guns?"

"Mostly it's bloody deer carcasses and the still." He grinned, his teeth bright in the moonlight.

"Oh, good," I said, teeth still chattering, heels crunch, crunching on the path. "I love culture." Suddenly I realized I was walking down a gravel path on top of a levee in heels to get laid, and how ridiculous it all was, and how unsafe it still might turn out to be, but every time I was unsure, Rusty put me at ease.

"Oh, we got culture at my place," he replied. "The finest deathcore metal and bologna sandwiches you've ever experienced, all at Chez Redneck," and he did a chef's kiss.

It made me laugh. Hard. I didn't even bother to hold back, like you do when you're on a date. I just doubled over and let it out, still walking because it was cold and I couldn't wait to get inside.

He watched me, grinning. "Has anybody ever told you how pretty you are when you laugh?" he asked.

"Oh, stop it," I said. Just then the wind picked up, pulling hairs from my ponytail and into my face. "Dammit," I said, brushing my hair away from my face with my hand.

"Stop what?"

"I already said I'd come home with you, Rusty. You don't have to bullshit me." I stumbled in the stupid heels and Rusty caught me by my arm, helping me stay upright.

He looked at me, curiously. "I'm not bullshittin' you. You need to pull back on that angry sarcasm a little bit, College Girl, and just accept a compliment, for fuck's sake."

I laughed. "Okay, Rusty."

"Kymer?" he asked.

"What?" I said, through chittering teeth.

"You're really pretty when you laugh." That smile of his, with those lips of his, was killing me.

"Thank you."

"There you go," he replied.

In spite of the city lights and the bright moon, stars twinkled here and there in the clear, chill blackness overhead, and a crisp breeze blew off the water.

As we walked under the river bridge, the sound of water rushing over the dam was louder. The bridge was split: two lanes heading south and two lanes heading north. As we passed under the roadway heading south, we could hear the dull sound of cars passing overhead with a sort of thump thump thump.

"Betcha never been on a date like this before, huh?" Rusty asked at that moment.

I laughed. "No," I said, raising my voice to be heard over the traffic and the water, "I have never been on a date underneath a bridge." As we passed under the gap between the roadways, a few stars peeked through. When we reached the northbound roadway, the sound of cars passing overhead was nearly drowned out by the sound of the river churning over the dam.

"Is it doing anything for ya?" he hollered, his voice echoing under the bridge, and all I could do was laugh in response.

"What's that building?" I asked. It was a concrete bunker, sitting on top of the dam.

"That's the housing for the electricity generators," he said, his voice still raised over the sound of the water.

"Hydroelectric?" I commented, surprised because Lawrence just wasn't a big town.

"Yeah," he replied. "Pretty cool, huh?" He pointed at the river, swirling and frothing on the low side of the dam. "There's some great catfishin' below the dam," he said. He let go of my hand and spread his arms. "Catfish this big down there. Eighty, ninety, even hundred pounders. They just sit down there in the mud, for years, eatin' all the dead stuff that comes over the dam."

"And does one noodle these catfish or catch them with fishing poles?" I yelled, amused.

He chuckled. "Well, you can't go noodlin' in the Kaw. It's just not safe. But you do have to have heavy-duty poles and reels to bring those suckers in, and apparently it takes hours to wear them out before you can finally land 'em. Never done it, myself, but I'm not very patient."

"But have you ever been noodling?" I asked. It was quieter now, as we walked away from the dam. The path had veered down below the levee in order to walk under the bridge, and now we had to walk back up to the top of the levee on the other side of the bridge. Rusty's hand tightened around mine as we made our way uphill on the path, my heels slick on the sandy gravel, but he firmed up his grip on my arm to help keep me from sliding backwards. I couldn't help but note it seemed to take him no effort to help me up the hill.

"Sure," he said. "My uncle's family has a place in the Ozarks with a pond on it. Have to go noodling when you're at Uncle Jack's." I burst out laughing. "Oh, come on," he said. "You didn't think I was going to say 'No,' did ya?"

"I honestly had no idea what you were going to say," I replied. "How much farther?" I asked, once we were back up on the levee path. The levee was darker on this side of the bridge, away from the lights of Rick's, and the dam, and the bridge, and as we began to walk, I could just make out houses down below the levee.

"I'm right over here," he said, "just a couple more houses that way," gesturing into the darkness. Once we were near his place, he helped me down the opposite slope of the levee—through the grass this time, no gravel path—into a back yard that seemed big for the cracker-box size of house sitting at the far side, just off a street.

As we walked up onto the small wooden back deck lit by a single door lamp, Rusty paused with his hand on the doorknob and said, "So, yeah, remember how I said I have a dog?"

"Yes," I said, teeth chattering and wishing he'd just open the door.

"He's a big dog. A big, dumb, slobbery dog, but I'll try to keep him away from you." Amazed, I watched as he opened the door without unlocking it first.

"You don't lock your door?" I asked, but at that moment a giant chocolate brown dog came bounding out of the darkness onto the deck and jumped up on me, paws on my shoulders, nearly knocking me over. He snuffled my face and hair with his fat pink nose, and I laughed, because it tickled.

"Godammit, Lugnut!" Rusty said. He grabbed the beast by his collar and pulled him off me, but Lugnut seemed unaffected by the rebuke. He smiled and panted, his fat tongue hanging out the side of his mouth. "Sorry about that. He doesn't have any manners at all." Lugnut whined at being restrained.

"It's fine," I said, brushing my dress off and smoothing my mussed hair back down. "I love dogs." Lugnut whined and wagged his tail furiously, straining against Rusty. "Get outta here," Rusty said, and I was amazed as he let go of his collar. The dog galloped into the yard and turned circles, sniffing, but the yard was unfenced.

"C'mon in," he said, flipping on a light. I stepped inside, and he shut the door behind me.

"You let your dog run free?" I was gobsmacked. If anyone had let their dog run free in our neighborhood in Bethesda, the authorities would probably be alerted.

"He always comes back," Rusty said, shrugging.

"He's at least fixed, I hope," looking around. It was definitely a bachelor pad: sparsely furnished with an old couch and a large screen television. A few empty beer bottles littered the scratched-up coffee table between the couch and TV. The living room carpet had seen better days. From the back door I could see into the tiny kitchen next to the living room, which was was almost bare, with nothing on the counters and an empty sink. The place looked fairly clean but had a definite doggy smell to it, and it occurred to me that if Victoria—or Zach, for that matter—knew what I was doing, their heads would explode, for a multitude of reasons. But Rusty was cute. And he was funny. And I was dying to get laid.

"Oh, no," Rusty replied. "No dog of mine is getting his nuts cut off," and he shuddered, as though the thought was unbearable.

"Oh, for fuck's sake," I replied, rolling my eyes and taking off my coat. I was mildly surprised there was a coat tree by the front door.

"What? The world could use more Lugnuts in it," Rusty said, casually. He took off his coat and flung it at the couch. Then he walked over to the fridge, pulled out a beer, cracked it open and took a long drink, belching after. "Excuse me," he said. "You want a beer? Sorry, we don't have any wine." He opened a cabinet. "We've got vodka. Or whiskey—little bit of rum," he said, peering at me around the cabinet door.

"No thanks," I said, rubbing my arms.

"You still cold?" he asked. It was the perfect segue for him to down the rest of his beer, set the can on the kitchen counter, walk over, and put his arms around me. We made out for a few minutes in the entryway. His lips were soft, and he tasted like beer, but I didn't mind. I did wonder how badly he'd wanted that beer, though.

I warmed up quick. The boy was a seriously skillful kisser, doing all the right things with his tongue. Our hands were all over each other— all outside the clothes—and after a few minutes, he disengaged from my mouth to ask, softly, "You wanna move to the couch?"

"Sure," I said, feeling very comfortable and also incredibly turned on. He held my hand and led me to the couch, he sat down first, and before he could make a move I sat on his lap, straddling him, feeling his bulge between my legs. I put my hands in his hair and kissed him hard. He slid his hands up my dress. After several minutes of that dance, I pulled away from him and whispered, "Could we maybe move to the bedroom? It'd probably be more comfortable."

"Yeah. Sure." I stood up so he could, and he took my hand.

"Just a sec," I said, grabbing my purse and putting the strap over my shoulder. As I followed him down the short hall, I retrieved the condoms from my purse with my free hand.

His bedroom was just off the living room, and once we were in there, we went right to work on each other. He didn't bother to turn on the light. The light filtering in from the living room, plus the moonlight from the window, was perfect. Not too bright, but not too dark, and the room wasn't that big; the bed was right there, as was his nightstand, littered with a couple of empty beer cans and some change, where I tossed the condoms. Thankfully, he took off his ballcap, placing it on the nightstand just before he slid my dress over my head. I reached down and unzipped his pants while he unbuttoned his shirt. I kicked off my shoes, peeling his jeans down, and then his boxer briefs. He was nicely turgid. I dropped to my knees and serviced him orally for a while until he lifted me up under the arms and placed me on the edge of the bed. He kissed me, reaching around to unhook my bra, fumbling a bit, something I was used to. As long as Zach and I dated, he could never quite master getting all four hooks undone on my D-cup bra.

"Don't usually have a problem with these," he mumbled, sounding embarrassed.

"Don't worry about it," I said. I reached around and with one motion had it undone and off. I tossed it aside. He kissed me, hard, gently easing me down flat on the bed from my sitting position. He pushed my legs apart, and went to work.

I didn't think it would be possible, but Rusty was at least as good at oral as Zach—maybe better—and he was willing to be down there a long time, until the pleasure was so intense I couldn't take it anymore. Up till that point, I hadn't insisted on a condom—which I knew was stupid—and now came the moment of truth.

"Please fuck me," I said, grabbing his hair. He moved to get on top of me, kissing me hard. I turned my face to the side. "Condom!" I reminded him, feeling for the condoms on the night stand and holding one up in his face.

"Oh, yeah," he said, taking it from me. "Sorry. I got carried away," and he chuckled a little. Once he had the condom on, he granted my request. With skill. The second time we had sex lasted even longer, until I was starting to get sore. Still, I had been well and thoroughly fucked, and now I felt like a tingly, exhausted rag doll, luxuriating in the afterglow of great sex. It was also getting very late, and I was supposed to open the museum gift shop in the morning.

We lay there for a couple of minutes, and for the first time since we met, there was mostly awkward silence between us.

"So," he said, lifting himself up and leaning on his elbow. "Was that okay?"

I laughed. "Yeah, that was okay. That was better than okay. Thanks. That was really... great."

"Really?"

"Yeah, really," I said, breathing out. "Look at me. I'm a sweaty, shaky, post-coitus mess."

"Post-coitus, huh?" he chuckled. "You're something else, College Girl," and he leaned down to kiss me.

I grabbed my phone off the nightstand. "Oh crap," I said, sighing. "It's three a.m. and my stupid car is still at stupid Rick's."

Rusty hopped up and pulled his underwear on. "I'll go get it," he said, sitting back down to put on his jeans.

"You sure?" I asked, sitting up.

"Well I'm not gonna let you walk all the way back to Rick's in your heels. Don't get me wrong—you look great in 'em, but let's face it—they make you easy prey. Especially in the dark." He finished buttoning up his shirt and said, "Throw me your keys," I leaned over the side of the bed, grabbed my purse off the floor and tossed him the keys once I found them. He caught the keys with one hand. "I'll bring back your car and you can give me a ride back to Rick's to get my truck."

He was back in ten minutes with my car, but then we made out for another half hour in my car before I said, "Hey, not to be rude or anything, but I really need to go. I have to work in the morning."

"Me too," he said, and kept kissing me. Finally, I pulled away.

"Really. I have to get at least a couple hours of sleep or I'll be worthless at work tomorrow," and I opened the truck door, stepping out.

"See ya soon, Kymer," he said.

We'll see. "Okay." I smiled at him, wondering if that would turn out to be true.

Rusty texted me the next morning while I was restocking the stuffed tarantulas at work: *Gess what I found???*

What's that? I texted back, and he sent a photo of one of my earrings, resting in the palm of his hand.

I wondered where that went, I replied.

Ur going to hv to come get it,,, lol

As winter began to melt away, green up, and morph into spring, things got weird.

Well, maybe "weird" is the wrong word. Just different. And by "things" I mean Mattie and Siren and me. The three of us had spent so much time together at the beginning of the year, but now our whole dynamic had shifted.

Mattie was seeing the guy he met at the Halloween party, Alejandro. Alejandro was a computer science major who happened to have a love for theater. Siren and I liked him a lot. Alejandro was hot. And so nice. He also had a great sense of style. Sometimes, I'd pick up Mattie and then Alejandro, so I could drop them off at Smoky Jo's for study dates, since neither Mattie nor Alejandro had a car. Usually

Alejandro was waiting out front, but one time Mattie and I went into the dorm to get him, and Alejandro's side of his dorm room looked like it came straight out of an Ikea catalog. He liked to wear Oxford shirts and penny loafers in the winter, and I'd never seen an actual human starch and iron a shirt with such skill. Not even my mother.

Siren was also seeing a guy from the Halloween party, but not the guy whose face she'd been attached to that whole night. She was seeing Jordan, the guy whose room the party had taken place in. The nice guy. Thankfully, he was also chill, because he'd been hanging out in our room a lot. But it worked out, because I was spending lots of time over at Rusty's, so when I was at his place, Jordan and Siren could smash in our room, and when I'd come home, Jordan would go back to his room. Well, most of the time. Sometimes I'd happen to be around when Jordan was, and they'd spend a few hours in Siren's bed together, under the comforter. Sometimes I got quite the eye- and earful, but I tried to ignore it. I would, however, shut and lock our door when they'd start doing it, because I didn't want anybody wandering in. Jeez, if Grace were to come in... she'd probably drop to her knees and start speaking in tongues.

I was seeing Rusty several nights a week when I didn't have to work. Most evenings I'd grab a quick dinner in the dorm cafeteria with Siren and Mattie if they were around, or some of the girls from our floor if they weren't, do a little studying and then head over to his place, usually around 7 or 8 p.m. We'd have sex, hang out, maybe watch an episode of some old TV show, have sex again, and then sometime around 11-ish I'd head back to the dorm. Every time I saw him, Rusty met me at the door with a beer in his hand, and he'd drink three or four while I was there. But I also knew most nights he stopped at Ricky's for two or three vodkas right after work, even before he started drinking at home.

We hadn't talked about our "relationship," or whatever it was we were doing, and frankly, that was fine with me. In fact, as far as I was concerned, things were perfect. I was doing mostly okay in school I thought, I was in pretty good physical shape with all the schlepping all over campus, I was working with Professor Berg to try to identify Flora's bee... I felt great, I looked great, I was eating right, and, oh yeah, did I mention I was having fantastic sex several times a week?

Around the middle of spring, Mattie began working on a short film for his final project in his film class. It was supposed to be no longer than five minutes. The script was called Space Vamp, and Siren had the lead role. She was a sort of superhero-sexy-space-vampire-come-to-earth who only killed pedophiles and rapists, so she could feed without guilt. But Alejandro was also in it, as well as a couple of Mattie's friends from his LGBTQ+ club. I liked to hang around to watch the filming, but I did not want to be in it. At least, not with a speaking part. He did ask me to be an extra in one scene. All I had to do was drink coffee while attempting to have a conversation with Mattie's gender-neutral friend Andie, who had spiky blonde hair and preferred the pronoun they. They dressed like a boy in khakis, cardigans and low-top Converse. They were super cute and got a little flirty with me, so I got a little flirty back. Later, Mattie told me they had a girlfriend.

This was the first Saturday the three of us had spent the afternoon together in a long time. Mattie's movie was due the following week, and it was the only day the three of us could get together. We were filming a restaurant scene in an empty part of the cafeteria in the student union. Mattie had asked his parents if he could film at their restaurant but wasn't surprised when they said no, since most Saturdays the restaurant was packed, and today was a game day.

"Cut! Cut, cut, cut!" Mattie waved his arm in the air. "Siren is doing perfect, as usual. You, Mr. Rapist! You need to look meaner. Sinister, even!" The scene we were filming was a date, and Alejandro was the rapist. His date was a queer-femme named Charlotte. "And you, Miss Extra Background Diner..." I looked up, surprised, because Miss Extra Background Diner was me, "... you need to get a different look on your face because you look like you are about to pee your pants while eating your finger. Do you need to use the restroom, Kymer? Because we can take a break."

"No, I'm fine," I said, realizing I'd been staring at the table, gnawing a fingernail and frowning, instead of keeping up the fake coffee and conversation I was supposed to be having with Andie. I reached for the cup of coffee in front of me and stirred it with a spoon. "I'm sorry, Mattie."

"That's all right, doll, but I want to get these takes in before the game is over, because campus will get wild. Are we ready? Okay. Action!"

Rusty was supposed to drop by to pick me up in a few minutes, and I wasn't quite sure what Mattie and Siren were going to think of him. I mean, I was pretty sure they weren't going to judge him for being blue collar, but I was sort of afraid they wouldn't like him. Okay, not sort of afraid, but super nervous, especially since I liked the guys they were dating. At the same time, I was trying to concentrate on the conversation I was having with Andie. Mattie said we should talk to each other at a low volume. "It'll look more real and I can edit out the background noise later," he said.

I focused on Andie, who had recently decided to get into street performance and was learning to eat fire.

"So, if you have long hair, you have to make sure to pull it back from your face and don't use hairspray, obviously. As you close your mouth around the flame, you have to remember to exhale, not inhale. Also, I always make sure I have ice water close by."

"So, you mean it actually burns?" I asked, nodding and smiling and taking a sip of coffee.

"Oh, shit yeah! It burns!" she said, and I almost spit out my coffee.

"Cut!" Mattie yelled. "That's a wrap, people. Very nice! We will resume filming tomorrow at noon."

"Where?" Charlotte asked.

"The final fight scene will take place on the top of the Vunos Hotel, down the street."

"Cool!" Charlotte said.

Mattie clapped his hands, and we all began to clean up. I checked my phone again. It was 8:13. Rusty had said he'd pick me up at 8.

"Hey, it was nice to meet you," Andie said, hugging me. They smelled really nice.

"You, too," I said, wondering if our paths would cross again. I was waving goodbye to Andie when Rusty walked through the Union doors. He looked uncomfortable. After he looked around a bit, our eyes locked, and he walked toward us.

"Hey," I said, trying to sound casual.

"Hey, College Girl. What's goin' on here?"

"We're just finishing up filming. It's an assignment for one of Mattie's classes."

"Well, bust my bubble and call me Glinda. If it isn't Jacob Murphy all grown up," Mattie said. From the little bit Rusty had talked about Mattie, I wasn't sure how well they knew each other. But they did a little guy hug, and I relaxed some.

"Me?" Rusty laughed. "Look at you! The last time I saw you, you were just a little shit. How tall are you now?"

"About six-five and completely fabulous, thank you."

"Too bad you can't play basketball," Rusty said, and I winced inside, but Mattie seemed unaffected.

"Oh, no, sweetheart," Mattie replied. "Those are not the kinds of balls I handle. Speaking of balls... this is my boyfriend Alejandro. Alejandro, this is Jake. We went to high school together." They shook hands, and while the three of them made small talk, I looked around for Siren. I couldn't figure out where she'd gone until she emerged from a bathroom across the Union and down the hall, having changed out of her vampire getup.

So, I was pretty floored when she walked up to us and Rusty said, "Hey, Siren."

"Heyyyyyyy... you ..."

"Jake," Rusty said.

"Jake! That's right. I couldn't remember your name out of context, you know?"

"Have you two met before?" I said. Because sometimes I'm slow like that.

"Yeah," Jake said. "At Bazongas."

"Jake comes in about once a week," Siren said. "Usually Thursday nights, right?"

"Yep," Rusty said, sticking his hands in his pockets. "That's payday."

"But..." she seemed to struggle with the words... "he's a great tipper, and... you're the one who helped out Jasmine that night that asshole grabbed her, right?"

"Sure did. That was Cliff. You gotta watch him. When he's drunk and in a bad mood, he can make some bad choices."

"Well, it was nice of you to pull him off of her."

"My mother raised me to be a gentleman."

"And it shows," she said, smiling. Only she said it in her sarcastic way. But you wouldn't know it was sarcastic if you didn't know Siren. "Can you excuse us for a second?" She grabbed my hand and pulled me off to the side.

"Hey, mama? I know you like this guy, but... I dunno. I think you can do better." My heart sank.

"Um... okay. Is he an asshole customer or something?"

"Oh, no, no, no. He always tips well, and he's polite. But he's there and not just for the booze. Like... he knows all of us by name."

I wasn't sure what she was getting at. "So... has he dated anyone there?"

"Well, no... but... he's definitely there for the atmosphere, if you know what I mean."

Just like all the pretty servers at Ricky's. Rusty knew every single one of them by name, and if I had to guess, he'd probably had sex with a fair number of them. "And... have you seen him lately?" I asked.

She thought for a second. "No. I guess I haven't. He hasn't been in for a few weeks now... probably about the time he started seeing you."

"I mean... I don't really care if he likes to go to Bazonga's," I said. I was surprised at what seemed like sexual judgment, coming from Siren of all people, and I didn't get it. "How's that any different than looking at porn?"

"Yeah, but these are real people... " She had this look on her face like she was frustrated she wasn't getting her point across.

"I mean, it's not like I'm gonna marry him. Why should I care if he looks at other girls?"

She looked surprised. "Are you sure you don't care? You're over at his house a lot."

"And you're with Jordan just as much." I couldn't figure out what she was getting at.

"Okay," she said, putting her hands up. "You're right. I'm sorry. You're a big girl. You can handle yourself."

"I mean... yeah, I think I can," I said. She was kinda pissing me off.

She hugged me. "I'm really sorry. I wasn't trying to judge. I just don't want to see you get your heart broken."

"Okay," I replied, wondering what had just happened.

"We're good?"

"Yeah, we're fine," I said. I glanced over at the boys, and Rusty caught my eye. He broke away and sort of moseyed my direction. "Should we get goin'? The band will probably get started soon." We were supposed to hang out at Ricky's.

"Yes, Alejandro and I need to get moving, too. We're going to see *Some Like it Hot* at the art-house theater downtown. Don't you girls do anything I wouldn't do!"

"Do you need a ride back to the dorm?" Rusty asked Siren. Always the gentleman.

"No, I'll hop a bus. Jordan and I are gonna stay in tonight. But you kids have fun! And use protection!" She used her stage voice and smiled at us, but it made me feel kinda ick to know she didn't really mean it.

Life went on like that for the next few weeks: school, homework, work, Rusty, repeat... and Siren and Mattie were caught up in their own lives, so I still wasn't seeing them a whole lot either. One Friday night, I was at Rusty's house, and instead of our usual fuck-and-go, he'd bought steaks and all the makings for salad. While he grilled the steaks, I made the salad, and the whole thing almost felt like we were a real couple. He even bought a halfway decent bottle of red wine. It was a beautiful spring evening. The temperature was perfect, until the sun began to go down, and the air became chilly. As the sun dipped behind the trees along the river, we started making out on the deck, hardcore. The first time we had sex that night, we didn't even make it to the bedroom; we had sex on the couch in the living room. Then we took a shower together and had mad-hot sex standing up in the shower. The third time we managed to make it to his bedroom. Afterward, we collapsed into each other on the bed. He held me next to his body so I could feel every hard muscle in his frame while he stroked my damp hair.

"I should get up and go before I fall asleep," I said.

"But I don't want you to go. I want you stay." He pressed himself into me and pulled me even closer. It felt so good... I didn't want me to leave, either. Dammit.

We cuddled all night—or at least most of the night—since Rusty had to be up at 5:30 a.m. to run the shop. It was the most wonderful night of all-the-feels I'd ever experienced in my life up until that point. Nobody had ever spooned me all night like that, and it was... intoxicating.

It was still dark out when he woke me with a goodbye kiss before going into work. "I'm gonna close the shop at noon today," he said. "Why don't you sleep in here and we can spend the day together?"

My first thought was that I needed to get up and get the hell out of there. On the other hand, it was Saturday, so no classes, and I was on the schedule to work Sunday afternoon.

"Is it that hard to decide whether or not you want to hang out with me?" Rusty said.

"No... but I'll need clean underwear, at least, so I might as well go home first."

"I already washed 'em. Put 'em in the washing machine when you fell asleep last night. They're in the dryer."

"You did not!"

"I did too. You can wear one of my t-shirts, and one of my ex-girlfriends left a pair of jeans here once. Pretty sure they'll fit you. They're on the chair over there."

I laughed. "You want me to wear one of your other girlfriends' jeans?"

"Ex-girlfriend. Like five years ago. If you want to go back to the dorm, that's fine. It's supposed to be a nice day today, and it would be really nice to come home and see someone besides Lugnut." He leaned down to kiss me, and we started making out. Then he pulled away abruptly. "Hell, I'll even take you to lunch at some annoying hipster café downtown, if you want."

Shit. I remembered I was supposed to hang out with Mattie and Siren while they filmed the last scene of Mattie's movie. But I wasn't in the scene... "Okay," I said. Lugnut jumped on the bed and licked my face with his big, warm tongue.

"See? Lugnut wants you to stay, too. I gotta get to work, but you go back to sleep," he leaned down, but once again, we couldn't stop kissing. Finally, he disengaged and stood up, shifting uncomfortably. "Damn. I think you started the launch sequence."

"How am I supposed to go back to sleep when my chassis needs servicing?" I said, giving him one of those fake sexy-girl pouts. Stupid, but it worked.

"Oh, Lord. Please don't start talking about cars. You are so sexy, and if you start talking about cars, I won't be able to leave. Just... hang on till I get back," and he rushed from the room.

"Okay, Rusty!" I called as he left the house. "I'll keep the motor running."

"Damn," he said, and I heard the front door click shut.

I fell back to sleep for another four hours. When I woke up, Lugnut was asleep next to me, snoring softly. I lay there for a while, petting Lugnut and looking over the room. It was in a medium-sort of state of messiness. Not too horrible, but not meticulous. Zach was meticulous. There were a couple of baskets of laundry sitting over in the corner. I wasn't sure if they were dirty or clean. The room smelled like dude, but in a good way... light sweat and cologne and deodorant. It was kind of sexy to wake up that way, in his bed, lounging in the smell of maleness. I was feeling really tingly and good until I remembered Siren's warning about him. I mean, I thought I was a decent judge of character, but... was I just blinded by the sex and the flattery? Was he a royal douche bag, and I couldn't see it?

Siren. Thinking about Siren made me remember Mattie's movie. I grabbed my phone and group texted them: Hey, guys. Rusty wants me to spend the afternoon with him. Did you still need me for the movie? And I felt a twinge of guilt for punking out on my friends for a dude. What the hell was happening to me?

Mattie responded: It's okay, sweetie. We won't need you today. Have fun!

I lay on the bed waiting for Siren to say something, but she didn't respond.

I pushed down my guilt and put my friends out of my mind. I had some time to kill before Rusty came back. There was a TV on the wall, but I didn't feel like watching it. I rolled over and studied his bookcase full of paperbacks. He had a lot of Stephen King, Piers Anthony and Clive Barker, and I noticed some of the other books we'd talked about on our first date. It was definitely the reading collection of a straight man.

After a while, I got up, retrieved my underwear from the dryer, my bra from the floor and began poking around in his room. I mean,

I'd spent quite a bit of time there recently, but since he was always with me, I never had a chance to really snoop. I opened all his dresser drawers but didn't find anything unusual... tube socks and a rainbow assortment of boxer briefs, shorts and a bunch of old t-shirts. I went to the closet to see what I'd find there... it was neater than I thought it would be. He had a collection of Hawaiian shirts, several pairs of jeans folded neatly over hangers, a couple pairs of khakis and two dress shirts. But this was apparently where he kept his good t-shirt collection, and it was impressive. He had at least twenty different KU t-shirts and about forty metal music ones. I flicked through them and picked out the most disgusting one I could find. It was a band called Vomit Rockit. The t-shirt featured a scary clown projectile-puking into a baby carriage. It was ridiculous. I grabbed it to wear. I wandered into the bathroom and laughed out loud when I saw my reflection. My hair was a rat's nest from all the sex, and my mascara had smudged. I took a shower, careful to scrub all the makeup off my face, and used lots of conditioner on my hair to finger-comb out the tangles.

When he came home, I was lying in the bed with damp hair spread out over the pillow, wearing nothing but his goofy t-shirt and my underwear. It worked.

"You look fantastic in my t-shirt," he said, taking his clothes off. He smelled lightly of gasoline and grease. "Just let me shower real quick." When he came back into the bedroom, he was already at full mast. I sat on the edge of the bed and attended to his erection for a bit until he lifted me up, placed me on the bed and went down on me. No guy had ever lifted me like that before, and even though it was kinda cheesy, I had to admit it was hot as fuck. We lay sweaty on the bed while he traced my stomach lightly with his fingers.

"You hungry?" he asked, after a while.

"Starving," I groaned.

"Well let's get dressed and get downtown. This would be a good time to get a table."

I laughed, and before he could get up, I took a photo of us lying in bed together. "What's that for?" he asked.

"Posterity," I said, checking the photo to make sure I didn't look like shit, but it was a cute photo, of both of us.

"Damn. I'm just another notch on your bedpost, ain't I?"

"Yep."

"How many notches you got?" he asked.

"How many notches you got?"

"A few," he said, shrugging.

"That's how many I got," I said.

We got up and dressed. The ex-girlfriend jeans fit me like a glove. They were cute, too, with strategic rips in all the right places.

"Damn," I said.

"Those work?"

"They're perfect."

"Yeah they are," he said, and he slapped me on the butt. "You should keep 'em. You should keep that t-shirt, too."

"Can I?"

"Hell yeah, you should. Did I mention you look smokin' hot in my t-shirt?" He put his arms around my waist and kissed me. God he was a good kisser. I melted.

"My t-shirt now," I reminded him.

"Sure is."

We took his pickup downtown and settled on gourmet burgers for lunch. We were both ravenous by the time we had food in front of us.

"Thank God the greens on this burger are seasonal," he said, taking a bite. "There's nothing worse than out-of-season greens on a burger." He sniffed one of the fries. "What kind of artisanal fries are these again?"

"Duck fat," I said, dipping one in garlic aioli. Delicious.

"Don't they have any ketchup in this communist burger joint? I ain't putting any mayonnaise on my fries."

I shoved a little cup at him. "Hand-crafted smoked paprika ketchup. It is dee-lish."

He snorted. "Heinz would be fine, thank you."

"At least your Kobe beef was raised locally."

"It better be, dammit. I like my burgers like I like my women.

Thick, juicy, and American," and he took a big bite of his burger.

I laughed. "You're a real patriot."

"I'm so American a bald eagle might fly out of my ass," he said, still chewing.

"That would be interesting." I lifted an eyebrow at him. He was clearly playing up the redneck as a defense mechanism for hanging out in a hipster burger joint. I looked him in the eye and said, "You're really funny, Rusty."

"So are you, College Girl," he grinned, returning my gaze. "I have to admit, this is one damn good burger."

"Told ya."

"Yep. For a fussy, pretentious, local, grass-fed, sustainable burger joint, this is pretty fuckin' good," he said, taking another bite.

I almost spit my organic soda across the table.

We spent the rest of the afternoon downtown. It was a beautiful March day, sunny, and the temperature had to be in the mid-fifties, at least. We browsed through a few shops and strolled through downtown, holding hands, until the shops began to close.

When we got back to his house, he pulled something out of his front pocket. "Here," he said, and he handed me a little white box. My blood froze. I didn't reach for it.

"What's this?" I asked.

"It's a just a little thing I found when you were trying on dresses," he said, offering it to me again. I took it, cautiously. I didn't know what to think. On the one hand, who doesn't like presents? On the other hand, if I opened that box and there was some kind of ring in it, I was going to throw up. But when I opened the box, there was a pendant inside—a small, gold and black scorpion encased in clear resin, in the shape of a teardrop, with a black silk cord attached—a real, preserved scorpion.

Rusty shrugged his shoulders. "It's not much, but I thought you might like it. What kinda scorpion is that, anyway?"

"I'm not sure," I said, studying it. "I don't know a whole lot about scorpions, truthfully."

"Some kinda college girl you are. Don't even know your scorpions."

"I'll have to look it up," I said, squinting at it, closely. The preservation was good. Really good. You could see every little hair. "This is beautiful, Jake. Thank you."

"You really like it?" he asked.

"Yeah." I said, putting it on. "I love it." Without thinking, I stood up on tiptoe and kissed him on the cheek. As soon as I did it, it felt wrong... too intimate.

He shoved his hands into his pockets. "Yeah, I guess you must. You never call me Jake," he said, giving me that smile of his that slayed me every time. He leaned over and kissed me on the forehead. "Why don't you stay again tonight?"

Feeling a sting of panic, I pulled back. "I can't," I said, my heart pounding.

"Why not?"

"I need to get back to the dorm." I didn't really, though.

"For what? It's Saturday night."

"I need to check on my bugs, and I have an English paper I should work on and a book for my Eastern Religions class I should be reading, and I have to work tomorrow, and Siren's probably wondering where the hell I am..."

"Okay." He gave me a funny smile. "I won't tie you up and keep you here, or anything." He shrugged. "I guess I have to get up in the morning, anyway."

"It's not that..."

"No, I get it," he said, running his hands up my shirt and deftly removing it over my head. "You're a strong"... he deftly unhooked my bra and had it off in a second... "independent woman." And then, of course, we were all over each other and proceeded to have maybe the best sex we'd ever had up until that point. It was stupid-good sex. Rusty was fun. He made me feel like I was the hottest chick on the planet. It wasn't that the sex itself was better, it was like... our chemistry was better. He smelled better. It was like being high. As addicting as it was, though, I was also feeling anxious about getting back to my actual life in college. Rusty was supposed to be my fuck buddy. Not my boyfriend. But this time when I left, instead of leaving quickly like I usually did, we lingered at the front door, making out. I could feel myself very much wanting to stay, and at the same time, very much wanting to get the hell out of there, delete his number from my phone and never come back. It was kind of awful.

Siren wasn't at the room when I got back, which bummed me out. All the lights were out, the room was cold and lonely, and I was restless, not knowing what to do with myself. I turned on several lights and flipped on the computer. The bugs seemed fine, but I fed everyone anyway, throwing out the food that had gotten old while I was gone and giving them new moisture cubes. I sent a text to Siren: *You working?* I waited a few minutes but she didn't reply, so I took a shower and changed into an old t-shirt and comfy shorts, and checked my phone again: *I'm closing tonight ugg*

Bazongas closed at midnight on Saturdays. That meant Siren wouldn't be back at the dorm until 1 a.m. at the earliest. I thought about texting Mattie to see what he was up to, but then I remembered he was probably with Alejandro, and I didn't want to bother them.

So there I was: all alone in the dorm on a Saturday night. I thought about wandering down the hall to see who else was in, but then I remembered the necklace Rusty had given me and sat down at the computer. After a few minutes of searching, I was pretty sure the scorpion inside was a Chinese Scorpion (Mesobuthus martensii). I also learned scorpions are served as street food in China and that the Chinese had been using scorpion venom in medicine for centuries. I wondered what scorpions tasted like... crunchy, I supposed. I held the necklace in my hand, peering at the perfect little arachnid wondering what it meant... as in, what it meant to Rusty. Was it an impulse buy? Or something more? It probably only cost a few bucks. He probably just bought it on a whim.

Since I was online, I decided to do a little research for a biology project, and then I watched one of my favorite old movies, Better off Dead, until I could barely keep my eyes open. It was one o'clock, and Siren still wasn't home. I turned everything off and went to bed, knowing she'd probably come in a few minutes and wake me up. My phone buzzed on the nightstand: *I relly loved spending today with you Collage girl,,,sleep tite!!!*

Oh jeez. I couldn't believe Rusty's timing. I didn't know if I could deal with it. I didn't respond. Instead I lay there, in the dark, determined to sleep, but not able to, my mind churning over Rusty. Part of me wished I had stayed at his house so we could watch some stupid movie and laugh together while he drank beer, and then have more stupid-good sex and fall asleep in each other's arms, while the other part of me knew I'd made the right decision to detach and come back to the dorm, even though I was bored and lonely.

I woke up late the next morning, and it looked like Siren hadn't come home. Worried, I checked my phone: *Spending nite w Jor didn't want to wake u*

I didn't see her before I left for work, and by the time I got back to the dorm after work, I could tell she'd been in the room because the stuff on her desk had been moved around, but there was no sign of her. My phone buzzed, but it wasn't Siren. It was Rusty: *Hey hot collage girl Im fixin to grile my famus burbon & pneaple ckn u shud come eat & after I will sex u up*

And how could I refuse an offer like that?

19

Spring Break Kansas

A t first I was annoyed when spring break rolled around, because I thought I was going to have to fly home again, but then I got a text from Dad: *Hi, Pumpkin! I was thinking that instead of you coming home for spring break, maybe Cade and I could fly out & meet you at Grandma & Grandpa's. Unless you're planning on doing Padre Island?*

Ha! Dad knew me better than that. There were several girls on our floor who were planning on going to Daytona Beach, but the thought of a week of drinking, hangovers and sunburns did not sound like a vacation to me. A week at the grandparents' sounded perfect, especially since Siren was going home to visit her mom, and Mattie had to stay in Lawrence to help his parents with the restaurant.

OMG that would be amazing! Love you!

Great! We'll plan on it, then!

I wasn't surprised that Victoria wasn't coming. She hated Grandma and Grandpa's farm. Cade and I loved it.

It was a five hour drive out to the central part of Kansas where the farm was, kinda-sorta near a town called 'Holcomb' with a silent B—where Truman Capote's In Cold Blood took place—but really out in the middle of nowhere. Nothing like living on the east coast, where you could pass through three states in less than an hour. My drive took me past Topeka, then by this truck-stoppy town called Junction City, then a town called Salina and into a kind of cool geographical area known as the Smoky Hills. The Smoky Hills were these gentle, kelly green rolling hills, against a brilliant blue sky that went on for miles. Then, all of a sudden, jutting up out of the picture-book hills, were these gigantic white windmills, like enormous flowers piercing the sky, and it was trippy. They were bigger than I would ever have imagined, and there were hundreds of them, with blades the size of the wings of a 747 slicing through the air. Eventually, the wind farms stopped, and I went through a few more towns, but the farther west I got, the farther apart and the smaller the towns got. Also the farther west I went, the flatter and flatter the land got, until it was like my Corolla was in the middle of a flat, green dinner plate, and the sky was a blue dome above me, dotted here and there with cotton-like clouds.

I finally pulled into Grandma and Grandpa's driveway that evening. Dad and Cade were already there. They had flown into Wichita, then rented a car and driven the rest of the way, which was still about a three-and-a-half hour drive.

The first thing I noticed when I turned off the car and got out was the noise. There was zero urban noise. None. Just the sound of the breeze in the grass and trees, and frogs and toads and bugs singing like mad. It was a background cacophony of chirping and buzzing and whirring and cheeping coming from the creek down at the bottom of the hill behind my grandparents' house, a sound you almost never hear in a city. The air smelled of sweet hay with a touch of manure in the distance. It was like I'd stepped into a whole different universe.

Grandma and Grandpa still had a working farm with cattle, chickens and wheat. They took care of the chickens and the cattle, and they also grew a huge vegetable garden. When Grandpa "retired," he leased out the wheat fields to another farmer, so someone else could take care of the planting and harvest. But they still worked their butts off every day, and they were in their seventies. I hoped to be like them when I got to be their age.

As I walked through the big yard up to the farmhouse door, I knew I'd made the right decision for spring break because Grandma and Grandpa spoiled the shit out of Cade and me... like, we couldn't stop them if we tried. I could smell Grandma's home cooking wafting out the screen door, and I didn't bother to knock. I just walked in. Everyone was there, like I knew they would be, hanging around the kitchen table: Dad, Cade, and Grandma and Grandpa. I was surprised Grandma was frying chicken that late in the day.

As soon as I was through the door, Grandpa burst into song: "There she is, Miss America!" like he always did. Apparently it was the corny song from the old Miss America pageants. He was always singing corny songs like that. He was skinny and rugged, tan, and wearing bib overalls. His head was bare, since he was indoors, but around the farm he wore a ball cap bearing the logo of the local co-op. When he went into town, he wore a straw hat.

Grandma dropped the tongs she was using to turn the chicken in a cast-iron skillet, wiped her hands on her apron and grabbed me in a death hug. It was cute; even though she worked from sunup to sundown, being hugged by my grandma was kind of like being attacked by a marshmallow.

"Oh, my goodness it has been far too long since I've seen you!" She engulfed me in her softness, the familiar scent of Grandma and rose-scented lotion slamming me with her love.

"Hi, Grandma," I said, hugging her back and feeling it. My favorite hugs in the whole world came from Grandma. When she let go of me, I pulled the KU t-shirt I'd bought to give to Cade out of my purse and threw it at him. It hit him in the face and fell in his lap. "You're welcome," I said, sitting down at the kitchen table. There I was, with my favorite people, at my favorite dining room table, the smell of Grandma's fried chicken sending me into emotion overload.

It was awesome.

Grandma was wearing denim capris with an elastic waist, a blue KU t-shirt, a KU visor and Jayhawk earrings because it was NCAA tournament time. She put her hands on my shoulders. "I hope to see you more, now that you're in Kansas. Your father says you're thinking of moving to Lawrence."

"Wow. Word travels fast!" I said, glancing over at Dad. He looked comfortable, lounging at the kitchen table, reading the local newspaper, without Victoria there to pick at him.

"How was the drive?" he asked.

"Long," I answered. "But great!"

"I bet you're hungry," Grandma said. "Sit down, and I'll get you a nice glass of lemonade. Supper is almost ready."

Supper was fried chicken, mashed potatoes and gravy, coleslaw and Grandma's home-canned pickled beets and sauerkraut, along with her homemade dinner rolls, fresh butter and plum jam. I liked to mix the saurkraut into my mashed potatoes. She and Grandpa grew the cabbage themselves, and she fermented the stuff in a crock in her kitchen in the summertime.

"This is a bigger supper than you usually feed us, Mom," Dad commented.

"Well, I knew you all would be extra hungry after all that traveling," she said, piling the table with food. "We'll get back on our regular meal schedule tomorrow."

After supper, we played penny-ante poker at the kitchen table until eleven o'clock. Cade and Grandpa both made out like bandits. My and Cade's bedrooms were upstairs, the rooms Dad and Uncle Bob had as kids. Both bedrooms still had the funky wallpaper from the 1970s. Dad's old room—the one I was in—had this space-themed paper with rockets and moons and planets. The wallpaper in Uncle Bob's room featured the logos of professional baseball teams.

There was a spare bedroom, too, where Dad could've slept, but he always chose to sleep on the chaise lounge on the enclosed porch out back. He said he slept better out there, in the country air. "It's supposed to get down to near-freezing overnight," Grandma scolded him.

"Great!" Dad said, grinning. "That's even better."

Grandma dismissed him with a wave of her hand. "You're bananas, just like your brother," she said. But she went and got him an extra blanket.

I was dead asleep when, around three o'clock in the morning, there was an insanely loud BOOM! that woke me. I sat up, my heart thumping. It was a thunderstorm, and I knew that meant Dad would have to move his pillow and blanket inside to the living room couch. The rain sounded like fat pebbles pelting the side of the house. Lightning lit up the room repeatedly, flashing like a strobe. The storm was crazy-loud for an hour or so—which meant it was right on top of us—and then the worst of it passed as the storm drifted on, the lightning getting dimmer, the thunder quieter. The rain changed from loud pebbles to a gentle patter, and I must've drifted off to sleep.

When I woke the next morning and looked outside, the sun was shining, but everything outside was soaked. I could smell coffee and bacon wafting up from downstairs, and heard the of spoons in coffee cups. A mourning dove cooed outside my window. It was still early—seven thirty—but the room was bright with sunshine, and I was wide awake, so I went down to breakfast. Along with coffee, milk and bacon, there was a choice of apricot, cherry or poppyseed kolaches (pronounced co-la-chees), the Czech version of a Danish, that Grandma had baked.

"Luckily, there was some thunder and lightning off in the distance that woke me up before the rain started," Dad was saying, as I sat down at the kitchen table. "Otherwise, I would've been soaked. That was one hell of a thunder-boomer." He took a bite of poppyseed kolache and chewed. I grabbed the last apricot kolache.

Grandpa chuckled and took a big swig of his coffee. "Rained like a cow pissing on a rock, didn't it?" and he winked at Cade. Cade laughed.

"Joseph!" Grandma yelled from the kitchen.

"Yes, Irene?"

"Do you really think it's necessary to share your dirty manure mouth with your grandkids?"

Cade fell out of his chair. "Manure mouth!" he laughed. "That's awesome!"

Dad shook his head at Cade and me. "I can't believe that's the same woman who used to tell Bob and I we were worthless as tits on a boar. She acts like you two are made of glass."

"I only said that when you were being real turds," Grandma yelled from the kitchen.

"Anyway," Grandpa cut in, "With that nice rain, the crick should be nice and full for you kids to play in today." He finished his coffee and stood up, putting on his baseball cap.

Cade and I looked at each other. "Yay!" I said. So funny that Grandpa talked about us like we were still little... truth was, though, we probably would play in the creek, because we always did.

"I'm going with you to feed the cattle and chickens this morning,"

Cade said, shoving the last couple bites of his food into his mouth and washing it down with his milk.

"That sounds wonderful," Grandpa said. He ruffled Cade's hair.

After breakfast, the men went off to feed the cattle and chickens while I stayed to help Grandma wash up. I'd asked her once, when I was little, why they didn't have a dishwasher. "Oh, I guess I'm just old fashioned," she said. "A dishwasher wouldn't really fit in with our décor. Besides, I think it's more fun to chat while washing the dishes. It's not the same loading and unloading a dishwasher." The entire kitchen—the table, the stove, the fridge, everything—was all rounded and streamlined and straight out of the 1950s. Grandpa had updated the fridge to run on modern coolant, and whenever anything around the house broke down, he fixed it himself. The abundance of nostalgia was intensely quaint. I loved that old farm house with all my heart. It had two stories, plus a cellar and an attic. It had all its old woodwork and hardware, and Grandma and Grandpa had filled it with antiques they used every day... the furniture, the pots and pans and dishes... everything. Even the radio in the kitchen was from the Sixties. The only modern things in the house were the computer and the television.

Grandma always washed, and I always dried and put away. The clean smell of warm dishwashing liquid filled the kitchen, pushing away the scents of coffee and bacon.

"I want to hear all about school!" she said, dishes clonking in the water. "Are you enjoying your classes?" She handed me a plate. I dried it with a tea towel and put it back in the cabinet.

"Yeah, I am."

We talked about the classes I was taking at the moment and how they differed from when she went to college. Then she hit me with: "Are you seeing anyone special?" and she handed me a warm, wet coffee cup.

"Oh... there is this guy I've been seeing recently."

"Your father told me you'd broken up with Zachary."

"Yeah. I didn't think it was a good idea to try to keep up a long-distance relationship."

"I think you made the right decision. Especially if you're moving to Kansas." She rinsed the pot she'd been scrubbing and handed it to me.

"Thanks. Me too," I said, drying it and placing it in the dish drainer.

"So who's the new fella?" she asked.

"Oh... he's just a guy..." I said, shrugging.

"Your age? Or older?"

"A little older."

"What's he studying?"

Ugh. The question I'd been dreading. "Nothing, actually. He owns his own business."

"He's graduated?" she looked surprised.

"No... he inherited the family business."

"Which is?"

"Fixing cars," I said, looking her in the eye.

She raised her eyebrows. "I see. A blue-collar man. Well... I have to say I do understand the appeal." That made me laugh.

"Have you told your mother?" she asked, handing me a plate.

"No. I haven't said anything to Mom and Dad... or Cade. I mean... I don't even know how long this is going to last, you know?"

"Understood. I'll keep it to myself."

"Thanks, Grandma."

We were quiet for a minute, and all of a sudden she said, "You are using birth control, aren't you? Because if you aren't, I'm going to give you what-for. There's no reason to risk getting pregnant, especially while you're in school."

The question shocked me so much I almost dropped the dish I was drying. I mean, Grandma and I were pretty relaxed around each other, but we'd never talked about sex.

"Yeah! Yes! Of course," I said.

"Condoms and the pill?" she asked.

"Umm... yeah." Lie.

"Every time?"

"Yes. Jeez, Grandma!"

"Well if you ever need any help with anything... anything at all. You call me."

"Okay, thanks."

"I mean that, now. Anything," she gave me a pointed look. "I won't even tell your parents if you don't want me to."

Wow. Was my grandmother offering to pay for an abortion if I ever needed one? "Thanks, Grandma. That means a lot."

She nodded. "My friend Celia got pregnant our junior year of college. She left and never did finish her degree. She had five kids and something like eighteen grandkids with all the marriages and divorces and what do you call them? Baby daddies. But that's how it was back then. They talked about girls going to college to get their M-R-S degree."

"MRS? What's that?"

"Missus," Grandma said. "It used to be that girls went to college to marry a college man, and they'd drop out before graduation."

"That sucks," I said.

She nodded. "Tell me about it. But it happened all the time. Thank goodness it's different for you girls now."

"So you didn't want to get your MRS degree when you met Grandpa?"

She chuckled. "Oh, heavens no. I did not want to marry a farmer."

"What? Why? You grew up on a farm."

"Which is exactly why I did not want to marry a farmer. Up before dawn, endless work, gardening and canning and sick animals and equipment repairs... I thought I wanted a city life. But your grandfather had no choice when it came to being a farmer. It's in his blood. Can you imagine him behind a desk? It would kill him. And anyway, I'm glad I ended up on the farm. It's where I was born, and it's where I'll die."

"So, what happened? Why did you end up marrying him?"

"Oh... the usual. Your grandfather was persistent, and eventually he wore me down."

I laughed. "You make it all sound so romantic."

"Oh, I'm teasing. I did like your grandfather, very much, from the very first date. I just didn't want to get married. My parents were adamant that I finish my degree. And your grandfather was fine with us waiting until we had both graduated before we got married, which was nice. "

"Grandpa sounds like a keeper," I said.

"He is. That's the kind you have to look out for... the keepers. Don't settle for anything less."

I woke up late every morning, and every morning Grandma left coffee for me in the old percolator coffee pot on the stove. She'd also leave a note letting Cade and me know what that morning's breakfast was and where we could locate it in the kitchen. Bagels on the counter, cream cheese & plum jam in the fridge. Be back for dinner! (heart) -Grandma

Because most mornings, Grandma wasn't home. She either volunteered at the food pantry in town, or had a meeting of the League of Women Voters, or attended her "coffee klatch" with friends at the local café. On weekends, when it wasn't the dead of winter, she helped her best friend Barb run a booth at the Farmer's Market. They called themselves the Fresh Market Grannies. Oh, she was also in a senior bowling league, the Silver Streaks. She still canned food in the summer, too: tomatoes and green beans and pickles in addition to jams. Grandma was kind of a badass. I loved her.

Most mornings, like this one, I was the last to get up, and usually the house was empty. I popped a bagel in the antique toaster and turned the gas burner on under the coffee percolator. Once the bagel was toasted, I spread a thick layer of cream cheese on it, with a thin layer of the plum jam on top. I knew when Grandma said she'd be back for "dinner" that meant she'd be back by ten to start cooking, so that dinner was ready at noon. Grandma and Grandpa always had their biggest meal at noontime, which they called dinner, while supper was usually a light meal of soup or sandwiches and veggies from the garden. Dad said that was how farm life was, because hard working farm people needed to refuel at lunchtime.

Cade and I spent a lot of time wandering the property, hanging out with the chickens, down at the creek catching crawdads, or exploring the loft in the barn. I hadn't spent so much time with Cade since I was maybe thirteen years old and he was ten. I guess once I was in middle school I got sucked into my social life with my friends, and he had his friends, and we definitely weren't as close now as when we were younger.

"So, how's school?" I asked him one afternoon when we were ankle-deep in the creek. The sun was shining, the temperature was in the mid-seventies, there was a light breeze, and the sky was a brilliant blue, dotted with a few fluffy white clouds. The day before it had been thirty degrees and cloudy, and it had even snowed a little. But that was Kansas for you, and I was glad I'd been smart enough to pack a variety of both spring- and winter-appropriate clothes. I picked up a crawdad, a big gray and blue one, behind his pincers like Dad had taught me, so it couldn't pinch me. It squirmed and strained, but couldn't reach my skin. I watched it wiggle for a minute and then set it back down in the water. It scooted backward and hid under a rock.

We call them crayfish in Maryland, but the Kansas part of my family had taught me the Midwestern vernacular. When I was little, Dad had also taught me that they were called "mudbugs" in the South, and being that crawdads are arthropods (invertebrates with exoskeletons) just like insects, they really were kind of like big, freshwater bugs.

Cade seemed to be picking up rocks, examining them briefly and tossing them back in the creek. He shrugged but didn't answer my question. That seemed odd. Normally I didn't have any trouble getting him to talk.

"What's going on, dude?" I pressed.

He threw a pebble downstream. "Nothing..." pause. "Dumb shit, I guess."

"Dumb shit as in, like, somebody is bullying you? Or dumb shit as in your friends are annoying? Or is the dumb shit a girl?"

He smiled an odd smile and chucked another rock downstream, this time hard. "It's kind of all three, actually."

"Oh my God. What are you not telling me? Do you have a girlfriend?"

"Okay, so, you know my stupid friend Josh, right?

"Your best friend in the whole world since forever? Of course."

"So he was dating this girl at school—her name is Forest—but I liked Forest, too, and after being his girlfriend for a few weeks, I kinda convinced her she should be my girlfriend instead."

"Cade!" I was shocked he would do that to Josh.

"I know. It was wrong. But... Forest is so... she's so smart, and she's funny, and she's awesome, and Josh is... kind of an idiot." Again, I was shocked. To see Cade have those kinds of feelings for a girl, over his own best friend... I didn't think he was capable of those kinds of emotions.

"Well, yeah, I mean, Josh is kind of an idiot. But he's your idiot. He's your best bud. Don't guys have like a code against stealing each other's girlfriends?"

"Yeah, I guess so. And I guess I fucked up and broke the code."

"What are you gonna do?"

He threw a bigger rock this time, one he had to heave with both hands. The splash was huge.

"Don't do that," I said. "You're scaring off all the crawdads."

"Sorry. I don't know. I mean... I really like Forest. And lately I've been thinking that maybe I'm outgrowing Josh. I don't see us having much in common in the next few years."

"Wait, what? You two were like best friends back at Christmas."

"Yeah, but he's been getting on my nerves for a long time. I'm not as interested in farts and monster trucks anymore, you know? Forest is into Monty Python. And Simon Pegg and Nick Frost movies. And D&D."

"She's a nerd, huh? Isn't Josh into that stuff, too?"

"Yeah, but he isn't good at it. He sucks at D&D and gets on everyone's nerves when we get together to play. And now, of course, our whole D&D group is super awkward because of the thing with me and Forest."

"Wait, he still comes to your D&D games?"

"Yeah."

"Are you talking to him otherwise?" My feet were numb in the cold water and starting to turn a little blue, but I was trying to ignore it.

He tossed a pebble. "Not really."

"Yikes."

"Tell me about it. We even had a fight. Like a fistfight." He chucked another rock, and it splashed downstream.

"A fistfight?"

"Yeah."

"At school?"

He kept throwing rocks. "Yep."

"Did you get caught?"

"Oh yeah. It was right in the middle of the gym at lunchtime. Everybody saw it. Zinkerman and Doddy broke it up."

"The principal?"

He nodded. "And Coach Doddy. He pulled Josh off me."

"Jesus. Then what?"

"Then... I got suspended for two days. So did Josh."

Amazing. The Charvat children were not troublemakers.

"Do Mom and Dad know?" I asked, trying to envision the brawl.

"Dad does." Throw. Splash.

"Victoria doesn't?"

Cade looked at me and grinned. "Dad didn't think it would be such a good idea."

"So how did you pull that off?"

"Dad told her he wanted to drive me to school those two days, and instead of driving me to school, we went into DC and messed around."

"Dad took off work?"

"Yeah. It was pretty cool. We went to the Air and Space Museum one day."

"So," I said, grabbing for a crawdad. It was small and black. "Obviously the making out with Forest must be worth it." Cade blushed and went quiet. I splashed him in the face. "You little pervert!" I teased.

"Shut up," he said, splashing me back. The next thing I knew, we were in a splash fight, screaming and laughing and flinging water like maniacs. Eventually we wandered back up to the house and sat down in a couple of porch chairs, so as not to walk wet through the house. We sat there together, dripping, chatting while the breeze blew and the sun shone on us and the cattle moooed in the distance. Dad came out onto the porch, the farmhouse screen door banging shut behind him.

"What have you maniacs been doing?" he asked, and Cade and I almost fell out of our chairs, laughing. It wasn't funny, but it was, because siblings.

Spring break fell right during the NCAA Men's Basketball tournament, which meant that nearly every night, and several afternoons, we watched basketball games. Grandma and Grandpa were what Kansans call "a house divided"—Grandpa had attended K-State, earned an agricultural degree, and was a huge K-State fan. Grandma had studied social welfare at KU. They met at a party at Grandpa's frat after a basketball game. They were so freaking cute.

This year, both KU and K-State had made it into the NCAA tournament, so there were several games for us to watch. Every day, Grandma, Dad and I wore our crimson and blue KU shirts, while Grandpa and Cade wore K-State purple and white. Grandma made popcorn for the games, and we cheered and screamed until we were hoarse. Even though I didn't really know what was going on, it was fun.

"C'mon boys!" Grandma would yell and clap. "Let's move those cabooses! Rock Chalk!"

"Cade, grandson of mine?" Grandpa said.

"Yeah Grandpa?"

"What do you call a KU graduate with half a brain?"

"I dunno, Grandpa. What do you call a KU graduate with half a brain?"

"Gifted!" he said, and Cade fell off the couch and onto the floor, laughing, because it was a thing they did.

"Very funny," Dad said.

Grandpa waved a hand in my direction. "Not my brilliant granddaughter, of course. However," he said, craning his neck around the edge of his recliner to look at me, "K-State has one hell of an entomology program. You could transfer any time."

"I'll think about it, Grandpa!" I had to yell over the KU fight song blasting out of the television.

"Don't listen to him, Kymer," Grandma said, waving her hand dismissively in his direction. "He forgot to take his medication this morning."

KU won, of course. I mean, it was close, but generally, in basketball, KU kicked K-State's ass. When football season came, though, K-State almost always handed our asses right back to us.

"We were robbed!" Grandpa said.

"Robbed, my eye!" said Grandma, gathering up popcorn bowls. "We trounced you fair and square."

Grandpa winked at me. "I think those referees need laser surgery on their eyeballs. Maybe their brains, too."

All that week, Rusty and I texted back and forth. Mostly goofy sex texts.

I wish I cuold help you lube up your chassey

I'm not familiar with that technique, but it sounds effective

Babe ,,, would I steer u wrong

But after a few days, he got a little more personal.

wish I could visit u out their ,,, I love farms,,, and old people

Oh, Christ. He was talking about meeting my family. Still, the thought of seeing Rusty do actual farm stuff at my grandparents' farm seemed... kinda hot. I'd always thought Grandpa was a little disappointed that Dad went into computers and not farming. But Rusty... I could see him out here, easily. Getting up at the ass-crack of dawn to feed the chickens and muck out the barn and throw a few hay bales... with no shirt on... till he was sweaty. Sigh. Plus he'd be able to fix all the farm equipment.

The thought was so sexually intoxicating I thought my lady parts might explode.

What are you gonna do to me when I get back? I typed, hoping to get the conversation off my family.

What ever u want ,,, for as long as u say

Promise?

promise

Sigh.

I'd brought my last empty terrarium with me on spring break, knowing it'd be easy to find an insect to put in it, even though it was still early spring. The trick was going to be choosing one.

On our last full day at the farm, I was tromping through a grove of trees near the creek, and found a Mourning Cloak butterfly (*Nymphalis antiopa*) resting on a hackberry tree, soaking up a beam of sun cutting through the branches. He was quite handsome, his velvety, chocolate wings with shining blue spots spread out flat to absorb as much solar energy as possible. He must've overwintered here in the grove, just waiting for the temperatures to rise. He was perfect, and very docile, since it wasn't very warm out. Siren certainly couldn't complain he was creepy. I decided to call him Sidney, like the actor Sidney Poitier. I thought Mattie would like that.

The next morning, which was a Sunday, we all left the farm early, right after breakfast. Dad and Cade had their plane to catch, and I had a long drive back to the dorm.

"Drive safe," Dad said, hugging me.

"See ya, sis-turd," Cade said. I grabbed him and hugged his skinny frame before he could get away.

The whole goodbye was kinda hard. So many feels. Grandma dabbed the corners of her eyes with a white handkerchief embroidered with violets. "It was such a pleasure to have you for a whole week," she said, giving me one of her patented smother-hugs. "I am so proud of the smart young woman you've become. I love you sooo much!"

"I love you, too," I said, returning her hug.

"I'll be texting you," she said.

"I look forward to it!"

"You take care of yourself," Grandpa said, hugging me. "Don't let those KU boys get too fresh." Oh, Grandpa. If you only knew.

"I won't."

It was a long drive back, but I blasted Eighties synth pop on the drive back to stay awake, and when I got to Lawrence, I took the I-70 exit and headed straight for Rusty's place.

He kept his promise.

20

It's Trich-y

About the time I hooked up with Rusty, I became highly aware of the fact that I was getting close to running out of birth control pills. Like, my prescription was about to expire, and I was going to have to get a gyno exam in order to secure a new one. Full disclosure: up to that point, I had never had one. A pap smear, I mean. Victoria took me to the doctor to go on the pill for my heavy periods and killer cramps when I was fourteen, and since I wasn't sexually active yet, I didn't have to have a pap. Fast-forward a couple years, and I had sex for the first time, but not with Zach. His name was Alex, a friend of mine who was a year ahead of me in high school. He was a super sweet guy who was anxious about not losing his virginity, so we took each other's, just because. Then we became fuck buddies, but we didn't tell anyone. That went on for about four months until Zach and I started making sexy faces at each other and Alex started dating Sophie the sophomore, so it all worked out in the end. Alex and I were still friends, though we didn't chat on the regular anymore. He was studying environmental engineering at Seattle University.

I was online, trying to figure out how to choose a local doctor and hoping Victoria wouldn't fight me about using their insurance to pay for it. Meanwhile, Siren was singing. "Tell me more, tell me more/ Like does he have a car? Uh-huh, uh-huh, uh-huh..." because she was practicing to audition for a production of Grease. After she'd finished the song for a third time, she asked, "What are you working on?"

"I'm trying to find a doctor," I said.

"Why?"

"I need my birth control prescription renewed," I said, putting my left hand under my chin while mousing with my right.

"Go to Watkins Health Center," she said. "They'll do an exam for free and give you a crazy-cheap birth control prescription. If you have a uterus, they practically throw the birth control pills at you when you walk in the door." She threw her arms out wide. "Look at me, I'm Sandra Dee," she sang, "lousy with virginity/won't go to bed/ Till I'm legally wed/I can't, I'm Sandra Dee!"

I have to admit I was skeptical about visiting Watkins, mostly because Mother Victoria had already poisoned my mind. "Now if you need to see a doctor while you're there, whatever you do, find a private doctor and don't visit the campus hospital," she'd told me. "Campus hospitals are dirty and crowded." Sometimes I still had this bad habit of believing what Victoria told me at face value because she was my mother, even though experience often proved her wrong. Besides, if I made an appointment with a doctor off campus, my parents would see everything on the insurance bill. Sure, Victoria already knew I was on birth control pills, but this way I could pay the bill myself and, more importantly, keep my own personal health care to myself, and that definitely appealed to me.

Watkins was busy with students, and I was surprised I didn't have to wait long before I was called back for my appointment. The clinic wasn't dirty, at all. It was actually pretty nice. So much for Victoria's prejudices.

The appointment was pretty straightforward. Not fun, but not horrible, either. A nurse led me to an examining room and instructed me to take my clothes off and put on the hospital gown she'd handed me so that it opened at the front. Another nurse practitioner came in to do the exam, and she instructed me to lie down on the examining table. "Scooch your bottom to the edge of the examining table. A little bit more... feet in the stirrups. There you go." She was a tiny, brusque woman with an Indian accent and her shiny black hair put up in a businesslike bun. She did a quick feel-up for lumps in my boobs, and then the speculum and pap smear, which was tolerable. While she was doing the exam, she asked me about former sex partners. (Three, all male, vaginal and oral sex, no anal.) "And of course, we're using condoms, aren't we?" she asked, and I hesitated. "We are using condoms, yes?" she repeated. "Because while the pill is an excellent form of birth control, it doesn't prevent sexually transmitted infections."

"Of course we are," I lied. We had used condoms, for like the first week we were having sex. And then... we didn't. One night, he didn't put one on, and I thought about saying something, but I didn't, and then after that there didn't seem to be any point.

"You're sure," she said, only it was more of a statement than a question, really.

"Um... well, mostly."

The nurse sighed. "Mostly does not cut it. Especially if you don't know your partner's sexual history. I'm sure you are aware of the range of sexually transmitted infections out there, and that some are incurable and can cause health complications."

"Yeah," I said. I felt so immature.

"You can sit up now," she said. I sat there on the examining table in the stupid gown while she gave me a talking-to and typed up all my medical deets. "Use condoms. Every time. And remember: When it comes to STIs, generally men are givers and women are receivers. It's much easier for women to contract sexually transmitted infections than for men. Often men act as carriers and don't develop symptoms. So a lot of the time, they're out there running around with stuff they don't even know they have. I'm going to order an STI screen in addition to your pap smear." Then she handed me a cup to pee in. "You'll need to leave a sample in here and then head over to the lab to have your blood drawn for the HIV, syphilis and hepatitis tests. We'll do the full STI and pregnancy screen and call you in a day or two with the results."

It kinda freaked me out, because I'd never been screened for STIs before. I had bought a pregnancy test once, after I realized I'd forgotten to take my birth control pills for a couple of days in high school. (It was during finals, though, and I'd been crazy busy.) When I got back to our room after the appointment, Siren asked me how it went, so I told her.

"You've had three sex partners and you've never been tested to see if you're clean?" she said. She looked at me like I was the stupidest person ever, and I felt like a complete idiot. "That's wild, Kymer. It doesn't seem like you at all."

"Well, how often do you get tested?" I asked, feeling defensive.

"Yearly, at minimum, and more often if I'm, you know, seeing more than one guy."

"You mean fucking," I said, dryly. It was mean. I don't know why I said it.

She gave me a look. "Of course I mean fucking. I'm telling you, this is not something you want to mess around with. Do you even know how rampant herpes and genital warts are? "

"I know."

"And Chlamydia! Chlamydia is everywhere these days."

"I know," I said, almost feeling like I was talking to Victoria. I wanted to put it all behind me and move on. They'd call me in a few days and tell me my tests were negative, and that would be that. No bigs.

21

Rock Chalk Floracus

The following day, Professor Berg called to me as I was leaving her class.

"Miss Charvat! Could I have a moment of your time, please?"

"Sure." I broke away from the crowd flowing out the auditorium doors.

"I know it's taken some time, but I have some news for you." I searched her face for a clue, but all I saw was Professor Berg's trademark neutrality. "I've been working very closely with my colleagues in the biology department, as well as the art department, and the history department. And at this point..." her pause seemed to take forever, "we are positive that Flora's diary is genuine." And she smiled.

"That's... that's amazing."

"It really is," she said, nodding.

"So... how did you do it? How did you all decide it's real?"

"Well, it's somewhat complicated, because it took all of us to make sure. The historians authenticated the paper and the leather cover, and they determined the handwriting inside is consistent with handwriting in that time period. The English department got involved, to confirm that the language, the spelling and sentence structure is all consistent with the time period as well. And of course we entomologists looked it over frontwards and backwards. But I suppose you could say the real break in the case, so to speak, was when Professor Lilliac—his specialty is botany—was looking over the diary. When Flora said she found the bee on the lip of a lady's slipper, you and I assumed that meant a shoe. But after studying Flora's drawings, Dr. Lilliac is confident the 'lady's slipper' Flora mentioned is a type of prairie orchid. Now prairie orchids are terribly endangered, and this very well could have been a species of flower that went extinct. Which means the bee is likely extinct as well."

What she said made perfect sense, but it super bummed me out. Extinction made me sad.

"I would like it if you and I could work on this problem next school year," she was saying. "I think we can probably prove within a reasonable doubt that this is an extinct species of bee. But as it stands now, there seems to be nothing in the current literature and databases of collections to suggest that this is a named species of bee. As the discoverer, it would've been nice if Flora had been able to name it, but of course it doesn't look as though that happened." She smiled again. "What it does mean, though, is that you get to name it."

"Me?"

She shrugged her shoulders. "You are the discoverer. And the tradition is that the discoverer of a new species has the honor of naming it."

"Well, I mean, I'd want to name it after Flora. That's only fair." As I said it, it dawned on me that maybe that was why the ghosts had contacted me. Because Flora's bee had been forgotten, and they wanted to set the record straight.

"I think that would be lovely," Professor Berg said. "You think about it and get back with me. We're going to have to have the name in order to submit our scientific papers."

"Scientific papers?"

"Of course. You've discovered a new species of insect. Or perhaps more accurately, a forgotten one. Regardless, we're going to have to write up the entire account and submit it to all the relevant scientific journals. It'll be a great learning experience for you." She smiled at me, adjusting her glasses. "Scientists have to know how to publish. You know what they say: publish or perish."

Wait a second... was Professor Berg calling me a scientist? It kinda felt like it, and it was weird. Weird but also fantastic.

I didn't even get twenty-four hours to be happy about it, because the next morning, Watkins called with the results of my STI test, and the news was not what I expected. In fact, it sucked. I had trichomoniasis. Tricho-fucking-moniasis. Trich! Me! I didn't have any symptoms, and the antibiotics were cheap, thank God, because there was no way I was going to charge them to my parents' insurance. I was so... humiliated, angry, ashamed... everything, that when I got off the phone I broke down and cried. I didn't even go to class that day. Siren didn't have to work, and she skipped her classes to sit with me, rubbing my back and braiding my hair.

"Kymer, this could be so much worse. It's a few antibiotics, and it'll be like it never happened. You'll be more careful in the future." What she said made logical sense, and usually logic makes me happy, but this time it didn't.

After blubbering for over an hour, I finally got to the point where I felt a little better. I got up to look at my face in the dresser mirror, and I laughed because it was all pink and blotchy, and my eyelids were almost swollen shut. Then I remembered what the nurse on the phone had said: "We strongly suggest that you inform all your previous sexual partners, so that they can be treated as well."

"Shit," I said. "I still have to tell Rusty." But it wasn't Rusty I was worried about. It was Zach. Did I have to tell him? I was pretty sure I didn't get trich from him, but it would be irresponsible—unethical—to not tell him. Then I remembered Chloe. What if Zach and I had both gotten it from Chloe? I had to tell him. He needed to know. But what if they both ended up being negative? Then all our friends in Maryland would know I had run off to Kansas and gotten an STI. How embarrassing would that be? I burst into tears again.

"Oh, mama," Siren said, "I thought we had gotten you through this a little," and she rubbed my shoulders.

"I'm sorry," I sobbed. "I feel so stupid."

"Oh my God, don't. It can happen to anybody."

"Has it ever happened to you?"

"Well... no... But that's only because I've watched it happen to my mother so many times that I'm super careful. I either use condoms or make a guy show me his papers from the health department."

"You're kidding," I said, blowing my nose.

"I am so not. My mother has had so much VD. Including herpes. Thankfully never HIV. And thank God for the local health clinic."

I couldn't help it. Even though I had just been bawling my eyes out, I giggled.

"What?" Siren asked.

"I was thinking about how different our moms are."

She laughed. "Oh my God. Your mother would be horrified by my mother."

"Maybe you and your mom should come home with me next Thanksgiving," I said, laughing at the thought of Siren's mom meeting mine. In the photo Siren kept on her desk, of her and her mother, smiling with their arms around each other's shoulders, her mother was an older, heavier, wrinkled version of Siren, with a deep tan and big, blonde hair, bleached like straw. And from the way her cigarette-stained voice boomed through Siren's phone, I knew Victoria would think she was trash. And then that made me a little sad again, because I knew the only way my mother would ever accept someone like Siren's mother in her house was if she were cleaning it.

I managed to pull myself together enough to go with Siren and Jordan down to the cafeteria to have dinner, since Siren didn't want to leave me by myself. The weird thing was, it was... nice. I hadn't eaten dinner in the cafeteria for a few weeks, and it was nice to have Siren and Jordan there to talk to and joke with, and to keep my mind off... everything.

I muddled through the next couple of days, trying to immerse myself in my classes and schoolwork. I also took a couple of days to think about the name of Flora's bee, but really, there wasn't all that much to think about. It had to honor Flora. I finally settled on Rock Chalk Floracus go KU. Halidactae, Augochloropsis metallica Rock Chalk Floracus go KU was the full name.

When I told Miss Berg she threw back her head and laughed. "I think that is absolutely glorious," she said.

It was sweet.

All of a sudden, my life became super busy. Professor Berg and I met three different times to write up the scientific paper on how I'd "found" the diary in the libarary, and all about the mystery bee entry and how we went about determining the diary was real, and also proving the bee was a previously unknown species. And when I say "we," I mean Professor Berg made me write up the paper myself, and she went over it with me until the language was perfect. When we were finished, she sent several copies to all the major scientific, biological and etymological journals. The university put out a press release about it, and for some reason, the media latched on to the story. At first, it was just the local media. One of the Kansas City television news channels came and interviewed Professor Berg and me in her office. Then the university's National Public Radio affiliate had us on one of their talk shows and our interview got picked up by other NPR stations around the country. After that, the story got a little national traction. It trended on Twitter one day, and then a couple of the national talk shows—one day-time and one night-time—mentioned it. And because the name of the bug was so unusual, they both managed to squeeze out a few good jokes about it. It was wild to hear my name come out of the mouths of a couple of real celebrities. They even mentioned Flora and showed her photo next to mine, and Mattie and Siren gave me endless shit about being "famous."

Oh yeah. The national attention threw my mother over the moon, of course. She was so proud of me it was freakish. Every time she found the story mentioned anywhere, she documented it. She bought every scientific journal and printed out every tweet and saved the television segments on her laptop. Like she'd never been that proud of me, ever. Truthfully, I hated it. It was like she couldn't be proud of me for what I was. She could only be proud of what I'd done. But whatever, she was happy, so I let her act like a maniac. Dad was great. Even Cade thought it was cool.

I was sort of ambivalent about all the attention. The day I was in the UDK, about a dozen random people on campus were like, "Hey! You're that bug girl in the paper," which I never really knew how to respond to, and for a couple of days, the girls in the dorm either congratulated me or teased me about it. "Way to show the rest of us up your freshman year, Kymer," Staycee yelled at me from down the hall, which was funny, but it was odd to be the focus of so many peoples' attention. Even my religion teacher, Professor Liu, brought it up at the beggining of class. "I see from the paper today we have an explorer in our midst." I was busy reading over my notes from the previous class, and didn't look up because it didn't click right away that he was talking about me. When I did look up because the class had gone silent, everyone was staring back at me. I smiled and gave a little wave. "Oh, yeah," I said. "Sort of." And then I stared down at my notes, trying not to blush.

"How exciting!" he replied, and then he went on with class, thank God.

It wasn't that the discovery of a new bee wasn't exciting. It was. It was probably the coolest thing I'd ever do in my whole life and now everything was going to be downhill from here. I just didn't need it broadcast. Being in the spotlight was not my thing anyway, and not being able to freely talk about the whole story made me feel a little bit like a fraud, but there was nothing I could do about that.

During the whole Flora/bee circus, I hadn't contacted Rusty about my STI test results. I was just so overwhelmed with the bee stuff and then the trich issue on top of it, I didn't know what to say to him. First off, I'd never even told him about the bug diary, so that was a whole thing I'd have to explain, and there was no way I was telling Rusty I had seen ghosts. It wasn't that I was worried about what he'd think of me, and I didn't really care whether he was a believer in ghosts or not. The bug diary felt too personal and complicated to get into with him. I wasn't sure I wanted to go there with Rusty.

Also, I was pretty sure Rusty had given me trich, but not absolutely sure. Siren was *positive* it was Rusty, and had said so, several times. "Mama, I know you like him, but I'm telling you, he's a player. Which would be fine, if he'd at least have the balls to be honest with you about it." She was so sure he was having sex with other women, and so angry he hadn't been safe or honest with me, she had me convinced—half the time, anyway—that she was right and I'd been a blind fool.

But what if *I* had given it to *him*? I also still hadn't contacted Zach, and I was *not* looking forward to that conversation. I knew as soon as

I told him, he'd of course tell Chloe—as he should, because she would also need to be tested—and then our entire friend group would know I had trich, and I really didn't want to learn any of my friends' opinions on the subject, because I had a feeling some wouldn't be supportive and I didn't want to find out who.

At the same time, I was trying desperately to convince myself that contracting an STI was no different than getting the flu, but I could hear Victoria's judgemental voice ringing in my head that I was no better than *some trash girl who'd been raised in a trailer park.* It was classist and stupid, but unfortunately still how lots of people thought.

But I couldn't continue to put off telling Rusty and Zach, no matter the fallout.

For a few days, Rusty sent me his regular texts, like telling me something dumb his workmate Earl had done, or a picture of Lugnut. After about seventy-two hours, though, he was upset I hadn't responded.

Hey collage girl!

Kymer did I do something to make you mad,,, whatever it is I am sorry

Kymer I miss U

Collage girl please,,, tell me what I did

can we at leist talk,,,I do'tn know what I did

lugnut misses U

Kymer?

I was reading *The Catcher in the Rye* for my English 102 class when that final text buzzed on my phone, reminding me I *still* hadn't told Rusty I'd tested positive for trich. I was almost glad to have an excuse to stop reading because Holden Caufield seemed like a spoiled brat to me. I put the book down and picked up the phone, my thumbs numbly typing out a vague-text because I still wasn't sure what I was going to say. *We need to talk* I typed out.

that dosnt sound good lol

It's not great

i'm fixin 2 go 2 ricks rite now,,,U wanna meet

Did I? No. No, I did not want to meet him at Rick's, though realistically, it was the kind of news probably better delivered in person. However, I was feeling like a giant coward. What exactly was the etiquette for telling your fuck buddy you had tested positive for an STI? Whatever it was, I was probably about to screw it up completely. I typed out my response and hit "send" before I could change my mind: *So I got a pelvic exam and STI screening the other day and as it turns out, I tested positive for trichonomiasis.*

His reply was instant: *is that what I think it is*

I sighed and texted back: *If you think it's an STI, you're right. I don't know when I got it or who gave it to me, but you need to get tested.* There. I'd said it. It was done. I gripped the phone with two sweaty hands, staring at it, waiting for a reply. I didn't need to wait long.

Are you saying you gave me trick?

It wasn't exactly the response I was hoping for. My thumbs stabbed at the phone keyboard. *No, that is not what I'm saying. I am saying I have it, ergo you probably also have it & you will require treatment. What we don't know is which one of us had it first.*

i think id know by now if I had a STI,,,lol

How often do you get tested? I texted back, realizing it was the first time I'd ever asked him that question.

years ago,,,its not like i date sluts

I stared at his text, stunned. How could that possibly be what he thought about women? That's when I lost it. *Are you even fucking kidding me right now???* My thumbs stabbed at the phone. *I'm only telling you because you need to go to a doctor and get treated. And you need to tell whoever else it is you're fucking that she needs to get treated too. And then you know what you can do? You can go FUCK YOURSELF.*

I put the phone down and cried for fifteen minutes before I could pick up my book and continue reading it. I didn't hear from Rusty the rest of that day, or the next, but the following day he texted:

I saw a doctor,,,can we pleese talk

I waited a full half-hour before responding: *Fine*

We agreed to meet at Ricky's. No way I was going to his house. When I got to Ricky's, Rusty was at the bar, drinking what looked like a Coke. That's when I remembered: He couldn't drink alcohol while he was taking the antibiotic. The nurse had specifically told me that drinking alcohol while taking that particular antibiotic generally caused nausea and vomiting.

"Hey Gorgeous!" he said when I walked up. "What'll you have?"

His charm, which I normally loved, was annoying as fuck. I told the girl behind the bar: "I'll have a chardonnay." I hadn't intended on drinking, but the thought of drinking in front of him when he couldn't made me super happy.

"So what are we talking about?" I asked, taking a seat on the barstool next to him.

"Look, I went to the health department yesterday, and I got tested. I had to tell the nurse my whole sex history, which was fun. She recorded it all in the computer, so now the Health Department knows how many girls I've banged. I had to think all the way back to when I was fourteen. Then they tested me for trich, and a bunch of other stuff... HIV, Chlamydia, gonorrhea ...." He ticked them off on his fingers.

"And?" I said impatiently.

"All the tests came back negative, like I thought they would."

I felt like I'd been punched in the stomach. He went on, "But the doctor said it's not unusual to get a false negative for trich, especially in men. So she went ahead and prescribed me the antibiotics just in case. Of course I can't drink for three days while I'm taking it, which sucks donkey balls. Might be the longest three days of my life."

"So it *is* possible you *do* have trich," I pointed out.

In a split second I saw his eyes travel up and down me, taking in my whole form before he scoffed out, "Yeah, I s'pose so." He took a drink of his Coke reflexively, as if it were a beer. I had a feeling it was the closest to a mea culpa as I was going to get, so I decided to let him off the hook, at least for the moment. Besides, I was curious about something. "You saw a woman doctor?" I asked, making a point to take a long sip of my wine.

He chuckled. "Yeah. It was kind of embarrassing, but at least she was good-looking."

"Are you ever not a total pig?"

"Me? No, I'm pretty much an asshole all the time," he chuckled again. Then he looked at me earnestly. "Look, I swear to you I am not cheating on you. I haven't slept with anybody else the whole time we've been together."

"That's not even the point, Rusty."

"It's not?" he gave me a look of mock surprise.

"Look, I'm not your girlfriend. If you want to sleep around, that's your business. But that means we have to use protection." Even as I said it, I knew it wasn't exactly the truth. I didn't *want* Rusty to be sleeping around, but, since I wasn't his girlfriend, it was his decision, not mine.

He looked at me for a second, a smirk forming at the corner of his mouth. "Not my girlfriend, huh? I like how you made that decision for me."

"Oh please," I said, rolling my eyes.

"What?" he asked. "Would it be so crazy for you to be my girlfriend? Or are you just slumming with me for fun? Samplin' the white trash experience while you're away at college?"

I laughed. "As if you're not bragging to Earl and whoever else that you're banging a younger college girl."

He paused, then chuckled, "Yeah, you got me there." He grinned and gave me a smoldering look that almost set my underpants on fire.

"I like you Rusty. I like having sex with you. I'm just not ready to be someone's girlfriend right now. I need to concentrate on school," wincing inside at how little I'd concentrated on school my freshman year.

"Oh man," he said, shaking his head. "I can't believe I fell for this."

"Fell for what?"

He gestured toward me. "You're just a ghetto tourist. All you KU students are just alike. You come here for four years, take our jobs and then leave. And you decided while you were here you'd just fuck a dumb mechanic."

"Oh give me a big, fat, fucking break. When have I ever treated you like a dumb mechanic? Ever?" He looked away, but didn't answer. "If you don't like hanging out with me, we don't have to keep doing this," I said, feelings welling up in my chest.

"Kymer you *know* I like hanging out with you," he took a gulp of his coke and leaned toward me. "But I gotta say, this trich thing is kinda fucked up. So let me ask you something: What the hell have *you* been doing behind *my* back?"

"Nothing." I practically yelled it, holding my hands out wide with innocence.

"You sure? 'Cause you're the first girl I ever slept with who ever accused me of giving her VD. Now don't get me wrong—I admit I been with my share of girls. But like I said, I haven't had any cause to get tested in *years*. No complaints whatsoever. Which really makes me wonder how many guys you've been with before me." He crossed his arms and sat back, as if challenging me to respond.

I downed the rest of my drink, set my wine glass down, got up and proceeded to walk out.

"Kymer!" he called after me, but I ignored him, walking as fast as I could and hoping he wouldn't follow me because I didn't want to talk anyore. Also, I was about to burst into tears, though I didn't want to, which was pissing me off. I understood Rusty was embarassed about getting an STI—so was I. What was pissing me off was he wanted me to be the bigger person and take the blame for it, and it felt so deeply sexist. He'd probably had an order of magnitude more sex partners than me, and I didn't judge him for that. But because I was the girl, and because I openly liked sex, I was supposed to take my honorary title of whore, just to save his overinflated ego. Well fuck that. I wasn't asking him to take the blame—all I wanted was for him to grow up and share it with me.

He caught me in the parking lot, as I was about to get into my car. "Kymer, come on, damn it! Will you please talk to me?"

"No," I said, slamming my door, starting the car and accelrating away in a satisfying spray of gravel.

When I got back to the dorm, I decided since my day had been blown up anyway, I might as well text Zach. How much worse could it get?

Hey. I need to tell you something. It's important.

It was a few minutes before he texted back, *What?*

I started the text and deleted it like five times before I finally texted, *I had an STI screening & it turns out, I have trichonomiasis. The treatment is easy. Just antibiotics. You and Chloe should get tested to be safe.*

He texted back, *Well that's just fucking great, Kymer. Thanks for letting me know.*

That's when I realized he probably thought I was suggesting I had given trich to *them*. Shit. I thought about sending another text to clarify, but then I thought—what's the point? I knew Chloe would make me out to be the villain, regardless.

I texted Erin, wanting to tell my side of the story before she heard the news from Chloe or Zach. *Hey. Sorry I haven't texted in a while. So long story short, I had to go to the school doctor to get more birth control pills and they gave me all the STI tests and the trichomoniasis test came back positive. So now I feel like a big whore and I had to tell Zach I tested positive of course and I'm sure Chloe will and I just wanted to text you first*

An hour went by before she replied. *Holy shit kymer wutttt??? lol*

My stomach fell. Great. More judgement.

Yeah, I know. I'm an idiot. I typed back.

Wait! No no no! I just mean UR life is exciting rite now, lol!!! UR still seeing that Rusty guy, rite?

I mean, I was

U think it was him then?

pretty sure

Then why tell Zach?

Because its the right thing to do I typed.

Tru she replied. Then: *Chloe is going to have a field day with this*

Right? I typed. *Ironically it's far more likely they gave it to me than I gave it to them. I didn't even start dating Rusty until after winter break!*

OMG Kymer fuck Chloe for real she is a total freak. I don't even talk to Zach anymore bcuz she won't let him out of her site

That was jarring to hear and I felt a wave of sadness for Zach wash over me, on top of Mount Misery where I was currently residing. *That's awful!* I typed.

I mean he's not complaining it's like they R pod people I don't even know them anymore and of course brent isn't speaking to me either

It was happening. Our friend group was falling apart. And it was probably all my fault.

Well that makes me feel like an asshole I replied.

Wut? Why?

Our whole friend group is blowing up & it prolly wouldn't have happened if I hadn't moved to Kansas

Oh please. I'm the lesbian remember?

Oh yeah I typed.

Lol!!! Erin texted back. Then: *At least the treatment is easy* and I was grateful for her support. I was tired of feeling the weight of bad girl guilt on my shoulders.

Thanks, friend

A few days later, Erin texted *So the creepy couple claims they both tested negative but I don't believe a damn thing they say anymore, lol*

I felt like a piece of shit for days, like I was some stupid, dirty... girl. How could everyone else's trich test be negative and mine the only positive? The answer, of course, was they couldn't. One of them had to be lying, or had a false negative test result, but that didn't matter. I was the only one admitting to being diseased, which gave everybody else plausible denyability. On top of all that, Rusty kept texting me. For a couple of weeks I ignored his texts completely, but once, in a moment of weakness I texted back: *Will you at least admit you could have given me trich?*

There was a pause. *I realy do'nt think so,,, your the one in college,,,*

I responded: *Don't text me again. Ever.*

Seriously?,,,,

I didn't answer.

22

Stupid Love

As the weeks went by, all the bug diary brouhaha finally stopped and thankfully, I'd managed to (mostly) forgive myself for getting trich. I was a sexually active young woman who'd gotten an STI. Big deal. I'd contacted my sex partners like a responsible young adult and been treated for the infection and moving forward, I vowed to do better.

There was just one problem. Now that I wasn't seeing Rusty, I suddenly had all this time on my hands, and it sucked. Siren and Mattie were still all wrapped up in Jordan and Alejandro, so I didn't see them much, which made it even more difficult to ignore the fact that I'd suddenly gone from having fantastic sex to absolutely none. Worst of all, I *missed* Rusty. I missed his face and his smell and his body and his hilarious redneck colloquialisms and the way he looked at me like I was the most desirable woman alive. But I was still furious with him.

One evening, after closing up the gift shop at the Natural History Museum and riding the bus back to the dorm, Siren wasn't there. The room was dim except for the throb of lava lamps on my desk and the streetlights streaming through the windows. I flopped down on my bed and stared at my bugs. Caroline the mantis was chewing on a cricket she had firmly in her grasp. Chrysler the beetle was sitting immobile on a twig. Sidney the butterfly was getting a drink from a moisture cube with his long proboscis. The tiger moth hadn't yet emerged from its cocoon, and I hoped it was still alive in there. I didn't even have Flora's bug diary to flip through, anymore. Looking at my little bug family made me feel a little better, but I still felt pretty freaking sorry for myself.

I was pathetic.

My phone buzzed on the nightstand. I snatched it, hoping desperately that it was Siren or Mattie.

It was Rusty.

Hey gorgus,,,I know you do'tn want to talk to me but I miss you so bad

I thought about it for a few seconds and then I texted back: *I miss you too.* What can I say? I was weak.

How are you? he asked.

I'm okay. I lied. At the moment, I was anything but okay. I was depressed and lonely and though I was happy to be out of the spotlight, the sudden lack of attention and human interaction made everything feel bleak. *I'm pretty bored right now, though,* I added and that was the truth. But it was also an understatement. I actually felt like I was dying inside.

U cuold come keep me company,,,

Oh could I now?

We do'tn have to have sex or anything I swear,,, I miss talking to U

You're so full of shit.

Ya im a asshole,,, remember?

I remember

im a asshole who misses your gorgus face

You're still full of shit

I know,,, I have missed more than your face,,,

Oh yeah? Like what?

like your magnifacent tits

That made me laugh. *Hahaha!*

I missed them so much,,, I have had to resort to interigateing the suspect

Hahahaha!

severil times a day

The texting went on like that for a while, and of course, I ended up at his house, like a dumbass. We sat on his back porch in the moonlight drinking beers and talking about nothing, because we both knew we didn't want to talk about anything real, because we both knew if we talked about anything real, we'd end up screaming at each other instead of screwing. And we both wanted to screw. So we talked about inanities—the weather, Lugnut, his work, my work—until we'd finished our beers, and the next thing I knew we were in his bedroom, tearing off each other's clothes.

"Um… " I said, when most of our clothes were on the floor. I held my hand up like I was in class.

"Um, what?"

"We should really use a condom."

"Why?" he said, looking genuinely confused.

"Because we should."

"Well… I mean… we both took our antibiotics," he said. I had a hard time keeping my gaze off the bulge in his blue boxer briefs.

"Yeah, but we haven't seen each other for a while," I said, getting impatient.

"So?"

"So we don't know for sure what the other one has been doing."

"I haven't been doing anything. Have you?"

"No."

"So, there you go."

"Rusty, seriously. We need to use a condom."

"Christ, I don't even know if I have any… "

I reached for my purse. "I have some."

"Why are you still carrying condoms around? Who are you seeing?" His words hit me like a slap.

"Are you kidding me right now?" I asked, staring at him. Lugnut jumped off the bed and trotted out of the room. Rusty shrugged, but didn't answer, which, I realized, was his answer. I began picking up my clothes.

"C'mon, Kymer, don't get pissed off at me again."

"Then say something that doesn't piss me off," I said, putting on my underwear.

"Well… what do you want me to say?" He threw his hands out as if to say, *What man could possibly know what you want, woman?*

"I want you to agree that if we are going to have sex, you will use a condom and not be a dick about it," I said it calmly, even though it made me so angry I had to spell it out to him. I just wanted him to respect my bodily autonomy so we could keep having sex. Why was that such a big deal?

"Well, yes, ma'am!" he responded, his voice edged with sarcasm, and my heart fell.

"Yeah," I said, pulling on my jeans. "I am definitely leaving."

He slammed his hand on the dresser. "Dammit!" And I knew he knew he'd messed up getting laid. Out in the living room, Lugnut barked, alarmed at the angry tone in Rusty's voice, and that's when I knew I was out. I put on my blouse and grabbed my purse, thinking that any second, he'd turn on the charm and apologize. I walked out the front door, shutting it firmly as I left. I even sat in my car for a few seconds, hoping he'd come after me. He didn't. So I drove back to the dorm.

Siren still wasn't home when I got back. I crawled in bed and cried myself to sleep.

23

Dirty Shirleys

It was the first Saturday night the three of us had spent together in several weeks, and we were in Mattie's room, lounging on the floor in our jammies. Mattie was mixing up our Shirley Temples, only Siren had bought some cherry vodka for us.

"You know what a Shirley Temple with vodka is called?" she said.

"No, what?" said Mattie. He was making our drinks on his dresser top. He set out the trio of tall glass tumblers, put exactly four cubes of ice in each glass, poured in the bubbling diet ginger ale and tinged it pink with grenadine. He topped them off with the cherry vodka, added three maraschino cherries per drink, and finished them with red swizzle sticks. He wore a faded Beyoncé concert t-shirt and black sweats.

"Dirty Shirleys!" Siren said, and she giggled.

"Oooo, I like that," Mattie said, and handed us our drinks.

Siren was wearing a onesie and her bunny slippers, sitting on a purple bean bag, hugging the big, green fuzzy pillow that was her favorite.

"How is Bazongas?" I asked. I was in my flannel bottoms and a long-sleeved t-shirt that said, I heart nuclear waste. I was lying flat on my back on the fuzzy purple rug with my head on a large, lime-green teddy bear Mattie had named Kermit.

She shrugged. "It's not terrible. I just wish I didn't have to put in so many hours there. I barely have time to study. If I don't figure something out, I'm going to drown in student loans. I'll never get them paid off."

"Didn't Travis say he'd help you?" I asked, sipping at my drink. It was strong.

"He says that, but when the loans come due, I don't think I can really expect him to help me out," she shrugged. "He could be married or something by then. He might have a kid."

"That's true," I agreed.

"And for another thing, I don't think I like the idea of being in debt to Travis. He already thinks he can boss me around. So I've been seriously kicking around the idea of getting into SuperFans to pay for school."

"Girl!" Mattie said. From his reaction, he clearly knew what she was talking about. I didn't.

"What's SuperFans?" I asked.

"It's this app where people can subscribe to your videos." She said it as though she was talking about waiting tables.

"What kind of videos?" I asked, sipping my drink.

Siren gave me a look. "Cute cat videos, Kymer. What kind of videos do you think?"

"*Sex* videos?" I exclaimed, immediately regretting the judgement in my tone. "Sorry," I said, staring down at my glass, watching the bubbles rise to the surface of my drink.

"Yes, sex videos," Siren flipped her hair off her shoulders. "So what? Everybody is doing it." She took a sip of her drink. "These are yummy! My only hesitation is once something like that is out on the internet it never goes away. And I wouldn't want it to fuck up my acting career."

Ugh. When she said it, I felt like someone had punched me in the stomach. The thought of Siren having to go into sex work to pay for school felt so... wrong. Not that she should be ashamed of the work... just that it could be her best, maybe only, option. It was so... unfair.

Then Mattie said, "Maybe you could wear a mask in your videos," and we all died laughing. "No, I'm serious, though. Like you could get some cute, black-velvet cat-eye mask... it could be mysterious."

"Sure," I said. "She could do magic tricks, too."

"Magic tricks?" Mattie said. "Like what?"

"I dunno. Maybe doves could fly out of her vagina."

"Ooo! Kymer getting salty!" Mattie said, smiling, and took a sip of his drink.

"Kymer!" Siren yelled, but she laughed and punched me in the arm. It hurt. I deserved it.

"I guess I *could* wear one of those rubber masks over my head and be someone else," she said.

"You could be Marilyn Monroe!" Mattie said.

"What if some freak wanted her to be Clark Gable with a vagina?" I asked, and we collapsed laughing. Then I said, "I think she should wear one of those fancy Mardi Gras masks with all the bird feathers and sequins."

"Girl, there are all kinds of fetish directions you could take this." Mattie stirred his drink thoughtfully. "You could wear one of those freaky sex hoods with the eyes and mouth that zip open and closed. Ooo! You could be a sex monster. No! A sex alien."

"No, no," I said, barely able to catch my breath. "You should wear a hockey mask."

"And she could pull-start a gas-powered chainsaw!" Mattie said. We all fell on the floor, dying. Then Siren said, "I bet there is a HUGE untapped redneck porn market," and we all collapsed again, except thinking about rednecks also made me think of Rusty.

"Or bad movies," said Mattie "Maybe we should start a porn movie company!"

"Oh my God, yes!" Siren said. "We could do campy porn rip-offs of iconic movies and call it Parody Porn."

"That's too literal," I said. "It should be something like... Spoogie Spoofs."

"Ewwwww!" Siren said.

"We could do *Romeo and Juliet*!" Mattie said.

"We could do *Gone with the Wind*!" Siren said. She grabbed my shoulders, leaned in and said in a deep, Southern drawl, "You should be kissed, and often, and by someone who knows how."

Mattie got up on his knees, clasped his hands together, prayer-like, and said in a high, squeaky voice, "As God as my witness I'll never be hungry again!" and then he mimed a blow-job. My stomach hurt from laughing. Siren had tears running down her cheeks.

"Girl, with your acting talent and my directing genius, there are literally no limits," Mattie said, settling into a bean bag.

"What about Kymer?" Siren said.

"She can get us the nasty, crusty bugs for when we do *Indiana Bone and the Dick of Doom,"* Mattie said, and Siren choked on her drink.

"Hey!" I said. "Bugs are beautiful."

"I love you, Kymer. Because you are so... extra. How are you doing these days without your love mechanic?"

"I mean, I guess I'm okay. I miss him. But... I mean... I think dumping him was the right thing to do?"

"I think it was the right thing to do," Siren said. She sounded so positive. I wasn't.

She looked at me. "Um... I haven't told you yet, but... Jake's been coming in to Bazongas again."

I took a big gulp of my Dirty Shirley and shrugged. "Figures."

"He's been asking about you."

"Asking what?" I said, taking another gulp of my drink.

"How you are," she said.

"What do you tell him?"

"I tell him you're doing great, and I leave it at that,"

"Thanks. I appreciate that, for real."

"He also wanted me to tell you he misses you," she said, peering at me over the edge of her drink as though she was trying to judge my reaction.

"Well, he must not miss me that much," I said. "It's not like I'm asking a lot of him."

"No, you are not," Mattie said. "Men can deal with condoms. It's not that difficult. And you're worth it. Good for you for sticking to your guns. I mean, it's not like you were in love with him, right? Like, you don't want to marry him or anything, right?"

"Oh, hell no," I said. "I don't think I want to marry anybody, ever."

"I didn't think so. I just thought I should ask," Mattie said. "Do you want to get married, Siren?"

"Sure," she said. My mouth dropped open. Mattie cocked his head to one side and considered her.

"Really?" I asked.

"What?" she said, wrinkling her brow. "Just because I like to date a lot doesn't mean I don't eventually want to settle down."

"I just didn't think you'd want to," I said.

"Yeah, I do. Not now. And not for another ten years, at least. I want to be an older bride, have a small wedding, pop out one kid, and be done." She crossed her arms to punctuate the statement.

"You want kids?" Mattie and I said it at the same time.

"One kid," she specified. "I'm not dealing with all that sibling rivalry bullshit. Travis is a pain in the ass."

"He loves you, though," I said. "And so does your mom. You both are really lucky to have such close families."

"I am grateful for my family," said Mattie. "And I am so glad they've ended up supporting me, even though things seemed a little iffy for a minute there."

"Does Moms like Alejandro?" Siren asked.

"She loves him!" Mattie said, sipping his drink.

"Really?"

"Really. Loves him to pieces. And see, Alejandro's family is Columbian, and he can cook. So he and my mother have been swapping recipes. I think she may even have a little crush on him, but he is cute as hell, so I really can't blame her."

"That's awesome!" I said.

"It is. Although the crush thing is a little... awkward. But last week he taught her to make empanadas."

"What kind?" Siren asked.

"Beef and chicken. With all kinds of exotic spices and olives and potatoes and vegetables. I don't even know what all was in there. They were delicious!"

"What about Pops?" I asked.

"What does he think about Alejandro, you mean? He likes him. They can talk about KU basketball together. And the Chiefs. And smoking meat. As long as my Pops can talk with a man about sports, barbeque or fishing, he's good."

"So... how are things going between you two?" Siren asked.

"Me and Pops? Or me an Alejandro?"

"Alejandro," Siren said, rolling her eyes.

"This might sound kind of sentimental or whatever, but... I am really happy. Like I don't know if I've ever been this happy. Alejandro is so sweet."

"Aw!" I said, and I smiled—because I really was happy for Mattie—but I also felt a twinge of jealousy.

"But I mean... how are things... going?" I wiggled my eyebrows at him.

"Going with what, exactly, Kymer?" he said, looking over his glasses at me.

"You know. The sexy time," I said, taking a sip of my drink.

"Oh, sex? Oh..." He stirred his drink, then said coyly, "We haven't done that yet."

"You haven't?" Siren and I blurted it out at the same time. "It's been months," Siren added.

Mattie took a sip of his drink. "Well, we've decided to wait a little bit. I mean, we've done some stuff... but we haven't actually done the deed."

"Why not?" Siren asked.

"Well not that it is any of you nosy bitches' bidness, but we're waiting because I'm a virgin."

"No way!" Siren said.

"For real," Mattie said, taking another sip.

"So, what do you do?" Siren asked, which made me laugh out loud.

"We talk. We watch movies and listen to music and do homework. Sometimes we make out. You know. Things. Whatever. The things people do. What about you, Siren? How's your sex life?"

"They are constantly getting busy," I said. "Constantly. They don't even care if I'm there. It's just non-stop sexy-time."

Siren shrugged and laughed. "That's pretty much completely accurate."

"But you're not seeing anybody else, right?" Mattie asked.

"No. Jordan and I are pretty into each other."

"Do you guys ever talk?" I asked. I was teasing, but she looked a little hurt.

"Of course we talk." She rolled her eyes.

"About what?"

"About everything. Politics. School. Current events. He's really sweet and easy to talk to. We get along really well. He really gets me. And I think I get him, too."

"I don't think I've ever heard you talk about a guy that way," I said.

She shrugged. "Yeah. I don't know, though. He's so young."

"So are you," I said.

"Yeah, but I'm not young like him. I mean, he's nineteen. This is his freshman year. He should be out having fun."

"This is your freshman year," I said.

"Yeah, but it's different for me. I've already had plenty of fun... and..."

I realized where she was going. "You like him, don't you?"

She sighed, and I was amazed when she wiped a tear away from the corner of her eye. "Yes." Her voice came out in a squeak.

"Oh, girl, come here," Mattie said. He put down his drink and hugged her. A second later, I decided to make it a group hug, and Siren let out a noise that was somewhere between a sob and a laugh.

"You guys. You're going to make me cry, damn it, and there's nothing I hate more than when my mascara runs." She wiped her fingers under each eye and fanned her face with her hands. "No crying," she said. "No crying. I don't know why I'm crying. Except he's... perfect."

"Siren, honey, why are you worrying so much? Just have fun and enjoy it. Enjoy him. Jordan is a good guy," Mattie said.

"He really is," I agreed. "You're really lucky you found him."

"I know," she said, taking a big breath. "I'm hormonal right now. And rehearsals have been a bitch." Siren had a part in the drama department's spring musical, Grease. She had landed the part of one of the Pink Ladies, Marty, but she was butting heads with the director some, and even though she didn't have the biggest speaking part, she had to perform in several of the musical numbers. When she was in our room, we listened to the Grease soundtrack nonstop while she practiced the lyrics and dance moves, which was actually kind of okay with me. I could block her out when I needed to study, and when I wanted to take a break, she was entertaining to watch. She was so good. But with rehearsals, her job and Jordan, I hadn't seen her all that much as of late. The show would be up in a week.

"I bet Kymer is happy she's not famous anymore," Siren said. Mattie laughed. It had not been lost on anyone that of the three of us, I was the one least equipped to handle being in the public eye.

"That whole thing was so crazy," Siren said, undoing her ponytail and redoing it. "How did you get that diary again? You said some old lady gave it to you?"

"Yeah, Kymer, I need the dirty deets, because I haven't heard any of it. Does anyone need another drink?" Mattie asked, and Siren and

I handed our glasses to him for a refill. "What old lady? I never saw any old lady. When did she give it to you?" He set the glasses on the dresser and set to work making another round of drinks.

"Don't make mine too strong," Siren cut in. "I have rehearsals tomorrow."

"How about you, Kymer? Another drink?"

"The first one you made was perfect," I said, wanting to get properly buzzed.

"Okay," Mattie said, "but getting back to the subject, who gave you that bug book?"

My mind raced... they were my friends... I trusted them... I wanted to tell them the truth. Even if it sounded insane. Also, the cherry vodka was kicking in. So I told them. Well... I told them about Carrie, anyway. I didn't tell them about Lewis Lindsey Dyche, because... that seemed like too much.

"Okay, so remember when we tripped at the library?" I started. Mattie handed us our drinks, and the two of them sat riveted, as I told them everything that I'd experienced that night. Siren settled into the beanbag she was sitting on and began sucking her thumb, something she did when she was concentrating. When I'd finished, she took her thumb out of her mouth.

"Jesus Christ, Kymer, that is intense," Siren said, her brow furrowed. "How come you didn't get a photo or take video or something?"

Her question almost knocked me over. Why hadn't I tried to get video evidence? "I guess... I was too freaked out. I could barely think while it was happening. Honestly, I didn't even know if she was a ghost, you know? Until I saw her photo on the way out of the library, I just thought she was... a person."

"I swear my heart is beating a mile a minute," Mattie said, his hand on his chest. "That is the best ghost story I have ever heard. That is better than when my Great Aunt Ruthie claimed she could talk to her dead husband through the old transistor radio in her kitchen."

I laughed, and Siren almost spit out her drink. "Wait, what?" she said. "Oh, now you have to tell us that story."

"There's nothing more to tell, really. One Christmas she surprised us all by letting us know that she could hear Uncle Howard on the radio communicating to her through the songs."

"Did she talk back to him?" I asked.

"Oh, yes," Mattie nodded his head emphatically. "Apparently she had whole conversations with him."

"So did somebody do something?" I asked, intrigued.

"There wasn't really anything we could do," Mattie said, shrugging. "She seemed perfectly sane in every other way. She was in good health and could take care of herself. But to her dying day, she insisted she spoke with her dead husband on the regular."

Siren and I died laughing. "So, yeah," I said, wiping the tears from my eyes. "I know you two probably think I'm losing my mind, but I swear that's how I ended up with the bug diary," I said. "Although I have seriously considered that I might be losing my mind."

"Like schizophrenia or something?" Siren asked, sticking her thumb back in her mouth.

"Yeah," I said. "Maybe. Maybe I never saw Carrie Watson. Maybe my brain concocted the whole thing."

"You are not schizophrenic," Mattie said. He shook his head emphatically. "No way."

"How do you know?" I asked.

"We have two regulars who come into the restaurant who are schizophrenic. You don't act anything like Harvey or Simon."

I laughed. "That doesn't mean I'm not in the early stages of it, or something. It does tend to present itself around our age."

"It does," Siren said, nodding. "Happened to a guy in my high school. He was three years ahead of me, but he totally started hearing voices and everything. He got taken out of school and never came back. Nobody knows what happened to him."

"Well that's comforting," I said, taking a drink.

"But you have the bug diary," Mattie said. "That's real."

"Yeah... I... don't know," I said.

"Well, I believe you," Mattie said.

"Me too," Siren said. "I believe in ghosts, though. You don't want to mess with ghosts."

"See, that's the thing," I said. "I don't believe in ghosts. Or at least, I didn't."

"What about now?" Siren asked.

"I... I don't know. I mean... I was tripping. Maybe I found the diary on a shelf and dreamed everything else." And maybe the pot made me see Dyche, I thought, even though I knew it wasn't true.

Siren laughed. "You are the only person I know who would demand evidence from herself."

I shrugged. "That's how science works."

"Oh my goodness! Speaking of science—okay, well, not speaking of science but speaking of *moi*, I have some news, too!" Mattie said.

"What's your news, sweetie?" Siren said. She stood and stretched, and in my buzz-induced state I marveled at her lioness-like litheness. She had arms of a Greek goddess.

"So, you know my film professor, Dr. Wilmoth? He liked *Space Vamp* so much he entered it in the Pop Corny Film Festival, and I got in! I get to go to Colorado this summer!"

"No fucking way!" I said.

"Yay!" said Siren. "Aspen?"

Mattie's shoulders sunk a little. "No... Manitou Springs."

Siren laughed. "You will love Manitou. Seriously. It's like Lawrence but with less deodorant and more drugs."

"Oh good! You had me worried for a second," Mattie looked over his glasses. "Well... except for the deodorant thing. I'm not sure about that. But you've been there, Siren?"

"We camped there for a week when I was a kid. It was some kind of hippie music festival thing my mom wanted to go to. It was fun, but we were lucky our old Buick made it there and back. The town is really cute and artsy. You'll love it. Hey! Maybe I could go with!"

"Of course you could go with," Mattie exclaimed. "You're the star of the movie!"

The two of them chatted about Manitou Springs, and the next thing I knew I was thinking about Rusty. It had been three weeks since I'd last seen him, and I was doing better—much better—but I was caught off guard at how difficult it was for me to shake my feelings for him. This was not part of my college plan, at all. Catching feelings was not supposed to be part of the deal. It made zero sense. Zero. I was young. I was free. I was cute. I was attending the college of my choice. I was supposed to be having the time of my life. I was supposed to be having the sex of my life. So what the actual fuck had happened?

I zoned out, thinking about Rusty's tight stomach, his rock-hard arms and his tattoos and his smell. Ugh. I really wanted to have sex.

And I really wanted to have sex with Rusty, specifically. But I wasn't willing to put up with Rusty not wearing a condom and blaming me for the STI. Also, I didn't like that I'd caught feelings. I needed to figure out an arrangement with... someone else. And this time, things had to be different. I wasn't sure how, exactly, because I wanted to be attracted to someone enough to have sex with them, but not so attracted as to lead to... I hated to even think the word... love.

"Kymer!" Siren yelled, and I startled. I realized they were both laughing at me, but, y'know, not laughing at me.

"She was for real in another universe," Mattie said. "Aw. You're thinking about your ex-mechanic, aren't you?"

"Yeah. It's been kind of... difficult," I admitted. "The thing is, I don't know even know why it's been difficult. We have nothing in common. It should have been the perfect setup. Great sex without feelings."

"And he gave you an STI," Siren said, taking a drink. She wasn't going to let me forget that.

"Probably, but we don't know that for sure," I said, and Siren rolled her eyes in response.

"Of course he did, Kymer. I'm telling you, Jake is a straight-up dog," For good measure she added, "Woof!" and Mattie fell over laughing.

"I mean... " Mattie said to her, "I don't know if I'd go that far. Jake was nice to my sister Eva for that week or however long when they went out in high school." He stirred his drink. "At least I think so. She never said different, anyway. He's always been nice to me, and not all the rednecks were nice to a gay boy back in high school."

"I don't trust him," Siren said, crossing her arms, and I bristled some. Still, I had to admit Siren's instincts were usually correct.

"Do you think you would've developed feelings for Jake if he hadn't developed feelings for you?" Mattie asked. It was a great question. I thought about it for a few seconds.

"No," I said, finally. "No, I don't. Damn him. Why did he have to do that to me?"

Siren uncrossed her arms, leaned over and hugged me. "I hear you, Sister."

24

You Can't Stay Here

Sometime around the third-to-the-last week of school or so, Isabelle, the Isabella tiger moth (*Pyrrharcia isabella*), emerged from the cocoon she'd spun when she was the wooly bear caterpillar. Like most moths, she was kind of small, and a sort of unassuming, feathery-golden color, with a few bold, black spots that looked like jewelry. It was kind of a classic look, I thought. Understated but elegant. Since, like many moths, she didn't eat, I decided I'd keep her around in her terrarium, at least until the end of the school year. I hoped she would think of it like a nice hotel room where she could relax for a few weeks and not worry about being eaten out in the wild.

Around that same time, Dyche Museum put Flora's diary on display. I was kind of surprised they'd managed to finish the display before summer, but the really cool part was I got to help work on it! I mean, not really, but sort of. I got to meet some of the graduate students who were learning how to do museum exhibit design, which I didn't realize was something you could get a degree in, but as it turns out, it is. Anyway, they let me hang out and showed me the techniques for building the exhibits in a workshop in Dyche Hall I didn't know existed. In fact, it was so cool, for a few seconds, I thought about switching majors.

When I was at work in the gift shop, I'd sneak upstairs to look at the Bug Diary display when I could. The diary was on a stand, open to the bee page, with a spotlight on it. But they had also made large reproductions of a few of the diary entries, to be read and enjoyed by the public as part of the display. They'd also included a photo of Flora and a picture of Snow Hall as it had looked back when she had attended KU. The display explained the story of how the diary had come to be found, and my name was mentioned, along with Professor Berg's, of course. Thank God they didn't include my photo.

It was silly, maybe, but it all felt so right to see Flora finally given the credit she deserved. It also felt good to be able to visit the diary. Even though I missed having it all to myself and being able to look at it any time I wanted, I didn't need it in my personal possession. I knew it belonged on display. Besides, KU was Flora's home, and that's where the diary belonged, you know? At home.

In those last few weeks of school, I realized Siren and I were going to have to find a place to live. There was no way I was going back to Maryland for the whole summer, and the end of the year was coming up quickly, so I researched apartments online. Siren caught me on one of the websites one afternoon.

"What are you doing?"

"I'm trying to find us an apartment. I never realized it was so expensive." I talked to my boss at work, and she said I could work full time at the museum over the summer, but even so, it would still be difficult to pay my share of rent and bills.

"Why are you looking at those horrible corporate apartment complexes?" Siren asked, her nose wrinkled.

I was surprised. It hadn't occurred to me to look at anything else. "I don't know," I said. "Because they're well-maintained and clean, and hopefully not full of dangerous wackos?"

"No," she said, shaking her head. "We do not want that. Go look at the reviews. Places like that make you jump through a thousand hoops at move-out time and then cheat you out of your deposit anyway."

"Well, where do you suggest? I'm not living in some... hippie-ass commune." I said.

"We're not going to live in a commune, doofus. Start looking at apartments for lease in old houses. There are some apartments downtown, too, above the businesses."

The first place we looked at was a dark, musty apartment in some skeevy guy's basement. He seemed really jazzed about the idea of Siren and me living there. "You girls could use the back yard for sunbathing or whatever," he said. "I don't mind."

"I bet you don't mind, weirdo." Siren said as we drove away.

A few days later, we looked at half of a condo in one of those creepy neighborhoods where every condo is exactly the same, each one split right down the middle. The development was full of speed bumps, and the average age of the residents seemed to be 108. The little old lady who was trying to rent out the one side of her condo was sweet, but I didn't think Siren's weed smoking and the noise of either of our sex lives was something she'd want to put up with.

"We'll think about it," we said, waving goodbye.

"She is so fucking cute," said Siren. "But I don't think I could stand it there."

I agreed.

The third time, though, was the charm. We rolled up on this massively creepy Victorian house in the area of town known as Old West Lawrence, just a few blocks from where Mattie's parents lived. About a quarter-section of the back of the house had been cordoned off and made into its own apartment, with a cute little kitchen and bathroom and two bedrooms. There was even a funky little balcony off the tiny living room that looked over the busy, one-way street below. We'd be near campus, and downtown, and even Smoky Jo's. It was perfect. The owner was a textile artist. She was an old hippie, a woman in her mid-60s or so. Apparently she was kind of famous. Her massive, gauzy, sparkly creations looked like water or earth or clouds, depending. Her name was Theresa Rosenstein, and she was so cool. She invited us in for herbal tea and French macarons, and before we left, we gave her the first month's rent right then and there. We were so jazzed to have secured an apartment—a cool apartment—we celebrated by getting ice cream cones downtown, and I realized that I was now officially a Lawrencian and a grownup, living on my own. I could come downtown any time I damn well pleased to buy ice cream, and Victoria couldn't bitch at me about watching my diet. I was a free, college-aged, American woman.

Next year would be amazing.

The final week of school was bananas. Everybody was trying to pack up, and study, and take finals at the same time. It seemed like all the girls in the dorm were chugging energy drinks, wandering the halls until late at night, trying to get everything done. So it kind of made sense that someone pulled the fire alarm one night, just before midnight. I mean, everybody was already sleepless and stressed out, so why not file outside and get some fresh night air we didn't have time for? Siren and I looked at each other. We were both studying. Siren rolled her eyes. "Seriously?"

"At least we're awake," I said.

We grabbed jackets and put on slippers to go outside, because the rule was that everyone had to exit the building during a fire alarm. Only when the fire department had shown up, and firefighters had searched every single room to make sure they were empty and there was no fire, would they let us back inside the building. Fire alarms usually meant we were outside for at least an hour. The last time we'd had a fire alarm was in January. Several people had wrapped themselves in comforters, on top of hats and gloves and coats, on top of jammies. Everyone huddled close. People jumped up and down in place to stay warm. Girls whimpered and whined about the cold. Guys laughed and ran around and kicked each other in the butt. And it was all in the flashing red and blue lights of the fire truck and the campus cops, making it a kind of twisted club atmosphere, without music.

"Fuck," Siren said. "I can't wait to move out of this dorm. These girls are sweet, but... all these kids are a little green, you know? And this business of pulling fire alarms in the middle of the night is fucking bullshit." She stuck her thumb in her mouth.

"Yes," I said, grateful that it was May and sixty degrees out. "Yes, I do."

Thankfully, they only left us standing outside for about forty-five minutes. But there was no point in trying to take the elevators back up because there were so many of us and the elevators were so slow. So we all tromped back up the stairs.

"Oh my God, why do I have to live on the eighth floor?" someone called out.

"Try the ninth," Siren replied.

"Try the tenth," another voice responded.

By the time we were back in our room and in bed, it was two o'clock in the morning. I had a final at 8 a.m.

The day before the last day of school, we had a ninth-floor dorm party in the commons area, so everyone had a chance to say goodbye or trade digits in order to stay in touch.

"Okay, I know we're all super busy, so I just want to thank you all for taking the time to meet here," Cheyenne the RA yelled out to settle everyone down. She had put out fresh cookies from a local bakery and the condom bowl on a table. "We had an amazing year together, and I feel really blessed to have met you all."

A chorus of "Awwws!" went up and hugging commenced. I retreated to a corner, watching the love-fest, hoping to avoid the touching. Siren was chatting with Staycee as though Staycee didn't irritate her in the least, as though she didn't regularly mention that the sound of Staycee's voice was enough to make her want to kill herself.

I was doing a good job of going undetected until Grace caught my eye and walked toward me. "It was very nice to meet you, Kymer. I hope we can keep in touch. We could get lunch or coffee or something sometime," she said, and her Oklahoma twang was sort of pleasant.

"Yeah, definitely," I said, wondering if I really meant it. But we went ahead and exchanged digits, so I was now officially electronically linked to Grace the Freak.

And maybe, I decided, that wasn't such a bad thing.

25

Flora

My very last final on the very last day of classes was, of all things, an Intro to Eastern Religions final. I'd taken the class to fulfill one of my humanities requirements. It was more interesting than I thought it would be, and I was sort of taken with the idea of Buddhism, and the very practical idea of the Four Noble Truths, which are: the truth of suffering; the truth of the cause of suffering; the truth of the end of suffering; and the truth of the path that leads to the end of suffering. Or, as Professor Liu explained it to us, suffering exists; it has a cause; it has an end; and it has a cause to bring about its end. I liked the practicality of it, as a spiritual tool to get through life that might actually work. I was surprised at how much I ended up liking the class and Professor Liu. I mean, I'd never want to study religion, but he made the subject fascinating. We also learned about Hinduism and Sikhism, as well as Shintoishm, Taoism and Confucianism. I'd never had much use for religion, so I was surprised at how much Buddhism intrigued me. I mean, not intriguing enough for me to actually pursue as a life philosophy, but still.

When I left Smith Hall, I decided to walk back to the dorm. It was a gorgeous day. The sun was warm, the breeze was light, and there were so many spring flowers blooming on campus you could smell them in the air: lilac, mostly, but also crab apple and pear trees.

I stopped in front of Spooner Hall, across the street from Dyche Hall, and watched for a good twenty minutes or so as the honey bees flew down from their window on the third floor of Dyche to forage in the flower beds in front of Spooner. Every few seconds, a bee with clean legs would land in front of me, and get to work gathering pollen on a purple hyacinth or a red tulip, while a bee whose pollen baskets were loaded with neon-orange pollen would take off and float slowly back across the street and up to the window, clearly weighted down with pollen. They made sure to gain altitude quickly, flying back and forth above the oblivious students who filed back and forth on the sidewalk underneath them. Watching the two species cross paths, each with its own agenda to contribute to its corresponding hive mind, was too cool.

Eventually I moved on, taking my time to get back to the dorm, soaking up the day. But when I got back to the dorm room, I felt on edge and bored. I had packed up everything of mine I could. There were no tests left to study for. I didn't have Flora's diary to read anymore. My bugs were all fed and watered. Mattie and Siren were both at work and would be for a few hours. I thought about wandering down the hall to talk to Grace or Staycee, but that wasn't really what I wanted to do. I thought about going downtown, but I knew if I did, I'd just spend money I needed to save for the apartment.

At that particular moment, I found myself missing Rusty. A lot. I felt... lonely. Like a loser. Like a lonely loser who didn't matter. Just to torture myself further, I scrolled through the photos on my phone until I found the selfie of us in bed together. He was so casually handsome, his hair mussed a little, with that cheeky sparkle in his eyes. I remembered how snuggling with him that morning had been almost as good as the sex. I closed my eyes and breathed in, ruminating on his scent. Had I been too demanding of him? Too bitchy? Was I throwing away a decent friendship and a great fuckbuddy for no good reason? An idea began to grow in the back of my mind... an idea I knew I shouldn't entertain, but I couldn't help it. It gnawed at me. I made a decision.

I checked my makeup and touched up my face and hair. I grabbed my car keys, left the dorm and drove over the bridge. I wasn't sure yet if I was going to go inside Ricky's, but I couldn't seem to stop myself from driving through the parking lot, just to see... my heart did a little flip when I saw Rusty's pickup parked outside. I parked and went inside, spotting him immediately. He was sitting at his usual spot at the end of the bar, with a beer, watching some ballgame on one of the televisions up on the wall. And as usual, the place smelled like stale beer and fryer grease. I took a barstool beside him.

"What's up?" I said, trying to sound casual.

He looked at me, surprised. "Hey, you! What are you doing here?"

"Oh... I'm bored."

"Chardonnay?" The bartender asked me. Her name was Gretchen, which I'd picked up from hanging out with Rusty so much, which is also how she knew what I liked to drink. That gave me pause.

"Yeah, thanks," I said, pulling cash out of my purse.

"Save it," Rusty said. He called to Gretchen. "Hey, Gretch? Put it on my tab, will ya?"

"Sure thing," she said.

He looked at me like he was hungry. "You look great," he said.

"Thank you," I said, and with perfect timing, Gretchen set my wine glass down in front of me. I took a sip, trying to look as cool and nonchalant as possible. I thought I succeeded.

"I've really missed you," he said. "A lot." He put his hand on mine, and gave me his best puppy-dog eyes. I felt my thighs warm.

"Yeah," I said, not knowing quite what to say. "I've missed you, too."

"Of course you have," he said, taking a swig of his beer. "I'm irresistible."

I couldn't help it. I laughed. "That you are."

The longer we talked, and the more drinks I had, and the more drinks he had, the more flirty we got. I had wine after wine after wine. Every time my glass was empty he'd say, "Hey, Gretch. Can she get another one?" and a new glass would appear in front of me. I knew he'd buy me alcohol all night if I'd drink it. I also knew I was drinking way too much and should stop.

We sat there for two hours, and I wondered why he hadn't suggested we go to his place. I let myself get caught up in the flirting and the alcohol, trying to not think too much about why I was there, because the truth was, I didn't know why I was there. I mean... I wanted to get laid, for sure. But... did I want more than that? I wasn't sure.

Out of the corner of my eye, I saw a gorgeous brunette sashay our way. She stopped at Rusty's barstool. It was Jess, the bartender who'd served us on our first date. She was wearing skintight jeans and a tight sweater, but no apron. Clearly she wasn't working tonight.

"You ready, Jakey?"

"Oh... hey," he said, as though he was surprised to see her.

I felt my face redden. "You two busy tonight?" I asked.

He looked uneasy. Jess looked fantastic. Like she should be in a shampoo commercial. I couldn't help it. I hated her.

"Uh, yeah... we were going to hang out tonight with some of the other bartenders at Jess's place. You wanna come?"

Ooof. Really? Invite me to Jess's place with some of the other bartenders? Who would also all be female and great looking? "No thanks," I said, smiling. I slid off my barstool. "I have plans." Lie.

"You sure? We're going to drink and... stuff. Should be fun."

"I'd love to," I said, smiling at Jess. "But I really can't. I have a date." She smiled back at me, clearly not upset I wouldn't be joining them.

"Date, huh?" Rusty said, laughing. "You sure rebound quick."

"Takes a slut to know a slut, I guess. See you later." I blew him a kiss and wobbled out of Ricky's without looking back. I was glad I didn't fall down on the way out. Why did I come here and make myself look like a desperate idiot? Why?

The sky had clouded over while I'd been in the bar. I went to my car and began pulling out of the parking lot, but I was way too drunk to drive. Damn it. I didn't want to, but I locked the doors, left my car in Ricky's parking lot and drunk-walked the couple of blocks to the bus stop over by Marvin's Auto Shop. Luckily, I didn't have to wait long, as the wind was picking up, whipping my hair into my face, making it hard to see. So much for looking cute. The sky was starting to look ominous, too. The first bus that stopped said it was going to the Vunos Hotel, clear on the other side of campus, about as far away from the dorms as possible. But with the way the sky looked, I felt like I didn't have any choice. I got on, not sure when the next bus would come by.

Thankfully, the bus was empty, and I took a seat near the back. Part of me felt like crying, but at the same time, I felt kind of dead inside, so I didn't. It wasn't raining yet, but the sky was getting darker and darker, and thunder rumbled in the distance, the clouds lighting up here and there. The bus trundled over the river bridge, and when it stopped downtown, a group of five sorority girls got on.

At least, they looked like sorority girls: expensive clothes, perfect hair... All of a sudden, the bus sounded like a party. They were all in short dresses and heels, and they took up the entire middle of the bus. They screeched and laughed as the bus trundled straight up the San Francisco-like steepness of Eleventh Street, all of them standing, teetering on their heels, clutching poles, on their way from the bars downtown to the dance club in the basement of the Vunos Hotel: The Grotto. I let them get off the bus first, their perfume cloud enveloping me in their annoying joy. I briefly fantasized about sticking out my foot to trip one of them, but of course I didn't.

As soon as I got off the bus, I knew it would be a race across campus and back to the dorm. It was one of those weird, spring Kansas evenings when the air felt unstable—gusty and heavy with moisture. The clouds overhead were angry and active, moving around way more than they should, and near the horizon, a growing band of darkness was rapidly eating the sky. I started race-walking through campus, past the Student Union, then Dyche Hall, then Lippincott Hall and Watkins Library, and after just a couple of minutes, I was starting to sweat. As I passed Wescoe, angry thunder rumbled from behind the thick veil of clouds. A blast of cold wind took my breath away, and a few fat rain drops began to dot the sidewalk. So I jogged, concentrating on staying upright. I was still drunk, and the only thing keeping me from barfing was the cool wind in my face, as the temperature had suddenly plummeted about ten degrees. The sidewalks were now completely empty. Campus was eerily dead.

I was almost through campus when freezing cold rain dumped out of the sky, soaking my hair and clothes. I screamed and ran into the entryway of Snow Hall, cramming myself up against the door, trying to avoid the driving rain, but it was useless. The rain pelted my skin like cold needles, and I stepped into the vestibule to get out of the deluge. Wiping away the hair stuck to my face, I looked up and there, resting on a light fixture, was a Luna moth (*Actias luna*) tucked away safe from the storm. *How did you get here?* I knew it was a little rare, but not impossible, to see Luna moths in Kansas, and I wondered how it had managed to find its way into the vestibule. Sheets of water washed down the glass of the doors and I started to shiver, chilled from the icy rain. There was a blinding flash of light and a millisecond later BOOM! The thunder cracked so loud I jumped.

It was looking as though I was going to be trapped in Snow for a little while, but I'd never been in the building before, despite walking past it nearly every day.

Shivering, I glanced inside the building to see if there was some place to sit, but the glass had fogged over. I reached out, wiped away a peep hole in the condensation, and was surprised to see a woman standing in the foyer. She was wearing a long-sleeved, light blue dress that almost reached the floor, lace adorning the cuffs and the neck. Her dark hair was pinned up in a topknot, with a few loose curls framing her face. She was facing me, and when our eyes locked, I knew exactly who she was and why the glass had fogged up.

It was Flora. Of course! She'd taken biology classes in Snow.

I pushed my way out of the vestibule and into the building, feeling the now-familiar rush of sultry, thick air. "It's you," I said. I rushed toward her then stopped short, afraid I'd somehow disturb the atmosphere or something equally wacky and cause her to pop out of existence.

She cocked her head to one side and smiled. "It's you."

"I'm so glad to actually meet you," I said, for once appreciating the stifling warmth of the ghostly presence. "I love your diary."

"I knew you would. I've been wondering if someone would come along someday—someone with whom I could commune—and here you are."

Now was my chance to ask the big question. "Why me?"

She smiled. "Because you were the one who could see us and hear us, and you were the one who would see this task through to the end."

My mind raced with all the questions I wanted to ask. "I don't mean any disrespect, but how did you forget to name an insect you discovered?"

"Oh, Kymer. How I wish I could take you back to Kansas at that time. It was so beautiful and so wild. We could barely keep up with the cataloging of it all! Everywhere you looked was some new creature or plant just begging to be identified. We simply overlooked this particular little bee. "But it's important for people to know this species of bee lived, and was forgotten about, before humanity even had a chance to acknowledge its existence. The web of life on earth is intricate and fragile, and I must say it's dismaying to see the web continue to collapse... I fear it may not stop."

"Yeah," I said. "Me too." But there wasn't time to be sad, because I knew Flora would be gone soon, and I knew there were things I should be asking, but it was hard to think because I was drunk... and that's when I had an epiphany. "Hey! How come every time I see you all—you ghosts—I'm fucked up? I mean... impaired?" I hadn't meant to curse.

She gave me a stern look, with the slightest hint of a smile at the corners of her mouth. "Yes. That's one of the factors. There are others. Some are external, others are internal. But it's... complicated." She folded her hands.

"Wait... internal like what? Like physical characteristics or mental?"

She was full-on suppressing a smile now, trying not to laugh, and it occurred to me how wild it was to see a ghost smile. "Let's call them... attributes, both physical and metaphysical. As I said, it's all very complicated, and I'm not sure you're ready for some of that information. But I am glad you ended up being our contact on the mortal plane. I'm admittedly old-fashioned, and you're a little... unorthodox... but I must say I admire your confidence and your love of biology. I'm also glad to see how our gender is fairing at the university these days. And in the world, for that matter."

"Does that mean you're not here all the time, then? On my plane of existence?" I asked, gesturing to the ground. I wasn't going to make the same mistake as with the other ghosts. There was no way I was going to let Flora go without asking some pertinent questions, drunk or not.

"No," she shook her head. "No, I'm not."

"Then where are you? Where do you go? What's it like?"

"Kymer," she said, giving me that schoolmarm look. "That's even more complicated than why it is you and I are able to interact for a few precious moments in this plane."

"But we're scientists, right? You have to tell me. I need to know."

"You—your people, in your time—you don't even have the language for that yet. Perhaps someday humans will be able to access other realities and planes. I want to thank you again, most sincerely, for all your hard work, and most of all, your curiosity. But we should both get moving now. It feels as though a twister is coming, and not even I, nor Carrie Watson have the power to stop a Kansas twister."

She sort of floated backwards, and I knew this was it. She was leaving. "You should take shelter in the basement of Snow, right now," she said, drifting. "You'll be quite safe downstairs. Snow is built like a fortress."

"Wait!" I said, realizing that once again, I'd neglected to take a photo or video of a ghost. But if I was the only one who could see and hear them, maybe it wouldn't work anyway, and it seemed rude to ask if I could take her picture, so I decided not to.

"Yes?" she said. But her voice was fading.

"I just wanted to say... thank you."

"For?"

"For being brave enough to leave home and go to school so other women could, too."

"My most sincere pleasure," she replied, but her voice sounded far away.

"Will I see you again?" I took a few steps forward and heard, from what sounded like the bottom of a canyon:

"I honestly do not know. I cannot see the future from where I exist. Study well, Kymer!"

The air went back to normal, and I knew she was gone. I turned to look outside, and though the rain had eased from a downpour to a light sprinkle, somehow the sky had gone from dark gray to a sickly green color I'd heard my dad describe many times. As I pushed through the door, the tornado sirens went off. The temperature outside had risen again, and the air was heavy and warm with moisture, but the wind was a little chilly as it whipped around me, wrapping my hair over my eyes. Lightning crawled across the sky in spidery veins. Then I did something really stupid. Instead of going back into Snow to take shelter, I ran. I ran faster than I'd ever run in my life, thankful it was all downhill. I passed two, maybe three cars on the way down, but not a single human being. I sprinted without thinking about the fact I was still drunk and a little woozy, not giving myself time to become unsteady and fall down. I was just a few yards away from Oliver Hall when the sky broke open with rain. By the time I made it into the dorm, I was drenched. A couple of girls were behind me, screaming through the parking lot, which was beginning to flood. I made it to the doors first, and held the door for them.

There was a RA in the entryway. He waved us in. "Get in quick!" he barked. "We're sheltering in the basement."

The basement of Oliver consisted of the laundry room and a study room with some tables and filing cabinets where you could look up old tests various professors had given over the years, with a small common space between. To see the whole dorm packed into the basement was wild. Kids stood everywhere there was a spot, and the din was incredible.

"Let's not sit on the washing machines, please!" Cheyenne yelled at some dudes, who hopped down. I wove through the mass of people, dripping, until I spotted Siren and Mattie standing next to the detergent vending machine.

"Oh my goodness, you poor thing!" Mattie called out when he saw me.

"What happened?" Siren said.

"I got caught in the rain on campus," I said, annoyed. My alcohol buzz was gone, it was hot with everyone smashed in together, and I felt nauseated. My clothes were glued uncomfortably to my body, and clumps of hair stuck randomly to my face.

"What were you doing on campus? I thought you were finished with everything after your religion final," Siren said.

"It's a long story," I said.

"Well, let's hear it, then," Mattie said, crossing his arms. "Looks like we are fixing to be here for a bit."

I told them. I told them I'd been alone and lonely that afternoon, and in a weak moment, I'd gone to see Rusty. "And then I might have gotten way too drunk and made a complete idiot of myself in front of him."

They looked horrified. "You did not," Mattie said, holding his face in his hands.

"Yeah, I did."

"Why would you do that?" Siren asked.

"I don't know. Because I'm stupid?"

"You didn't go home with him, did you?" Siren asked.

"No," I said, trying to wipe the hair off my face. "He left with another girl."

Mattie's eyes got big. "He did not!"

"Good," Siren said, firmly. Then she looked at me with pity. "Oh, Mama. When are you going to learn you're too good for him?"

"Am I?" I said. "Because I feel like shit." I sunk down to the floor, tired.

She sat down next to me and gave me a hug. "Of course you are. Next time he comes in to Bazongas, I'm gonna pee in his beer."

That made me laugh. We ended up being in the basement of Oliver for forty-five minutes while a tornado touched down just south of town. Luckily, no one was injured or killed, but I was a little bummed I hadn't had a chance to see it. Then again, I reasoned, since I now lived in Kansas, hopefully I'd have other chances.

The last day of school was almost as crazy as the first, with parents and students coming and going up and down the halls, hauling out boxes and lamps and computers and microwaves and everything else. Most people were moved out by noon, by parents who wanted to get on the road back to wherever they came from. Siren and I, on the other hand, waited for the dorm to clear out that morning, then took our time carrying out our boxes in the afternoon. Pops and Mattie's brother Isaac came to help him move, and after they'd cleared out Mattie's things, they helped Siren and me.

We loaded a few of our bulkier possessions—like the computer, printer, mini-fridge and microwave—into Isaac's truck, and I loaded my clothes and books into my Toyota. Siren's Ford Fiesta was stuffed—and I mean stuffed—mostly with her clothes and makeup cases. After we managed to get all our crap dumped in our new apartment, it was late in the afternoon when we went back up to the dorm room to clean and check for anything we'd left behind. It was austere and echo-y sounding, with all of our stuff out of it. It reminded me of the day we'd moved in.

The production of *Grease* had gone really well for Siren, and she was still riding the high of the show. In fact, some hot-shot play producer from Kansas City had been at one of the performances, and Siren had caught his eye.

"He was so impressed with my performance, he wants me to audition for *Into the Woods* at the KC Dinner Theater this summer. He asked me himself," she said. She was on cloud nine, chattering away as we opened drawers and checked under the beds one last time. She grabbed an old t-shirt and began dusting with it.

"That's awesome!" I said. But how are you going to handle rehearsals in Kansas City with your job?"

She sighed. "Oh, that's not a problem. I'll just have to give up all the best shifts at work to do the play. You know, Friday nights, Saturday nights and Sundays. Hopefully, the pay I get for the play will help make up for the tips I'm going to miss out on. Oh, and I should probably tell you... I broke up with Jordan."

That shocked me, since she'd spent time with him just two nights ago. "What?"

"Well, I don't know," she said, wiping the dust off the top of her dresser. "Maybe 'broke up' is too strong. We decided we'd take a break."

I was pretty sure "taking a break" in Siren's world meant they were done. "We decided, or you decided?" I said, rubbing a spot of spilled nail polish on the tile in the closet with cotton balls and nail polish remover.

She laughed. "Okay, mostly me."

"So, what's his name?"

"What's whose name?"

"The other guy you're interested in."

She frowned, looking insulted. "Why does there have to be somebody else? There doesn't have to be somebody else."

I laughed. "Because I know you. I mean, no judgement. But what's his name?"

"Fine," she said, sweeping a couple of dust bunnies out from under her bed. "It's Dante."

"Dante?" I'd heard that name before. "You're getting it on with your T-Bird stage boyfriend?"

"I mean... we did make out for hours during rehearsals."

"Hours?"

"Well... we wanted it to look good. You know, on stage. It's not as easy as it looks."

"Oh, you succeeded. You guys were hot," I laughed.

"I know, right? He is *so* hot."

"How's Jordan taking it?"

"Um... I mean, I think he'll be okay. He's adorable. He'll meet someone quick."

"He is that," I replied. I had most of the purple nail polish cleaned up, but there was a lavender stain on the floor. Thank goodness it was in the closet. I hoped they wouldn't hold it against us.

Siren stood up, holding the broom Cheyenne had been kind enough to loan to us. "Is that it? Are we done?"

"I think that's it," I said. We'd removed everything from the room except the bugs. It was already getting warm outside, and I didn't want them to fry in the car while we were busy cleaning.

Siren grabbed Sidney and Isabelle from the shelf above my bed. "You can take Chrysler and Caroline," she said.

"Give me Isabelle," I said.

"How come?"

"She doesn't need to move to the new apartment." I opened the window and took the top off her terrarium. She didn't move. "Go on, Isabelle." I put my finger in her terrarium. After a little coaxing, she climbed on, her tiny feet tickling my fingertip. Then I stuck her out the window. She crawled around on the tip of my finger for a few seconds, until a gust of wind blew her off. She fluttered unsteadily through the air, losing altitude but definitely still flying. She beat her wings like crazy, rising and falling, fighting and flitting, pushed around by the warm spring breezes swirling around the dorm.

"Go, Isabelle!" Siren yelled, and we watched her make her way into the world, until she disappeared into a thicket of sweetly scented lilacs.

Look for the further adventures of Kymer, Siren and Mattie coming soon from Anamcara Press.

About the Author

AMBER FRALEY IS YOUR TYPICAL GEN
XER suburban Kansas wife and mom
of one who grew up a book nerd in a
dysfunctional family and now writes
about those experiences as hilarious
therapy. She's the author of the darkly
humorous essay collection From Kansas, Not Dorothy, and the viral essay
Gen X Will Not Go Quietly, as well
as numerous human interest articles
in regional magazines. Growing up in
Lawrence and Wichita, Amber spent her formative years with her face
in a book or at the mall with her friends. She loves the Kansas with all
her heart, is frequently awkward in public, and desperately wishes to
see a tornado and live to tell the tale.

Follow her on Facebook, read her public blog on Medium.com or visit
her website at https://www.amberfraley.com/

Acknowledgments

The Bug Diary wouldn't exist without the help of so many family and friends who helped it come to fruition. Thank you to my friends Stephanie Weaver, Tracey Kastens and Mark Davoren who read early drafts of this book and helped me make edits. Their attention to detail was invaluable. Thanks to my friends Erin Hatton and Linda Brandenburger and Scott Thomas who read early drafts and encouraged me to keep going. Thanks to my dear artist friend Lana Taber Grove who for providing so many spot-on, gorgeous illustrations to go with my writing over the years, including this cover. It has my heart. Thanks to my daughter, Jordan Fraley, who helped me with the current slang the kids use these days and thanks to my husband Jim Fraley for his immense support in every sense of the word. Thanks to Nathan Pettengill, the best editor a freelancer could hope for, for his editorial input and professional encouragement for years and years and years now. Finally, and most importantly, thank you to my college besties Michael Tidwell and Phoebe Zimmermann for letting me tag along in so many wacky adventures, and for routinely making me laugh until I couldn't breathe. I couldn't have made it through those years without you.

OTHER BOOKS YOU MIGHT ENJOY FROM ANAMCARA PRESS LLC

ISBN: 9781941237-33-5
$18.99

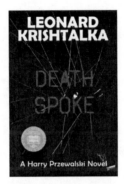

ISBN: 9781941237-30-4
$18.99

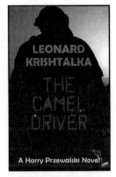

ISBN: 9781941237-32-8
$18.95

ISBN: 9781941237-13-7
$18.95

ISBN: 9781941237-18-2
$16.95

ISBN: 9781941237-08-3
$24.95

Available wherever books are sold and at:
anamcara-press.com

Thank you for being a reader! Anamcara Press publishes select works and brings writers & artists together in collaborations in order to serve community and the planet.
Your comments are always welcome!

Anamcara Press
anamcara-press.com